THE
FARAWAY
PEOPLE

STACEY DIGHTON

CRANTHORPE
—MILLNER—
PUBLISHERS

First published by Cranthorpe Millner Publishers (2023)

ISBN 978-1-80378-173-0 (Paperback)

www.cranthorpemillner.com

Cranthorpe Millner Publishers

OTHER BOOKS BY STACEY DIGHTON

Pale Face and The Raven
The Hawk and The Raven
The Maidens of Fey and Other Dark Matter

For Lily, my writing buddy and constant companion.
We miss you xx

PROLOGUE
FRIDAY, 22ND JULY 2022

Alison raced through the forest as rapidly as her screaming lungs would allow. Brambles clawed at her face and arms, nettles attacked her ankles, and sharp, wire-like twigs slapped viciously at her chest. She was breathing heavily, her heart hammering incessantly. Hot blood rose to her face as her skin turned hard and prickly. Torrential rain was streaming through the dense canopy overhead. The freezing cold water had soaked through her thin T-shirt, causing her body to shiver and her lips to tremble. It was absurd. Just two days ago she was standing on crisp, golden sand, tossing a coin on whether to go back into the cool ocean waters or collapse onto a beach towel and soak up the baking hot sunshine.

Where was Michael? What the hell had happened to him?

Night had descended. The forest was bleak, and frankly terrifying. She could hear a distant groan, as if someone was in horrible pain. There was a thud and the squelch of footsteps in thick mud. She cried out as a bat flew across her path, and she stumbled over a raised root, sliding down an incline and landing hard on her backside.

'Shit! *Shit*!'

The clasp of her sandal had torn in half, and the shoe was now hanging limp, useless. She grabbed it and threw it angrily into the undergrowth.

'Bloody cheap crap!'

She unclasped the other and tossed that too. She was crying now, tears rolling down her cheeks and mingling with the rainwater. She wiped her forearm across her eyes and stood, almost slipping in the mud once more.

'Michael! Where the hell *are* you? I'm out here in these bloody woods, all on my own! This is so like you, just abandoning me like this! You're such an arsehole!' She was shaking with rage, but she was afraid too, like, really afraid. Her voice became a hoarse whisper. 'Michael? Please. I'm... lost out here.'

It was hopeless. She sounded hopeless.

That bitch; those monsters. They'd called themselves neighbours, friends even. She'd fallen for it, been taken in by the woman's charm and her fake promises. What the hell had she been thinking? How could she have been so naïve, so pathetically foolish? Michael had tried to tell her, but had she listened? No, she hadn't. She'd allowed herself to be seduced. To be... well, to be bloody groomed.

Suddenly there were eyes all around her: red and orange, hundreds of them floating in the black, glaring at her, malicious and hungry. She heard the sound of sniggering and scowling, like a thousand hissing snakes – the *babies*.

The air had turned putrid and dense, like a toxic fog. She backed away and turned on her heels, retreating the way she had come, stumbling and staggering. She could hear a wailing, a sobbing, but she couldn't place it. She realised with a growing sense of despair that it was her. The sound was coming from *her*.

Childlike voices drifted from within the darkness.

Alison. We can see you. We can smell you. Come back to us, Alison, come back home.

'Stay the fuck away from me! I don't want you anywhere near me, you fucking freaks! I—' Tears continued to pour down her face. Rain ran from her slick hair and into her eyes. 'I don't believe in you!' She pushed through a dense thicket but tripped on a rock. She cried out but managed to keep her balance by pin-wheeling her arms and spreading her legs. She slid down a muddy slope, her body gathering pace at a frightening speed. She reached out and found a hanging strand of ivy that she clung onto in grim desperation. Her feet continued to slip and move in the mud, but

2

she wedged them onto a slug of limestone. She began to laugh hysterically as her uncontrolled journey came to an abrupt halt.

She glanced over her shoulder. The eyes had gone, as had the cruel laughter. She was getting out of this. She was now so determined to make that her truth. Surely it had all been just a crazy hallucination, a nightmare. When she eventually woke up, she was going to slap Michael for being such a dream idiot, and then they would have coffee in bed, and maybe they would make love. She needed him close to her. She needed to feel the warmth of his skin. It had been so long.

She stepped through the wall of ivy, pushing it aside like a heavy drape, and gasped. She was at the cliff's edge. The land fell away sharply towards ferocious waves that roared savagely beneath her feet. It was that place; that terrible, blood-soaked hellhole. The ocean ravaged the rocks with an unyielding onslaught. The sky was black, the water charcoal-grey. A sweeping, silver beam from a distant lighthouse flitted across the undulating waves. The swell rose and fell with a growing intensity. The horizon appeared endless, her route to escape just a distant promise. The hiss from the ocean sounded like a desperate scream. Alison slipped at the edge, almost tumbling feet-first into the darkness.

That was when she saw it. It was gargantuan, a giant behemoth rising from the depths. Pounding waves lashed over enormous, heavy hooves. Its hands were encased in a swarm of black locusts, its huge equine skull resembling something from a freakish horror movie. It leered down at her. Drool hung from its teeth and lips, elastic and yellow.

'Oh… oh, *God*!'

She turned her head, only to be confronted by the sea of red and black once more. The eyes. They resembled a twisting loop of grotesque Halloween decorations. The laughter resumed. She heard her own voice from a million miles away, frantically reciting a once forgotten prayer.

'I believe in God, the father almighty, creator of Heaven and

3

Earth, and in Jesus Christ, his only son, our lord, who was conceived by the Holy Spirit, born of the Virgin Mary…'

Something warm and wet fell onto her shoulder and she raised her head. Her vision was obscured by a huge, terrifying face: the skin cracked and bleeding, black, soulless eyes unmoving, dark crimson teeth hanging with festering skin. She smelled its breath. It reeked of death.

The beast smiled.

DAY 1
SATURDAY, 30TH JULY 2022

Hattie Penrose opened the passenger door of the gleaming white Audi Q7 and stepped out onto the driveway.

'Seven hours of non-stop nineties pop is just a little too much for me to take, that's all I'm saying,' she said, shaking her head.

'Oh, come on!' Hattie's sister, Bea, cried. 'Don't tell me you didn't have a thing for the Backstreet Boys back in the day, or that you've never shaken your hips to the Sugar Babes or Five.' She launched herself from the rear passenger seat and dragged her partner, Rachel, behind her. 'Take That? You loved Take That! We both know you had a huge crush on Robbie Williams.'

'Yeah, yeah, okay. All that's true, and thanks very much for reminding me how old I am, but while we're all crammed into one car with the kids playing up, and you and Rachel bickering about who said what to who and when, and then throw on top of that the fact that Richard can't stop faffing with the sat nav, because for some reason he never bloody believes what it's telling him,' Hattie took a breath, 'well, even Mozart's piano concerto in D minor would get a bit much.' She hauled a large suitcase from the roof-box and tossed it onto the driveway as her sister dodged out of the way.

'Careful with that thing, Hats. It's heavy,' Bea said. She puffed out her cheeks. 'I can't believe how much you've packed. It's a week, you know? We're not emigrating.'

Hattie's husband, Richard, stooped and grabbed the case. He lifted it to his shoulder. 'She's never been able to master the art of minimalism, Bea. You of all people should know that.' He turned to his son, a teenage boy with curly blond hair and the pink stains

5

of pubescent acne on his cheeks and neck. 'Jonno, grab the wash bags, will you?'

'Bea's not much better, Richard. Don't let her fool you,' Rachel said, laughing. 'We spent a long weekend in Rome earlier this year and she managed to fill a double wardrobe with all her stuff.' She slung a large rucksack over one shoulder and grasped a heavy holdall in the other. 'I, on the other hand, made do with a pair of dungarees, three tops and a skirt.'

'Oh, come off it, Rach. That's a load of crap, and you know it.'

'Bea!' Hattie cried. 'Sally's in the car.'

'She's asleep and she didn't hear a thing. Anyway, crap's not a real swear word.'

'If you're going to insist on being a bad influence…'

'Hattie, dearest,' Bea said, grinning, 'that's my speciality.'

Hattie brushed a blonde curl from her eyes and looked up at the two-storey cottage. The place was rustic all right, just as they'd told her it would be. It was well off the beaten track, too. A sign at the foot of the driveway proudly declared the old converted cornmill as 'Spriggan's Retreat'. *A retreat would be perfect*, she thought. *A retreat is just what we need. If only we could.*

'Anyone for a beer?'

'Bea! We haven't even unpacked yet,' Hattie yelled, dismayed. Even though Bea was only slightly younger than her, she acted like she was in her teens, not her early thirties.

Rachel emerged from the kitchen, an open bottle of Peroni in each hand.

'Come on, sis,' Bea exclaimed, as she accepted one and took a large swig. She smiled and wiped spilled beer from her mouth. 'We're on holiday, after all. It's time to loosen up a bit, isn't it? Enjoy yourself!'

Richard poked his head through the kitchen door. 'Is there any more of this stuff to bring in? Only, I'm gasping.'

'Your daughter, Richard? You know? The short one with freckles?' Hattie exclaimed, her eyes wide.

'Oh yeah. I forgot I had one of those.'

'The Penrose party, I presume!' a demure lady with long, silver-streaked hair declared loudly as she emerged from behind a hydrangea. She was attractive in an unconventional way, and was wearing slim blue jeans and a loose-fitting chiffon top. 'You're a little later than expected.'

'Yes,' Hattie said, her daughter in her arms. 'That's us, and sorry. The traffic was truly awful.'

'Oh really, it's no problem at all. We were just getting ready for dinner, and I heard your vehicle pulling onto the driveway.' She eyed each of them in turn. 'Have you travelled far?'

'We're from Kent, so about three hundred miles, give or take,' Richard said, helping himself to a beer after all. 'The 303 was about as unreliable as ever.'

The woman shook her head. 'That road never gets any easier, I'm afraid. I'm Glanna, Glanna Cormoran, and my partner, Noah, is in the main house. He'll pop over to say hello a little later, I'm sure.'

Hattie took her hand. 'I'm Hattie, and this is my husband, Richard. My sister, Beatrice.'

'Bea,' Bea said, correcting her.

'Sorry, yes, Bea. And this is her partner, Rachel.'

'Oh, how wonderful,' Glanna beamed, hugging each of them in turn. 'And the children?'

'This little one is our five-year-old daughter, Sally-Ann.'

'How do you do, Sally-Ann?' Glanna said. She reached out to touch the little girl's cinnamon-coloured hair, but Sally-Ann pulled away, tucking her head into the crook of her mother's arm. 'I'm expecting my own child, as you can probably see,' she said, rubbing her tummy. 'The baby's due any day now.'

'Oh, wow. You don't seem anywhere near big enough.'

'How nice of you to say that. I actually carry very lightly. I've always been this way,' the woman said, giving a wry smile. 'You could say it's a family curse.'

7

'So lucky,' Hattie said. 'I was like a water balloon with Sally-Ann. Anyway, this is Richard's son, Jonathon. We call him Jonno.' The boy emerged from the kitchen with a glass of cola. He looked up and raised a hand awkwardly.

'Ah, from a previous marriage, I assume?'

'Er, no, we didn't make it that far, actually,' Richard said. 'It was just a fling, really. You know? One of those brief encounters. Yep, it happened when we were both young and stupid.' Hattie nudged him. 'But it gave us Jonno and, of course, for that we're very grateful.'

Glanna smirked. 'Quite. Anyway, it's a pleasure to meet you all. I'll leave you to unpack and settle in, and I'll pop back over in the morning to give you some hints and tips on where to visit, what to do, what not to do, that kind of thing.'

'Oh, Glanna, that would be perfect,' Hattie said.

Bea nudged Rachel, shooting her a wink.

'No bother at all,' Glanna said, and pointed to a wooden gate. 'We're just through there, in the big house. If you need us, just holler or bang on the door. I warn you, however, you might need to be patient. We have three teenagers, and they can be a little boisterous at times. Oh, and there's my mother too. She's old and senile and can come across as quite scary. She's harmless though, I promise.'

'We completely understand,' Hattie said, pausing. 'Well, it's lovely to meet you, isn't it, Richard?'

'It sure is. And don't worry, we'll keep it down,' he said, shooting a glance at Bea.

'Oh, no need to worry. As I say, we're used to a little noise. Just do me one small favour.'

Hattie set Sally-Ann down, and the little girl turned and ran to her auntie. 'Of course.'

'Please don't put anything other than loo roll down the toilet. We're not on the main waste system here, what with us being so far out of town and all, so we have a very, *very* large cesspit to cope with the sewage from all these buildings.' She turned up her nose. 'Anything bulky just clogs up the pipes, and we have to get the bloody thing drained. The smell can be downright repugnant.'

Richard nodded. 'My parents have the same set up, so we're used to it. It's no problem at all.'

'Well, then you'll know. Oh, and just one other thing.' Glanna pointed to the roof of the cottage. 'The attic. It's off limits, I'm afraid, because of that godawful thatched roof. Bloody thing needs taking down and tiling if you ask me, but the council have their rules.' She seemed to lose herself for a moment. 'Anyway, we couldn't bear to think of someone inadvertently striking a match up there, and then *woof*!'

'Jesus!' Bea said, giggling. She placed her head on Rachel's shoulder.

'The whole place would burn to the ground in minutes.'

The group fell silent. Hattie pushed away the terrifying thought of her family fleeing from a ferocious blaze as it tore through the aging building's timber structure.

'Just stay away from the attic and there's really no danger at all.' A sudden gust of wind threw Glanna's long hair across her face. Her pristine appearance suddenly became unruly, chaotic. 'You'll enjoy it here at Spriggan's Retreat, of that I have no doubt. You'll find it quite enlightening. Enriching, perhaps.'

Hattie glanced at her husband.

'Anyway, that's enough of me prattling on. All that's left for me to do is to bid you good afternoon and leave you to enjoy what's left of the day.' And with that, she raised a hand and departed.

''Bye,' Hattie said, followed by an insincere 'goodbye' from her sister. Bea turned to the others.

'Well, she was odd, wasn't she?'

'Oh, leave it, Bea, will you?' Hattie said, grabbing Sally's hand in hers and opening the gate.

'I liked her,' Rachel laughed. 'She had a... quaint charm.'

'It's the isolation. It makes these country bumpkins a little eccentric,' Richard said, aping a thick Cornish accent. 'Or as mad as old hatters. It's either that or its all the inbreeding. Didn't you notice her third leg?' he laughed. 'Anyway, let's finish up here and head down to the water.' He pointed to the ocean. 'I think a swim is in order, don't you?'

Bea whooped. 'I'll get my cozzy on. Come on, Rach.'

'Don't worry,' Rachel replied. 'I'm right behind you.'

'Dad!' Jonno yelled from an upstairs window. 'Come up here, quick!'

Richard looked up. 'What's the matter, son?'

'There's a rat!'

*

The rat, as it turned out, was pretty light on its feet, and by the time Richard made his way up the crooked staircase and into the box room at the front of the house, it had disappeared.

'Big, you say?' he asked.

'As big as a cat, I swear.'

'What type of cat?'

'A brown one.'

'No, not what colour, what type? What size?'

Jonno was hunched over and peering under the bed. 'I don't know. A big cat.' He sat up and held his hands about two feet apart. 'This big.'

'That's one hell of a rat, son. And, you say it escaped under the bed?'

'I told you that already!'

'Okay, okay. I believe you.' Richard gestured for his son to sit. 'Well, it's gone now. If you see it again, let me know and we'll do something about it, okay?'

Jonno slumped onto the mattress. 'I hate rats.'

'Oh, nonsense. They're just big hamsters, that's all. Nothing to be afraid of.'

'They go for your throat, you know? If you corner them.'

'Rubbish. Who told you that?'

'Alex at school. His dad owns a farm, and they get hundreds of them in the barns.'

'Well, Alex is full of bull. He's just winding you up. Pay no attention. I can honestly tell you this as your father,' Richard touched his son's arm, 'they're more scared of you than you are of them. You probably won't even see it again. Now that it realises the place is occupied, it'll probably stay well out of our way. Anyway, we're going to walk down to the cove and take a dip in the water. What d'ya think?'

Jonno sighed. 'I don't know.'

'Oh, come on. You can't just sit in here and fret about a stupid rodent for the rest of the day. We'll take the bodyboards.'

Jonno looked up, hopeful. 'And the snorkels?'

'Obviously!'

*

Spriggan's Retreat was tucked into the crook of a little bay called Bodhmall's Rest and was only accessible by a four-mile-long, single lane road that wound intricately southwards from St Austell. The beach, a small stretch of golden sand that sat at the base of a steep footpath, was privately owned and shared with three other properties. It was surrounded on either side by tall cliffs carved out of limestone and clay, but the water itself was clear blue and as smooth as glass. When they arrived at a little after four in the afternoon, the beach was deserted.

'Our own private beach? How about that, guys! Well done for finding this place, Hats!' Bea yelled, dropping her towel and running headlong towards the water. 'I'm going in.'

Rachel turned to Hattie and shrugged. 'She's bonkers, your sister.'

'Tell me about it.'

11

Rachel tore off after her, leaving Hattie and Richard to set up camp.

'Well, what do you think?' Hattie asked.

'I think it's nice,' Richard said.

'Nice as in "we're going to have a nice time" nice? Or "I'll grin and bear it" nice?'

'What does that mean?'

Hattie let go of Sally's hand and watched as she ran towards the water, her half-brother in tow. 'Don't let her go in too deep!' she yelled at Jonno.

Jonno looked over his shoulder. 'I'm not stupid, you know.'

Hattie sighed. 'Is he ever going to like me?'

'It's just his condition,' Richard answered, pushing their parasol into the sand.

'That's nonsense and you know it. He resents me.'

'For what?'

'For taking up some of your precious attention.'

'You need to relax. We're on holiday after all. You're so—'

'So what?'

'So tense. All the time. Just try to let it go.'

'I can't.' Hattie shook her head. 'Don't you think I've tried?'

'Well, we came here to get away from it all, physically *and* mentally. I for one have every intention of doing just that.' He grabbed the bodyboard. 'Are you coming in?'

Hattie plucked a paperback from her bag and dropped onto a beach towel. 'No, you go ahead. I'm just going to sit here, read and take advantage of the peace and quiet. Have some fun with the kids, please. They've been looking forward to this.'

He stooped and kissed her on the forehead. 'I love you. You do know that, don't you?'

She forced a smile. 'I do.'

*

12

Eli liked the car. It shone like a crystal, and its wheels were big and black and had really deep grooves. He ran his fingers along one of them and thought of his toy racing cars. He made vrooming noises.

The Faraway People were out. They had arrived, disappeared inside the Rotting Place, and then came back out with boards and balls and towels and all sorts of other things. He thought they were going down to the beach, probably to swim in the sea, which made him want to be sick. The thought of the salty water inside his mouth made him gag, and the idea of little fish swimming around his feet and brushing up against his toes made his eyes water and his throat hurt.

He glanced at the gate that led back to the big house. It was closed. He knew the Kid-Bastards were away: the boys with their guns, and the girl with her little tricks. Sweet Mother was busy indoors too. He had time.

He withdrew the key from his leather pouch and hopped over the picket fence. He was excited to see what he might find inside the cottage, besides the rats, of course. He'd seen them before; seen them plenty of times. He'd killed a few too, with his traps. He'd found them with their eyes bulging and their tongues sticking out.

He opened the door and the smell hit him like it always did. He raised a hand to his mouth. It stank of damp and mess, like something was dying slowly inside a pool of brown and icky pond water.

There was an open bottle on the kitchen counter, only half drunk. He lifted it to his lips and tasted it. Ugh! It was bitter and fizzy, and he hated the feel of it in his mouth. He spat it into the sink. He saw the open suitcase on the sofa. It was full of clothes and things. They were scattered on the floor as if the family had been in a hurry. It looked like they were a messy family. Sweet Mother wouldn't be pleased. He raised a pair of shorts to his nose and breathed in. They smelled of flowers and the sea. That also made him gag, and he threw the shorts on the floor.

He looked at the wall in the hallway, and at the crayon pictures

13

he'd drawn for Sweet Mother. She'd pinned them up there for all the families to enjoy. They were portraits mainly: the fat girl with the pigtails; the chubby boy with the cracked spectacles; the big man with the red hair and beard.

Eli didn't like to go upstairs in the Rotting Place, but he was curious. The boy had been up there. He'd seen him hanging out the window and shouting something at the tall man. The steps were old and creaky, and they frightened Eli. He didn't want to fall down and hurt himself.

He took a deep breath, trying to be brave, and grabbed the handrail with both hands, hauling himself up, one foot after the other. Sweat rose to his cheeks and forehead. The physical exertion made his shoulders ache and his jaw hurt. Each step squeaked and groaned differently to the last, as if the wood was about to splinter and snap in two. Eli imagined himself falling through a gaping hole, the sharp wood clawing chunks out of his skin as his terrified, bloodied torso came crashing down onto the ground, his skull shattering into a thousand pieces, his brain splattering up the walls in a mushy mess. When he reached the first-floor hallway he collapsed in a heap.

After a moment to compose himself, he looked up. The boy's room was ahead, and the door was open. He skulked tentatively along the hallway, always glancing over his shoulder and into the open doors of the other rooms. Those rooms were still dark and full of shadows, and they called to him, the voices swimming around in his head like fish in a bowl. He wanted to get out of there as quickly as he could, but his curiosity pushed him on.

The boy's room smelled of turds. All boys smelled of turds, and this boy was no exception. Eli retched and a little sick came up in his throat. It tasted of the fizzy, bitter drink from the kitchen and he retched again. This time some sick escaped from his mouth and ran down his chin. He wiped it away with the palm of his hand, which he then smeared down the leg of his shorts. They were dirty anyway.

14

The boy had a gun. Well, an air-rifle. Eli wasn't allowed to play with guns, but he picked it up anyway. The smooth, cold metal felt exciting to the touch. He raised the rifle-sight to his eye and pointed the barrel at the window. He made little *putt-putt* noises as if he was shooting at passers-by; one of the Kid-Bastards, maybe; one of the boys.

He put the gun down and looked at the other things. There were books with brightly coloured pictures on: one with a fire breathing dragon, its eyes red. Flames spurted from its mouth. There was another that had soldiers and guns and boats. The pictures were fun, but the words were of no interest to Eli. He couldn't read anyway. He was going to learn, but he just hadn't had time. He pushed the books to one side and grabbed a flat glassy thing, which sprung to life when he lifted it to his face. There was a picture of the boy and the tall man and some other woman (not one of the women that got out of the car) but someone else. There were other little pictures on the flat glass thing, and Eli touched it. Suddenly, there were moving pictures, and the glass thing was speaking to him and playing music. It frightened him, and he threw it onto the bed. Only, the corner of the glass thing hit a bedpost. Eli heard a crunch, and the noise suddenly stopped. His mouth fell open, his lips trembling. He wanted to cry but he held it together.

'I told you, Aaron, that rabbit's mine. I shot it first!'

Eli looked out the window. It was the Kid-Bastard boys.

'Oh, get lost, Freddie. You couldn't hit a deer if it was giving you a lap dance. You can have the bloody rabbit, just don't pretend that you killed it.'

Eli picked up the glass thing and put it back where he found it. The glass was cracked, just a little bit. He hoped the turd-boy wouldn't notice.

'Get it away from me, I don't want it. You can keep it for yourself if you love it so much.'

'Oh, get lost, you loser. Hey,' Eli watched as Kid-Bastard Aaron spied the car, 'nice wheels.'

The two boys dropped their guns and the rabbit, and they started to circle the vehicle.

'Whoa, this family must have a bit of money. What d'ya think?'

'I think you're right, mate. This lot must have plenty of paper.' The older boy did a little dance. 'Do you think they've brought any girls?'

Freddie grinned. 'Oh, I hope so. Not like the last ones, though.'

'No, definitely not. Stuck up bitches. Especially that one with the stud in her nose.'

Freddie puffed out his chest and snarled. 'And they were fat, too. Like two big hippos.' They both laughed at that. 'I'm glad they're gone.'

'Me too. We're well shot of 'em. Wait a minute,' Aaron walked towards the picket fence. 'The door's ajar. Do you think they're inside?'

Eli backed away from the window. Stupid idiot. He'd meant to close the door behind himself.

'Dunno. Shall we take a look?'

Freddie raised his hands. 'Mother won't like it.'

'Mother's not here, you big baby. You coming or what?'

Eli peered along the upstairs hallway and realised there was no way out. He was going to get caught inside the house by the two Kid-Bastard boys, and they would do what they always did to him: they would hurt him.

'Hello. Anybody home?'

Eli looked out the bedroom window and saw the two boys standing at the doorway below: Kid-Bastard Aaron with his face at the open crack of the door, Kid-Bastard Freddie standing just behind him.

'I don't think there's anyone here, Fred. Shall we go in and take a look?'

'I don't know—'

'Oh, come on, you pussy.'

Eli heard the door open, followed by the sound of footsteps on

16

the wooden floor.

'They got beer. You want one?'

'Well, I—'

'Take a swig of that. It's posh lager.'

Eli glanced towards the window. He could jump, but he didn't like heights. Sweet Mother said his bones were brittle. He looked at the gun. Maybe he could shoot the boys and make a run for it, but he knew they would catch up with him. They'd be angry too, and they would hurt him ten times more than usual and make him cry and puke. He wanted Sweet Mother. He wanted her so bad.

'These knickers are nice, Freddie. There must be girls here after all, and skinny ones too.'

'Awesome. Do you think they're country girls?'

'Nah, not with a car like that, and especially not with knickers like these and that posh lager. These are upmarket girls, all right. Classy bitches.'

Eli looked under the bed, but the rats lived under there, and they had beef with him. He wasn't going to risk getting bitten and clawed and infected with scabies or rabies or worse.

'You wanna look upstairs?'

Eli felt his heart rate escalate and his lips start to tremble once more. He rummaged in his pocket for his knife. It was there, just where he left it. If he needed to use it, he would, just to protect himself. That was okay, wasn't it? He wouldn't be punished for that, would he? Surely Sweet Mother would forgive him. Wouldn't she?

'I don't know, Aaron. We're gonna get caught.'

'Don't be stupid. They're probably out on a walk, or down at the beach, or summit.'

'But Mother?'

'Mother's not here, and neither is Noah. We got this place all to ourselves.'

Eli spotted the loft hatch in the plastered ceiling at the end of the hallway, and he felt a faint twinge of hope. They would never

17

look up there. He took a step towards it and inadvertently trod on a loose floorboard. It let out a little creak.

'What was that?'

'Rats maybe?'

'No, that was too loud for a rat.'

'Maybe one of the kids are still home?'

'I don't think so.'

'Then… what was it?'

'I don't know.' There was a pause. 'Let's take a look.'

Eli heard the sound of the boys taking the steps two at a time, heard the creak of the handrail, the thud of feet on crooked timber, the heavy breathing of two fully grown Kid-Bastards with thick muscles and heavy hands. He saw the dirty brown tufts of Kid-Bastard Aaron's curly mane, saw his muddied fingers as they gripped the wall at the corner of the stairs, and his heavy boots as they mounted the hallway.

Eli pushed the hatch closed behind him and held his breath.

*

Rachel floated peacefully on her back. The late afternoon sun caressed her ebony skin, and the cool ocean waters lapped over her shoulders and onto her cheeks.

'This is gorgeous.'

'You said it,' Bea said. She was floating alongside Rachel.

'I could stay out here all night.'

'Me too.'

Rachel felt Bea's fingers delicately caress her forearm.

'What do you think?' Bea asked.

'About what?'

'About Hattie and Richard?'

'I think they're a bit on edge, especially your sister.'

Bea murmured in agreement. 'She's always been highly strung, ever since we were kids.'

18

'Yeah, but the way your parents are, it's—' Rachel paused. 'I'm sorry, but they're hard work. It must affect her. It must affect you, too. In fact, I know it does.'

'Yeah, I guess. You kind of get used to it. What do you make of Richard?'

'He seems nice.'

'A little too nice, maybe?'

'What do you mean by too nice? How can someone be too nice? No. He seems fine to me.'

'I know. It's just, well, it's probably me. I sometimes think there's something about him. He's not been the perfect husband, you know. Not by a long shot.'

'Well, nobody's perfect. Especially not the two of us,' Rachel laughed. 'Look, he's always been nice to me, so on that basis, I like him. Your parents on the other hand...'

'Yeah, yeah. I get it.'

'Well, the way they spoke to you, Bea. What they did. Are we even gonna talk about that?'

Bea righted herself in the water. 'I'd really rather not. Look, I know it was unforgiveable, what they said, how they went about it, but you have to realise who they are, where they've come from.'

'That's no excuse, and you know it.'

'Yeah, I do, I really do, and that's why we're here.' Bea started to massage Rachel's neck and shoulders. 'To get away from everything. To relax.'

'Mm, that feels good.'

'I thought it might.' Bea's hands wandered a little lower, and Rachel pushed her away.

'Get off me, you slut,' she said, throwing water in Bea's face.

'Hey, stop that, you...' Bea laughed and splashed back, 'you bitch.'

'Hey, whatcha doing?' It was Jonno.

'Oh, erm—' Bea exclaimed, startled. 'Hey, Jonno.' She smirked at Rachel. 'Aren't you a little out of your depth?'

19

'I can swim,' he said.

'Yeah, but there's swimming and there's swimming, kid.'

'Hey, I ain't a kid!'

'Well, if you act like one—'

'I'm sure your aunt didn't mean it like that,' Rachel interjected. 'Did you, Bea?'

'No. No, of course not.'

Rachel glanced back towards the shore. Richard and Hattie were talking to an older, long-haired gentleman. She wondered who it was. She was sure there hadn't been anyone else on the beach a few moments ago.

'But if you get a cramp out here,' Bea continued, 'or get tired or whatever, well, you could drown.'

'You could get cramp just as easily as I could. Or get tired.' Jonno was indignant. 'You could drown too, you know. Both of you.'

Rachel swam over to him. 'No worries, Jonno. You can stay out here with us.' She winked at Bea, still half keeping an eye on the stranger on the beach. 'We were going to swim over to the rock pool, see if we can't find some crabs or mussels or something. You wanna come?'

'Dad says I have to be careful around the rocks.'

'Well, you will be.' Rachel smiled. 'We'll be careful, and you'll be careful too.'

'That's right,' Bea said, grinning. 'The three of us. We'll look after each other. Come on.' She pushed off. 'Last one there's a big, smelly poo.'

Bea raced towards the rocks, throwing her arms into the water, and kicking her legs furiously. Rachel thought she looked hysterical, but she launched herself after her. Jonno was quick, and he came up alongside Rachel, his skinny arms thrashing into the water. They passed Bea as the rock pool loomed closer. She felt Bea grab at her feet in a clumsy attempt to sabotage her race to victory. She looked over her shoulder and yelled an obscenity, and

Bea swore back at her, water spraying over her partner's long brown curls and into her eyes and mouth. Rachel hadn't meant to fall for her; the scatty, pasty-looking bird who took everything in her stride, but she had, just the same. It didn't help her situation, not in the slightest, but what could she do? It wasn't as though she'd wanted it. Quite the opposite. She'd deliberately tried to avoid it.

'Argh! *Argh*! Bea! Help, Bea!'

Rachel glanced to her right and saw Jonno floundering, his face a mask of desperation and panic. His arms flapped and flailed in a chaotic attempt to keep himself afloat. Bea stopped dead in the water.

'Jonno, calm down, calm down!'

'I'm, urgh, I'm—' the kid was choking. 'Shark, there's a—'

Rachel quickly raced around Bea and approached Jonno from the rear. Bea was frozen. It was clear she didn't know what to do, which was hardly surprising. She'd had no training.

'I'm drowning, help! Bea, help me!'

Rachel pushed Jonno's body upwards in the water, and she gripped him across the chest from behind. Jonno fought against her, but she held him close and kicked backwards.

'Come on, Jonno. We're going to head towards the rocks. Just go with me, we're going to be okay, I promise.'

The boy calmed down a little, and Rachel eased him towards the water's edge. Bea seemed to shake herself into action and paddled behind them.

Within a few moments they were sat on a large, smooth rock. Jonno's head was slumped between his knees, water spilling from his open mouth. Bea swam up beside them. She shot an inquisitive glare at her partner.

'Jonno, Jonno! What the hell happened?' she asked.

'Something—' He paused for breath. His chest was still heaving, and his eyes were bulging. 'Something touched my leg. Something weird.'

'Just seaweed, I bet.' Bea said.

'It had teeth and scales and horrible eyes.'

'A fish, then. Maybe a fish.'

'It wanted to bite me. I know it did.'

'I don't think that it—'

'It *did*! I'm not lying! I felt it. It grabbed my leg in its mouth. It wanted to eat me! It did! I *swear*!'

'Okay, okay, we believe you,' Rachel interjected, putting an arm around him. 'But you're on dry land now. You're safe.'

He was panting and shuddering. They both gave him a moment. 'Rachel's right, Jonno,' Bea said, breaking the silence. 'You're safe now, you're with us.'

'I guess.' He looked back at the shore. 'I want to go back to Dad.'

'Of course.'

He stood and shook the water from his hair.

Bea pulled herself up onto the rocks. 'Where did you learn how to do that?' she asked Rachel.

'Two seasons at the local swimming pool. I was Lifeguard of the Month, July 2010.'

Bea planted a huge kiss on her lips. 'Is there anything else I need to know about you, Rachel Woodley?'

'Well, Beatrice Jane Piper,' Rachel said, winking, 'you're just going to have to find that out for yourself.'

*

Richard lounged on the wet sand and patiently filled the castle-shaped bucket with a plastic spade. His daughter, on the other hand, was running up and down the edge of the water, scooping up clumps of sand in her tiny fists, throwing them into the bucket and yelling "sandcastle!" at the top of her lungs. His wife was sitting much further back. She was thumbing through a glossy magazine and peering over the edge of her sunglasses every now and then. Richard thought she was either enjoying watching the two of them playing together or, in some clandestine way, she was casting a slide rule over his parenting skills. He suspected it was the latter.

He was pretty impressed with his own work: a large, enclosed mound surrounded by a deep moat, a bridge at one end and a summit decorated with a dozen replica castles, all stacked in a pyramid-style shape, like some sort of medieval citadel. Richard could imagine himself living in that citadel, probably in the central tower in an ornate, private chamber. He would gaze out over his empire and watch as evil hordes would attempt to breach the impenetrable gate in the middle of his large surrounding wall. He liked the sound of that.

He and Hattie had decided to come here on the spur of the moment. Everything had just got too much for them. They'd both been arguing pretty much constantly for months. Little things at first, inconsequential things, like whose turn it was to unload the dishwasher, who had left the wet towel on the floor of the bathroom, why the bedroom light was left on all bloody day. Then those little things had become bigger things, and those bigger things had become interwoven and tangled up in other things. It was a mess, a confused mash of upset and tension, and then the resentment had started to creep in. 'Why didn't you stick up for me?' 'Why weren't you here?' 'How could you let this happen?' 'Who do you think you are, lecturing me like that?' 'Well, she's not your wife, is she? I am!'

When the thing with Bea had kicked off, it had been a welcome distraction. He hated to admit that to himself, but there it was. It had given them something to direct their anger towards, rather than at each other. Bea had been distraught, and rightly so, and her sister had backed her all the way, as had Richard. They'd formed a little protective ring around both Bea and Rachel, who they barely knew. What they had was unity, and unity was something that had been missing from their marriage for the best part of a year. He cherished that. The holiday was a way of solidifying that feeling, or so he hoped; a break, some time away from everything, time for all of

23

them to connect in some unconscious, speculative way, but that would be meaningful and lasting and impenetrable. Like the gate in his wall.

'Daddy, look.'

He glanced up at his daughter who was pointing inland.

'What is it, darling?'

'There's a man over there. He's talking to Mummy.'

She was right. Tall and slender with long, flowing grey hair, a grey moustache, cotton shirt, cargo shorts and sandals. He looked like a cross between the Big Lebowski and Catweazle. Richard stood and thrust a hand towards his daughter.

'Come on, darling. Let's go over and say hi.'

He caught the conversation mid-flow.

'So, yes, three of the four properties have been here for many hundreds of years and have been owned by the current families for almost all of that time. Several generations of course.' The man laughed.

'That's fascinating. Really, *really* interesting. So, your ancestors lived in the…'

'The Night Watchman.'

'Yes, in The Night Watchman. Such a wonderful name. It must be really comforting for you to know that you're sleeping in the same bedroom, watching the TV in the same lounge, cooking in the same kitchen.'

'Oh, very much so. And—' The man spotted Richard. 'Well, hello there.'

Hattie looked up. 'Richard, Sally. This is Mr Treg—' She paused.

'Tregeagle.'

'Sorry, yes. This is Mr Tregeagle. He lives in the house up there.' She pointed. 'The beautiful house at the edge of the cliff.'

'Oh, you're too kind. And please, call me Pascoe, or Paz. Whichever you'd prefer. I answer just as well to both.'

Richard held out his hand. 'It's lovely to meet you, Paz. I'm

24

Richard, and this is our daughter, Sally. Say hi, Sal.' Sally pushed her face into her father's thigh and shook her head. 'Sorry, she's a little shy.'

'That's no problem at all. I remember being that age.' Paz laughed. 'Well, at least I think I do. It was such a long time ago.'

'Yeah, you and me both.' Richard looked up at The Night Watchman which was indeed dangerously close to the edge of the cliff. Its plastered exterior was slightly yellowing as if stained by nicotine. It had half a dozen large, lead-paned windows, a steep, tiled roof and a turreted annex on its eastern side which looked misshapen and crooked. Ivy was making a nuisance of itself around most of its exterior, and brambles hung over the fence. 'So, that's your place, then.'

'Yep, for my sins. The upkeep is a bit of a burden, I can tell you, but it keeps me and the missus busy, what with all the weeding and the painting and the fixing and the mending.' He exaggerated a sigh. 'It's a full-time job.'

Hattie smiled. 'I bet it is, but what a lovely location.'

'Yup, it is that.'

There was an awkward silence.

'You're staying at Glanna's place?'

Richard nodded. 'Yes. Spriggan's Retreat. We've only had time to have a quick look around, though. We came straight down here to the beach, what with the kids being crammed in the car for hours today.'

The old man bent down and ruffled Sally's hair. 'I bet you were feeling like hens in a coop, weren't you, my lovely?'

Sally shook her head and shuffled behind her father's legs.

'Oh, come on, Sally. Paz is just being nice to you.'

The old man stood. 'It's okay. I have that way with kids. I think it's the long hair.' They all laughed. 'She's a good one, Glanna. Been in that house forever – her family, I mean. Longer than mine even, perhaps longer than most in this little corner of the country. A good 'un, all right. She stays on the right side of wrong, for the most part.'

Hattie shifted closer to her husband. 'The right side of wrong?'

'Yup, whatever that means.' Paz laughed once more. He idly drew two fingers along his moustache. 'Anyway, I came down here to let you know about the gathering. It's tomorrow night. In the summer months, after the Solstice, those of us who live in the four properties here in Bodhmall's, well, we have a weekly Sunday night get-together on that little patch of ground between us. We call it No Man's Land, on account of it belonging to no man. Or woman, for that matter. There'll be music and a barbecue and some locally brewed ales and cider. Even something a little stronger if you fancy it.' He nudged Richard. 'Some pop and cake for the little 'uns too.'

Hattie glanced at her husband. 'Well, we don't know what we'll be doing yet, but thanks for the offer.'

Richard shrugged. 'It might be kinda fun.'

'That's the ticket, old son,' Paz exclaimed. 'Anyway, it starts at eight.'

'Eight?' Hattie shook her head. 'I don't know, that's a little late for Sal. She's normally asleep by then.'

'Oh, come on, Hats,' Richard said. 'We can bring a buggy, and she can crash in that if she gets tired.'

Paz nodded. 'There's a big ash tree in the middle of No Man's Land, and you can push her buggy underneath that if she falls asleep. It's peaceful, I can assure you. I've had a few afternoon dozes under there myself.'

'I don't—'

'Paz,' Richard interjected. 'My wife and I would be delighted to accept your invitation. We'll see you there at eight.'

'Excellent, most excellent indeed.' Paz bent down and pinched Sally's cheek. 'Kathy will be delighted.' He stood and shook sand from his shoes. 'Well, I'll be on my way, but just one more thing. Sunset in these parts is around nine thirty this time of year, hence the late start. We'll all be partaking in a little Cornish singing when that happens. Don't be alarmed, it can be a little... unsettling to the

26

newcomer.'

'Unsettling?' Richard glanced at his wife.

'Well, not unsettling as such. Maybe odd is a better word. Anyway, you're welcome to join in. In fact, we'd love it if you would. I'm sure you'll pick it up.'

Richard smiled. 'Sounds like fun, doesn't it, love?'

He could see Hattie was seething.

'Well then, if not before, I'll see you tomorrow evening at the party!' Paz yelled as he headed off up the steep incline.

Hattie turned to her husband and hissed, 'Richard, what the hell was that?'

He shrugged. 'I thought—'

Suddenly, Bea appeared at her sister's side.

'Did somebody say party?'

*

She watched as the skinny boy paddled up to the two women: one with long brown curls and milky-white skin, the other a black-skinned lady, with shoulder-length braids. The pair of them were more than just friends, she could see that much. She wasn't so stupid as to think the same couldn't like the same.

She giggled as the trio raced towards the rocks. The black lady streaked ahead, while the boy did his best to act like the big guy and catch her. She hated how boys did that, always trying to act like they were the stronger of the species when it's obvious that strength isn't all about biceps and pectorals and bench presses. Strength was in the mind, in how far you were willing to go. She was willing to go all the way, every time. Some people thought she was a spiteful girl, vicious and callous, but oh, she was far worse than that. All they needed to do was ask the cripple. The stories he could tell, if he dared.

The pasty lady grabbed the black lady's foot, which gave the awkward boy the edge. He might have even gone on to win if she

27

hadn't already sent a message to Morgawr, the pet she wasn't supposed to have. She'd dragged her out there, all the way from Falmouth. All it took was a simple charm. She had the knack, you see. Her mother had it, she had it, a few others. It was in her blood, in the very fibres that held her together. She couldn't remember the moment that she'd realised, it had been so long ago, but now it just felt like slipping into a favourite nightie or an old pair of jeans. Her friend, Morai, said she was a natural, that she was blessed. The old lady encouraged her to use what she had in a way that she chose, which was very different to her mother. Mother liked her to do as she was told.

Morgawr gave the boy a shove, a nibble, no more. It was simple but it did the trick. Her dark form was visible just beneath the surface of the water – her beautiful tail, her smooth grey-blue skin – and then she was gone. The boy went totally mental, almost having a heart attack right there in the water. She nearly wet herself from laughing. It was hilarious.

The black lady saved him from drowning, which was a pity and a blessing all in the same breath. The pasty lady was about as useful as a bucket with a hole in it. Evie moved from her position on the hilltop and crouched by the cliff's edge. She laughed out loud as the boy coughed and spluttered. He was retching like a baby. It was pathetic, really. He was scrawny and spotty and hadn't quite grown into his body yet. He was fresh, like newly laid snow. She was going to have some fun with him, her boy. She liked him.

*

'I thought he was with you,' Richard said.

'Yeah, and I thought he was with you,' Hattie replied. 'He's your son, after all.'

'And what's that supposed to mean?'

'It's a biological fact, Richard. I'm not his mother.'

'Well, not by blood, but you're married to me, and that makes

28

you his—'

'Yes, stepmother, and you know how I hate that term. It makes me sound like an old hag in a witch's hat and a black robe. Look, it was one of those things. He'll bounce back from it.'

'I'm just saying, we could both be a bit more attentive towards him, that's all. What with his condition, and with Sally and everything else taking up so much of our time. It's only natural that he'll start to feel more and more—'

'More what?'

'Pushed out.'

'She's our daughter, Richard. What the hell are we supposed to do?'

Jonno had already run off ahead. Sally was holding his hand and whooping and giggling as they snaked in and out of the tall trees that lined the gravel track leading back towards the house. Jonno was making aeroplane noises and shouting in some mock British fighter pilot accent, and their daughter was lapping it up. Bea and Rachel were lagging behind and were out of earshot.

'Can we act like a team with him? That's all I'm asking,' Richard said.

'A team?'

'Yes, a pair. Not two separate individuals.'

'So, you're blaming me?'

'No, I—'

He looked lost for words and that pleased Hattie. How dare he accuse her like that? She'd done everything she could for the boy, including getting him moved to a school much closer to their home and significantly more in tune with his needs. Had his own mother done that? Had she? No, she'd married some wealthy distribution tycoon, moved to Chigwell and all but forgotten about Jonno. Was it her fault that they now had a daughter of their own, who, at five years old, sucked up so much of their time and attention?

'I'm not at fault here, Richard. You were there with the pair of them, and you should have kept watch over what your son was up

29

to.' She folded her arms. 'Period.'

'Let's just leave it, shall we?'

'Yes, shall we?'

The forest opened up onto a gravel road that looped around a large circular patch of grassy land with a grey tree with long, angular branches at its centre. Hattie thought that it must be the ash tree that Paz had told them about. At each of the four points of the compass sat a property. The Night Watchman was the southernmost residence and the one closest to the sea. To the east, and to Hattie's right, was a two-storey building constructed from stone called The Sailor's Curse. It was built into an incline and stone steps led from the basement to the ground floor doorway. Small windows faced out towards the sea, and a large, sparsely decorated balcony opened up towards the common at No Man's Land. To the north was Spriggan's Retreat and its parent property, Excelsior Lodge. This was Glanna's and Noah's home, and it was almost entirely hidden behind a thick, overgrown hedgerow. Hattie could just about make out a steep stone chimney, crudely tiled roof and tangled cloak of wild ivy. To the west was a house that looked out of place among the others. A modern-looking glass sign was fastened to a red brick wall with tall stone pillars. A neat, italic engraving declared the property as The Weary Traveller.

'That house is a little weird, isn't it?' she said, deciding to change the subject.

'What, the cottage that looks like it might have actually been built this century?'

'Well, yes. It's just a bit jarring, like it's been put in the wrong place.'

'The wrong decade, more like,' Richard said. 'I expect the owners are newcomers to the area. Probably a wealthy career couple who decided to move out here to get away from the big city lifestyle. It happens all the time. Counter-urbanisation, they call it.' He shook his head. 'Pretty soon the whole country's going to be one big sprawling mass of motorways, retail parks, postmodern, prefab apartment blocks and coffee shops.'

She laughed. 'Says the guy who can't go anywhere without first stopping off at a Costa and grabbing a takeaway skinny latte and an almond croissant.'

'That's different, and you know it.' He broke into a smile and slapped a hand on his stomach. 'I have a figure to maintain.'

'What? A figure forty-eight?'

'Ooh, that's harsh,' he said, grinning and pushing his thumbs into his tight waistband. 'But fair, I guess.'

Hattie paused. That was more like it. That was what they'd come out here for – well, one of the reasons anyway – to relax, to breathe and to actually converse with each other. And to forget, of course. There was always that. She went to take his hand in hers, to pull him towards her, maybe kiss him tenderly the way they used to, but Bea and Rachel appeared from out of nowhere.

'So, what's the plan, sis?' Bea yelled.

'We were mid-conversation, but,' she glanced at her husband, 'what do you think?'

'Well,' Richard said, 'I, for one, can't be bothered to cook, and there's fat chance of us getting a takeaway delivered out here.' He winked at Bea. 'How about we take a drive into town and find ourselves somewhere to eat?'

'Ricky, my old son,' Bea said, grinning, 'now you're talking.'

Hattie felt her own smile reach her eyes. Maybe they would come to enjoy their week together, after all. Just the six of them, out there in the wilds, away from the poison and the vitriol and the hate. And there was that other thing too, the thing that was really going to change their luck. Change it for the better.

Suddenly, Jonno came running towards them from the direction of the cottage. Sally was cradled in his arms and was shrieking. 'Dad, come up here!' he shouted.

'Jonno, be careful with her. She's not a doll!' Hattie yelled.

'I need Dad.'

'What is it, son?' Richard asked.

31

'It's the cottage.'

'What about it?'

Jonno was breathing hard, his face pink. 'I think there's someone in there.'

*

Eli watched from his little hideout nestled within the eaves. There was a gap between two of the joists overlooking the driveway, and he could see the Faraway People next to their shiny car: a tall man, three loud women, a boy who looked about as scared as a rabbit caught by a fox, and a little 'un. The tall man was talking in an angry voice to the two Kid-Bastards. The scared kid (who Eli now recognised as Turd-Boy) was holding out the glass thing that Eli had accidentally cracked. The tall man was pointing at it and then gesturing towards the Kid-Bastards. Kid-Bastard Aaron was shrugging, and Kid-Bastard Freddie was staring at the floor. Eli smiled. They were taking the blame, which was just as cool as a cucumber for Eli. He wasn't in any hurry to confess. No way horsey, or however the saying went. He might be slow sometimes, but he wasn't stupid.

Sweet Mother appeared along the pathway that led from the Rotting Place to the main house. Eli felt his heart flip a little. She was beautiful, his sweet mother. The sun shone right out of her eyes like laser beams, and the smell that wafted over him when she passed was of spring flowers and freshly cut grass. He knew his life in Bodhmall's would be unbearable without her. She was why he stayed around, even with all the snitching and bullying and the beatings and kickings. It was her, not his own brother, who kept him there.

Sweet Mother grabbed Kid-Bastard Aaron by the ear and dragged him towards her. The tall man held out his hands, and the loud woman with the yellow curly hair shook her head, but Sweet Mother wasn't going to be told what to do with her own child. She reached out her other hand and grabbed Kid-Bastard Freddie by the arm and pulled hard. Freddie went down like a barrow of bricks and jumped up just as quick too, his face red and sweaty. Eli held a hand to his side. His ribs hurt from laughing.

Sweet Mother shoved the Kid-Bastards towards the Faraway People, and the boys glared at the floor as if there was something gross down there. He watched their mouths move in slow motion and imagined the pathetic apology that was most probably spilling from their lips. He wished he was down there with them, savouring every sweetly delicious word. They deserved it, even if they didn't do it. They were going to be in for a beating tonight, that was for sure. They wouldn't be able to sit down tomorrow, not without a soft cushion. He giggled again.

Sweet Mother held out her hand, and Turd-Boy handed her the glass thing. Eli didn't know what it was – the thing with the moving pictures and the noises – but it looked really expensive, and he thought the Kid-Bastards were going to have to work extra hard around the place to pay for it. It would take weeks, months even. Eli laughed again and rolled onto his side.

Just then, a rat, one of the younglings, ran right up to him. Its beady black eyes watched him closely.

'What? What's up, fella, you hungry?'

The rat blinked and then held its nose to the air, its whiskers twitching.

'You are, aren't you?' Eli reached into the pocket of his shorts and pulled out the remains of a ham sandwich. He'd been saving it for later. 'You want some of this?'

He held it out, and the rat looked at it suspiciously.

'You can have it all, if you want.'

He placed the sandwich down on the floorboard and shuffled backwards into the darkness.

'Go on. Take it.'

The rat approached the sandwich, placed its tiny nose up to the stale bread filled with slowly wilting ham and oozing mustard, and

33

then backed away.

'What's wrong, little fella? Don't you like the mustard? I'm not a fan either, it's too stingy, but the sandwich was on the sideboard, and Sweet Mother says I have to grab what I can get, otherwise I'm bound to starve.' That wasn't entirely true, but he'd learned to eat whatever was going, whenever he could.

The rat looked up, had another good whiff of the sandwich, and then turned and ran towards the farthest corner of the loft.

Eli sat up on his haunches. He could hear noises downstairs and realised, too late, that the commotion out front had ceased, and the Rotting Place was now fully populated with the Faraway People. He cursed the rat, he cursed the sandwich and he cursed the Kid-Bastards. At this rate he was going to be stuck there in the dingy, stinky attic all night; up there with the ghosts and the damp and the horrible, festering smell.

He peered over to where the rat had scurried, silently swearing and grumbling, even though he knew he'd be in for it if Sweet Mother heard the nasty words that were coming out of his mouth. Suddenly something caught his eye, something shiny. He shuffled forwards on his hands and knees, taking extra special care not to lean on a loose board or a crooked joist. Turd-Boy was just below him in his bedroom (Eli could hear him talking to one of the loud women).

As he edged closer to the gleaming object, an uncertain knowing came to him. He'd seen that shiny thing before. He'd admired it from afar, and then he'd had the chance to see it and its other half up close. The last time he'd laid eyes on it was when the Kid-Bastard girl and the Terrible Babies had been out there in the forest, when the awful thing that he didn't talk or even think about had happened.

He kept moving forward nonetheless, dragging himself along the twisted, decaying wood as quietly as he could, the shiny thing getting a bit brighter, the scurrying and squeaking noises from the rat family getting a bit louder. The smell was getting worse too; the

34

horrible, deathly, putrid rotting smell. It was the cottage. It was decaying all around him, like the leftover squidgy meat on a chicken carcass. Eli went to retch, but he pushed the side of his hand into his mouth and bit down. He couldn't make a noise, no matter how sick he felt, or how badly he wanted to puke.

A rat ran over his fingers, and he pulled his hand away. He leaned back and gazed at the shiny thing. It was as he remembered it; all silver and sparkly and just as beautiful as the brightly coloured flowers that lined the edge of the lawn in Sweet Mother's garden. He gasped and realised, with a grim knowing, that it was him. Eli didn't know how he'd made it up there into the attic, especially after what had happened to him, but it was him all right. His skin turned tingly, and fear rose in his throat like a fiery worm. He held his shaking hands to his lips, but it was no good. He had to see for himself. He lifted his gaze and glared up at the face.

The face of the Red Man.

*

The shower was hot and soothing, and it calmed Rachel's mood. The thing with the two country-bumpkin kids had been weird and unexpected, and it had unsettled her. *I mean, who does that*, she thought. *Who the hell just goes and brazenly invades the personal space of their guests. Their paying guests, no less.* Her privacy was important to her, vitally important, especially in the profession she was in. She couldn't have people rummaging through her stuff, no matter how young and innocent they might at first appear, and she wasn't foolish enough to think those two little arseholes were innocent. It was in their eyes. They were devious little shits, and she knew she was going to have to keep a watch on them. If they'd decided to take a look in her handbag they would have been in for a shock, and that would have meant this whole charade of a family outing would have turned ugly, pretty quickly.

What was it with Hattie and Richard anyway? Why were they

even together? It was obvious even from her fairly distant vantage point that Hattie resented the shit out of Richard's son, and Richard thought Hattie was a cold, emotionless bitch. It was either that, or they just got off on being horrible to each other, which wasn't unheard of, and was perhaps closer to the truth. The little girl was sweet though, and so was the boy. It was too often that way, wasn't it? The kids ended up being the collateral damage in the brutal battle that people called marriage. She could relate to that. She'd been collateral damage too.

She washed shampoo from her hair, and soap from her eyes, and switched the focus of her thoughts to Bea. Bea had been a surprise. A pleasant one, but a surprise nonetheless. It wasn't supposed to have turned out this way. Bea was just supposed to have been her *in*, her gateway. Of course, all that had gone out the window after that first spark-filled dinner, followed by a wonderful second date. That magical, phantasmagorical night. After that, it was like someone had pressed go on the merry-go-round, and they were off. Little by little, and day by day, Rachel had grown more and more fond of Bea. She liked her, like, a lot. Perhaps she even loved her, although that was something she was going to have to spend some more time thinking about. Bea made her laugh until her sides hurt, made her feel emotions that she never even knew she had, and when they kissed, it made her tingle all over. No one had ever affected her like that before. Regardless of the consequences and the threatening emails, and the tense phone calls from people who ought to know better, she intended to cherish it and guard it until it either bloomed into something eternal and gorgeous, or it faded like an old pair of well-worn jeans. Eric would just have to deal with it, and that was that.

She leaned into the stream of hot water and felt her muscles relax just a little. Yep, now she knew that the family living here had kids that couldn't keep their noses out of other people's business, she was going to have to be more careful. No one, not one living soul, could find out about Eric and Operation Glow. People's lives depended on it, not least hers.

All of a sudden, the shower door opened, and Rachel gasped as cold air invaded the hot cubicle.

'Room for one more?'

'Bea, you can't come in here. What if your sister hears us?' Rachel was laughing, but she really meant it.

'Don't worry, they're downstairs and completely preoccupied with Sally.' Bea placed her hands on Rachel's hips, and she traced a finger along the curve of her buttocks. The electricity fizzed immediately across Rachel's skin.

'What about the boy?'

'Headphones on, eyes closed.' She kissed Rachel's neck.

'And the dinner reservations?'

Bea pushed the hair from Rachel's face, their body's coming together in a delicate caress as the water poured over their torsos. She leaned in, their lips almost touching, her sweet breath on her skin.

'Dinner can wait.'

*

Dinner, as it turned out, was pretty damn delicious. Richard had driven, even though they had all volunteered, but he was a bit of a control freak and couldn't possibly let anybody else drive his top-of-the-range, souped-up with all the extras, Audi Quattro. It even had a personalised number plate – P3N R0S3, of all things.

'Oh my God, guys. These mussels are to die for,' Rachel said, spooning in plump shellfish that had been doused in white wine and garlic sauce.

'I agree,' Richard replied through a mouthful of bread. 'They're just as good as the ones you get at the seafront in Whitstable. Isn't that right, Hats? At that place we go to?'

Hattie was cutting up sausage for their daughter, who had somehow managed to get ketchup all over her white and pink dress.

'Huh? What's that?'

'That place. You know, by the waterfront? What's it called again? I can never remember. Anyway, these mussels are as good as anything you can get there, which is really saying something.'

'My burger is oily,' Jonno sneered, wiping his face with a napkin. 'Really oily.'

Bea leaned over the table and looked at his plate. 'Looks okay to me, kiddo.'

Jonno pushed it away. 'It's gross.'

'Nonsense, son.' Richard cut a chunk from the burger and ate it. 'That's a good burger, that is. There's nothing wrong with that.'

Jonno folded his arms. 'I'm not hungry.'

Bea raised her eyebrows at Rachel, who decided to change the subject.

'This place is nice.' They were in a pub situated at the point of Mevagissey harbour, a rustic-looking establishment called The Lookout, and it was three quarters full, with sun-kissed holidaymakers and a smattering of semi-inebriated locals.

'It's a bit basic, but it will do for our first night,' Hattie said, and handed the knife and fork back to Sally. They all laughed at the ketchup-drenched chip hanging from one corner of the little girl's mouth.

'It's quaint and homely and I like it,' Bea said. She'd gone for the chicken burger, and she'd already eaten all of her chips and most of the chicken. She'd foregone the bun, which Rachel suspected was because she was leaving room for a few gin and lemonades later on.

Hattie eyed her sister. 'What did you make of that earlier? With Glanna and her boys?'

Bea shook her head. 'A couple of illiterate shits, if you ask me.' Hattie glared at her. 'Sorry, I didn't mean to say that. Oiks – I meant to say oiks.'

'They were just curious, I guess,' Rachel interjected. 'They probably wanted to see what we were like, and what expensive, top-of-the-range gadgets we had. They've probably never even left the village before.'

'Well, whatever their motives, they're paying for the repair of that iPad,' Richard said and took a sip of his beer. 'If they do that, we'll say no more about it.'

Hattie set down her knife and fork. She'd barely touched her Caesar salad. 'I agree to a point. Boys will be boys, and I'm sure it was an accident, but the way she dealt with it. Glanna, I mean. Did you see her? Her eyes? The anger? How she grabbed and pushed them? And while she's pregnant too.' She shook her head. 'She was too aggressive. They were scared, the pair of them. Is it any wonder they've turned out that way? Archaic parenting, that's what it was. From the Middle Ages.'

'Maybe, or maybe boys like that just need a firm hand,' Richard said.

Hattie was having none of it. 'Oh, that's utter rubbish.'

'I mean it,' Richard continued. 'Kids that age think they can do whatever they want, whenever they want, with absolutely no consequences or repercussions. Look at what happens in schools these days. Kids bringing knives to class, as if it's the most normal thing in the whole world. And if a teacher touches them, or speaks to them in the wrong tone or, perish the thought, uses a word that they might find offensive? Well, then the parents complain to the governors, and if it pushes one of those hot, media-friendly buttons that everyone's so sensitive to, then they're out of a job without even a handshake or a "thank you for all your years of dedication and service".'

'And so they should be,' Hattie said.

'You're kidding, right?'

'No, I'm not.' Hattie was insistent, and Rachel noticed that the table behind them was starting to take an interest. 'When does a little tap on the hand become a smack? When does a smack become a push? When does a push become a punch, or something far worse?'

'Oh, you're being over dramatic.'

'Am I? Really? I've seen what becomes of the type of parenting that you're peddling, Richard. The capital punishment kind.'

Richard took another sip of his beer. 'I never said anything of the sort.'

'Really? That's what it sounded like.'

'Well, I guess you heard me wrong, didn't you.'

Bea stepped in. 'Anyway, we're all a little tired and a bit irritable. Why don't we just change the subject?'

Jonno was still sulking over the quality of his dinner. 'Are we having pudding?'

'Not if you don't eat that burger, son,' Richard said, pointing at Jonno's plate.

'I told you, it's horrible. If I eat that, I'll be sick.'

'Well, why not give it a try, and we'll see what happens.'

Hattie erupted. 'And there you have it, everyone! Capital punishment parenting at its very best.'

'And what do you suggest I do? Ask him really, *really* nicely to eat his dinner?'

'I'm not eating it.'

'You are, son.'

Jonno folded his arms and turned his head. 'Not.'

'Are.'

'Not.'

Richard reached over and grabbed the burger. 'You bloody *are*!'

Jonno pursed his lips and turned around in his chair.

'Oh, for heaven's sake! Will you just *eat*?' Richard threw the burger back on the plate, spraying lettuce, tomato and onion all over Rachel's lap.

'Oh dear,' Rachel said, calmly picking salad from her crotch.

'Rachel! I'm so sorry,' Richard cried, leaning over and grabbing a napkin. He made a clumsy attempt to wipe food from her cream trousers. It was too late. Grease and tomato juice had already seeped into the fabric.

'It's fine. It's fine, honestly,' Rachel said, glancing at Bea who was now giggling into her glass. 'A little white wine and some Epsom salts and they'll be as good as new.'

Hattie also couldn't hold in a chuckle. 'Not a good start to our holiday, is it?'

'Oh, I don't know,' Rachel dabbed tears from the corners of her eyes, 'it could have been worse.'

'*How*?' Bea and Hattie both exclaimed in unison.

'Jonno could have eaten that oily burger and thrown up all over me.'

*

The rest of the evening went off without a hitch. The three women switched to rhubarb and ginger gin (Hattie with tonic and the others with lemonade). Jonno and Richard made up, sunk a few Cokes, and bonded over a ham-fisted game of pool. Sally fell asleep on two chairs that Hattie had pushed together to create a makeshift bed.

'So really, what is it with you two?' Rachel was curious.

'We two?' Hattie raised her eyebrows.

'Yeah. You two. You and Richard.'

'Whatever do you mean?' Hattie grinned and took another sip of her gin. Rachel could see she was getting more than a little merry, which was good because she was half-pissed herself.

'Oh, come on. You know. The bickering. The fights.' Rachel smiled. 'What's that all about?'

Bea leaned back in her chair and laughed. 'Oh, they've always been like that, ever since they first met. It's the way you both like it, isn't it, sis?'

Hattie nodded and winked.

'Doesn't it get exhausting?'

'A little.'

41

'Stressful even?'

'Not really.'

'Well, let's take that little debate over dinner.' Rachel leaned over the table. 'That argument. It seemed a little—'

'A little what?'

'Oh, I don't know. Maybe I shouldn't—'

'No, go on. Say it. I won't be offended.'

'A little unnecessary.'

Hattie reached out and took Rachel's hand. 'Well now. That depends on your point of view, doesn't it?'

Bea held up a finger as a blond-haired, surfer-dude of a barman walked over.

'Did you need something, ladies?'

'A round of the same, please.'

The surfer-dude looked down at Bea and smiled confidently. She shook her head.

'Just the drinks, please, sweetie. We don't need pudding.'

Hattie erupted into a fit of laughter, spitting gin all over the table. 'Bea!'

The barman grinned and collected the empty glasses. He was blushing. 'No, I didn't mean to—'

'She's just messing with you, handsome. Don't take any notice,' Rachel said and touched Bea's arm. 'You're not really her type.'

Hattie smirked. 'I, on the other hand...'

Bea's mouth dropped open. 'Harriet Penrose, nee Piper! Whatever has come over you?'

Hattie lifted her gin glass to her lips and raised an eyebrow to the surfer-dude. 'I'll let you know later on, eh, sweetie?'

Rachel and Bea erupted.

'*Hattie*!'

*

Where was he? Evie needed something seeing to urgently, and only the cripple could do it for her. He wasn't in his dusty, smelly coop above the barn, or in the kitchen where she usually caught him with his head in the larder. His absence was starting to annoy her, and if he wasn't careful, she'd be forced to take her pissy mood out on him.

'It wasn't us, Mother!'

'Oh, it never is, is it? Don't take me for a fool, Frederick. You and your brother were caught red-handed.'

'He's telling the truth,' Aaron said. 'We were just messing around. We never even went into the bedroom.'

There was a swish and a crack, and Evie heard one of her brothers howl.

'I swear on my life. We never—'

Thwack!

Evie winced, but she smiled nonetheless. She knew the stupid boys must have been up to their usual tricks and got themselves caught, the same way they always did. They may have got the brawn, but they'd been short-changed in the brain cell department, and then some.

'Okay, okay. I'm sorry. *We're*—' Aaron was pleading with his mother. '*We're sorry.* Aren't we, Freddie?'

'But, Aaron. We didn't—'

Thwack!

'Ow! That one really hurt!'

'And there'll be more where that came from if you don't make amends for what you did. Shaming our family that way, and with our guests too! The pair of you need to grow up!'

'I think they've had enough, Glanna.'

It was Noah. Evie hated Noah. He was a wuss.

'I'll be the judge of that. They're my boys, and they'll take their medicine. Won't you, Aaron? Frederick?'

Silence.

'*Won't you!*'

43

Thwack!

'*Ow*! Yes, yes! We will. We're sorry, and we'll pay to get the thing fixed, and then we'll take it back to the Penrose family and we'll apologise to them again. We will. *We swear*!' It was Aaron, and he sounded like a little snivelling baby. A growing number of red welts were now painfully visible on the pairs' bare buttocks. Evie held a hand to her mouth and peered through the open window of the kitchen. It was pathetic, really. The two of them. Aaron, a nineteen- year-old man with wavy, brown locks, thick shoulders and the faint line of a moustache, and Freddie, just seventeen, with short, black hair, big ears, and the lingering scar of a corrected cleft lip. They were strong from long hours working the farm, but they cowered in front of Glanna like a couple of weak-minded peasants.

'You two. You just can't help yourselves, can you? Don't you remember what happened last time, with those two girls? The strings we had to pull, the apologies we had to make. Noah had to practically beg the police to let it go.'

Evie sneered. That wasn't even close to the truth.

'We're really sorry, Mother. We were wrong to go into the cottage. We know that now don't we, Freddie? And the girls, that was wrong too. We... we won't let it happen again.'

Evie scowled as Freddie started sobbing into his hands. Their mother placed the long length of bamboo onto the kitchen table. She wasn't going to fall for the crocodile tears, was she?

'You'll work extra hours with the farm hands, and you'll muck out too, every morning at four-thirty.'

The boys nodded.

'And you'll be docked a month's wages.'

'A month?'

Glanna placed a hand on her makeshift cane once more and raised her eyebrows.

'A month it is.' Aaron glanced at his brother. 'Thank you.'

'And that other thing? That thing we spoke about?' Glanna nodded. 'You'll take care of that, too?'

44

Freddie looked up at his brother quizzically. Aaron knew what their mother meant, and so did Evie.

'Yes, we will. First thing,' Aaron confirmed.

Their mother smiled and turned to Noah. 'Then, it's done.'

Noah sighed, shook his head, and left the room without uttering a word. Evie shot daggers at his back as he exited. He was a problem that needed resolving, even if their mother couldn't see it.

'To your rooms, boys. *Now*!'

Aaron and Freddie rose to their feet, hitching their trousers carefully over their swollen backsides.

'And Evelyn?'

Evie gasped. She'd been busted. 'Yes, Mother?'

'You can come inside, too. Right now.'

*

'Do you take card?'

Richard stood at the bar, waiting to settle the bill. His family were slowly getting their things together. Hattie was gently waking their daughter while encouraging the others to finish up. Jonno was all jacked up on bar snacks and Coke, his broken iPad a distant memory, and Bea and Rachel were on the drunk side of merry, their high-pitched cackling increasing in volume.

'We do, sir. Chip and pin finally made it down to the southwest,' the landlord said, his laughter tinged with more than a hint of sarcasm. He was a wiry, well-dressed man with a handle-bar moustache and thick-rimmed glasses. 'Nice family you have there. Just down for your holidays, are you?'

Richard nodded. 'Thank you, and yes we are. Just for the week. We arrived earlier today.'

'Very nice too. I could use a holiday myself,' the landlord said, punching the price into the till. 'You should be able to put your pin in now, sir. Are you staying here at the harbour?'

Richard grimaced. A hundred and ninety-five pounds. How

45

many gins had they had? 'What? No. We're a little farther along the coast.'

The landlord tore the receipt from the till-roll, and he gave the customer copy to Richard. 'Aah. Okay. Portmellon or Penewan, is it? Both nice places, maybe not as nice as Mevagissey, if you forgive me for saying, but pleasant nonetheless.'

'No, it's neither of those, actually. It's a much smaller place. We were a little bit short of choice, given that we only decided to come down a week or so ago.'

The landlord gave a knowing nod. 'Yes, all the nice places seem to get booked up very early in the year, I'm afraid. Staycationing, I believe they call it. What a load of nonsense. A holiday's just a holiday to me.'

'Yeah, you've got that right.'

'I'm not complaining, though.'

'I bet.'

'You all set?' Hattie asked. She was holding Sally in her arms, the young girl slumped sleepily across her chest.

'Yep. All done. I was just chatting to—'

'Wally.' The landlord held out his hand and Richard took it.

'Nice to meet you, Wally. I'm Richard, and this is my wife, Hattie.'

'A pleasure. A lovely daughter you have there.'

'Thank you very much,' Hattie said, glancing at her husband. 'She really is our little red-headed princess. Anyway, we best be off.'

'Your husband was telling me that you'd struggled to find accommodation down here.'

'Yes, but luckily a friend recommended a place. It's very nice, actually, isn't it, Richard?'

'It sure is.'

Hattie passed Sally to him. 'Bodhmall's Rest is a nice, quiet village. We're very lucky.'

'Bodhmall's?' the landlord exclaimed and placed his hands on the bar, his face suddenly a little grey.

'Is there something wrong?' Richard asked.

'No, no. Nothing wrong, it's just—'

'Just what?'

'What property?'

'The old cornmill.'

Wally dabbed at his moustache. 'Spriggan's?'

'The very same. Do you know it?'

'Yes. The Cormoran place.'

'I think that's their name, yes.' Richard replied.

'They've all lived there for years,' the landlord continued. 'I think it's just Glanna now, although maybe the old girl's still alive.'

'Yes, that's right.' Hattie interjected. 'Glanna's a nice woman. She's actually expecting a baby, but I'm sure you know that. And her mother's still there too, although we haven't met her yet.'

Wally's eyes narrowed. 'I thought old Dolly would have passed years ago. She must be ninety and change.' He paused. 'I'd steer well clear of that family if I were you.'

'What? Why would you say that?' Richard asked. 'I mean, we did have a little trouble with the sons, earlier, but—'

'It was nothing.' Hattie interrupted. 'Just a couple of over-enthusiastic boys.'

'Sons? Those two? Well, I guess you could call them that.' Wally leaned across the bar. 'Listen, it's a strange place, Bodhmall's. Very strange, even for Cornwall, which I agree has its fair share of weird goings-on. But Bodhmall's? The stories have stuck, as have the headlines.'

'The headlines?' Richard was starting to get a bad feeling.

'Look. We have a room, here at The Lookout. We don't normally hire it out, and some of you would have to make do with sleeping on camp beds, but it might be better for your family.'

Hattie shook her head. 'What? No! I mean, whatever for? We have a perfectly good cottage in Spriggan's. Why would we want to—' She glanced at Richard. 'Why on earth would we want to

47

come out of a cottage that's plenty big enough for all of us, just to squeeze into one room here?' She forced a smile. 'I mean, it's very nice of you, Wally. Really. But no. Thanks.'

Wally turned to Richard. 'I urge you to re-think this, Richard. I really do.'

Hattie snapped. 'Am I here? Can you see me? I've already said no thanks. And my husband agrees, don't you, Richard?'

'Of course,' Richard replied hastily. 'Yes, of course I do. Look, Wally, unless these people are convicted criminals or have some kind of deadly virus that we ought to know about, then I really think there's no need to frighten my wife with hearsay and rumours, do you?'

Wally reached under the counter and grabbed a piece of scrap paper. He snatched a pen from the till and began to carefully draw a rough circle, then six equally spaced petal-like shapes that stretched from the circle's centre to its perimeter. When he'd finished, he pointed at it with the tip of his pen.

'Have you seen this shape in Spriggan's? Anywhere at all?'

'Oh, this is nonsense,' Hattie scowled.

'Daisy wheels,' Wally said. 'Hexafoils, if you will. Think, Richard. Have you seen them anywhere at all? In the property? On the grounds?'

Richard studied the crude drawing. It was a familiar pattern. Maybe it was something he'd seen in reference books or on the Internet, but had he seen it since they'd arrived at Bodhmall's? He didn't think so. 'No, I don't think I have. What do you think, Hats?'

'Oh, I don't believe Wally wants to know what I think,' she snarled, tugging at her husband's jacket. 'Shall we go? Now?'

'If you see this mark,' Wally continued, 'then you must get yourself and your family away from Bodhmall's immediately. Do you hear me, Richard? You, your wife, your little girl. All of you. You come here, or go to St Austells, or just go home. It doesn't matter. Just get away from that place.' He shook his head. 'We can't afford another incident, not around these parts. Too many

48

disappearances, too many bad headlines. The tourist trade just wouldn't recover.'

By this time, Hattie was practically dragging her husband from the building. Richard reluctantly conceded ground as Wally hollered after them:

'Daisy wheels, Richard! Watch out for the *daisy wheels*!'

*

Eli climbed out of the rear bathroom window in the darkness, just as the headlights of the Faraway People's vehicle swept onto the driveway. He turned, pushed the window closed, and ducked behind the hedge.

The lady with the wavy brown hair got out of the car first, her pale legs barely holding her up.

'And he said there'd been too much of what?'

The lady with the angry voice and short blonde curls emerged from the front passenger seat. She too was a little unsteady.

'Bad headlines, disappearances even.'

'Ooh, sounds exciting,' the pretty black lady said.

Turd-Boy peered up at the cottage. Eli thought he looked tired. 'It sounds a bit like an old horror film,' he said. 'Like *The Exorcist* or *The Haunting of Hill House*, or something. Maybe we should listen to him.'

The tall man reached into the back seat and retrieved the little red-headed girl. 'Oh, don't pay attention to it, Jonno. It's just crazy talk, that's all. It's typical in these old out-of-the-way places. There's nothing going on, so the locals just make stuff up.'

Eli's lip curled. It sounded like the tall man was being rude about his family.

'Yeah, I agree with your dad.' It was the brown-haired woman. She stumbled across the driveway towards Turd-Boy and grabbed his arm. 'But when you go up tonight, Jonno, check under your bed before you turn the lights out. There could be a grisly old witch

49

under there.'

The angry woman hollered, 'Bea! That's enough. You'll scare him!'

The tall man opened the gate and approached the front door. Eli cowered behind the bush. He wondered if the Faraway People knew about the Red Man in the attic, or about what the Terrible Babies did to him.

'Well, I think we've had enough adventure for one day, don't you?'

'I agree,' the black lady said. 'I, for one, will be sleeping like a log tonight. Your wife and sister-in-law have managed to get me a little merry, Richard.'

Brown curls sniggered. 'Me too. I feel like my legs have turned to jelly.'

They all laughed, and one by one the Faraway People disappeared into the cottage. Eli watched them, sneering. He turned and spat on the ground. They were rude Faraway People, very rude. They'd made fun of his family, laughing and joking about them like they were stupid backwards people. He would tell Sweet Mother.

He turned and peered up at the roof. There was a dim glow from within the eaves, just a little glimmer of light. It was the silver, shiny thing, Eli was sure of it. It was beautiful, magical even, and the Red Man said he could have it all to himself. Just him, just Eli. But he had to do something first, something that would be tricky, but a thing the Red Man said he needed, and needed real badly.

Eli had to bring him the little girl.

DAY 2: THE TIME BETWEEN
SUNDAY, 31ST JULY 2022

Absolute silence. The fuzzy darkness thinly coats the hours that exist sometime after midnight and long before dawn. A movement under bedsheets, a muttering of dreams.

A figure stands motionless beside the bed; a slim, sexless outline. An arm gradually extends. A hand clutches a vial, while fingers and thumb slowly remove the cap. Powder falls like crimson snow, a mere dusting on the surface of the water. It dissolves gradually, creating only the smallest of bubbles. It leaves no trace. Only the water remains. The lipstick-stained glass rests on the bedside table where she can reach it.

The silhouette retreats into the shadows until it is gone.

She sits up. Perhaps she senses a disturbance, perhaps she hears a sound. She is barely awake. She glances at her husband, rubs her temples as she sips from the glass. She yawns, tugs at the duvet, and rolls onto her side. Within a few moments sleep returns. Her lips are still damp.

BEFORE RACHEL
FRIDAY, 6TH SEPTEMBER 2019

She was back in the club. The lights were bright. It was hot and she needed air, but she knew she was going to have to suck it up like a big girl. This job hadn't come easy, and she wasn't about to throw in the towel at the first bump in the road. Yes, the offices were heavily guarded; yes, she was the only black female officer on the taskforce; yes, Lyndsay Arthur was a dangerous guy with a past so chequered you could play chess on it; and yes, she was pretty sure her boss hated her (or doubted her capabilities at least), but she had worked her ass off for this bust, and she wasn't going to balls it up. The guy was a top-billing, end-of-level baddy, and he just had to be stopped.

She glanced across the dancefloor and eyed her partner, Tommy. He was watching the thick-necked bouncer, a guy she'd given the nickname, House Brick. He was blocking the entrance to the backstage area. She idly fingered the name badge on the lapel of her blazer and took a breath. She glanced at her watch. It was one forty-five in the morning, and she knew Lyndsay had a car out front waiting to take him to his father's place in Manchester. Either they pinched him now, or the whole operation was going to have to move two hundred miles north and switch to the Lancashire team. She wasn't about to let that happen. There was no way she was losing this bust to those northern cowboys. Tommy raised his eyebrows, and she nodded her reply. It was time to move.

He turned to the guy dancing next to him, an unlucky kid in a peach-coloured, tight-fitting polo, with neat blond hair. Tommy didn't hesitate. He swung a fist at his jaw, and blondie went down. Within an instant, two other club-goers confronted Tommy and a scuffle ensued. Thomas 'Boiling Point' Harris was no slouch when it came to a dust-up, and the kids were way out of their depth. None of that mattered, because right on cue, House Brick came steaming across the dancefloor with an athleticism that belied his size. He cracked Tommy on the temple with a rock-like fist, and Tommy crumpled in a heap.

'What the hell's going on here?' she hollered over the pounding house music.

'Fucking bloke just smashed this kid in the face!' House Brick yelled as he held the other kids back. 'He's coming with me down the alleyway so me and the boys can give him the fucking kicking he deserves.'

'No, leave him,' she said, looking down at Tommy, who was slowly coming to. She sighed. The things they did for the job. 'We don't need another investigation by the Old Bill. They've been itching to shut us down all year. I'll take him to the rest area out back, and I'll wait with him until he comes round. I'll soften him up a bit, make him a coffee, and try to patch up the split in his eyebrow.'

'But the prick started a fight in the club! Unprovoked too. He deserves what's coming to him, Tammy!'

Tammy Lush, front of house manager for Neon City. That was her cover.

'I get it, I really do. And ordinarily I'd agree, but Lyndsay won't thank us when one of his clubs sits idle for three months while we battle it out in the courts. If you and the others hadn't put that lawyer in a coma back in the spring, we wouldn't have this problem now, would we?'

She thought that comment would hit the spot, and it did. He backed off.

'What's the point of even having me and the lads in the club if we can't police the rules?' he sulked.

'There's a difference between policing the rules and assault and battery, and you know it. Just leave the grown-ups to sort out this mess, will you? Go back and keep watch on the dancefloor with the others, like you're supposed to.'

House Brick swore under his breath and stormed off.

'You okay?' she asked when he'd gone.

Tommy sat up on his elbows. 'Where am I?'

She smiled. 'Sorry, I didn't think he would smash into you like that.'

''Sokay. Didn't hurt.' He winked. 'Much.'

'My heart bleeds for you. Now, act like you're pissed and put your arm over my shoulders. We're going in.'

She guided Tommy through the mass of animated clubbers and headed towards the ladies' loos. The backstage door was in the corner, just off to one side. She nodded at another bouncer she'd nicknamed Bucktooth.

'You need any help with this one?' he asked, scowling at Tommy through crooked, mock gold-encased teeth.

'No, I'm good. Thanks.'

Bucktooth reluctantly let them pass, and they pushed through the door into a dimly lit corridor. She kicked the door closed and whispered to her partner.

'Stay in character. They have cameras all along this stretch, and in the offices too. The kitchen's clear, though.'

Tommy, who was still a little concussed from the heavy sucker punch he'd just eaten, nodded. 'Got it. And you think the laptop is where?'

'In Lyndsay's office.'

'Which is?'

'Third door on the left.'

The strip lights flickered on and off in time with the beat of the loud drum-and-bass music bellowing out of the club's PA system next door. It gave the corridor an eerie strobe-like effect. That, coupled with the smell of stale cigarette smoke and sweat, put her on edge. The green carpet was stained with dark patches, as were the lime-green painted walls. She wondered how many of the stains were dried blood.

They veered into the kitchen, and she shut the door behind them.

'Where did you stash the weapons?' Tommy asked.

'Two pistols, taped to the underside of the sink. Both with full clips, and one spare between us.'

'That's not a lot of ammunition.'

'If this thing ends up in a shootout, Tommy, we've failed.'

He reached into the kitchen cabinet and found what he was looking for. He eyed the pistol, a 9mm Glock 17.

'I get it,' he said. 'But I'd also like to have a fighting chance of getting out of here alive.'

She took the pistol and checked the clip – seventeen rounds. With Tommy's gun and the spare clip, that was fifty-one rounds between them. By her last estimation, Lyndsay had three bodyguards, plus him, plus his accountant, Zef Abraham. If they were all carrying, that meant they were a hundred and fifty percent outgunned. She didn't like the odds, but they were the only odds on offer.

She pulled her phone from her jacket and punched in her passcode. There was no 5G signal in the club, but she had access to Lyndsay's personal Wi-Fi hub, something she'd had to earn by the worst means possible: by sleeping with the guy. It hadn't been her proudest moment. Did she like it? No. Did she hate herself for using her body like that? Yes. Had she scrubbed herself in the shower for like an hour and a half afterwards? Yes, and she'd gone through three bars of soap in the process too. She groaned and keyed in the Wi-Fi passcode. Within an instant, she was connected.

'Henry will kill the cameras from the van,' she said. 'Once that's done, we'll have two minutes to gain access to Lyndsay's office and find his laptop. All the evidence we'll ever need to prove Lyndsay Arthur is heading up the biggest drug and human trafficking cartel this side of the Atlantic is on that computer. All the months of undercover work, Tommy; all the hours spent on overnight stakeouts, in the car, in the office, walking the streets and pushing crappy, drugged-up informants for details; all the time spent away from your family, from your kids.' Tommy was a single father with two young daughters, Isobel and Ebony. 'All the heartache. It all comes down to this one defining moment. It comes down to you and me, Tommy. Just the two of us.'

He rammed a clip into his pistol and nodded. 'Then let's do it, boss.'

She sent a message to the van out front, and within seconds the confirmation came back.

'Cameras Down.'

She turned to her partner, forced a smile, and stepped out into the corridor.

DAY 2
SUNDAY, 31ST JULY 2022

'*Ugh*!'

Rachel sat up in bed, sweat pouring from her forehead, hair sticking to her cheeks. She'd been crying.

She shot a tentative glance at Bea. She was asleep beside her. Rachel carefully retrieved a phone that she'd taped to the inside of the dresser. She shook off the remains of the not-so-distant memory she no longer wanted, and swung her legs onto the floor. She stood, taking care not to disturb the duvet, and glanced back at Bea. She was stirring. Rachel leaned over and kissed her on the cheek.

'Go back to sleep, baby. I'm just going to the loo.'

Bea muttered, 'Okay. Come back to bed when you're d—' and then she was gone again.

Rachel opened the bedroom door and peered along the corridor towards the other two bedrooms. Jonno's room was next to theirs, and Hattie and Richard's room was diagonally to her left. Sally's room was next, and then the bathroom door lay dead opposite. She skipped across the hallway and gently sat down on the toilet seat. She pushed the door closed behind her.

Her phone only had ten percent charge, so she knew she was going to have to be quick. She punched in her code which unlocked her phone. She then went to her browser and typed in the URL she had memorised. Within a few moments the central server access screen was visible. She entered the password – GLOW808 – and waited for her email homepage to appear. The network at Spriggan's was painfully slow, and she watched with growing frustration as the wheel of death continued to spin.

While she waited impatiently, she thought of that night, of the mistakes she'd made. She'd been naïve, *stupid* even, to go in there the way she had. She'd been so eager to please, so determined to impress. They'd given her time off afterwards, time she didn't need. It just made it worse, and allowed the regret, the *guilt*, to take hold. It ate away at her like acid, burning and gnawing at the lining of her stomach until the pain was too much to bear. She had to get back to it – to get even – for Tommy.

Suddenly her phone sprang to life. She looked down and smiled. She had a new message. She clicked to open it.

Sent: Sunday July 31ˢᵗ 3.14 a.m.
Sender: Eric Chapel
To: Beth Mckinley
Message Subject: Intel

Beth, as much as I hate this little relationship you've forged with the sister-in-law, it seems to have borne some fruit at last. Contact was made this morning, a little after 1 AM. Harry called my home phone to let me know. Can you believe it? At this hour? Liz was less than impressed, let me tell you. Anyway, I wanted to get it to you straightaway.

Usual email address, haribe@gmail. Same call sign – Mr Quin. The ping locates it somewhere in your vicinity, most probably within the property you're staying, although we can't be 100% sure of that. It reads as follow:

'This is a message for The Weasel from Mr Quin. I'm in place and ready to go, just as we agreed. Work your magic by Wednesday, and I'll take care of the rest. Everything's in place, you just need to come through. Don't worry, they'll never know a thing. We'll be long gone before anyone gets a sniff of what we've done. Don't fuck up, or our mutual friends will not be happy.'

You called it, Beth. Right from the start. This whole trip has been carefully set up to make a deal happen. Don't underestimate this Quin character. If you're right, he'll have a direct link to whoever replaced the recently deceased Lyndsay Arthur, and that makes him just as dangerous. Take all necessary precautions, and if you even get a whiff that your cover is compromised, hit the evacuation code and we'll get you out of there.

I'll contact you if we hear more.
Eric

Rachel – because Rachel was how she now referred to herself after almost a year of immersing herself in the character – shut down her phone. She let out a long, slow breath. She hadn't even realised she'd been holding it this whole time. Quin was there all right, right there in Bodhmall's. Right under her nose. He was so close she could taste the gunpowder; could feel the waxy sheen on the banknotes; could smell the blood on the carpet. She grinned. Lyndsay may have been taken out by someone in his own gang, but that didn't mean her job stopped there. Whoever now ran the Belvedere Saints was just another bad guy as far as she was concerned. A bad guy that was peddling illegal pills that killed people. That killed kids. She was going to make damn sure that he was stopped, whatever the cost. For Tommy; for his girls. Even if she had to be the one to put a bullet in his head.

*

'So, what time's the party?' Bea asked. She was up and moving and frying bacon over a hot stove.

Hattie was at the kitchen table, her head in her hands. She had a pounding headache which was hardly surprising. How many gins had they consumed? And what the hell had she said to that young surfer guy in the pub?

'Eight, I think,' she mumbled.

Bea was in her chequered pyjamas and Yoda slippers. She

looked ludicrous. 'Great, I love a good party.'

'I don't think it's the kind of party you're thinking of, Bea. It's more of a—' Hattie paused. 'A ritual, I guess. They're going to chant and sing as the sun goes down, if you can believe that.'

Bea flipped the bacon onto a tray and cracked eggs into the pan. 'Awesome, sounds delightfully pagan.'

'It sounds odd, that's how it sounds.' Hattie sipped her coffee. She glanced towards the door as Richard entered. 'But hubby here has managed to blag us all an invite, so we absolutely have to go.'

'What's that now? The barbecue? Later on? Yep.' Richard grabbed a slice of crispy bacon and bit off a chunk. 'I'm looking forward to it.'

Jonno came in and slumped into a chair. 'What's with all the kids' drawings on the wall?'

'Oh, I think they're sweet,' Bea said.

'I think they're weird,' Jonno huffed.

'Do you think they'll do one of the six of us?' Bea asked.

'Oh, God, I hope not,' Hattie said. 'I'd hate to be pinned up there for everyone to see.'

'It's only a drawing, Hats. I don't think you need to worry about how your hair might look,' Bea said, laughing. 'Or your make-up. Who do you think draws them, anyway?'

'I don't know. One of the kids maybe?' Richard offered.

'What? You mean those two boys? Really? Are they a bit backward or something?'

'Bea!' Hattie yelled. 'Don't use that term. It's cruel, it's outdated and it's wrong.'

Bea held up her hands. 'Sorry, it's just that, you know, they're a little crude, aren't they?'

'Whatever,' Jonno said, disinterested. 'I don't care. What's for breakfast?'

'Duh,' Bea pointed at the frying pan. 'Take a wild guess.'

'I don't like bacon.'

'No shit.'

'Bea!'

Richard interjected. 'Jonno likes scrambled eggs, Bea. Don't worry, I can make them. I know how he likes them. Plenty of butter, eh, son?'

'Is Sal still asleep?' Bea asked.

'Yep. Must have been the long drive and the late finish last night. I didn't hear her stir at all.' Richard winked at his wife. 'And I know you didn't, Hats. Not after you consumed all that alcohol.'

'Did you check in on her?' Hattie asked.

'What? No. I didn't want to disturb her.'

'So, you didn't think to stick your head in the door before you came down?'

'Did you?'

'Richard!'

He shrugged. 'What could have possibly happened to her in the few hours since we went to bed?'

Hattie leapt up. 'She could have jumped out of the window or fallen down the stairs. It's a strange house, you know.' She really couldn't believe her husband at times. 'Have you heard of cot death?'

'She doesn't even have a cot. Don't you think you're being a little dramatic?'

'Dramatic? It's our bloody daughter, Richard! Our five-year-old daughter!' She pushed past Jonno and flew up the stairs, two at a time. Her head was throbbing, and all her husband could think about was bacon and barbecue and stupid countrified rituals. As she rushed along the hallway, Rachel appeared from the bathroom, a towel around her body.

'Morning, Hattie. Everything okay?'

Hattie ignored her and raced into Sally's room. Her mouth fell open. The bed was empty.

'Sally? *Sally!*'

Richard was suddenly at the door with Rachel beside him.

'What's wrong?'

61

'She's not there, idiot!'

'No, she's not.' Richard pointed to the base of the bed, where two little feet were sticking out. 'She's there.'

Hattie dropped to the floor and reached for her daughter. 'Sally, darling. We thought you'd run off.'

Richard turned to Rachel and smirked. '*I* didn't.'

'Mouses,' Sally said.

Hattie frowned. 'What's that, my love?'

'Mouses. They ran under the bed.'

'Mice? Under the bed?' Hattie looked at her husband. 'Richard?'

'I suggest you come out of there, sweetheart. Let Daddy say hi to the mice.'

Jonno joined them at the door and shot his father a smug grin. 'I told you there were rats.'

*

'Well, I'll never. Rats you say? That's never happened before,' Glanna said. She was standing at the front door of the cottage and slowly running a hand across her stomach. The sun hung low in the sky behind her.

'Well, they're here all right. In two of the bedrooms at least.' Hattie had taken a couple of paracetamol tablets and her headache was thankfully starting to subside. Even so, the early morning hunt for her daughter had put her in a bad mood.

'Well, don't worry. I'll have a word with Noah. He'll send one of the boys round to put some poison down.'

'Oh no. Not poison. What if our daughter touches it?' Hattie shuddered. 'Don't you have any humane traps?'

'Perhaps. We certainly have traps.'

'No, I think you misunderstand. I don't mean traps that hurt the animals. They'd be just as dangerous to put around the house as the poison. I mean traps that catch the rats but don't harm them. You know?' Glanna shrugged, and Hattie quietly wondered whether their host was on her wavelength. 'You can get them at any pet store, or online.'

'I'll talk to Noah. I'm sure he'll know what you mean.'

'Thank you. Yes, that would be good. Thanks.'

'Anyway, changing the subject. Did you have a nice evening?'

Richard appeared from the lounge. 'We sure did. We popped into Mevagissey and had dinner at The Lookout.'

'The Lookout?' Glanna raised an eyebrow.

'Yes, the pub in the harbour. Nice place. The owner seemed to know you and your family.'

'Oh, did he now?'

'Yep.' Richard placed a hand on Hattie's shoulder. 'A friendly chap. I think he said his name was Walter, or Wally. Yes, that was it, Wally, wasn't it, love?'

Hattie nodded. She was watching Glanna closely. She looked so graceful in a long, flowing kaftan, her dark hair tumbling over her shoulders, lipstick expertly applied, but there was suddenly an odd twitch at the corners of her mouth.

'I believe I do know of him.'

'He knew your mother, too.' Richard continued. 'Dolly, isn't it?'

'Mother Dolores, yes. Her friends and family call her Dolly.'

'Oh, I'm sorry. I didn't mean to—'

'No bother,' Glanna said, and waved a hand dismissively. 'Anyway, I'll go and see about those—' she pointed at Hattie, '*humane* traps, you say?'

'That's them,' Hattie confirmed.

'Well, you learn something new every day. In the meantime, if you want a recommendation, I would suggest you spend a long day at our beach before tonight's festivities. The sun is supposed to be quite spectacular today, and the sea is forecast to be extra calm too. Quite a day for a swim.'

'Oh, we're planning a hike, actually,' Hattie said. 'Well, it's just

Richard, Sally and I.' She glanced back into the kitchen, where Rachel was cleaning up behind Bea. 'My sister and her partner are going to do a little garden sunbathing, and Jonno—' she shrugged. 'Well, Jonno will occupy himself, I'm sure.'

'A hike?'

'That's right.'

Glanna paused, and Hattie noticed the twitch once more. It was slight but it was there, nonetheless.

'Wonderful!' Glanna exclaimed. 'Well, there's a trail that leads right through the woods, out to Dozmary Point, which I would highly recommend. There's a café on the clifftop that does a beautiful crab sandwich, if you like that sort of thing.'

Richard clapped his hands together. 'Yes, we do. Thank you very much.' He turned to his wife. 'Well, it sounds like we have ourselves a plan, Hats.'

Hattie nodded. It did sound good. Just the three of them.

'Well, there you have it,' Glanna said, and turned to leave. 'And please let the girls know that if they need anything, anything at all, then all they have to do is come through the gate and up to the house. I'll keep an eye out for them.'

'We'll do that.'

'Enjoy that walk, now,' she said, peering over Richard's shoulder. Their daughter was skipping past with her large, moth-eared teddy bear in tow. 'Watch out for the piskies, though, won't you, my love. They're crafty and cunning, and once they fix their eyes on you, there'll be no turning back.'

Hattie shuddered. Was the woman joking, because she wasn't smiling? 'Oh, please don't,' she said. 'If you put the wind up her, she won't want to come.'

Glanna's face broke into a broad grin. 'Then let's just say I was playing around. Silly old Glanna.'

Another pause, another silence.

'Anyway,' Hattie raised her eyebrows. 'Let us know when you have those traps, and Richard will put them around the house.'

'Nonsense,' Glanna exclaimed. 'We never ask our guests to do our dirty work for us. Noah and the boys will have the job done before you know it, and they'll return your son's computer thingy too once it's been repaired, something for which I cannot apologise enough.'

Hattie waved it off. 'It's fine, honestly. It was just one of those things.'

'My sincerest thanks for your kind understanding. Now,' Glanna nodded, 'enjoy Dozmary, and say hi to Hilda at the café, if you wouldn't mind. Tell her Dolly and Glanna wish her good grace and a peaceful path.'

As Glanna disappeared, Hattie pushed the door closed. She turned to her husband.

'What was all that about?'

Richard reached under the stairs and grabbed his walking boots. 'She certainly has character.'

Hattie smirked. 'Yeah, and so did Ted Bundy.' She kissed him on the cheek. 'Now, shall we see how good this crab sandwich is?'

*

The trail was roughly marked, and it snaked westwards through densely populated woodland. The forest bordered the edge of the coastal cliffs and stretched around two miles inland. The route was hilly in places, and Hattie was grateful that she'd continued to pay her gym membership back home, even if she'd frequented that dreadful place less and less recently. Richard pushed Sally's empty buggy, while their daughter skipped merrily by his side.

'This is nice.' Hattie said.

'Yes. It is.' Richard shot her a sideways glance. 'It's exactly why we came here.'

Hattie nodded. It was peaceful, serene even. No angry words, no demands, no sniping. They walked that way for a little while without speaking, just the sound of Sally singing a song from nursery, coupled with the constant twittering of birds.

'You know,' Richard eventually broke the silence, 'if Sally wasn't here—'

'But she is.'

'Yeah, but if she wasn't, if we were on our own, like when we first got together,' he laughed. 'Woo. You remember that night, right?'

'I do,' she said, smiling. It had been fun, if a little industrial. 'But let's not talk about things like that in front of our daughter.'

'What's that, Mummy?'

'Nothing, darling. Daddy's just being silly.'

'Silly Daddy.'

They both giggled.

'But still. You can't erase the memory,' Richard winked. 'And I've been living off that memory for some considerable time, let me tell you.'

'What's that supposed to mean?'

'Nothing. Just, you know?' He shrugged. 'Wouldn't hurt to get back to that now and again, that's all.'

Hattie gasped. 'Back to what? Grazes on my bum, twigs in my hair and bugs in my knickers. No thanks!'

'Well, if not that, then maybe something else. You know? Spice it up a bit?'

Hattie stopped, her hands on her hips. She felt a little insulted. 'Are you getting at me, Richard?'

'What? No?'

'Because it sounds like you are.'

'I'm not. I promise!'

'Stop shouting, Daddy,' Sally said. She'd grabbed a long branch and was swinging it around her head like a sword. 'You'll wake the bears.'

'Sorry, sweetheart. I wouldn't want to wake the terrible, bloodthirsty grizzlies from their little snooze now, would I? They might see the three of us standing out here in the woods and decide to,' he held his hands in the shape of bear claws and growled, 'eat us for their dinner!'

Sally shrieked and ran around the base of a tree, her father in hot pursuit. After three or four laps, Sally became distracted by a passing dragonfly, and Richard stopped and bent over, his hands on his knees.

'I'm getting too old for that,' he admitted.

'Quite.'

'I'm sorry, darling. I didn't mean anything by what I said.'

'Yes, you did.'

'I didn't. Honestly, I didn't.'

'That's a lie, but whatever. Let's just keep moving.'

Hattie seethed as she mulled over their conversation. She would never admit it to him, but he was right. It hadn't exactly been earth-trembling of late. Far from it. *Fifty shades of grey*? More like a couple of shades of magnolia. He'd been busy with the company, and she hadn't exactly been in the right frame of mind, what with all their money issues and the incident with her parents. When they did finally set aside some time in the bedroom, they either got disturbed by Sally wandering in and climbing under the covers, or Jonno waking up in the middle of one of his night terrors. The environment wasn't exactly conducive to experimentation. And there had been that moment, of course; that horrible moment of poor decision-making on her part.

'Do you hear that?' Richard asked, changing the subject.

'Do I hear what?'

He stopped. 'Nothing. Not a thing.'

Hattie paused, tilted her head. 'It's nice.'

'Yes, it is. I guess.'

Sally tugged at her father's leg.

'What is it, Sal?'

'I want a drink.'

'I agree with our daughter,' Hattie said. 'I'm parched. How much farther is it to this café?'

67

'Beats me. I'll check.' Richard pulled his phone from the pocket of his shorts and glanced at it. 'Damn, no signal.'

'Try the 5G network.'

'That's what I was doing.' He shook his head. 'Not a single bar.'

'Nothing at all?'

'That's what zero bars means, Hats. No signal, no connection, and I don't think Wi-Fi's really an option in the forest.'

'Ha-ha, very funny.'

He persisted. 'Excuse me, Mr Squirrel. I don't suppose you happen to have a broadband router somewhere in your treehouse, do you? You do? Excellent. The network passcode is AcornsRnuts? Well, of course it is. Thank you very much, my good fellow. That really has got us out of a spot of bother.'

'Don't be a prick, Richard,' Hattie griped. He was annoying her, but she couldn't stop her mouth curling into a smile. She kissed him.

'Now, that's the Harriet Piper I fell in love with, right there.'

He pulled her towards him, but she shook him off. 'What do you mean?' she hissed. 'So, you don't love me right now? Right this second? You just love some distant memory of who I used to be? I haven't changed, you know. I might be a little harder, a little less soft around the edges, but I'm still the same woman, Richard. She's still right here, inside me, at least.'

'Then let her out sometime. Just like you did there, when you kissed me. Don't be afraid to open up and let people in. Let *me* in.'

'People hurt people, you know?' she said. 'Sometimes deliberately. I say that because I never knew that before, I really didn't. Maybe I was naïve, I don't know, but once you find that out, you can't forget it.'

Richard kissed her forehead. 'I'm not people, Hattie. I'm your husband.'

'They're my parents.'

'They'll come around.' He took her hands in his.

'Maybe I don't care.'

'Then maybe that's fine.'

She fell into him then and they hugged each other tightly. She needed it. She needed to feel something, *anything*. She had been numb for so long, as if someone had reached in, grabbed her emotions chip, and brutally wrenched it from her. She had become so removed from everyone and everything, and she didn't know how to change. She just didn't have a clue. Perhaps that's why she did what she did. The touch of another. She just needed a warm body, someone to remind her of who she was. She'd hoped this trip would make it all go away – the guilt, the self-loathing, and the hatred she felt for her parents.

'Sally?'

Hattie looked up. 'What?'

Richard's face was ashen. 'She's gone.'

*

Jonno was bored. His Aunt Bea was outside with Rachel and laughing over some blurry celebrity picture in a gossip magazine. He found the idea of lazing around in the garden immensely tedious. That and the fact that his dad and Hattie were out there in the wilderness with his half-sister. It basically meant that he was left on his own, stuck in the dusty, smelly old dump of a cottage with nothing to do but listen to music that he'd already heard, watch TV on a tiny flat screen that only had five channels, or read crappy, thirty-year-old books about stuff he had no interest in. What's more, it was really hot and uncomfortable, and he was sweaty. He hated that. He hated the heat, and he hated this holiday.

He'd said he didn't want to come. He'd said he would be much happier staying at his mum's, even though he wasn't Terry's biggest fan. He'd even said he would stay at his granddad's place, although he knew his dad would never go for that. They didn't exactly get on; a family secret in a long list of secrets that his dad and Hattie assumed Jonno wasn't aware of. In fact, now that he

69

thought about it, they assumed a great deal about what he did and didn't hear, and what he did and didn't take in. He knew a lot, an *awful* lot. Like where all that money came from, the money that he'd found in a suitcase under the stairs back at their house. And why they'd ended up at the backside of nowhere in a place that smelled like old people and mouldy water.

He opened the fridge, took off his T-shirt, and stood in front of it. The chilled air felt good. He reached into the freezer compartment, grabbed an ice cube from the latticed mould and popped it into his mouth. Whoa! That was too cold, so he spat it onto the floor.

He glanced out the window and watched Aunt Bea stand up and twirl around while Rachel laughed. He liked Aunt Bea, even though they weren't really related at all, and he liked Rachel, even though there was something about her that made his teeth hurt. They hadn't listened to him about the thing in the water, but that was okay. He probably wouldn't have listened to himself either, but he knew what he saw. He knew what he'd felt. It was a dinosaur or something, a giant snake. He shuddered.

The rear garden of the cottage was lined with fir trees that separated the small, neatly planted space from what he assumed was a much larger garden that lay beyond the picket fence – the one that belonged to the creepy woman and her boys, the boys that had broken into his room and cracked his iPad. That had really upset him. That iPad was his lifeline to his friends, to his mum. He'd thought about thumping them for doing what they'd done, had even dreamed about it that very night, but even in his rage he knew that they were much older and much bigger than him, and that the most likely outcome was a black eye and bloodied nose.

Jonno shut the door to the fridge and walked out into the hallway. He glanced at the crude crayon portraits. His eyes were drawn to one with a little girl with dark hair and freckles. She looked lonely. She stood with her parents. The dad was depicted as an older man with grey, thinning hair, the woman younger with a slight frame. The girl had a crooked grin and sharp eyes. In another, there was a boy wearing over-sized glasses. He was dressed smartly. He stood with what looked like his mother and grandmother. They too were dressed in smart clothes: pleated trousers, white blouses, hair immaculate. In all the pictures the adults' faces were faded, almost invisible. The crap drawings made Jonno wonder about all the families that had stayed there before. Why had they picked Spriggan's Retreat, of all places?

Jonno's gaze shifted to the small, partially frosted window by the front door. He peered out. The sun was high in the sky, and he could feel its persistent barrage of volcanic-level heat driving downwards towards the cottage. He thought of what the weird lady had said: "Don't go into the attic, don't strike a match". He hoped the sun did what he daren't and torched the whole place so that they could all get back in the car and go home.

Jonno was startled by the appearance of a strange-looking boy. It was like a scene from an old film: *The Hunchback of Notre Dame*, or *The Elephant Man*, or maybe even *The Descent*. He hadn't actually seen any of those films, but he'd read about them, and he'd seen clips on YouTube, on his broken iPad. This boy wasn't exactly any of those characters, but he was definitely from the same gene pool.

Jonno watched with a morbid fascination as the boy approached their car from the bushes. He wore khaki shorts and a grey, sweat-stained T-shirt with a camo vest. His dark hair was almost Mohican-like, with little black tufts sprouting from either side. One leg was straight and perfectly normal, the other twisted awkwardly at the hip and turned outwards. One shoulder was bulbous, the arm bent with the hand resting on the boy's chest, the fingers deformed into a grotesque claw. His eyes were too close together, almost touching, the irises almost completely white. His nose was very thin and long, and his mouth was small and turned upside down, as if the boy was permanently sad. His ears hardly had any lobes at all, and there was a thick, purple vein running down the side of his neck

71

which pulsed and throbbed.

Jonno watched as the boy surveyed his surroundings. Firstly, the boy looked back along the driveway; secondly, he turned and took one long, inquisitive look at the front door. His eyes moved to the window, the window that Jonno was standing at. Jonno instinctively dived for cover. Then, after a moment, he peered sheepishly over the windowsill. He could see the boy thinking, presumably wondering whether he was truly on his own. His albino eyes blinked once, twice and then he reached into the pocket of his vest. He withdrew a short wooden object, from within which the boy extracted a long curved blade. Jonno gasped. The boy took a few more steps towards the cottage, and Jonno took an equal number of steps backwards.

He considered his three options. Option one: go get his Aunt Bea and hope to God the sight of an adult would scare the intruder off. Option two: confront the boy himself while armed with his trusty air rifle. Finally, option three: run and hide and hope that whatever murderous intent the boy had would soon abate. He didn't like the way any of those scenarios played out in his head, especially the one where the boy with the scary eyes dug the knife into Jonno's throat, and sprayed blood and gore all over the driveway. He was strangely relieved when the boy bent down, grabbed hold of the Audi's front wheel arch, and plunged the knife into the tyre; an act he repeated on all four wheels.

Once the boy was finished, he stood, wiped the knife on his shorts, closed the blade and tucked it back into his vest. He took one last look at the cottage, exposed a sneering smile, turned, and then disappeared back into the bushes.

Jonno gingerly got to his feet. He let out a long sigh of relief, and then stifled a laugh; something that caught him off guard. The whole scene had been terrifying, tragic even. The disabled vandal, the unfortunate intruder, the hunchback of Bodhmall's Rest. He found it all a bit comical, even if that did make him a bad person who laughed at the misfortune of others. It wasn't just about the kid with the disability, which was unfortunate enough. His dad, though – his dad was going to come back from his little family picnic and find out that his forty-thousand-pound car was now completely and utterly useless. Now, that was priceless.

Perhaps, he thought, *this holiday isn't going to be so dull after all.*

*

'Sally!'

'Sally! Where are you?'

'Sally, stop playing around, sweetheart. Mummy and Daddy are really worried about you. You're *scaring* us!'

'Sally, come back here *this instant*! If you come back to us right now you won't be in any trouble, but if you don't—'

Hattie was going out of her mind. How could this have happened? They'd only turned away for a minute, thirty seconds even. It wasn't long enough for her to do a complete disappearing act like this. What if she'd been chasing a bird or a butterfly? Hattie thought back and remembered the brilliant blue dragonfly that had caught her attention. What if she'd strayed too close to the cliffs? What if she'd tripped and fell and... She couldn't even think about the ending to that sentence.

'I'm going to try looking further along the path. Are you okay to keep looking here? Hattie? Are you okay with that? Baby, are you listening?'

'What? Yes, of course I am. Please, Richard,' she grabbed his face. She could feel that he was trembling too. 'Please find her.'

He kissed her on the throat. 'I will. *We* will.' He turned and ran ahead. 'Sally! *Sally*!'

Hattie stepped from the path and worked from tree to tree. 'Sally, are you there, darling? It's okay, it is. It's fine. We know that you didn't mean to run off, you were probably just singing and dancing and got lost, that's all. If you can hear me now, please come

73

towards my voice. Please, Sally. *Please*, baby!'

The forest was so quiet. No birdsong, no insect noise, no screams and shouts from holidaymakers, no engine noises from aircraft overhead. It was as if someone or something had pressed an invisible mute button and deliberately turned off all sound. Hattie shuddered. It was eerie, freaky even. Sally was out there in it, all by herself and probably just as terrified as her parents, and yet they were simply impotent. They couldn't find her, and Hattie knew if it went on much longer the sun would start to set and Sally would be out there at night, all on her own, and she would be so cold and so afraid, and she would cry out for her parents and they wouldn't be able to hear her or find her, and it would just be so, so horrible.

There was a movement to her right, and she whirled towards it. Something small and quick had caught her eye, but when she peered into the trees and brambles there was nothing.

'Sally? Is that you? Baby, are you there?'

She walked to the spot where she thought she'd seen movement.

'Sally? Are you out there, sweetheart?'

She stepped on a rock and slipped, grabbing hold of a slim branch just in time to prevent herself from tumbling to the ground. '*Shit*!' She steadied herself. 'Sally! Please!'

There was another movement to her left, and she span to face it. Once again, there was nothing.

'Sally, if that's you, will you stop playing around. This isn't funny anymore. Mummy's just hurt her ankle.' She had too, the pain was screaming at her. 'And now she's starting to lose her temper!'

A noise from behind her, like a child's laugh.

'That's *enough*, Sally!'

If Hattie was angry at her daughter, her voice didn't give it away. Quite the contrary. Her voice was hesitant, uncertain and afraid. She glanced back the way she'd come, but Sally's buggy was no longer there, and neither, for that matter, was the path. The forest seemed endless, stretching far away into the distance, and the light was starting to fade too.

'Richard?'

Another snigger; one from her right and another, slightly higher pitched laugh from behind. Something or someone was taunting her.

'Who is that?'

Hattie slipped once more, and this time she fell to one knee. Her hand slammed into something sharp, and she cried out as thick bramble thorns penetrated the skin.

'*Ow*!'

She looked up, and there, maybe forty feet or so in front of her, was the shadowy form of a child reaching out from behind a narrow trunk. It held out a hand and waved at Hattie, and she lifted her bloodied palm and waved back. She spoke in a whisper.

'Sally?'

'Are you coming, Mummy?'

It was her daughter's voice, but different.

'Where, baby?'

'Are you coming to get me, Mummy?'

'Of course… of course I am.'

The child beckoned to her. 'Then come to me. I'm just here. Right here. Right where you can see me.'

Hattie started to cry. 'It doesn't sound like you, Sally. Your voice, it's… strange.'

'Here I am, Mummy. Why won't you come get me? Don't you love me? Don't you love me anymore, Mummy?'

'Yes, of course, I—'

'Then come to me. Just stand up, silly, and walk to me. You can do it.'

Hattie wiped tears from her cheeks and snot from her nose. She was afraid, but she didn't know why. It was her daughter after all, she'd found her. Richard had gone off like a firework, like he always did, and Sally had been right there all along, right under their noses. She stood.

'I'm coming, baby.'

The child started to sing.

'*Ladybird, ladybird, fly away home—*'

Hattie started to walk towards her daughter, and yet it felt almost as though she wasn't moving. Sally's silhouette was floating towards her, her bare feet just inches above the leafy carpet beneath.

'*Your house is on fire—*'

That song, she hadn't heard Sally sing it before, but the melody, it was so beautiful and yet so familiar. Her daughter was closer now, maybe thirty feet away, and Hattie longed to hold her in her arms, to smell her hair, to kiss her soft cheeks and clutch her so tightly that she would never be able to leave her again.

'*And the children are all gone—*'

The light started to penetrate the canopy, and Hattie could make out some of her daughter's features: her beautiful blue eyes, her red hair, the freckles on her forehead and cheeks.

'Sally, my darling.'

'*All except one, and her name is Sally-Ann—*'

There was something wrong. Sally wasn't smiling. She was gnashing her teeth together as if she was having one of her tempers, and her brow was furrowed, her eyes like slits. The song was coming from her in some disembodied way, but her lips weren't mouthing the words. There was just the awful chattering sound of teeth coming together repeatedly, and the persistent, feral grunting of desperately, urgent hunger.

'*And she's cooking for dinner in the frying pan!*'

Hattie held out her arms as her daughter came within reach, the lyrics of the nursery rhyme drowned out by the sound of her own joyful sobs.

'It's Mummy, Sally. Come to Mummy.'

Sally, or the thing that she believed to be Sally, leaned forwards and Hattie could now see its grey skin, its red eyes, and its black, flitting tongue.

'*We see you, Mummy. We want you, too. Come with us, and we'll show you the path home.*'

Hattie cried out as something grabbed her shoulder. She rolled onto her back and looked up at the ominously black silhouette that bore down on her. She screamed.

'*Hattie*!' the thing yelled.

'Leave me alone! Just give me Sally! I just want my *daughter*!'

She swung her arms around frantically, one of which connected with her attacker, but the thing grabbed at her and pulled viciously at her clothes.

'Hattie, it's me!'

She fought with all her pitiful strength, but the creature was far too strong, far too powerful. She felt the energy draining from her body. Her cheeks were hot, and her vision was cloudy, but she felt the creature lift her from the floor as if she were nothing.

'It's me. Your husband. Richard. I… I think you fainted.'

Hattie almost choked on her own breath at the sound of Richard's voice. She held her hand up to shield her eyes from the brilliant glare of the sun.

'I found her. She's back there along the path with Hilda. You know? The lady that Glanna told us about?'

Hattie tried to speak, but her throat was bone dry. 'Hilda?'

'Yes, you remember?'

'The children, the song?' she asked. 'The ladybirds and… and the fire?'

'I… well, that's a little odd, Hats. But… maybe you're dehydrated, or the heat's gotten to you or something, but it's OK. We can get you something to drink, something to eat.'

'But… but where—'

'Sally, you see? She's such a clever girl. She knew where we were going all along.'

'Where we were… going?'

'Yeah, she—' Hattie watched as her husband pointed to a

77

plump, red-faced woman who was standing on the edge of the forest with their daughter at her side. She was beaming with a broad sunshine of a smile. 'She found Dozmary Point.'

*

Freddie emerged from the thicket, his face and arms covered in mud and mulch. Sweat ran from his forehead and into his eyes, and he wiped his dirty fingers across his brow. He was shaking his head in disgust.

'That was gross.'

Aaron leaned with his bare back against a tree and pulled a pack of cigarettes from the pocket of his jeans. He lit up. 'Maybe the foxes got to him.'

'I don't think it was the foxes that did that.'

'Nah, me neither.'

Freddie thought of Evie and the children, what she could make them do.

'You think we dug a deep enough hole?'

'Well,' Aaron exhaled, 'it will have to do. I, for one, am not digging any more. I'm knackered. And, anyway, we've filled it in now.'

Freddie sat down on an exposed trunk, his mouth open and his hands on his hips. 'Mother will be pissed if he gets found. Noah too.'

'Oh, Noah can go fuck himself for all I care. It's always you and me doing the grunt work anyway. What does he ever do, aside from playing with his chemistry set and reading his boring books?'

'But—'

'Look,' Aaron bent down and took his brother's face in his grimy palms. 'We came out here, and we did what was asked. Mother will just have to be happy with that, won't she?'

Freddie pushed Aaron's hands away. The acrid smoke from his brother's cigarette was making his eyes stream. 'And what if…

what if he comes back?'

'You saw him, right? How the hell is he coming back?'

'I don't know. I just thought—'

'Look, what did Mother ask us to do? What was the task?' Aaron flicked his butt.

'Well, she—'

'Did she, or did she not, tell us to get rid of the body?'

Freddie sighed. 'Yes. She did.'

'And?' Aaron perused the ground around them. 'Do you see any bodies? Any at all? Because I sure don't.'

Freddie stared at his dirty trainers. 'No, I... I don't see any bodies.'

'So, there you have it.' Aaron smirked. 'Task accomplished, bruv.' Aaron climbed the short incline and grabbed a shovel and a heavy pickaxe. 'Let's head back. We skipped breakfast, and my stomach's groaning like a vicar in a brothel.'

There was a flash of colour to Freddie's right, and he whirled towards it. He peered into the gloom, but there was nothing; just trees, leaves and the morning's lingering mist. He decided it was probably a squirrel. Or a rat. Another sodding rat.

'What if he somehow shows up?'

'Who?'

'What do you mean, who? The husband.'

Aaron turned to his brother. 'What, like a zombie?'

'No, not like a zombie, exactly.'

'What then? A ghost? Freddie,' Aaron grinned, exposing all his crooked and yellowing teeth, 'the dude is dead. Like, *proper* dead. People don't come back from that.'

Freddie nodded reluctantly. His brother was right. It was pretty final, death. He remembered the guy's face: the rage in his eyes, his red hair, crimson cheeks, and the muscles tensed in his neck. He was a bomb just waiting to go off. They'd had no choice. They say the dead are finally at peace, but Freddie couldn't agree. The guy hadn't been peaceful at all. She, on the other hand – the wife – she'd just looked sad. That image, the blonde lady with the pretty face in such a state of confusion, and the angry man with his body ripped and shredded like slow-cooked meat. He knew it would never fade.

'Come on, Blair Witch. I'm starving,' Aaron said, and tossed the pickaxe in Freddie's direction. He snatched at it, narrowly evading its sharp point as it swung between his open legs.

'Careful, you idiot! You could have injured me down there.'

Aaron laughed. 'Ha, wouldn't have made a difference. You haven't used that little thing since the shop girl with the lazy eye decided to cop you a charity shag.'

'Hey, watch it! What the hell would you know about that?'

The pair of them trudged their way through the dense woodland, pushing each other and hollering abuse. Some way behind, in the darkest part of the thicket and with his hand resting on freshly laid earth, the Red Man was crying.

*

'And don't forget to grab the sun cream on your way back.'

'I won't, don't worry. How could I? You've said it a hundred times already. Now, just let me go to the loo, won't you?'

Rachel burst through the kitchen door, leaned over the sink, and splashed her face with cold water. It was sweltering hot, maybe thirty degrees, and she'd been literally cooking out there. The things she did for her job.

Bea had her nose in one of her beloved Agatha Christie detective mysteries. She appeared totally engrossed. Rachel, on the other hand, had dozed off for like an hour. When she gradually came to, she'd sensed that the moment was right. The others were out, and they surely would be for a while yet. Bea was still head down in her book (*Jesus*, she thought, *how could anyone concentrate for so long on all those streams of tiny words?*), and Jonno was otherwise engaged. Eric had said it was here. *Right* here. She needed to find something before the day was out. She was

80

running out of time.

She dried her face and hands on a clean tea towel and turned to the open doorway. Richard kept his laptop in the bedroom – she had seen him cowering over the screen's bright glare that very morning – so she decided to start there.

She poked her head into the lounge. No Jonno in there. *Maybe*, she thought, *he's in his bedroom*. She decided to check.

She grabbed the handrail and climbed the stairs. The place really was old, and it smelled like it too.

Rachel moved quickly along the upstairs hallway and thrust her head into Jonno's room. He wasn't in there either, which she thought was odd, but it was convenient for her. She swept back out onto the landing, and after a quick glance into the bathroom, opened the door to the master suite. The room was quite large with plenty of room for a queen-sized double bed, built-in wardrobe, and narrow writing desk, and Richard's laptop sat open beneath the slim, single-glazed window. She moved swiftly across the large rug at the foot of the bed and hit the space bar. The screen came to life, and immediately a picture of Hattie, Richard and Sally beamed up at her. She paused to consider the password. It was obvious really. Even if she hadn't had the foresight to peep over Richard's shoulder when she and Bea had visited for dinner a month or so ago, she felt she could have got it within three or four attempts. It was the tried and tested combo – daughter's name, followed by her date of birth: *Sally210617*.

She glanced over her shoulder before hitting *enter*. There was nobody there. She was still alone, but she knew she had only maybe five minutes before Bea came looking for her.

She found the email icon and double clicked. Again, the local Wi-Fi did its best to drive her insane as the blue circle of doom whirled and whirled like a digital Catherine Wheel of torture, but thankfully, after a few moments, the browser came to life and she was inside Richard's personal inbox. She scanned the list of names. Eric had given her the call sign *Mr Quin* and the email address *haribe@gmail*, so she speed-read the emails in Richard's inbox for any sign of either. After she came up blank, she searched his sent items. Not much activity in the last week, and prior to that there were a lot of work emails and personal stuff sent to both sets of parents. She clicked on the search bar. She typed *Quin,* which frustratingly came back blank, so went for *Haribe* instead. There was nothing. *Weasel* gave her the same disappointing result. She decided that there must be another email account, so she opened Richard's search history.

She scrolled through the boring stuff: news, sports, business updates, some pretty standard porn – nothing sinister – and then she spied an interesting link. Anticipation built, and she licked her lips. She brushed a stray braid from her face as her finger hovered over the keypad. Could this be it? Could it be that easy?

She hesitated before double clicking. Again, the circle of doom. Again, the gasps of muted frustration. This time, the circle wheeled over and over, until Rachel was thrumming her fingertips on the desk and pulling at her cheeks and hair. She couldn't see the garden from this part of the house, and so she listened keenly for the sound of a door opening or of footsteps on the hard flooring. She swiped a finger across the keypad again, but the circle still whirled. She considered searching for the router, but what was the point? Re-booting it would take far too long, and even then, there was no guarantee of success. She wondered whether her best option would be to leave it for the day and pick another moment, but would there ever be a better chance than this? With the house empty and the laptop right there? She cursed her bad luck. Of all the times for the connection to freeze. Shitty, backwoods, musty-smelling, rat infested, creaky old creep-show of a house. Of all the places for this deal to go down, why did it have to be here?

'This is just bloody brilliant.'

Suddenly the screen flickered and jumped, and an email page leapt into life.

'Yes, *yes.*'

She cracked her knuckles and peered eagerly at the screen. The address read *dickyP@mail.co.uk*. Not the account she had hoped for, not even a cool, difficult-to-crack codename, but she pulled out her phone and took a photograph anyway.

She opened the contacts list and was surprised to find only one: *tdeville666@hotmail.com*. Five emails to the same person, three replies.

DickyP – Payment sent. It should be with you by the end of the day. Do what you do.

TDeville666 – Thanks – all received.

Dicky P – This month will be a little light – I hope that's OK. We'll meet at the usual spot.

TDeville666 – That could cause a few problems. Let's talk about it face to face.

Dicky P – It was great to see you again. As I said when we met, give me a few days. I think I have a way to meet the shortfall.

TDeville666 – That would be very good. We'll need it. If you're serious about this – as serious as I am – then we need to act quickly.

Dicky P – I've got it – sorry it took a little longer than expected. Transferring it now.

Dicky P – We made it. The drive was way too long and Hattie seemed even more uptight than usual, but otherwise the trip was uneventful. When can I see you? We need to talk. I want to up the ante.

Rachel opened each correspondence in turn, read them with a keen interest and sent a copy to her private email address. She then deleted the sent items from Richard's mail account. There was no mention of any of the contacts or leads that Eric had given her, but there was definitely something off about the exchange. The secret account, transactions that sounded financial, a covert meeting. It was enough to pique her interest, even if it wasn't quite what she'd expected. Who was Richard planning to meet? Was it The Weasel? Was this the link between Lyndsay Arthur, Mr Quin and whoever now sat at the top of the pyramid? Was Richard the facilitator, the fence? She had to find out, even if she knew it might cost her on a personal level. She desperately wanted that not to be the case, much more than was healthy in this situation, but she couldn't lose sight of what she'd set out to accomplish. It had been way too long, and she'd lost too much along the way.

'Rach? Are you still up there?'

'Shit—'

She shut the window and opened Richard's Google account. She heard footsteps and the door to the lounge opening.

'Rach? I'm burning out here. Are you still on the loo?'

'Just finishing up. God, you're so impatient.'

She clicked on *search history* and hit delete. More footsteps, this time in the lounge.

'Well, you've been bloody ages, you know. I thought you might have fallen down the hole.'

'I'm drying my hands, just give me a sec.'

Rachel closed all the open windows and scrolled to the start icon. The screen froze again.

'Oh, *come on*!'

A groan from one of the steps.

'I'll come up and grab the sun cream if you like. I know where I packed it—'

'*No*! I mean, it's okay. I've got it right here.'

Rachel bashed the keypad, but the screen just stared at her, the agonising circle of doom whirring and taunting.

'Factor fifteen?'

'The very same.'

'Well, that's no good for me, Rach. You know that. I burn with anything less than factor thirty. Look, I know where—'

'*Thirty*! I've got thirty! My mistake.'

The circle disappeared and the menu bar opened. Rachel wiped sweat from her face, hit *sleep*, closed the laptop and raced across the bedroom, hastily tiptoeing across the landing to the room she shared with Bea.

'You're confusing me. I'm coming up.'

Rachel frantically opened the green zipper bag at the foot of the bed and pulled out moisturiser, hand cream, body spray, hairbrushes. Where was it? Where the hell had Bea put it?

The footsteps had made it to the top of the stairs now. Rachel could feel her heart almost exploding through her ribcage and her breath coming in shallow bursts. She threw face wipes, cotton buds, eyeliner pens, tubs of foundation, and tubes of lipstick all over the floor in urgent desperation. This was ridiculous.

Bea rounded the corner and pushed the door open.

'What's going—'

'*I've got it!*' Rachel whirled round and held out the tube of sun cream, her face hot and sweaty, her hair stuck to her forehead and her smile wide and forced. 'Factor thirty, just like you asked.'

Bea's eye narrowed and she glared at her. *I've been rumbled*, Rachel thought. She held her breath, ready for the inevitable.

Bea smirked. 'I hope you're going to clean up this mess.'

*

Jonno sat in the attic and peered through the gap in the ceiling. He'd decided to take a look up there after the scary-looking boy had slashed the Audi's tyres. He'd figured he might need a hiding place if the boy decided to come back and do some more serious damage. He looked like he was more than capable. The roof fascinated him with its promise of chaos and destruction. Its flammability was like a magnetism to him. He'd even taken Rachel's lighter with him, just to feel the soothing heat of its smooth casing in his pocket. He sat there in the darkness, inches from the dried kindling, knowing it would erupt if he just ignited one little, titchy flame. It was a sense of power he rarely felt in his day-to-day life, and he realised he liked it, like, *a lot*. The ongoing existence or otherwise of this mouldy, festering place was in his hands. He had control.

Rachel, on the other hand, was out of control, creeping through his dad's room and shoving her nose into his personal stuff. He watched as she cursed and grunted, grinned as he heard Aunt Bea come into the house, giggled as Rachel rushed to conceal what she'd been up to, and groaned in disappointment as she appeared to get away with it.

But she hadn't, had she? No, not by a long shot. She may have saved him from drowning in the ocean, but that didn't excuse her from spying on his family. And anyway, he already knew what she'd found. He'd seen it before. The money, the secrets, the deception. It was all around him. Everybody lied, he'd learned. Even those that shouldn't. It was ingrained in people, as real as blood and sweat and pain. It coursed through everyone like a virus, permeating fingertips and tongues, spilling from open mouths like bad breath. His dad had lied to him about his mum; Hattie had lied about why she was so angry all the time; Aunt Bea had lied about what had gone down with that accountant guy, and Rachel had lied about who she really was. Ipso facto, everybody lied. There was just no getting away from it.

He'd realised some time ago that where there are lies there is generally truth, and the holder of the truth gains the power; the power of ultimate control. There was something else he'd learned too. Control is a funny thing. One minute you have none, and then suddenly you have it all. He had control over his dad, even if he didn't know it yet, and up there in the attic, with Rachel's lighter gripped firmly in his hand, he had control over the house. Better still, he now had control over Rachel.

He intended to exercise it.

*

86

'Did you do it?'

'I did.'

'Did he see you?'

'I fink so.'

'The boy?'

Eli nodded, smirking. 'Turd-Boy.'

'That's good. I assume you left the knife?'

'Yep. I dropped it in the bushes at the side of the track. In the dirt, by the wall like you tole me to. Nice and obvious, but not too obvious.' He scratched at an itch and peered up at her. He thought she was pretty, in spite of everything. She smelled good too. 'It'll be found if someone wants to go looking for it, don't you worry yourself about that, Miss Evie.'

She smiled back at him. It was a nice smile, although he always thought it a bit crooked, like a line that hadn't been drawn straight. In any case, she looked pleased with his work, which was good enough. He'd made sure he did exactly as she'd asked, to the letter. Everything, just like she'd said. He knew what she wanted, after all. She wanted to play with her new toy – the boy who smelled like turds – the one she scared so badly he almost drowned himself. She'd told him all about it, the way it had made her feel. She told Eli lots of things, sometimes things Eli didn't want to hear, things he really didn't want to have rattling around in his big old head, but he just sat and listened anyway, looking attentive and agreeable and nodding along just the same. What's more, he'd seen this particular trick before, the one where she teased the new kid. Push him, tickle him and stretch him to see how he reacted. Would the kid tell? Would he even care? Would he come after Eli himself? Kid-Bastard Evie stooped down and whispered. He liked that.

'Let's let that little pot boil and see where it takes us. It'll be fun. Now,' she straightened, 'on to other things. I need to talk to you about my two idiot brothers.'

Eli recoiled. He didn't want anything to do with those two.

'What about 'em?'

'I need you to keep an eye on both of them.'

'What fer?'

'That little episode the other evening, with the periwinkles.' Again, he felt himself shrinking. The Red Man – the thing he'd asked for: the little girl.

'That poor couple.'

'Yes. Indeed.'

'She was nice to me.'

'Everyone's nice to you, Eli. You have a way.' She took out a pad and pen and handed it to him. 'Here, keep notes.'

He took them in his good hand and peered at her, curious. 'Notes?'

'Yes. Look, I know your grasp of the written word isn't exactly grammar school standard, but your sketches will do, even scribbles. I want to know where they go and what they get up to. Especially after dark.' She glared up at Excelsior Lodge. 'My mother's up to something, and she's got Tweedle Dumb and Tweedle Dumber doing her dirty work for her. I have to know what it is. *Exactly* what it is.'

'But... what if I get caught?'

'Well, silly,' she said, winking at him, 'don't.'

*

'How are you feeling?'

'Better, I think.'

'You poor dear. This heat really does do odd things to people, especially if you're not used to it.'

Hattie sipped her lemonade.

The large lady with the green apron and rosy complexion continued. 'The forest can be really quite confusing, even to the locals. I've told the council several times that the path needs to be laid properly, and that they need to put some signs up, some landmarks at the very least.'

Hattie nodded, but she was only half listening. The memory of that horrible thing masquerading as her daughter… She tried to focus on the cool drink in her hands, and of Sally, of course. Sally was there with them and that was good.

'This is delicious, Hilda. It's really something.' Richard was devouring a sandwich while spilling fresh crab meat all over the table. 'It's just divine. Hats, you really need to try this. You'll love it. It's even better than back home.'

The café was empty, aside from the four of them. The panoramic view through the windows at the front exposed the cliff edge and the gently shifting surface of the ocean. The bright sun was a crisp yellow and the sky a deep forever blue. A gull swooped past on the slipstream as though it hadn't a care in the world. Hattie was envious.

'I'm not hungry.' She shot a sideways glance at the woman. 'Sorry.'

'Not at all, love. You've had quite an episode. It's little wonder that you've lost your appetite, what with you losing your baby girl and then collapsing with heat exhaustion like that.'

'It wasn't the heat.'

'Of course it was, darling.' Richard dabbed at the corners of his mouth. 'What else could it have been? You fainted.'

'I saw something. It'll sound weird I know, but something—' she winced, 'there's something in those woods.'

Richard laughed. 'You were delirious, love. From the heat. What you saw – *whatever* you saw – well, it was a figment of your imagination. Isn't that right, Hilda?'

'It's true, dear. It's happened here before, more than once. People come into the café in a right state, telling me stories about all sorts of creatures and strange shenanigans. I sit them down, get them a drink and something to eat, and by the time they leave it's all been forgotten, and they go back to their holidays and have a wonderful time with their families. It's the air down here, you see.' Hilda scraped Hattie's uneaten sandwich into a waste bin. 'It does things to people. It unlocks their creative side, or something like that.'

'I know what I saw.' Hattie stood and went to her daughter. She was lying on the floor in front of the window and scribbling on a sheet of paper with coloured crayons.

'And I believe you,' Richard said as he stood to gather their things. 'You had an awful fright, we both did, and it's no surprise that it manifested itself as something horrible and terrifying. I was terrified too.'

'Your little girl really is an angel,' Hilda said, pouring herself a coffee.

'I know,' Hattie agreed.

'She came right into the café, right out of the blue. It caught me by surprise, I can tell you. She grabbed me by my hand and pleaded with me to go with her to find her mummy. I was shocked, but I went, of course. Who wouldn't? She led me down the hill, across the stream and into the woods. Then she directed me along the trail as confidently as one of the locals would. I was astonished when she brought me directly to you and your husband. Someone so young, too.'

Richard was nodding. 'It was a miracle, really. I was frantically scouring the woods when I saw them both walking along the path, as if they were out for a stroll or something. Sally here was practically dragging Hilda to you, wasn't she?'

Hilda smiled.

'I don't like this place, Richard.'

There was a moment of silence.

'Look,' Hilda removed her apron and smoothed down her skirt. 'Why don't I call you a taxi? I can get you back home quickly so you can put your feet up, and then your lovely husband here can wait on you while you get your bearings back.'

Hattie thought that sounded good. She wanted to be anywhere but here. She needed to get her daughter as far away from that café and those horrible woods as possible.

'Great idea, Hilda,' Richard said. 'If you wouldn't mind arranging that for us, that would be perfect. I think my wife needs to rest.' He reached for his wallet, and Hilda immediately held out her hands.

'Please, no. The sandwiches and the lemonade are on me. I couldn't even think to charge you, after you've both had such a terrible start to your day.'

Richard shook his head. 'Oh no, that's very kind of you, but really, I'd much rather we pay our way.'

'I wouldn't think of it. No, thank you very much.' Hilda waved a hand dismissively. 'Now, where did you say you were staying? I can book you a taxi online. I'm really quite the dab hand with technology these days, you know.' She tapped her keyboard and smiled. 'There it is. Now, all I need from you is the house number and postcode.'

Hattie stooped and tucked Sally's drawing into her pocket.

'We're staying at Bodhmall's Rest.'

*

Jonno found the knife on his third reconnaissance sweep of the driveway. After waiting long enough to be sure that the boy wasn't coming back, he made a decision to check the damage to his father's tyres. They were pretty bad, like, catastrophically bad, and he knew his dad was going to have a heart attack when he saw them. The boy had obviously known what he was doing, pushing the knife in and then twisting and pulling it diagonally upwards. The tears were deep and long.

He'd instinctively wandered towards the gap in the bushes, the spot where the boy had exited the scene of the crime, and he'd clambered through them. He climbed onto the stone wall and dropped to the rough track on the other side. He glanced up and down the path and then traced a finger along the stonework as he walked towards No Man's Land, circling the large tree, looking in at each of the properties in turn, and then arriving back at Spriggan's. He did this twice more, each time taking in more of his surroundings: the jarring differences between the four properties, the wooden bench that sat to the north of the grassy area, the strange-looking monument on its southern tip. On his third circuit, something caught his eye. There was a bright reflection off something on the ground, by the base of the stone wall. Curious, he stooped to see what it was. He felt a pang of excitement. He held out a hand to it, felt his breath catch in his throat as his fingertips brushed its surface. The wooden handle felt solid and well used, the edge of the knife smooth and dangerously sharp. His tongue felt dry, and his teeth ached. He looked around once more but there was no one there. He stood and pocketed the knife, feeling the pleasing weight of the solid wood and the chill of gleaming metal against his thigh. He felt the excitement of danger and secrets, too.

He turned to head back to the cottage, to the safety of his room where he could properly assess his illicit treasure, and that's when he saw the boy. He was standing further along the path, by the edge of the big house. His gait was awkward, angular, his expression unmoving. He was looking directly at Jonno.

'Shit.' A hard lump formed in his throat, and he felt the urge to turn and run. The knife burned hot in his pocket. He held his breath and felt the quickening thrum of his heart.

The boy stood for a moment that way, just staring at him, as though he found Jonno unusual. Then he abruptly turned and disappeared into the forest.

The old Jonno would have placed the knife back on the ground and returned to his bedroom, never thinking of this episode ever again, never even allowing it to pass through his thoughts. But that was old Jonno, the Jonno that existed no more. That Jonno had melted away as soon as he realised he had gained the power. This newer, more formidable version of himself didn't back away from a challenge, not ever. This version of Jonno tackled things head on, and so he decided, with an air of glued-together confidence, to follow the scary-looking boy.

The woods were dense, and the ground was uneven. A couple of times he nearly fell, undoubtedly hurting himself in the process, but despite his dad regularly calling him a clumsy lummox, he was actually pretty nimble, and he moved swiftly and ably among the trees. He could see the boy weaving a line towards what looked like a clearing. The sun burned a laser beam of orange light through a hole in the thick canopy.

He placed a hand on the knife and then sharply pulled it away again. Did he really think he had it in him to use it? To cut someone? Stab them, even? When it came down to it, would he really be able to hurt somebody? He'd never even punched anyone before.

The trees started to thin out as Jonno approached. The boy had been standing directly in the centre of the clearing, staring up at the sun, the light illuminating the angular features of his misshapen head. However, when Jonno finally emerged at its perimeter, scrabbling up a mound of rubble and loose earth, the boy had disappeared. Jonno stood there, half behind the base of an oak tree, and waited. The clearing was empty, besides a couple of animated squirrels that seemed to be engaged in a battle over some hazelnuts. Jonno took the bull by the horns and boldly walked out to the middle. The squirrels stopped, looked at him, and then departed in a pair of grey-tailed flashes. He was alone.

There was a snap of twigs, the whistle of movement. He span towards it – nothing. He felt a coldness rise to the surface of his skin, even though the heat was at least twenty-five. He was sweating and shivering all at once. He wanted his things, the comfort of his stuff, the hardened, impenetrable armour of his daily rituals. This wasn't him. He'd made a mistake. Another crack sounded, the clatter of birds departing their nests, leaves being wrenched from branches, forest debris flying. He almost sunk to the ground in a sobbing, retching mess, but he somehow held it together. He attempted to grip the knife, but it felt like soft feathers between his trembling fingers.

A prod between his shoulder blades, the feel of hot breath on his neck, a hoarse grunt in his ear. He closed his eyes and envisioned the boy standing behind him in the clearing, so close they were almost in an embrace; white eyes unblinking, a clawed hand gripping a bloodied blade.

He turned slowly.

*

'So, your brother-in-law.'

'The one with a stick up his arse?'

'Yes, that's him, the very same.' Rachel laughed through a mouthful of ice cubes and tea. 'What exactly does he do for a living again?'

Bea closed her paperback. 'For a living?'

'Yeah, you know, work and stuff. I mean, he's got a Q7, so he must have a few quid in his bank account. The detached house, double garage, private school for Jonno. Doesn't exactly scream poverty, does it?'

Bea peered at Rachel over her sunglasses. 'I thought you knew. He has his own business, Penrose & Son. And Hattie? Well, she works with kids. I think they do pretty well between them. They're not rich, if that's what you're asking.'

'No, no. I'm not asking that at all. Wouldn't bother me if they were.' Rachel knew she was treading a fine line between interest and inquisition. 'Just, you know, Penrose & Son. What even is that?'

'Whew, I don't know. Buying and selling, I guess. He's away a lot on business trips. He goes all over the place – Africa, South America, and the Far East.' Bea opened her book, signalling she was growing tired of the subject. 'I think Hattie prefers it that way.'

'Mm, I guess.' Rachel considered her next question carefully. 'I'm assuming it's all above board? This business of his? Nothing

94

dodgy, or anything like that?'

Bea dropped her book. 'What, you mean like illegal?'

'Well, you know?' Rachel forced a laugh. 'Nothing serious – I'm not suggesting he's a mafia don or anything – just that maybe he's dabbled in some under-the-table deals, some secret handshakes, perhaps paid for a few favours. That kind of thing.'

'Ooh, now that is an interesting thought. Richard 'Pablo' Penrose, devious criminal mastermind. The kingpin of the east Kent underworld. Raking in millions of pounds through illicit deals. Drugs, prostitution, armed robbery,' Bea leaned towards Rachel, hands curled in mock claws, '*murder*!'

'Oh, piss off. I was just being curious.'

'Stop being so bloody nosy,' Bea said, wagging her finger. 'You want to know what he does, ask him. I haven't a clue. When he starts spouting on about work, I either switch off or leave.'

'Yeah, whatever.'

'Oh, come on. I was only kidding.' Bea tried to kiss Rachel on the cheek, but she turned away, feigning annoyance. 'Look, I believe he trades in collectables, fine goods. Some art, historic artefacts, sculptures and books. It's basically old stuff, the kind of junk that only the wealthy can afford. People that have got more money than sense, if you ask me.'

Rachel raised her eyebrows and sipped on her iced tea. She already knew all of this of course. 'He must make a lot of contacts in that line of work. Powerful people.' She shrugged. 'I would guess so, anyway. People with money tend to have power. They go hand in hand, don't they?'

'Yeah, maybe. Ooh, there was one guy.'

'Yes?'

'Big bloke, quite old. Early fifties? No, wait. He might have been older than that. Anyway,' she turned to face her, 'he had a nice car; a Maserati or a Lamborghini, I don't know. It was one of those cars that looks hard to get in and out of, and it was bright orange too, like a tangerine, that's why I remember it. Anyway, Richard sold him something pretty damn expensive. I know that, because he and Hattie were going on about it for weeks. I think it paid for the swimming pool in the garden.'

'Wow. Yeah, I did wonder about that. It's a nice pool.'

'Yeah, well, the deal turned sour. Apparently, the guy really didn't like the condition of the goods that were shipped to him. He was pretty pissed, in fact. It got real scary, real quickly. Two blokes turned up one night at the door. I was inside with Hattie, Jonno was at his mum's, and Sally was in bed. We were watching the TV when we heard a lot of yelling, the slamming of doors, and then a scuffle.'

'Woah!' Rachel exclaimed. 'What, like a fight?'

'Worse. They did a number on him. Broke two of his fingers, fractured his eye socket, and split his mouth open. He was a mess.'

'What? You mean these guys were pals of the bloke with the orange car?' Rachel was taken aback. This hadn't been in the file. *How the hell had they missed this?*

'Something like that. I definitely think they worked for Lambo guy, even though Richard would never admit it. There was blood everywhere. We took him to A&E, but he just told them that he'd been attacked in the street. He refused to get the police involved, much to Hattie's annoyance.'

'That's just awful.' Rachel suddenly had a feeling this Lambo guy was going to be very important to her case. 'What happened after that?'

'Don't know, nothing was ever said about it, and I didn't ask. Richard said he'd sorted it somehow, but the atmosphere in the house was pretty tense for months afterwards. Then again, that's nothing unusual.'

'And this Lambo guy?' Rachel pushed. 'Did he have a name?'

'It was never mentioned, or if it was, I didn't catch it. But I do remember the numberplate on the car. The tangerine mobile, that's what I called it. Anyway, I'll never forget it, especially after what happened. It was creepy.'

Rachel leaned closer. 'Creepy? How do you mean?'

'You know – scary. This old guy and his goons, showing up at the house and kicking the living daylights out of Richard, terrifying his family. His numberplate matched his persona, like he was making some kind of sick joke or something.'

Bea recalled the details and Rachel's heart stopped for just a moment. The clues were beginning to click together like little plastic bricks. Bit by bit she was building a path that would lead her to the top of the criminal enterprise and to Tommy's killer. She sipped furiously on her drink, attempting to organise the jumbled thoughts that were racing around in her head. The numberplate matched the email address of the contact she'd found on Richard's laptop: TDEVIL666

*

A voice from behind.

'Whatcha doing?'

Jonno cried out and span around, almost falling over. It was the freaky kid all right. He must have been standing there all along.

'I—' Jonno was lost for words. He stared at the boy's disconcerting features: his long head, twisted leg, milky albino eyes. He was frozen to the spot. The boy slowly looked him up and down. A long line of spittle ran from a slanted mouth. He seemed oblivious to it.

'You have my fing.'

'You're—'

He pointed at Jonno's shorts. 'My sharp fing. I saw you put it in your pocket.'

Jonno came back to reality. 'Oh, yeah. Sorry.' He reached into his pocket and touched the warm handle of the blade. Was he really going to give this guy a knife? 'I'm sorry, I just saw it lying there on the ground. I assumed someone had lost it and—'

'I had.' The boy held out his good hand. 'And now I want it back.'

'Of course.'

Jonno once more considered his options. Option one: give the guy the knife and hope he didn't turn his head into a shish kebab. Option two: stab the guy to death and figure out some ingenious way of disposing of the body. Just the thought of those two horrifying scenarios, neither any better than the other, made his head hurt. He tried to collect himself, but it was a haphazard attempt. Everything was a fog. His dad said that when Jonno got like this it was because he was letting the weight of the world press down on him like a heavy boulder. When that happened, he told him to think of the boulder as a giant helium-filled balloon, and to imagine it floating away. Jonno closed his eyes. He thought of the balloon – a big blue one with happy birthday printed on the front in large silver letters – and took a long, deep breath. When the fog cleared and the weight lifted a little, he picked an option.

'There you go. Sorry for any confusion.'

The boy eyed the blade, scratched at a cauliflower ear, and shrugged.

'You keep it.'

'But I—'

'I've got plen'y.'

Jonno looked down at the knife in his hand. He tried to hide his gratitude, play it cool. 'Okay, whatever.'

'I'm Eli, by the way.'

'I'm Jonno.'

'You wanna see sum'fing, Jonno?'

He was still reeling. Eli's generosity had thrown him. 'Sure, I guess.'

'Cool. Follow me.' The boy turned and disappeared amongst the trees.

Jonno kept pace with him, although Eli was much quicker than he looked. He half-ran, half-swung through the woods. Jonno felt his lungs bursting as he scrambled up a slope, pushing through thick undergrowth and leaping over rocks and gnarly roots. They emerged at what looked like the rear of Excelsior Lodge, the moss covered, tiled roof of the bigger house just visible above the trees, the smaller cottage barely peeping out from among the hedgerows. He heard his aunt Bea's laughter. It was such a happy, familiar sound that he found himself drawn to it. Maybe sunbathing in the garden hadn't been such a bad idea after all.

Eli turned to him, his expression a half-sneer/half-smile. 'Come on, it's just through here. Quickly.'

They passed through a tatty wooden gate into an open yard, a rusty brown combine harvester parked as if abandoned, a truck raised on red blocks, its wheels missing. Eli rounded a corner and entered a large barn, its wide doors standing open like the jaws of a mighty beast, its teeth made from bales of hay that lay scattered in the gloom. The boy glanced over his shoulder and beckoned Jonno towards him.

Jonno paused and looked back towards Spriggan's. He briefly considered whether or not to follow him. He remembered the knife slicing through the tyres as easily as cutting through soft cheese; recalled Rachel hunched over the laptop, and later, scurrying around to find the sun cream. Above all, he remembered that he had the power. He placed a hand on the knife and strode forwards.

It was hard to see inside the barn. The smell was oaty and musty, like out-of-date cereal. He tripped on the remains of a bale, and heard laughter from above.

'I'm up here.'

Jonno looked up and saw Eli hanging from a handrail at the edge of a mezzanine floor. There was a wooden ladder leading upwards.

'Wh... why? What's up there?'

'You'll see.'

Jonno placed a hand on the ladder and swallowed. He hated heights. The sharp daggers were back inside his skull and his brain hurt. *Balloon, balloon, balloon* he repeated over and over in his head. *It's just a stupid balloon.*

99

He placed his foot on the first rung, and then his other foot on the second. He felt his own body weight, the gravity sucking him towards the earth like an enormous magnet. The boulder sat awkwardly on his shoulders. It was rocking from side to side. He couldn't let it fall. He gritted his teeth and tensed his muscles, hauling himself upwards while everything around him tried to drag his body back to the ground and crush him with its awesome mass. His eyes were now at the level of the mezzanine floor, and he could see a mattress, crayon drawings, and more knives and tools. There was a window overhead that faced Excelsior Lodge. Eli was standing there.

'Come over here. You'll definitely wanna see this.'

Jonno grunted and pulled himself across the floor, his legs still flailing behind him. Eli grabbed his hand and pulled, and Jonno felt himself flying across the loft as if he were weightless. The boy was super strong.

'Take a look over there, quickly, at that window. Be careful now. You don't wanna get caught.'

Jonno stood sheepishly next to Eli. He could smell the boy's dense body odour. He peered at the house. Excelsior Lodge was large, but it was in need of some urgent care and attention. The walls were almost invisible behind a blanket of thick ivy, and the frames of the doors and windows were mottled brown. White paint flaked away from rotting wood like scabs. Overgrown weeds lined the base of the building, and a crumbling path led along its edge towards the rear garden. Eli pointed with his good hand to a window on the second floor. He smiled, revealing more spittle.

'There she is.'

'Who? What?' Jonno saw movement behind the dark window. A body, a *female* body. Alabaster skin, long ebony hair, a face that displayed a confident, natural beauty. He felt something unknown rise in his chest. The girl – no, the woman – leaned her slim body towards the glass, her hands resting delicately on the windowsill, her face tilted upwards, her black bra barely covering her breasts.

Jonno felt the boulder lift from his shoulders and float gently upwards into the ether.

Eli leaned over and whispered in his ear.

'Meet Miss Evie.'

*

'I don't want to go, Richard.'

'Oh, come on. It'll be fun.'

'I'm still not feeling that well.'

'It's just what you need.'

Hattie recalled Hilda's horrified expression when she'd told her where they were staying. 'What do you think that was all about?'

'What's that, love?'

'The way Hilda pushed us out the door as soon as the taxi showed up. It was like she was trying to get rid of us, almost like we were diseased or something.'

'Oh,' Richard laughed. 'I think you're overreacting. We'd probably just outstayed our welcome, that's all. I mean, she had just found our daughter and paid for our cab, hadn't she? I don't think we could have expected any more from her.'

'I guess,' Hattie said. She picked up Sally's drawing from the coffee table. 'What do you think this is?'

Richard took it from her. 'Mm. It sorta looks like a giant horse, crossed with a human or a goat, or something.'

'That's what I thought. Why would she draw something like that?'

'I don't know.'

'It's weird.'

'Yeah, but—'

Hattie knew what he was going to say. Since she'd been able to talk, their daughter had been fascinated by monsters, dragons and ghosts. They'd even cut out sweeteners and food additives from her diet because the research Hattie had undertaken suggested that kids

101

with overactive imaginations could really be affected by them.

'You think she's okay?'

Richard smiled. 'She's more than okay, Hats. She's perfect. She's unique. There's nothing wrong with that.'

'Mm, I suppose.' She placed the drawing back on the table, turning it over so that the horse-monster wasn't glaring up at her anymore.

'Anyway,' Richard continued, 'this gathering. I think it's exactly what you need. Some food, some drink, and a singsong with the locals.' He pointed out the front window. 'It's right on our doorstep. We don't even need to drive.' Suddenly his face turned white, his eyes wide.

'What's up?'

'The car.'

'What about the car?'

'The bloody *car*!' He lurched for the door. 'What the hell?'

Hattie followed him outside. 'What is it, Richard?'

He pointed at the wheels of the SUV. The car sat awkwardly on the driveway, listing to one side as if wounded. Black rubber lay like folds of loose flesh on the gravel.

'Someone's slashed the tyres!' he yelled as he walked around the vehicle. 'All four of them!'

'I don't understand.'

'What's not to understand? The car's been vandalised, darling. Isn't it obvious? Can't you see it with your own eyes?'

'Okay, yes I can see it, there's no need to be so patronising. I didn't bloody well do it.' He always acted like that. As if everything was her fault.

'*I know*, I know. I'm sorry.' He stood with his hands on his hips. He looked like he was about to cry.

'What's going on, guys?' It was Bea.

Hattie pointed to the tyres.

'Oh, bloody hell.'

'Yep, my thoughts exactly.'

'They're going to cost a small fortune to replace,' Richard mumbled to himself. 'I don't even know where the nearest garage is.'

'Glanna will know,' Bea said. 'I'm sure her and her husband can help.'

'I bet it was her boys,' Richard hissed. 'Those two little bastards. I bet they did this to get back at us about Jonno's iPad.'

'Oh, come on, Richard. You don't know that,' Hattie said.

'Then who? There's no one else here.'

Bea interjected. 'It could have just been some kids passing through. Perhaps they saw your expensive car through the gates and thought it would be funny to have a go at it.'

'Funny? *Funny*?'

Bea shrugged. 'Well, you know what kids are like.'

'No, it was the boys. I'm sure of it. You wait 'til I see them.'

'Everything okay in there?' Paz yelled from the road.

'No, not really,' Richard grumbled.

Suddenly there was a boom of a stereo and the hubbub of people.

'We're just getting going out here. Join us when you're ready. No rush of course.'

Hattie gripped her husband's hand. She now thought the gathering might be a good idea after all.

'Come on. Let's worry about the car in the morning.' She kissed her husband on the cheek. 'I suddenly have the urge for some barbecue.'

*

The big ash tree had been decorated with bunting that had seen better days. Picnic tables stood loaded with condiments, paper plates, and various homemade beverages. A gallon drum had been split in two, its shell filled with hot coals, red meat sizzling on the grill. An antique speaker played folk songs that were unfamiliar to

103

Hattie – lilting, unsettling melodies. Paz was holding court.

'Richard, Hattie and family,' he waved them over. 'Come, come. I want to introduce you to the others.'

Hattie glanced at her husband. He was still visibly seething. 'Let it go, let's just try to have a good time,' she said.

'I'll do my best. No promises.'

'You got us the invite, don't forget.'

Paz grabbed Hattie's hand, which made her feel mildly uncomfortable. 'This old villain is Bertrand. He and his wife own The Sailor's Curse, that dirty old property on the side of the hill that's in urgent need of repair.'

She turned and nodded to the older man. He was bald, except for a rat's tail that hung from the rear of his head in a tight plait. His pate was brown from too much exposure to the sun. He wore hooped earrings in both ears and was dressed in an ornate kaftan and leather sandals. He clasped her hand in both of his. Again, discomfort.

'It's a pleasure,' he said, turning to Richard and embracing him. 'And don't listen to this old fool. The house is fine, if a little tired. You'll notice he hasn't mentioned the state of his place. It's riddled with woodworm as big as your thumb.'

'It's lovely to meet you too,' Hattie said. 'And we think your house is beautiful.' She turned. 'This is my sister, Bea and her partner, Rachel.'

The pair offered a 'hi' and 'hiya' in turn.

'And this is Richard's son, Jonno, and our daughter, Sally-Ann.'

Bertrand hugged them all. Hattie thought he clearly didn't observe rules on personal space. 'It's truly wonderful to meet you. You have such a beautiful family.'

A lady in a thin white gown approached, her hands held together as if in prayer, her head bowed. Her hair was silver and short, her face and arms painfully thin. She had a tattoo on the side of her face, an ornate swirling pattern of colourful lilies. 'This is my wife,

Amelia,' Bertrand said. 'I'm afraid she doesn't speak, but she can sign if you're able to read it. Otherwise, I can translate for you.'

'Actually, it's fine. I know sign,' Hattie said, smiling and nodding. She'd learned it at the school. 'It's lovely to meet you, Amelia.'

Amelia raised her hands, nimbly constructing shapes with her fingers and palms.

Hattie translated slowly. It had been a while. 'Nice... to meet you all, but I... must... warn you. Whatever... you do... don't... eat... the food.'

'Woah there, Amy, my love,' Paz cried, mocking indignation. 'That hurts, it really does.'

'Don't mind her,' Bertrand said, forcing a smile. 'She has a warped sense of humour.'

'Nonsense. She's no such thing.' Another lady approached, with thick hazel curls, a round face, a button of a nose, and brightly alert eyes behind thin-framed spectacles. She was wearing a long chiffon skirt and khaki vest. She looked younger than the others, maybe forty. 'Don't listen to the pair of them, Amy. They're just a couple of foolish man-children.' She turned and thrust out a hand. 'Katharine Tregeagle. Pascoe's my husband, a burden I carry every single day, I'm afraid. It's a pleasure to make your acquaintance. Welcome to our little community.'

Hattie took her hand and made the necessary introductions.

'Okay, okay. Where's the beer at?' a gruff voice bellowed.

Hattie turned to see Glanna's two boys, along with Glanna herself and a wiry-looking man she presumed to be Noah. There was also a pretty young woman with long dark hair and a smattering of star-like freckles on her shoulders and cheeks. The boys paid them no attention and headed straight for the picnic tables. She sensed Richard tensing beside her.

Katharine gave a terse nod. 'Glanna.'

'Kathy.'

'I see Paz has kicked off already.'

'We knew we had an additional six people to cater for,' Katharine said. 'More food to cook, takes a little longer.'

Glanna pursed her lips. 'We have the sow. Noah prepared her this afternoon.'

'Bertrand,' Katharine said, 'will you be a love and fetch the rotisserie?'

'This is for you,' Glanna said, turning to Jonno. 'I hope it goes some way towards making amends for what happened yesterday.'

Hattie started to object. 'Oh, there's really no need—'

'No, I insist.'

'What is it, son?' Richard said as Jonno stared at the package, transfixed. 'It's okay. Go ahead and open it.'

'I'm afraid the people at the store were unable to repair the screen on the tablet the boys regretfully damaged,' Glanna said. Jonno pulled at the bow and hooked a finger along the edge of the wrapping paper. He couldn't get inside quickly enough. 'We have that one of course, if you want it back, but we thought it best to replace.'

Jonno shrieked. 'It's the latest Pro! Look at the screen, Dad. It's huge!'

'Woah, look at that.'

'It has a lot of storage,' Glanna offered. 'Or so the young man in the shop told me. Two hundred and fifty-six ginglebots?'

Jonno laughed. 'You mean gigabytes?'

'Yes, that was it.'

'Glanna, you shouldn't have,' Hattie said. She didn't know much about computers, but she guessed it must have been expensive.

'It was the least we could do. Noah here insisted.'

The man with the long hair and wispy beard leaned forward. 'Hi, I'm Noah by the way. I was waiting for the introduction, but it doesn't look like one's going to be forthcoming.'

'Oh, my manners. Sorry, yes this is Noah, my partner.'

'Nice to meet you,' Hattie said. 'And congratulations. On the baby, I mean.'

Noah nodded stoically. 'Yes. Quite the event.'

'Anyway,' Glanna continued. 'My two boys you've met. And,' she turned to the girl standing to her right, 'this here is my youngest, Evelyn.'

The young woman gave a wry smile. Hattie was taken by her hazel eyes. There was something about them.

'Can I offer anyone a drink?' Katharine interjected.

'Katharine, darling,' Bea said, 'I thought you'd never ask.'

*

Eli spied the girl. She was with JTB, which was Eli's new name for Jonno the Turd Boy.

JTB had acted all weird when Evie had put on her pre-planned little show. It was if he'd been under some kind of love spell, swaying on the spot and sweating like he was burning up. Kid-Bastard Evie was pretty, but she was also mean. JTB wouldn't know that of course. She liked hurting things, and she smelled funny, like honey, sugar and jam.

JTB had wanted to know all about her of course, but Eli only told him what Evie wanted him to: her name, her age, and the fact she was one of the Kid-Bastards (he didn't use that phrase of course. No one needed to know about his little nicknames, thank you very much). He still hadn't decided whether he wanted JTB to be his friend yet. He was a bit odd, and besides, Eli didn't really do well with friends.

The Red Man sat next to him in the dirt, his face crusted with dried blood, and gloopy, dark red stuff. A crevice ran from the corner of his permanently agape mouth to a blackened temple. He eyed Eli through one dark marble of an eye. He looked angry.

'I don't even know why you want the girl, anyway. She's just a young 'un, and she runs around and screams a lot.'

The Red Man's expression was unmoving. They sat silently and

107

watched as the gaggle formed on No Man's Land.

'Look at 'em all, pretending to be friends when secretly they all hate each other. What a fake bunch of fake people. All except Sweet Mother of course. She's smarter than the rest of 'em put together, including Kid-Bastard Evie who finks she's smart but she's really just as dumb as the boys. Maybe even dumber. At least those two don't preten' to be sum'fing they're not.'

Eli watched them all play host to the Faraway People. Bald-Head and the Kid-Bastard boys skewered the dead pig and hung her on the hot thing, her mouth hanging open as if she was waiting to be fed. The quiet lady served punch from a large glass vat. Eli gagged. The punch made his stomach hurt. Noah and Sweet Mother stayed a safe distance from the others, but Eli knew that she was just biding her time, getting the lay of the land. She was the boss after all, even if the others didn't always show it.

JTB was playing with the glass thing. His dad looked just as excited as he was. Eli sniggered as JTB spotted Kid-Bastard Evie standing just a few feet away. She was wearing a dress that showed off her dotty skin. Boys seemed to love those brown dots, but they just looked like mud splats to Eli. They were dirty and gross. JTB's face lit up, as bright as a bonfire, as she walked past. Eli knew this was deliberate on her part. The glass thing almost spilled out of JTB's hands.

He watched as the girl with the red hair ran and whooped around the tree, the angry woman standing with the quiet lady and not paying the little girl much attention. She seemed to do that a lot.

'It's not safe, there's too many people,' he muttered.

The Red Man urged him on.

'They'll see me,' Eli continued. 'I stick out from the others, the way I look.'

The Red Man gave a shake of the head, the wave of a blackened hand. He was holding the shiny thing. The orange glare of the setting sun glistened off its smooth surface, and the diamonds shimmered and fizzed. Eli watched as it moved in the air, graceful

108

and elegant. The Red Man held it close for Eli to see. He felt his jaw click as he unconsciously ground his teeth together. He wanted it.

'Okay, okay, but not now,' he sighed. 'Tonight. I'll do it tonight.'

*

A new trio had arrived. Hattie watched as they strode towards the makeshift bar from the direction of The Weary Traveller. They looked like the human embodiment of the house: perfectly pressed clothes, identical spectacles, emotionless and cold. The older pair looked as though they were in their late thirties or early forties, the younger man in his late teens. The woman had dark chin-length hair, piercing blue eyes, a thin face and long neck adorned with a pretty silver necklace. The older of the two men was clean-cut, slim with short black hair and an overtly straight gait. The teenager, by contrast, seemed to be carrying a few extra pounds and had the faint hint of a moustache.

Amelia eyed them over her wine glass. She set it down and turned to Hattie. She began to sign.

'Here… they come. The… Addams Family.'

Hattie smiled. 'Oh, I don't know about that. They look pretty normal to me.'

Amelia shook her head and eyed the approaching woman with caution.

'They… can… be a bit… strange.'

The trio were suddenly right on top of them. They peered down at the assortment of refreshments. The older man glanced at Hattie, an eyebrow raised.

'Hattie Penrose,' she declared. 'Very pleased to meet you, Mr…?'

'We'd like some punch. Three glasses, half-filled.'

'I… er.' She glanced at Amelia who was shooting her an I-told-

109

you-so smirk. 'Okay, of course, that's no problem at all. Here you go.' She spooned the punch into three plastic goblets and handed one to each of them in turn. 'One for you, and for you.' The woman seemed transfixed by Hattie's hair. 'And here's one for you. There, that's all three.'

'Thank you,' the man said, then gave a curt acknowledgement to Amelia before turning away.

'They're a bit odd, aren't they?' Bea said, appearing at the bar.

'Yes. And rude too.'

'Mm. Anyway, can I have two red wines and a beer, please? We're helping Paz with the barbecue. I think Rachel's taken a bit of a shine to him.' She groaned. 'She does love the older blokes.'

Hattie smiled. 'Listen, can you keep an eye on Sally for me? She keeps tearing off and I'm a little preoccupied here.'

Amelia grabbed her arm and signed. 'It's... fine. I... can... manage. Go... play... with your... daughter.

'Oh, really?' Hattie said. 'Are you sure? I don't want to leave you in the lurch.' Amelia nodded.

'If... they don't... like it... they can... serve themselves.'

'Okay, yes, that's very true, I suppose.' She glanced at Sally, who was now lying on the floor and picking daisies. 'Thank you, Amelia. I shouldn't be too long. I think she'll tire soon, and then I can settle her down in the buggy.'

'Actually, you might want to collect your daughter and come with me,' Katharine said suddenly, before grabbing her arm.

'What? I... okay, I guess.'

Katharine cocked her head towards The Night Watchman. 'I have something I want to show you.'

*

'What you got there?'

Jonno heard the girl's voice and knew instantly it was her. He looked up at her silhouette, the sun behind her, her face a dark mystery.

'It's a—' He glared at the object in his hands, but he couldn't even begin to remember what it was called. 'It's a—'

She laughed. It was a beautiful sound. 'Don't you even know what it is? It's been holding your sole attention for this past hour.'

She was right. He hadn't even realised that his father had walked off and was now talking to the strange woman who owned the cottage.

'Of course I do. It's just—'

'Just what?'

'I'm still thinking.' Those sharp daggers in his head again. That bloody boulder too. The ground suddenly felt very welcoming to him.

There was a flash of movement, a lock of hair on his shoulder, the smell of honey and cinnamon. She was next to him.

'Here, let me take a look.'

He handed the object over to her instinctively.

'It's a tablet, silly. Look, if I swipe this way I can get to your emails, if I swipe that way I can get to your browsing history. You won't have any, of course, as its brand new, but you know what I mean.' She gave it back. 'It's nice.'

He nodded. His mouth felt as dry as dirt.

'You lost your voice or something?'

He shrugged.

'You're a little nervous around girls, aren't you? How old are you?'

He held both hands open, all ten fingers, and then another hand, all five.

'Fifteen, eh? Ha, I'm older than you. I'm sixteen. Seventeen in two months.'

His mouth fell open. She looked like a woman in her twenties. She was so… mature, so certain of who she was.

'Mother tries to control me like a little kid, of course. She doesn't seem to realise I'm more or less an adult now, and smarter than my two older brothers.' She pointed to them both. They were swigging beer and drunkenly tending to the sizzling animal. The sight of the dead pig made Jonno want to bring up his lunch. 'They'll start singing soon, this lot.' She yawned. 'Boring.'

He suddenly found his voice. 'What... what do they sing about?'

'Oh, old stuff, mainly.' She picked at the grass. 'Gods and spirits, that kind of thing.'

He laughed, and she laughed back. 'Sounds weird.'

'It is.' She touched his hand. He was so shocked, he almost pulled it away. 'What about your family? How do they, you know, treat you?'

Jonno paused. The boulder seemed to gain a little mass. 'Okay, I guess.'

'You don't sound too sure.'

'My dad's okay. He looks after me. Hattie's not my mum. She scares me a little. I don't think she likes me.'

'Oh.'

'My Aunt Bea and her girlfriend are nice, and I love my little sister, even though she takes up a lot of their time.'

'It must be hard.'

He felt himself sink into the blanket, felt the sharpness resume in his temples. 'I don't know.'

The conversation paused, and Jonno wondered whether that was it. He wasn't very interesting after all, and she was everything he wasn't: confident, graceful, and eloquent. What could she possibly see in a stupid, anxious kid who preferred to be tucked away in his room, playing computer games and listening to music through battered old headphones? She'd be an idiot to find him anything other than gross.

'Jonno?'

He nodded, resigning himself to failure.

'You wanna get outta here?'

112

*

'Glanna, I need a word if you don't mind.'

'Of course, Richard. You want to talk here or—' she pointed to a bench by the path. 'Would you rather we sit?'

'I don't care.' He'd had a bit to drink. The punch really did carry one.

'Well, then let's just stay right where we are.' She smiled. It was a little unnerving. 'May I ask whether you've tried the hog roast?'

He nodded. 'You may, and yes, I have. It's delicious. Look,' he paused. 'It's about my car.'

'Your car?'

'Yes. It was very expensive – Hattie would say an unnecessary extravagance – but, you know, I run a high-end business that demands a certain image. My clients expect it. I can't be turning up in some battered old hatchback, asking these guys to pay me the kind of money I'm charging. It would look, well, wrong.' He had no idea why he was telling her this. 'Anyway, that's beside the point.'

Glanna's expression was unmoving. 'Quite. And, I agree.'

Richard took a swig of his punch. He decided to get straight to it. 'Good. Look, it's about my tyres.'

'Tyres?'

'Yep. Tyres. Someone slashed them, the tyres that is.'

Glanna's mouth fell open. 'What, here? At Bodhmall's?'

'Yep, right here. On your driveway, in fact.'

'Oh my. That's awful.'

'Awfully expensive, more like.'

'But how? When?'

'I was hoping you were going to tell me that.'

'What's going on?' It was Noah.

'Someone has vandalised Richard's car. His tyres have been slashed.'

113

'Oh no. That's terrible. Who would do such a thing?' Noah exclaimed.

'I have my suspicions.'

'Really?' Glanna asked. 'Then you must tell us. Who?'

Richard tried to choose his words very carefully, but they tumbled out like pennies from a jar. 'Do you happen to know where your two sons were today?'

'My sons? Why? What… what have they got to do with this?'

Richard took another swig. 'Don't you think it's awfully coincidental? The boys broke my son's tablet just yesterday. You punished them for it – I mean, I presume they're paying for the replacement – and then, just one day later, I find my Q7 with all four of its tyres completely destroyed.'

Glanna gasped.

'That's one serious accusation,' Noah interjected. 'Do you have any evidence to support it?'

Richard paused. Did he? 'Well, no, not really, only circumstantial. As I said, it all adds up. The circumstances, I mean.'

'So, no evidence at all then?'

Richard was back-footed. 'Do you have CCTV? Tell me you have cameras dotted about the place, an expensive property like this.'

'No, why would we? Nobody comes through here. Just our guests.'

'Yes!' Richard cried. 'That's exactly my point. It had to be a local!'

Noah's tone hardened. 'So, if not the boys, then one of us? Is that what you're saying? You think one of us did it? Shall we ask everyone? I mean, we're all here, aren't we? Everyone, listen up!'

The crowd turned to them, and Richard felt their eyes on him. His face suddenly felt very hot.

'No!' He yelled. 'Please, no.' He appealed to Glanna. 'I'm not saying that. *I'm not.*'

Glanna reached out a hand and clasped his. Her grip was firm.

'Then what is it that you're saying, Richard? I must confess, I'm a little confused. Either you think one of us, one of the boys maybe, committed a terrible act of vandalism on an expensive item of your property, *or* you're asking for our help with finding someone who can repair the damage.' She leaned closer to him. 'Now, is it the former?' Closer still, close enough for him to feel the warmth of her breath on his face. 'Or the latter?'

He swallowed. 'The latter, I guess.'

Her gaze held his for a moment longer than was necessary, and he looked away. What had he done? This woman was no criminal, far from it. She had the look of someone who cares, who nurtures. He'd overstepped the mark, he knew that now.

'Okay, then that settles it,' she said, breaking the spell. 'Noah knows a mechanic, don't you, dear?' Noah nodded. It was a reluctant affirmation. 'We'll call her first thing and see about replacing those tyres.'

'Glanna, I'm sorry. I—'

She held up a palm, fingers spread. 'We'll hear no more about it. What's done is done. We can move on from this, can't we?'

He nodded. He felt defeated, deflated like one of his shredded tyres. He had no idea what to do or say next. Fortunately, the neat man from The Weary Traveller appeared between them.

'It's almost sundown.'

Glanna glanced at the sky. 'So it is.'

'Will you and your family be partaking?' he asked Richard.

Richard had no clue what the guy meant, but he nodded, more out of relief than any kind of affirmation.

'Then... to the monument!'

*

Hattie was standing in the garden of The Night Watchman. Sally was at her feet and playing with an over-enthused dog, a little grey and white Highland Terrier called Willy.

115

'You have a lovely home.'

'Thank you, that's so nice of you to say,' Katharine said. 'But it's not really mine to have, of course. It's been in the Tregeagle family for many, many generations. I'm just an interloper. Paz calls me his sleepover friend.' She laughed.

'Maybe so,' Hattie said, 'but you must love it. Living here, I mean. Overlooking the sea, it's so peaceful. And such a quiet neighbourhood too. No motorways, no hustle and bustle, no pollution or overpopulation. It's heavenly.' Hattie was envious.

'It has its moments.'

The conversation paused. Hattie listened to the gentle hiss of the ocean, accompanied by the faint strains of music and laughter from the party.

'Look, Mummy. Goldfish,' Sally said, pointing to the pond.

'Be careful, darling, don't fall in.'

'Oh, it's only a couple of feet deep,' Katharine assured her. They wandered further along the uneven path. 'I keep asking Pascoe to fill it in, but he loves his fish. Lord knows why. I think it's an eyesore.'

Hattie peered into the water. The pond really was quite small and almost entirely blanketed by algae. A water skater skimmed over the surface, heading towards a sole lily pad. It was languid in its journey. As it reached its destination, a long pink tongue flicked out from behind a group of petunias. Almost as quickly as it had arrived, it was gone, devoured. She caught a glimpse of the frog as it sucked the twisted torso and broken wings into its mouth. It glanced at Hattie, blinked twice and then disappeared into the murky water.

'You wanted to show me something?' she asked.

'Ah, yes. Indeed.'

Katharine beckoned her to the little white fence bordering the southernmost tip of the property. A few feet beyond, the ground fell away sharply, tumbling downwards in a mass of rock, red clay and tangled foliage.

'It's beautiful,' Hattie said.

'Is it?'

'The view, I mean. It's stunning.'

Katharine pointed towards the boundary. 'Every year we have to move that little fence of ours, just a centimetre or two back this way towards the house.' She took a deep breath. 'It's like the sea wants to take back what's hers. Pretty soon this will all be a pile of brick, concrete and timber lying somewhere down there on the ocean floor. Only our memories will remain.' She paused. 'If we're lucky, that is.'

'Oh, I'm sure that would take years, decades even.' Hattie bent down to her daughter who was yawning. She stroked the dog. 'Can't the local council do anything? Install a sea wall, maybe?'

'Paz wouldn't allow it. Or the others. He says it would be unnatural. If the sea wants the house, then it should be allowed to take it, he says.' Katharine's voice dropped to little more than a whisper. 'It's already taken so much more.'

'So much more?'

'Oh, things, people I've lost. I feel them in my stomach, in my heart, but there's a mist where memories should be. Those precious memories,' she shook her head. 'It seems that once they're gone, they're gone for ever.'

'What do you mean?'

'Oh, it's nothing. Just my silly, nonsensical ramblings,' she said, but her eyes betrayed her.

'Katharine, I don't understand.'

'You don't need to.' She turned to Hattie. 'Look, I brought you here to tell you this one, really important thing.' She was close to her now. 'Protect this wonderful living organism that you call your family. All of it. The little details that are precious to you, but also those that aren't. They're all important, all a small intricate part of the greater whole.' She gripped Hattie's arms. It hurt a little. 'Once the rot sets in, you'll never get rid of it, believe me. It's all-consuming, all-destroying.' Her gaze was steadfast, her voice pleading. 'Never live in fear. Never wake up every morning in a cold sweat. Never feel the terror of everything you love just crumbling from these cliffs and falling into the ocean, washing away like so much seaweed and sand. Cherish what you have – *everything*. The good *and* the bad!'

'I—'

'Promise me.'

'I—' she glanced at Sally. She thought of Richard, of the mess she'd left back home. 'I promise, I guess.'

Katharine pulled her close, and she wrapped her arms around her. They stood that way for a few moments. Hattie felt like crying, but she had no idea why. Suddenly there was the sound of a loud horn and the crowd cheering. Katharine held her by the shoulders at arm's length and smiled.

'It's time for the blessing.'

*

They were in the forest. It was getting dark. Evie was in front of him. He could just about hear her, but it was too dark to know exactly where she was.

'Where are we going?' he asked. He didn't like the dark. He never had. He couldn't even sleep in it.

'You'll see soon enough.'

'I don't like this, Evie.'

'Don't be such a baby.' Her voice had a hint of malice. He looked down at his tablet and wished the battery hadn't died on him. He couldn't even use the torch on his phone. He'd left it in his room.

'My dad's going to wonder where I am.'

'Then let him wonder.'

He tripped on a rock and almost went down. *Great*, he thought. *Smash the replacement iPad, why don't you? That would be just perfect, wouldn't it?* He groaned. He wished he was back in his room in the musty, pukey cottage. He wished he had his air rifle with him. Above all, he wished he'd never come on this stupid holiday.

'Nearly there.'

'Nearly where?'

'I can't wait to show you. You'll love it.' She laughed, but really it was more of a cackle.

His head hurt and his eyes felt like they were too big for his skull. His teeth ached. He felt the soft tread of invisible creatures scuttling and squirming around his feet. Snakes, rats maybe. He heard a child's muted laughter, but then it was gone. A bug slapped against his cheek, and something bit his leg. He felt the salty swell of tears at the corners of his eyes. He knew he couldn't cry.

'Evie, I—' his voice betrayed his burgeoning terror. He bit down on his hand.

'Here. I've found it.'

Jonno's foot caught on something metallic, and he tripped again, half sprawling. He tumbled into Evie who had stopped only a few feet in front of him.

'Hey, watch it. I'm right here, you know?' She laughed again, but this one was friendlier.

He waited for his eyes to adjust to the gloom. He could see her now; the faint trace of her hair, the curve of her shoulders. 'Where are we?'

She grabbed hold of something above and pulled herself upwards. There was a creak as she lifted a leg over a metallic lip. She spun round and took his iPad from him.

'You coming, or what?'

He was curious. The object was long and cylindrical. Something wide and flat blocked the way to his right. 'What is this?' He ran a finger along it. It was hard and sharp. Rust and paint flaked away.

'You can be my co-pilot,' she said, reaching down and holding out a hand. He took it and instantly felt the softness of her skin. His

119

eyes shrunk back to their normal size once more. She pulled as he hoisted himself into the open space. She was stronger than she looked.

'Is this a—'

'Yep.'

'An aeroplane?'

'World War Two fighter plane, actually. A Hurricane.'

'Really? How?' He felt the leather of the seat, the jagged metal structure.

'Don't know. Never asked.' She wiggled the joystick and made machine gun noises.

'Shouldn't this be in a museum?'

'Probably, but I won't tell if you don't.'

He glanced behind them. He could see what was left of the tail fin and rudder. 'It's—' he struggled to articulate his emotions. 'It's *awesome*!'

Suddenly her hands were on his face, her lips on his. The kiss was long and awkward, but he didn't care. He could have stayed that way for ever.

'This will be our little secret place, Jonno. A quiet place, just for you and me. You'll never tell, will you? Never?'

He shook his head. He would never.

Suddenly, a loud blast sounded. Evie turned and leapt from the cockpit. He felt sick with overwhelming emotions. She peered up at him, and he knew, in that moment, that he loved her.

'Come on, the sun is setting,' she said. 'It's time for the blessing.'

*

The locals called it a monument, as if it were a statue of historic significance or a natural phenomenon of some outstanding beauty. It wasn't that at all. *Decoration* would have been more appropriate. Or a *display*. Yes, that was it, a display, like you might make at primary school with papier-mâché, elastic bands and tinsel. Rachel didn't know what to make of it, although she knew it was weird, and gross too; weirdly gross. It looked like it carried the skull of a deer or a horse, one that had seen better days. It was fastened to a black pole which rose about four feet from a metal stake in the ground. Antlers protruded from the head, decorated in a garland of holly and ivy, red ribbons hanging down and resembling a bloodied mane. A black robe hung from where the neck should be, and symbols or runes were sewn into the robe with silver thread. The hands that protruded from its centre were skeletal and human-like. They were open, their palms held upwards. Within one palm was nestled a small bunch of ripe blackberries, within the other, a copper dagger.

'The Oss.' It was the man with the rat's tail – Bertrand.

'The what-now?' Rachel asked.

'The Oss. It's our offering to the spirits.'

'The spirits? What, like ghosts?'

'No,' he laughed. 'Not exactly. The term *gods* would work, but that's not right either. No, they're more like an invisible thread that binds us; the people, like you and I.' He gestured towards her. 'The land, the sea, the universe – everything. The tapestry of life, I guess.'

Rachel stifled a giggle. '*Oookay*. Well, come on then. What is it?'

'Is what?'

'This... thing?'

'The skull? It's equine,' he offered, as Rachel shrugged. She had no idea what that meant. 'You know, from a horse?'

'You killed a horse?'

The lady who didn't speak shook her head. She started to sign.

'Not exactly,' Bertrand said. 'She died. Her name was Betsy. She belonged to Glanna's mother, Dolores. She was a stubborn old mare, much like Dolly. It was her time. It's the ultimate honour for her, you know?'

'I think I'd rather be buried.'

Bea arrived and took Rachel's hand. 'We're going to sing, Rach. Isn't this fun?'

Rachel smiled. Bea was so full of zest, so easily entertained. Where had she been all her life?

Paz passed them and went to Hattie. Rachel watched as he raised a large conch shell that appeared to be filled with a clear, viscous liquid. He dipped his fingers and thumb into the shell, raised a hand to Hattie's forehead, and then drew an invisible shape. Hattie looked too dumbfounded to react.

'Deep peace of the running wave, the flowing air, the quiet earth.'

The others let out a low humming sound. Rachel looked at Bea, her eyebrows raised, but her partner was transfixed. Paz moved onto Richard, and again he dipped his fingers into the shell.

'Oh, I don't think that—' Richard attempted to say, but it was done before he could finish. Again, the low hum.

Paz moved around the semi-circular congregation, drawing on each of them in turn, repeating the same phrase, followed by the same reaction. Jonno and the young woman had returned from wherever they had gone. Jonno's face was a bright crimson. The girl carried a wry smile on her lips. Rachel could see that something had happened between them, and she suspected the girl was the instigator. She hoped the kid was okay.

She was last in the queue. The liquid felt hot on her forehead, Paz's fingers calloused like fine sandpaper. The glow from the fading sun painted patterns in his eyes, the embers of a dying bonfire. She suddenly felt unnerved, a little chilled. She crossed her arms over herself.

They turned to the ocean, the thin line of brilliant orange flickering just above the horizon. The others clapped their hands together once. Rachel jumped, and Bea uttered a surprised, '*Oh*!'

They began to sing in words that Rachel didn't understand, their hands raised to the sky, their faces bathed in a furious yellow. The

122

congregation turned and began to weave in and out of each other, those from the left weaving to the right and vice versa. Bea grabbed hold of Rachel's hand and pulled her along beside her. The language was alien but the tune was eerily familiar. Bea imitated the melody and she gestured for Rachel to follow suit. Rachel wasn't a singer, but she decided to join in – what the hell.

Paz lifted the Oss from its metal stake. The horned head became a ghostly silhouette in the darkening sky.

'*To the sea*!'

They cheered, sang and danced along the gravel pathway in a conga-like procession, spinning around and waving their arms in the air. Rachel felt dizzy, but Bea appeared to be throwing everything she had into it.

'This is so great, Rach, isn't it?'

Rachel didn't think so, but she followed suit. This was taking her undercover assignment to a new level, but what else could she do? She spied the man with the spectacles, his eyes wide and his mouth open in a wide maw. His wife was behind him, her expression filled with anxiety and confusion, and their son was by her side, grunting and growling like a wild animal. The two boys from Excelsior Lodge were half-giggling, half-chanting. The larger one, Aaron, winked at her as he passed. Noah bashed a wooden drum with his open palms. Glanna held her long kaftan as if it were a giant wing, her voice tremulous with thick vibrato. Hattie and Richard were arm in arm. Rachel thought they almost looked happy. Jonno followed the dark-haired girl as if on a long invisible string. She was exultant, almost aggressive. He was sheepish, slightly embarrassed. The quiet lady spun past them theatrically, her mouth open, her eyes focussed on something not quite there. Bertrand trailed her, his own eyes closed, his lips parted in a sneering grin.

The group danced through the woodland as they descended the slope towards the ocean. The Night Watchman was up ahead, The Weary Traveller someway behind them. The tide was high, but the waves were slight. The thin stretch of sand looked like a long slither of orange peel.

Paz approached the water and stood in its shallow depths. He held the Oss in front of him at shoulder height, his arms outstretched. The others formed a line along the shore. The singing stopped and the low hum resumed.

'Warmth of the solstice, fill our hearts with joy. Blood of Bolster, flow into the ocean and provide us with your glorious, unrivalled sustenance.'

The locals hollered a loud, '*Hoi!*'

The sun had almost disappeared now, but Rachel knew that it would have one final say before descending below the horizon. She watched as Paz turned with the Oss held above his head like a mighty spear. He was now a long, loping silhouette, his hair blown to the side like dark withering fingers. The scene was almost cathartic. She peered into the ocean and thought she saw it bubbling and boiling. It had become a dark crimson, almost bloodlike. There was a coppery scent on the breeze. She suddenly felt like she wanted to vomit.

'Do you see that?' she asked.

'I—' Bea was uncertain.

The hum grew louder. Noah quickened the beat of the drum.

The smattering of clouds overhead seemed to move and join into an awful shape. Rachel thought she could see red vengeful eyes, a wide grin and fangs drenched in blood. She heard Hattie cry out, and Richard attempting words of comfort. Jonno was shuffling uncomfortably in the sand.

'Be one with us! Become us, as we are you!'

The wind had intensified now, and Paz was having to yell to be heard. Rachel looked at Bea once more. Was she crying?

'Horned god, bring us sustenance and the glory of the hunt! Morrighan, protect us from those that would do us harm! Nuada, receive our blessing for we are forever in your debt! White Lady, you are no longer welcome here. Visit us *no more!*'

124

'Hoi!' the crowd yelled.

'Blesséd be!' hollered Paz.

'Blesséd be!' they shouted in return.

Paz turned and hurled the Oss into the water. The clouds parted as the sun flared, sending a yellow flame soaring across the horizon like a soundless explosion. Somewhere in the distance there was a mighty roar. The others cried out as they collapsed onto the wet sand.

Darkness descended.

*

Eli stood next to the child's buggy. The little girl was sleeping, like a baby doll. Her cinnamon hair was striking. He reached down and touched it. He felt a ripple, like soft lightning running through his fingers. She stirred, and he backed away and hid behind the tree.

What did the Red Man plan to do with her, anyway? She was harmless, wasn't she?

He thought of the shiny thing – the diamonds and silver. The *diamonds* in particular. Eli would keep the thing in his secret place. Not even the Kid-Bastards would find it there, no one would, although he might show Sweet Mother. She would understand. She knew all about treasure and secrets. She had loads.

Eli peered at the little girl from his spot behind the tree. The others were still at the beach, but he knew he didn't have long. Once darkness fell, they would come back in a hurry. It got real cold, real quick when the sun disappeared. He knew that from personal experience. The barn was freezing at night.

The girl arched her back and yawned. She was cute.

Eli approached, and then ran back behind the tree. He was undecided on the best course of action. Should he pick her up and take her in his arms or just push her along in her wheelie thing? Would she scream? Or would she just sit there silently like a china doll? He knew that pushing her would be the easier of the two

125

options, but he also knew it would be difficult to navigate across the uneven forest floor. Oh, why couldn't the Red Man just come to them? He made a snap decision. He would carry her. He rushed to her side, bent down and looked closer at the harness. He wondered whether he just needed to push the black catch. He studied it some more. No, there were clips either side. That would be tricky. How could he be expected to unlatch both clips simultaneously with just the one good hand? *Maybe*, he thought, *I could use my teeth*. He glanced back at the path. There was no one there, which was good. He crouched on one knee and leaned forward. He knew it was going to take all his concentration.

'Hey, who are you? You're not my mummy.'

Eli sat up with a start and fell clumsily on his backside. 'What? You... you scared me!'

'You look funny.' The girl laughed.

'That's not very—' he pushed himself forward on his hands. 'Well, so do you.'

'Where is she? Where's my mummy?'

Eli stood. 'Perhaps you should ask her that. She left you here on your own, didn't she?'

'I want her.'

'Well, she's not here. Sorry.'

'What's wrong with your hand? Did you hurt it?'

'Yes, a long time ago.' He glanced down at his crumpled fingers. 'But it's okay. I've got used to it.'

'Do you need a plaster?' She pressed her own hands together, as if they too were injured.

'No, I don't need a plaster. It's fine.' He reconsidered his plan. 'Do you want to go for a walk?'

'With you? I don't want to. It's too dark.'

He reached into his pocket. 'I have a torch.'

'Will you take me to her?'

'Take you to who?'

'My mummy, silly.'

He felt something pull at his heart. He pushed the feeling aside and reminded himself of the shiny thing. 'Of course,' he lied.

The girl held her index finger to her thumb in an O shape. 'Okay,' she said, and grinned.

'Cool,' he said. 'Let me just take care of that.' He reached towards the harness, but she pushed his hand away.

'I can do it myself, thanks,' she said. 'You have a funny hand.'

He took a step backwards, suddenly self-conscious. Without thinking, he tucked his hand in his shirt. She jumped down and went to him, holding out her own hand. After a moment of indecision, he took it. Again, something pulled at his heart. They walked past the barbecue, between the picnic tables and around the rotisserie. As the warm yellow glow of the garden lights began to fade, Eli switched on his torch. Immediately, the ground in front of them was bathed in a bright, blue-grey circle. The little girl's grip tightened.

'I'm scared.'

'Don't be.'

'I don't like the dark.'

'Oh, it's nothing to be afraid of. It's just like daytime but without the sun.'

'I like the sun.'

'Here,' he bent down and withdrew something from his pocket. It was a little ball covered in cloth with a crude, sewn-on face: two crosses for eyes, a black button nose, a slanted mouth and fluffy orange hair. 'This is for you,' he said, smiling.

'What is it?' she said, taking it.

'I make them. This one's s'posed to be you.'

'Me?'

'Yes. See, it's got your hair.'

Sally touched her head, then the orange tufts. 'My hair.'

'It'll keep you safe, even in the dark.'

That seemed to comfort her. 'I'll keep it forever.'

He didn't know what to say to that. It made him feel warm inside.

'Why do you look like that?' she asked.

The warmth disappeared. 'Like what?'

'Like you were left unfinished.'

Unfinished? He liked that. It sounded so full of hope. 'I don't know. Just unlucky I s'pose. I came out this way. You know, when I was born.'

'Did your mummy take care of you?'

'I never knew my mummy.' He didn't remember her, not even a shred of memory. 'She died giving birth to me.'

'Oh, that's sad.'

'I guess.'

'What about your friends?'

'I don't have any.'

The little girl stopped and looked up at him. 'You don't have any friends? What? None at all?'

He thought of JTB and their encounter earlier that day. Was he a friend? Could he be? Did Eli even want him to be?

'I'll be your friend,' she offered.

'Oh, I don't know—' He brushed something wet from his cheek.

'But only if you find my mummy. And my daddy too.'

Suddenly there was a noise along the path: lights, singing, clapping hands, and the sound of a drum. He glanced towards the forest and imagined the Red Man looking down at them, waiting. Eli looked at the little girl, at her copper-coloured hair, her pale, almost luminous skin. Her hands were so small, like cotton balls.

'I—' he stammered. 'I don't fink this walk is a good idea after all. I have somewhere else to be, and anyway, it's too dark for lil' girls to be out on their own.'

'But—'

'No buts. Just you wait here. Every fing'll be fine. You'll see. Just fine. Just as cool as a cucumber.'

He released her hand and brushed her from him like a stain. He turned on his heels and ran towards the comfort of his loft. He felt

128

the eyes of the Red Man all over him, like tiny pins being pushed into his flesh. Eli would come to pay for his betrayal. If he was sure of anything in this world, it was just that. The Red Man would want what was owed, and then some.

*

'What the hell was *that*?' Rachel exclaimed, a glass of red wine in her hand. She was leaning half-pissed on the kitchen counter. 'I mean, that was some weird freaky shiz, right there.'

Bea laughed, throwing a shawl over her shoulders. 'Oh, I don't know. It had a certain rustic charm.'

'Charm? *Charm*? Giving thanks to horned gods and white ladies and praying for blood to flow into the ocean. The *ocean*? That didn't seem odd to you?'

'I can't even think about that right now,' Hattie said. 'I'm still too upset about Sally. How the hell could we have left her there like that? She was all by herself. What were we thinking?' She was still beating herself up for being so careless. Was that the right word? *No*, she thought. *Once was careless. Twice was… well, some might consider it neglect, wouldn't they?*

'Oh, she's fine, Hattie,' Richard said. 'We were just having fun, that's all.'

'We're her parents, Richard. We're supposed to take care of her, but… we left her.' She couldn't shake the shame, but she also couldn't shake the memory of her conversation with Katharine. What was it she had said? "Be careful of the rot". She pictured their daughter, lying on the ocean bed as her skin began to decay, and barnacles attached themselves to her bloated corpse, her face becoming no more than an encased mass of shells and lichen. She shuddered. 'I just can't believe how we got caught up in all that nonsense. I mean, what was I thinking? What if she had got lost again? What if—'

'Oh, sweetheart, don't blame yourself. I was equally at fault,'

Richard said, and went to her. 'I guess all the dancing and singing got the better of us. We were never more than a couple of hundred feet away from her, at the very most.'

'But you hear about terrible things, Richard. In the news. Kids getting kidnapped, murdered—'

'But that didn't happen, Hats, did it? She's here, and she's fine.'

'Yes, I know, but still. It was like we were all in some sort of trance or something.'

'Nonsense! We were just having a good time. It's not like we did anything wrong.'

'They were welcoming at least, I guess,' she admitted, allowing herself a smile. 'And I guess it was entertaining too, despite how the night ended. Wasn't it?'

'I thought it was great.' He swigged on his beer. 'Got a bit scary there at one point, but hey, who are we to judge? We can get pretty scary ourselves, can't we?' He turned to Jonno, elbowing him in the ribs. 'And what was all that with you and the pretty girl, son? Someone got a crush on you, have they? The old Penrose charm rubbed off on you, has it?'

'Oh, leave off, Dad. We're just friends.'

'Don't tease him, Richard,' Hattie said. 'It's a good thing. At least he was out of his room and away from his gadgets.'

'I mean, who does that? Skins a horse's head and puts it on a pole?' Rachel interjected, her words heavily slurred. 'She even had a name: Betshy! They shkinned the head of a horsh called Betshy! That's just wrong on sho many levels.'

A fly passed by Bea's cheek, and she flapped at it. 'Where's the switch for the bug lamp? These things are all over the place.'

'And skeleton handsh?' Rachel continued, seemingly undeterred. 'Were they human handsh? And, if sho, who'sh were they? Did they shkin an old friend? Maybe a relative. Did they butcher an old uncle, or an aunt?'

Richard interrupted. 'Oh, come on now, Rachel. Don't you think you're being a little dramatic?'

Hattie thought they all were. It was late, it had been a bizarre evening, and they'd all had way too much to drink.

Rachel leered awkwardly at Richard and poked at his forehead. 'Peash of the wavesh. Peash of the air. Peash of the goat—' She burst into laughter and staggered into a stool. Richard caught her.

'Really, these flies are irritating,' Bea said, running her hand along the wall behind the bread bin. 'The switch for this thing must be somewhere.'

'Jonno, why don't you go up to bed?' Hattie said. She turned to her stepson. He was sipping on a Coke and giggling into it.

'I don't want to. This is funny.'

'It's very late.'

'I said I don't want to.'

'Richard!'

Richard laughed. 'Oh, leave him a while. He's old enough to see the grown-ups acting like idiots.'

'Yeah, Hattie.' Rachel said. 'Let him see ush acting like idiosh.' She was really slurring now.

'It must be somewhere around here,' Bea cried. 'Really, why hide it? I mean, what does that achieve? Nothing, that's what.' The persistent fly was still buzzing around her head.

'Now, about this girl, Jonno. What was her name again?' Richard asked.

'*Dad*!'

'Arwin? Eliza?'

'Just leave it, Dad, will you?'

'Get off his back, Richard,' Hattie said. 'You see, Jonno? This is exactly why I suggested you go up to bed. Your father's drunk, and he's acting like a prat.'

Richard looked wounded. 'I am doing no such thing.'

'Oh yesh you are, Dicky,' Rachel said, setting down her glass. 'You're teashing him.'

Hattie turned to her sister. 'Bea, I think your partner has had enough.' She scowled. Rachel was starting to annoy her. Where the

131

hell had that nickname come from, Dicky? 'Perhaps you two should call it a night as well,' she said.

'I will, once I've killed this goddam fly!'

'Dicky, dear? Do you mind if I call you that?' Rachel asked.

'Er, no, I guess not.'

Hattie did.

'Wouldsh you mind grabbing thatsh bottle for me? Or would you like to email your little friend about it first?'

Richard shook his head. 'I don't—'

Rachel tapped a finger to her nose but missed. 'Don't worry. Itsh our little shecret.'

'Rachel, what on earth are you talking about?' Hattie hollered, starting to feel her temper get the better of her.

Bea tapped the cage surrounding the lamp. 'How on earth do you get this thing going?'

'Oh, for heaven's sake, Bea. The switch is right over—' Hattie opened a cupboard door, revealing a rather grim-looking microwave oven. To its right was a big red switch. Hattie slammed her hand onto it. '*Here*!'

All of a sudden, the two UV bulbs nestled behind a white metallic cage fired into life. There was now a purple-blue tinge to everything. The fly immediately altered its course and flew straight towards it. There was a fizz and a sizzle.

Bea raised her arms aloft. 'Yes! *Yes*! The bloody beast is dead! All hail queen Hattie!'

Hattie wasn't listening. She was staring at her sister's forehead and the strange pattern that was now clearly visible in the ultra-violet glow of the lamp. She looked at Richard. He had the same pattern. Rachel and Jonno too. She stumbled to the hallway mirror and stared at her own reflection.

What was it that the guy from the pub, Wally, had said to them? Look out for the hexafoil – a circle with six equally spaced petals at its centre. Quite a rudimentary pattern, yes, but striking nonetheless. The kind of shape that could easily be drawn with a finger and thumb on the foreheads of unsuspecting strangers. Particularly if the artist was using invisible UV reflective ink from a shell. A conch shell, to be precise.

It was there on her forehead, as clear as the tip of her nose.

There was no doubt, no doubt at all.

It was a daisy wheel.

ALISON AND MICHAEL
APRIL-JULY 2022

Alison and Michael Periwinkle's arrival at Bodhmall's Rest was truly a last-minute thing. There's was a shotgun wedding, you see? Both divorcees, both without children, both looking for something fun but enduring. Drinks after dinner, dancing until the small hours at the local thirty-something hangout, smooching outside the kebab house, a fumble in the back of a taxi. She didn't normally put out on the first date, but she wasn't getting any younger, and he was exactly what she'd been looking for: tall, handsome, fun and with money in the bank. Two weeks later they were at Gretna Green, standing outside together in the pouring rain. Alison's mother was their sole witness. They tied the knot for what would be her third time, his second. What? Are you judging? It's not as though she was some kind of Liz Taylor wannabe. This was going to be it, you know? For life.

The fortnight they spent in the Seychelles was magical, truly. The sand was white, the sea a lush blue, the fish every colour of the rainbow and then some. Michael took her scuba diving, something she had never previously had the time or, more importantly, the money to do. Her first husband couldn't even swim, and her second was an alcoholic who gambled away their savings.

The hotel was extortionate but to die for. Crisp, white sheets, a balcony overlooking the ocean, and a bath that you could do laps around. And the food? Lobster, caviar, steak that you could slice with a butter knife. She had been careful of course. She didn't want her new, Internet wealthy husband to think her fat. Not after only a week of marriage.

Michael was older than her at forty-one. It was only a three-year age difference, but it was enough to make her start acting like a grown-up. She'd been avoiding that transition ever since she'd turned twenty-one and was told by the county judge that scoring a seventy on a breathalyser test while in charge of a speeding vehicle was irresponsible, and that she was plenty old enough to know better. *Am I ever*, she thought at the time, but she was never stupid enough to repeat her mistake. Inch by inch, her dad used to say.

Michael was thick in the chest – one of the things that attracted her to him – and tall at six-four. He wasn't muscular, but he wasn't a beanpole either. He was, what her grandmother would call, impressive. She felt protected when he was around, even though he was as passive as the Dalai Lama and abhorred violence. His thick hair was a dark auburn with streaks of light-ginger, his cheeks and chin always covered in a well-trimmed beard. His aftershave was expensively nice, his eyes bright blue and piercing. She had fallen in love with him the moment he had opened his mouth and told her, in the sweetest way, how attractive she looked. That was all she had needed. That one simple, throwaway compliment.

She hadn't wanted the honeymoon to end. She'd stood there outside the hotel, stomping her feet like a spoilt child as they'd waited for their taxi in the blistering sunshine.

'Oh, Michael. Do we really have to leave? I mean, really?'

'We can't stay here for ever, Ali. We both have jobs to go to and houses to sell.' They still owned their own homes but were planning to sell up and buy a nice detached four-bed, somewhere on the south coast.

'Can't all that wait? It's so boring. Come on. Just another week here. I'm sure that's all I'll need, you know? Just to acclimatise.'

'And then at the end of that week you'll want just one more. Look,' he placed his hands on her shoulders and looked into her eyes. She melted. 'It's been wonderful, it really has. The best two weeks of my life, and I've had a lot of weeks, trust me. But we have to get back to the real world, to *our* real world. We have a home to find, a future to build. We'll have more holidays like this, so many

135

more, and every one of them will be wonderful and magical because we'll be together. The two of us, for ever.'

She felt the tears come. He had such a way with words. 'You promise?'

'On my heart,' he held his hand to his chest, 'because it's yours.'

'I love you, Michael James Periwinkle.'

'And I love you, Alison Mary Periwinkle. All the way and back again.'

And, as they say, that was that. Except it wasn't. Once they got home and went back to hopping from one house to the other, spending their weekends looking for new homes that were either too big or too small, or the garden didn't catch the sun just right, or the neighbours were too stuffy, or the traffic nearby was way too hectic, etcetera, etcetera, she had herself another lip-poaching moment. It was her specialty after all, and what's more, it had been building. Perhaps, she thought with just a small amount of self-deprecation, that she just wasn't the homemaking type.

'I've had enough of this, Michael. It's getting to me, it really is. Let's just take off for a while.'

'What? Why? Where would we take off to?'

'I don't know. I don't care. I just can't keep spending every daylight hour working behind a filthy desk in a stuffy office, only to spend our evenings and weekends in your car, driving here, there and everywhere. We're just looking at houses that neither of us like. Honestly, if I smell another cup of coffee or a freshly baked loaf of bread, I'm going to puke.' She shoved her hands into the pockets of her beige chinos. 'It's depressing.'

'It's life.'

'Not my life. Not *our* life. *Our* life is supposed to be fun. *Our* life is supposed to be exciting. Remember? That's what we promised each other. No more mundane normality. I've done that, and so have you.' She bit down on her lip. 'It sucks.'

There was a moment between them; a moment of knowing. That

136

was exactly what they'd agreed. He knew it too, and he'd slipped. He'd let life take over.

'Look, I have an idea,' he said, finally. 'I have a friend.'

'Okay,' her interest was piqued.

'A guy I knew from school. Bit of a nerd, but I liked him. He got me the good weed.'

'Sounds like a keeper.'

'He really was.' He smirked. 'Anyway, he has a place. Well, he lives in a place with his partner, way down in Cornwall. Like, *way* down. It's a bit unsophisticated but it might be kinda fun.'

Alison was intrigued. 'What are you thinking?'

'Well, I have some business down that way, so perhaps we could spend a few days in the countryside. He's always going on about this quaint little cottage that they have on their land. They rent it out occasionally, and he said he'd give me a good rate, on account of him being an old pal and owing me a few favours.'

She went cold on it. 'I don't know. Sounds a bit dull.'

'They have their own beach.'

She thought that sounded much better. 'A private beach?'

He nodded. 'Yep.'

'Cornwall, you say?'

'Uh-huh.'

'The English Riviera.'

'Well, actually I think that's Devon, but you're close enough.'

She went to him. 'Michael, my love.'

'Yes, Ali, my sweet.'

She smirked. 'When do we leave?'

Hattie awoke at around eight, which was late for her. She had the early murmurings of a headache. Fortunately, she had a packet of paracetamol capsules tucked away in the top drawer of her bedside table. She removed her eye mask, threw two capsules down, and glugged on the glass of tepid water she'd brought up to bed. She reached out her hand, her eyes half-shut, and found that the space next to her was empty. She hoped Richard had the coffee on, and some toast. *Yep*, she thought. *Some toast would be good.*

She gingerly swung one leg out from under the duvet, felt the threadbare carpet beneath her toes, and then followed it with the other. She sat up. The morning sun was just about peeking through the gap between the heavy curtains, and it cast a thin beam of light onto the wall opposite. It looked like a gateway to another world, as if two disembodied hands might appear from within the warm glow and push the shadows away.

What had been in that punch? By the way her head was throbbing, she suspected someone had emptied their personal stash of spirits into that innocent-looking plastic bowl, topping it up with fruit juice and ice cubes to mask the taste. She burped and held the back of her hand to her mouth. A little sick came up and almost caught her by surprise. She shook her head. What had she been thinking? This was supposed to be a relaxing getaway, not a hen weekend. Alcohol didn't agree with her. She'd proven that on more than one occasion, none more so than that fateful Friday night in November 2021. The first work's do she'd agreed to go to since Sally had been born, and what a car crash it had turned out to be.

She thought of Stephen, the teaching assistant. He'd persuaded her to go on to a nightclub after all the others had bailed. It was pretty obvious he fancied her – she'd known that since the get-go – but she was only playing along for the sake of her own ego. Except, of course, at some point she had crossed the line she'd drawn for herself (let's face it, it had only been a faint one to start with) and he'd jumped across it with both feet. It wasn't his fault. She'd made herself pretty available, of that there was no doubt. For his part, he'd made her feel special and wanted, like a woman again. It had been a mistake. A really, *really* big humdinger. A pretty gargantuan fuck-up of the planet-destroying variety actually, but it wasn't the biggest. No, not by a long shot. The biggest mistake she'd made, and partly the reason she'd decided to book this last-minute, held-together-by-sticky-tape, long-shot of a week away with her nearest and dearest (not the only reason, but more on that later), was that she'd brought Stephen back to her place. No, not the house she shared with her husband and daughter. That would have been awful enough, but in some ways, it would have been preferable. No, for some reason, in her drunken state of heightened emotional diarrhoea, she'd decided to bring the poor guy back to the place where she'd spent most of her formative years. The bedroom where she'd listened to emo music for hours on end, dyed her hair black, and buried her nose in Anne Rice novels. Yep, that's right. Hattie Penrose, *nee* Piper, brought her one-night stand back for a quick, and way too noisy, shag at her parents' house.

She held her face in her hands and shook her head. Richard didn't know of course. How could she tell him? It wasn't like she wanted anything more from Stephen, and she knew for a fact that he didn't want it to go any further. She also didn't want her marriage to end, despite all the bickering and the backbiting. She cherished her house, adored her daughter and she still loved Richard. None of that had changed. It had been nothing more than a release, and a welcome one too. Becoming a mother hadn't come easy to her. She had been affected in ways that she hadn't anticipated, and Richard hadn't been as understanding as he might have been. She wasn't blaming him, wasn't blaming anyone or anything for that matter, but post-natal depression had happened, and it had lingered, and yes that had made her an angrier person than she'd been before, although she'd never been the warmest. Christ, her own mother wasn't the warmest. But Hattie had been happier before. She knew that sounded awful, admitting that she'd been happier before Sally-Ann had arrived, but it was the truth. The cheerful enzyme had been ever present before Sally's beautifully delicate head had appeared from between her legs. She loved her so much that it made her heart hurt and her muscles ache. She would do anything for her (commit murder, armed robbery, arson, embezzlement, *whatever*) but that didn't change the fact that for over five years she'd been pretty damn miserable and a bitch to be around. There, she'd admitted it. She was a *bitch*.

Her parents knew. They'd probably heard everything. It wasn't as if they'd been discrete. They'd both been up, dressed and drinking tea on the sofa when Stephen had left sheepishly the next morning. She would never forget the look on their faces. The judgement. Jesus, she may as well have killed someone; vandalised a church; scandalised the monarchy. Their eyes screamed disappointment, betrayal, shame. They couldn't even speak to her. She'd just showered, grabbed her things, and left.

She let Richard believe the argument with her parents was about money, which it also was, but not really. Not deep down. His business had been suffering pretty badly – culminating with the incident with those thugs – and so she'd asked her mum and dad for a fairly sizable loan. This had been before the one-night stand, of course. They had been considering it, the loan that was, and they were enjoying dragging it out. Her father never let either of his children have anything without a long, painful process of 'thinking it through'. It was his way of making sure they knew how much of a favour he was doing them, how much they needed him. Also, they would be under no illusion that it would need repaying and then some, both physically and emotionally. Of course, after the Stephen incident, he'd flatly refused. That had led to a blow-up at their house which Hattie had carefully stage-managed. The last thing she wanted was to not get the loan, and then for Richard to find out about her infidelity. The former she could handle, the latter not so much. Shortly afterwards, Bea came out to them all. It wasn't a surprise to Hattie, she'd known for ages, but it left her God-fearing parents shellshocked. That was when things had got really ugly.

'Mummy?'

She looked up, still half in a dream. It was Sally. She was standing in the bedroom doorway, dressed in her pink pyjamas and holding her scruffy teddy bear by one hand. 'Yes, baby?'

'Can I play with my friend today?'

'Your friend?'

'Yes, the boy with the broken hand.'

'I don't know what you mean, bunny.'

'Last night, he said we could go for a walk in the woods, but then he had to leave.'

Hattie stood, swaying a little. 'I think you must have dreamed it, my darling. We were at the party last night with our neighbours, remember?'

'Yes, I know. He played with me while you were by the sea. I woke up and he was standing under the tree.' She laughed. 'He's got a funny face.'

'No, bunny. There was no one there. We were all together, weren't we? We were maybe gone for a couple of minutes while we were down on the beach with the others, but when we came back you were standing on the path, waiting for us.'

Sally stomped her feet and dropped her teddy bear. 'I know, mummy! That was where he left me!'

'Oh, Sally, you come up with some strange stories, you really do.' Hattie wiped sleep from her eyes and held out an unsteady hand. 'Now, let's go downstairs and see what Daddy's up to.'

'I'm not making it up, Mummy! Look,' she pulled something from her pocket and held it up for her mother to see. 'He gave me this.'

Hattie stopped and turned. She looked down at the object. It took her a few moments to fathom what she was looking at. It was small enough to sit in Sally's palm, spherical, made from cloth and string and quite clumsily put together. Whoever was responsible for the needlework had attempted a face and hair – red hair, like Sally's. She caught a gasp in the back of her throat.

'What the—'

Sally grinned. 'My friend. See? He made it for me.'

*

Jonno lay on his bed and stared at the ceiling. The boulder was back. It was crushing his lungs. He could feel its jagged surface pushing into his chest, could smell the moss like a damp carpet. His mouth tasted of bugs and dirt.

Thoughts flitted around in his head like flies. She couldn't really like him, could she? Why would she? He was just a nervous, jittering idiot who never left his room. Why did Evie take him to the crashed plane? Had she really kissed him? He touched his lips and smelled his fingers. There was still the faintest scent of berries. He thought of their time on the beach, how terrified he had been. He'd felt as if the sky was going to swallow them all. And the sea. It had looked like cherry cola. Or *blood*. He'd staggered, almost fainted, but she had caught him. She was really strong for her size. Her eyes had been on fire, like electric. He had felt her skin dancing against his, as if there was something wriggling around in there.

He stood and removed his T-shirt. He had to see her to be sure. Whatever had happened last night, he liked her. He *really* liked her, and he'd never felt that way before. He imagined it was like experiencing a chemically induced high, because he couldn't shake it. Maybe he was addicted, like that kid at his school had been, the

142

one who took too many painkillers.

He looked at himself in the mirror. He was a skinny, pasty boy with spots. His dad said it was because he was too picky with his food. He tensed his muscles and heard himself let out an involuntary grunt. There was a slight ripple of bicep and the hint of a six-pack. He nodded his approval. He was no Eddie Hall, but it wasn't bad. At least he wasn't flabby.

He lifted an arm and smelled his pit. Ugh! It stunk like old socks. He was going to have to take a shower in the mouldy bathroom, which was an idea he wasn't fond of. What if Rachel or Aunt Bea walked in on him? That would be mega embarrassing.

Something ran across his foot, and he leapt into the air. He flapped frantically at his toes, stumbled backwards and clattered into the wardrobe. He lay on the floor, his eyes wide and moist. He spied the rat. It wasn't as big as the one he'd seen on their first day, but it was plenty big enough to sever his jugular. He held a hand up to his throat, but the rat didn't look at all interested. It collected a biscuit crumb from the patchy carpet and held it carefully between tiny paws. Jonno lay there, breathless, and watched in silence as the rodent meticulously devoured the crumbly feast. Once finished, it turned to him. Was that a nod? Jonno thought it might be. He nodded back. The rat's whiskers flickered and twitched in acknowledgement, then it turned and disappeared between the flaky skirting board and the damp-stained wall.

Jonno leaned on his elbows and let out a long breath. The place was infested all right, but maybe it wasn't as bad as he'd first thought. Rats were outsiders, and so was he. Maybe they didn't want to hurt him at all. He hated rats, that hadn't changed, but maybe he could stomach them. He impressed himself with that one thought. He could stomach rats. How mature.

He stood up, took another look at himself in the mirror, and turned to the window. He immediately raised his arms to cover his chest, and he felt his face flush with an intense prickly heat.

There she was, standing on the driveway next to his dad's

143

stricken car. She was dressed in tight blue jeans and a cut off T-shirt. She stared straight at him and smiled. She pointed at his bare chest and winked, turning her hand to beckon him. Jonno felt the inside of his mouth become a vacuum, and the pulse in his neck race to a gallop. He glanced at his washbag. He really hoped the shower was free.

*

Rachel sat on the edge of the bathtub and glared at her phone. Things were not going according to plan. She'd barely made any progress. She still didn't have any solid clues about the identity or location of Mr Quin, and, what's more, she'd almost spilled the details of the one semi-good lead she'd uncovered to the one person she shouldn't. And why was that? Because, like a little kid, she'd got herself flustered by what appeared to be some sort of crazy, local cult. What had got into her? She used to be better than this.

She scrolled through her messages once more.

Sent: Monday August 1st 0.10 a.m.
Sender: Eric Chapel
To: Beth Mckinley
Message Subject: Contact

Beth, this just came in. It looks like somebody's getting spooked.

'What the hell's going on? I haven't heard from you in four days. Is this deal still going ahead or what? I'm ready to blow the whole thing and walk. Suggest you get your shit together and sharpish. We've worked way too hard on this to see it collapse at the last minute. You said I could rely on you, so do yourself a favour – be reliable.'

END

Whatever you're up to down there, Beth, it's making a ripple. You'd just better hope that ripple doesn't become a whole tidal wave of trouble heading your way. Message me back with the details. I'll make the necessary enquiries. We're getting close. I can feel it.

Same as before – any hint of being blown, hit the 'come get me' code.

Eric

She read it again. She wished she shared Eric's same level of optimism. The message didn't tell her much at all, except that The Weasel had disappeared, and Quin wasn't happy. If Quin was Richard, then what account were the emails coming from? She hadn't seen anything like this on his laptop. Unless, of course, he had another encrypted email address hooked up to his phone. That was a possibility she couldn't rule out, but how the hell was she going to get access to that? And what she'd said to him last night – whatever the *hell it was* that she had said last night – it must have put the wind up him, potentially even blowing her cover. She swore under her breath. She was such an idiot. Tommy and the girls deserved so much better than this. She needed to do better, *be* better.

She realised she was going to have to up the ante, be bold, take some chances. With just a few days left, she couldn't keep carrying on the way she was, spending wasted hours on a sunbed, drinking cocktails and playing house with the new woman on her arm. Sacrifices needed to be made, no matter how she felt. She couldn't keep letting herself get distracted. It was unprofessional, dangerous even.

Her phone pinged again.

Sent: Monday August 1st 8.10 a.m.
Sender: Eric Chapel
To: Beth Mckinley
Message Subject: Urgent

145

Beth, some intel just came through. We suspect there's going to be a meet today. Your guy might try to make face-to-face contact. Whatever you need to do, make sure you follow him. Take pictures, but keep your distance. Don't get blown. This could be the moment we uncover the identity of the man at the top. It's what we've been waiting for.

Stay safe and keep in touch.

She realised she'd been holding her breath. She let it out slowly, her cheeks and neck suddenly clammy. Could she have just got that lucky?

Suddenly, the handle of the bathroom door rattled, and she dropped her phone. It clattered to the ground. She scrambled around on the floor, hoping that she'd remembered to lock the door behind her.

'Is someone in there?' a man's voice yelled.

Who was that? Richard? 'Yeah, it's me. It's Rachel. Just hang on a sec. I'm just flushing the loo.'

'Be quick, I need a shower.' It was Jonno. 'Like, *now*.'

She sighed. What was so urgent that the kid needed a shower immediately? As far as she could tell, he barely washed.

'No worries, mate. I'll just be a mo.'

She heard the boy grunt, frustrated, and then there was a desperate shout from the direction of Hattie and Richard's room.

'*Richard*!' she heard Hattie scream. 'I need you here! *Now*!'

*

They were all standing in the open doorway of the bedroom, Hattie, with one hand on her hip, the other holding the strange-looking ball-shaped thing. Sally was crying.

'I don't know, Sal, sweetheart. It does look kind of weird, doesn't it?' Richard said, trying to appease their daughter.

'Weird? It's freaky, Richard!' Hattie was angry. 'Freaky, that's what it is!'

Bea nodded. 'It is pretty strange.' She stooped down to her niece's level. 'Where did you say you got it again, Sally baby?'

Sally was sobbing uncontrollably, tears rolling down her cheeks, snot on her lip, and her chest was heaving in and out. Rachel joined Bea on the ground. 'You can tell us, sweetheart. It's okay.'

'My… my… friend.'

'What friend, baby?'

'Apparently someone with an injured arm, or hand, or something like that.' Hattie was dismissive. 'Look,' she glared at Richard. 'What with the incident with the iPad, the tyres, and that creepy thing in the woods—'

'Wait. What creepy thing?'

'Never mind, Bea. It's not important. Anyway, along with last night's freak show on the beach, those bizarre drawings on our foreheads, and now this,' Hattie gestured towards the peculiar object, 'it's all too much, Richard. It is. It really is. I say we cut our losses and get away from here as soon as possible.'

'No, mummy! I… I… want—'

'Hattie,' Bea said, shaking her head. 'Are you really sure about that?'

'I am.'

'That's not fair!' Jonno cried. 'Just because she's got something she shouldn't have! What's that got to do with the rest of us?'

'Oh, Jonno. It's not always about you, you know,' Hattie retorted.

'No, it's usually all about *you*, isn't it?' he yelled.

'What the hell's that supposed to mean?'

'Oh, I don't think you want me to say. Not in front of the others.'

'Woah! Woah!' Richard interjected. 'Will everyone just calm down a bit, please.'

147

Rachel watched carefully and let the coin spin. She hoped, for her sake, it landed the right side up. Bea hugged Sally tightly, the little girl's sobbing easing just a little. Rachel tried not to look at her partner. She knew it would probably make her like her even more, and that would only serve to cloud her judgement.

'Look,' Richard said. 'Let's not overreact here.'

'I'm not overreacting—'

He held up a hand. 'Okay, let's not go overboard, then. We've got off to a shaky start, that's true.'

'To say the least.'

'The locals are a little odd, there's no denying that, and the damage to our property has been,' he shook his head, 'unfortunate.'

'And expensive,' Hattie added.

'Well maybe, maybe not. Let's hope Noah can make good on his promise, and the tyres will be a little less pricey than I first thought. We'll see. But in any case, both he and Glanna were genuinely surprised last night, I do believe that, and I also believe they want to help us out.'

'I like them,' Rachel said, but it came across as insincere, even to her. She tried again. 'I mean, they seem kind of nice.'

'There you have it.' Richard pounced on it. 'Rachel agrees. They're kind of nice.'

'They are. And Evie too,' Jonno said.

'Huh. Yeah, sure,' Hattie sneered. 'What about last night, and those drawings on our foreheads? Those shapes were exactly what the pub landlord warned us about.'

Richard laughed. 'Oh, now hang on a minute, Hats. You didn't even like the guy. Now, you're suddenly all ears about these daisy wheels, or whatever it was he called them.'

'Well, you can't deny that they're exactly the same as the sketch he made, can you?'

'Well, no, but—'

'Exactly! You can't, and you won't.'

Bea stood. 'Look, sis. I'm with Richard and the guys on this one. We can't just run for the hills, just because of a few silly superstitions and strange goings on. We're in Cornwall, for God's sake. Everywhere you look there's a stone monument, witch's cauldron, or crop circle. I sort of like it, the spirituality I mean. It's kinda charming.'

'And this, Bea? What about this?' Hattie held out the ball.

'It's rather sweet, isn't it?'

'Look at it! Just look at the thing!' Hattie was shaking now. 'Who the hell gave this to my daughter?'

Sally pulled free from her auntie's grasp. 'I told you, mummy! The man with the broken hand and the funny face!'

There was a long period of awkward silence while everyone appeared to consider their respective positions. They each had their own little agendas, it seemed. Rachel studied them, trying to get a read. Bea gently soothed her niece, Richard fidgeted with his chewed fingernails, Hattie nibbled on the inside of her cheek, and Jonno shuffled from one foot to the other. Rachel listened to the steady ticking of the downstairs clock, the chirping of the birds flitting about in the garden, and the creaking and groaning of the frayed tether still holding this little broken family together. She wondered how much more that tatty piece of string could take.

'Oh, wait a minute.' Jonno broke the tension. 'Do you mean Eli?'

*

'Oh, hey there! Noah, is it?' Richard yelled, crossing the driveway.

'Yes?'

'Oh, hi. I mean, morning. Sorry to catch you on the hop like this. It's Richard,' He thrust out a hand. 'From last night?'

Noah's upside-down eyes peered back at him through thick, grimy spectacles. His hair hung in lank strands down his back, and he wore a loose shirt, and white linen trousers. He had leather sandals on his feet, which shuffled uncomfortably in the gravel.

149

'Ah, yes. The Penrose party.'

'Yep, that's right. The rowdy bunch. Ha-ha, yes. Noisy buggers, the lot of us. Great night last night, by the way. We really, really enjoyed it.' Richard felt himself nodding somewhat eagerly, and reeled it in. 'We all did. So raw, so authentic. Wow! Blew our minds.'

Noah stepped back as if readying himself for retreat. 'Well, we're used to it by now. The whole thing's probably lost a bit of its charm for us but, you know, it's our way of life so we just get on with it.' He turned to go.

'My tyres. I'm sure you'll remember. They were vandalised yesterday.' Richard pointed at his car. 'You see? Completely useless at this point. I really need to get them fixed.'

'Mm.'

'Your wife – she said you could help. She thought you knew a guy.'

Noah winced. 'For the tyres?'

'Yes, exactly. I really have to get them replaced, you see? They're Quattro Premium. Cost a bloody arm and a leg.' Richard leaned over and patted Noah playfully on the shoulder. 'You know, you'd be doing me a huge favour if you'd give him a call. Or her, of course.'

'It's a *her*. Usually, anyway.'

'*Her*, then. Great.'

'I'll, er, see what I can do.' Noah turned to go, but stopped, seemingly thinking it over, but eventually turned away again.

'Thanks. That's really good of you. It'll be a great help,' Richard said, and then with a Columbo-esque awkwardness, 'Er, there is… one more thing. If you wouldn't mind?'

'Yes?' Noah paused.

'You don't happen to know where this came from, do you?' Richard held out the little cloth ball, its crooked face peering up at them through its clumsy x-shaped eyes. Noah stared at it, unmoved.

'No idea.'

150

'Really? You're sure?' Richard persisted. 'Because my little girl was given it last night by some boy she describes as having a broken arm and a funny face.' He smiled. 'You know how cruel kids can be. It sounds rather odd, I know.'

Noah was still for a moment. Richard thought he saw something pass over his face, like annoyance.

'No. Really, I have no clue.'

'No clue?'

Noah shook his head. 'None at all.' Another shake.

'You don't want to take this back to the house? Maybe ask around?' Richard pushed the cloth ball towards him.

'Look, Richard. I'll make the call about your tyres, even though it really is none of our business. We couldn't even hope to afford a vehicle like that.'

'Oh, come on. With a place like this? The grounds? The buildings? You must be doing okay.'

'Inherited I'm afraid. A hand-me-down.' Noah took the ball and glared at it. 'I'll take this too, but I can't promise anything. Maybe the others will know who this boy is. That is, if he even exists at all.'

'That'd be great. Really. And the tyres too. You'd be doing me a huge favour. Huge. I mean, it wouldn't really be much of a holiday if we just found ourselves stuck here, staring at the walls for hours on end, playing board games and drinking ourselves into a stupor. We'd probably end up killing each other.'

'Quite.' Noah nodded and turned away. He glanced over his shoulder. 'Come to the beach with us later this afternoon, if you like.'

'The beach?'

'Yes, a few of us are heading down there. There's a cave that we swim out to, the boys and I. Petra, who owns the Weary Traveller? He and his son sometimes come with us.' Noah's face was only half visible, but Richard sensed a wry smile. 'You and your boy are welcome to come along. That is, assuming you're both

151

strong swimmers.'

'Well, erm,' Richard considered his son, his thin arms, and gangly legs. 'Yep, I'm pretty sure we'll manage.'

'Good. Let's say three p.m. then. And bring a camera.' Noah disappeared through the gate. 'There's lots to see.'

*

Rachel stood at the upstairs hallway window, and she watched as Richard held an uncomfortable conversation with Glanna's creepy-looking partner. She thought the guy was punching: all scrawny arms, scraggly beard, Jesus-creepers and googly eyes. Glanna, in contrast, was attractive with poise, demure in a Hollywood golden-era kind of way, but with a big dollop of New Age chic thrown in. She wondered what she saw in him.

Bea was out in the garden looking for bugs with Sally, and Jonno was in the kitchen, helping Hattie clean the breakfast stuff away. Bea's sister had calmed down eventually, reluctantly agreeing to continue with the holiday, on the proviso that Richard made enquiries about the mysterious one-armed toymaker. The whole week away was becoming a little too Hammer-horror weird for Rachel's liking, but what choice did she have but to stick with it? She had her priorities, after all.

Earlier that morning, while she'd sat and consumed her dry toasted bagel (all the while Bea teasing her about her bludgeoning hangover) she'd overheard Richard and Hattie talking. Richard had started by telling his wife that he needed to clear his head, citing everything that had gone on with the car and their daughter. She'd told him that was fine, as long as he was back by lunchtime; they were supposed to be spending time together as a family, after all. He'd said, no problem. He planned to go and have a word with the husband, Noah, ask about him calling the garage, see if he knew anything about the little freaky ball thing, and then once that was done, he'd head off for a walk around the cove. That little snippet had piqued Rachel's interest. It gave her that feeling, like this was the opening she'd been looking for. *Think of an excuse*, she told herself. *Throw Bea off the scent. Make up some bullshit lie about sleeping off the wine from the night before, or about going to take a really long soak.* Whatever, the story didn't matter. What mattered was the outcome. Richard was her best lead, and she needed to exploit him, however awful that sounded. She recalled the email:

"When can I see you? We need to talk."

Well, if that was his intention, to meet up with the mysterious TDeville666, then Rachel planned to make sure she was right there, listening to every goddam word.

*

'Did you do this?'

'Did I do what?'

'This?' Noah held out the little ball with the orange hair. 'Did you give this... this thing to that little girl? Don't you lie to me, Eli. I'll know if you're lying.'

'Well, no. I mean... what I mean is—' Noah's palm connected with Eli's cheek. There was a loud thwack and Eli's head jolted to the side. 'Ow! That hurt!'

'There's more where that came from.'

They were standing in the barn, Eli bare-back, wearing only his cargo shorts. His brother had rushed in while he was getting dressed, a darkness beneath his eyes and spittle on his lips.

'What the hell do you think you're playing at?' Noah asked, seething.

'What... what do you mean? I jus' give her a toy.'

'Don't take me for a fool, brother. This isn't just a toy. It's a charm.'

Eli backed away. 'No, it's jus' a toy, like I said. I promise, Noah. Honest.'

Noah launched himself at Eli, catching him across his chest and throat. 'I told you not to lie to me! Now, you either tell me what you're up to, or I'm going to go up to the house and fetch the irons.'

'*No!*' Eli yelped. 'Not the hot fings, *please* don't use the hot fings!' He pressed a hand to his chest, and touched the patchwork pattern of mottled, pink flesh. 'I didn't mean nuffin' by it, Noah. I was just being nice to her.'

'I don't believe you. You don't even believe yourself, do you? There's something going on here, Eli.' Noah shoved him against the ladder. 'And you're going to tell me exactly what it is.'

Eli looked up at him. He was unsure of what to do or say. 'I don't—' A fist this time, and the sound of something gristly giving way in his nose. He dropped to the floor as warm salty blood flooded into his mouth and spilled down his chin and neck. 'Please, don't hurt me no more, brother. Please!' He spat red gloop onto the hay and raised a trembling hand to his shattered nose.

Noah was breathing heavily. Sweat glistened on his forehead. He rubbed his knuckles. His hair had fallen across his face in greasy strands. Eli knew that he liked it, that he fed off the domination, the control. He tried to make himself as small as possible, as small as a mouse. He wouldn't cry, though. He never cried.

'You either tell me what you're up to, or this is going to get a hell of a lot worse. I mean it!'

'*I can't!*'

'You what?'

Eli didn't lift his gaze. He simply whispered, 'I can't.'

'Well, we'll see about that.' Noah grabbed a heavy rake from beside the stable door and raised it above his head. 'Even if I have to beat it out of you.'

Eli winced and raised his arms up to protect himself. 'No, brother. Please!'

'Leave him!' There was a silhouette standing in the doorway.

'He's been messing around with our guests,' Noah said.

'I know.'

'He's causing trouble again.'

'Nothing we can't handle.' The figure emerged from the haze, small feet on scattered hay, a clutch of dark, tumbling hair, and a veil around an elegantly swollen waist. 'Now give me that and go inside. Let me speak with him alone.'

'But, Glanna—'

'Go, Noah!'

Noah shoved the ball into her hands. He huffed loudly and marched outside.

Eli attempted a smile, but his face hurt, and blood was sticking to his lips. *Everything is going to be okay now*, he thought. *Sweet Mother will make it all okay*. She crouched in front of him. He could smell perfume and incense.

'Why, Eli? What were you trying to achieve with this?' She held the ball in the palm of her hand and ran a long finger over its crude face and orange hair.

'It wasn't my idea.'

'Then whose?' She touched his nose, held her hand up to her eyes. She gazed at the wet crimson smear on her fingertips.

'Those people. The ones that we hurt.'

'We didn't hurt anyone, Eli.'

He watched her, expressionless. He thought she was truly and uniquely beautiful. 'But we did, didn't we? The pretty lady and the man with the beard.' He recalled the look on the woman's face, the furious rage in her husband's eyes.

'I'm not understanding you, my love.' But he could see that she was.

'He came to me. In the Rotting Place. He spoke to me.'

'Who did, Eli? Tell me who?' She placed a warm palm to his cheek, and the truth fell out of him like bitter ash.

'The Red Man. He's coming for us.' He wiped blood from his mouth. 'He's coming for all of us.'

*

She edged along the crumbling path at the foot of the cliff, the water beneath kissing the slim gap between the sand and the sharp granite. White foam grasped at her ankles like damp fingers, and a southerly wind fought a raging battle with her braids. She wished she'd had the good sense to tie them back in a ponytail. The Night Watchman peered out towards the vast horizon, dark windows like pupils, its weather-beaten cheeks of brick and crumbling mortar.

Richard turned back towards her, and she swiftly ducked behind the bracken.

'Aw, but it's going to be a nice day today, Rach,' Bea had said. 'We could go for a walk, find a quiet spot somewhere. Maybe take a dip, you know?'

'Maybe later.' Rachel had retorted. 'I've just got a really bad headache. I don't feel like doing much at all at the moment. I think I just need to sleep it off.' She'd shaken her head, feigning annoyance. 'It's my fault. I had way too much wine.'

'Just a bit.' Bea had stuck out a lip. 'After lunch, then?'

Rachel had smiled. 'Of course,' she'd said, kissing her. 'I'm sorry.'

She knew it was a fragile plan at best. If Bea decided to check in on her, which was a distinct possibility, then she was going to have some explaining to do. She'd just have to worry about that later. All that mattered now was following Richard and making sure she wasn't seen. Pretty much everything she'd put herself through this past three and a half years hinged on this one speculative field trip. The mission was in the balance, this single moment of good fortune threatening, with faint promise, to tip the scales in her direction.

Richard, rucksack slung over his shoulder, rounded the curve in the rock face and disappeared from her view. She raced after him, taking great care not to slip on the gravel and send herself tumbling into the water. She placed a hand on a slab of cool grey basalt and peered around the corner. The wind here was at its strongest, the cliff completely exposed to the full power of the ocean. She pulled hair from her mouth, wiped moisture from her eyes. She'd dressed herself in a vest top, khaki shorts and hiking boots. She thought she looked like a slightly shorter, stockier version of Lara Croft, although God help her if she had to swing across a ravine or dive for sunken treasure.

Richard was climbing the rough incline towards the top of the cliff. The Night Watchman was to their left, the water now some fifty feet below. There was no cover along that rapidly rising path, so she waited. She decided to let him crest the summit and then take a chance on him not coming back her way. She looked at her watch. It was ten-fifteen a.m. She could probably push her absence until eleven-thirty, twelve at the latest. Beyond that, and her lie was bound to unravel rapidly.

He disappeared behind a large rock, and she decided to make her move. The distance was only forty feet or so, but it was an agonising dash. She slipped on a patch of moss, slid to her right and scraped a knee. She grabbed hold of the ground for purchase as stones clattered beneath, tumbling and bouncing towards the water. Blood ran down her leg and onto her white sock. She licked a palm and rubbed the long graze, all the while cursing under her breath.

Once she'd rounded the corner, she spotted Richard some way in the distance, striding purposefully down a well-marked path. The trail followed the cliff's edge, stretching east towards what looked like another, much smaller beach. The ground faded away beneath them and then rose once more towards a large wooded area. It was maybe a mile and a half ahead. The area around her was deserted. She and Richard were the only people on that path and there was no cover. She suddenly felt very exposed.

'Maybe if I keep my distance,' she reassured herself. She wasn't confident. 'You can do this. Just focus.'

A large bird of prey suddenly appeared at the ground in front of her, a baby rabbit caught in its razor-sharp claws. The stricken animal let out a loud piercing shriek and she leapt in the air.

157

'*Fucking hell*!'

Richard heard the commotion and turned to face her. She dived behind the boulder. 'He must have seen me,' she said to herself. 'Must have. Jesus-bloody-Christ.' Her heart was hammering in her chest. She heard her own rapid breathing. What if she'd blown it? What if she'd been spotted? 'Get yourself together, girl,' she said. 'It's just a bloody bird.'

She peered around the rock once more. The buzzard and the rabbit had disappeared, and Richard was now much further ahead. She stood, dusted herself down and decided to follow him.

They walked that way for another thirty minutes. Richard was a white and blue blob in the distance. The descent was steep, the climb even steeper. The little beach turned out to be nothing more than a shallow cove; grey shingle and brown seaweed littered the small slip of land, the tide almost reaching the base of the cliff. A rickety wooden bridge crossed a river that zig-zagged towards the ocean, foamy water tumbling over scattered rocks. The wind had dropped a little, but Rachel still felt its cool kiss on her cheeks. Her forehead and neck were now starting to simmer under the relentless glare of the rapidly rising sun. She regretted not wearing a hat.

Richard climbed over the slanted stile to the next field, the woodland now just a short way off. There was the sound of an engine, and Rachel crouched behind a crop of tall grass as a car approached them from the north. She couldn't see it – the ground rose just enough to hide it from her view – but she could hear it just fine. It sounded like a V8 or maybe something bigger. The deep roar grew louder and deeper, and for a moment she thought the invisible vehicle was going to tear through the barbed wire fence and come barrelling straight towards her. Then, at the last minute, it rounded a bend, and the sound faded to a low grumble. She stood, as Richard disappeared into a thicket of tall pines.

She uttered a '*shit*' and tore off across the rough terrain, bounding the stile in a somewhat unorthodox fashion. She sprinted towards the woods. Cows scattered in her wake as she shooed and harried them. She slipped, almost tumbling head-first into a huge pile of manure. Flailing her arms, she staggered and tumbled along the path and into the cover of the forest. The glare of the sun dissipated somewhat, and she found herself in a cool shade. Richard was nowhere to be seen.

The path penetrated the tall trees. It wound this way and that, and then forked either side of a large oak that split the trail in two. She realised she was going to have to take a chance. She paused and listened. She could still hear the low growl of a car and the faint strain of voices. *Head away from the shore*, she thought. Chances are, they would meet inland, away from beachgoers and prying eyes.

She followed the left-hand tributary. A squirrel ran across her path and disappeared up the trunk of a tall pine and ran along an outstretched branch. A family of sparrows fizzed by, followed by the luminous green zip of a dragonfly. After a few moments, the comfort of the shadows began to filter like dissipating smoke, and she spotted a clearing. No, not a clearing, a car park.

'You made it!' Richard's voice.

'Only just. Why the hell did you drag me all the way out here?' It was a woman.

'Did it take you long?'

'Oh, four hours or so. Luckily the traffic was kind.'

Rachel stepped off the path and into the cover of the trees. She trod carefully, trying to avoid twigs and dry leaves or anything that might give her away.

'Thanks. For making the trip, I mean.'

'Sure. I just hope it's worth it.'

'Oh, it will be. You'll see.'

Rachel could make out Richard's T-shirt. He had his back to her. The woman was ahead of him, obscured from Rachel's view by branches and leaves. The car was behind a hedge.

'How is he?' the woman asked.

'He's fine.'

'You're sure?'

'As sure as I'll ever be with him. You know, he keeps himself to himself. He's like his dad in that way.'

'Pff. You must be kidding.'

Rachel crouched and inched carefully towards them. She wanted to see the woman and get the numberplate of the car.

'He misses you, you know.'

'I miss him too.' Her voice sounded piled high with regret.

'You could come over. Any time.'

'I don't think that's wise, do you? After what happened.'

'That wasn't my fault.'

'Well, *he* doesn't see it that way.'

'I know that, but you need to make him understand. It was just a stupid mistake.'

'He's not really the understanding type.'

Rachel could see her now. Hazel hair pulled back in a long ponytail, with a sharp nose and chin, dark sunglasses, and pale complexion. She wore a peach summer dress, matching flats. There was something about her.

'Look, do you have it?' she asked.

'Yep. It took me a little while to get it together but,' he removed the rucksack, patted it, 'it's all there.'

'You're… sure about this?'

'I am.'

'And Harriet?'

Richard laughed awkwardly. 'You know she hates it when you call her that.'

'Hm. And?'

'And what?'

'Is she okay with it?'

There was an awkward pause. 'Of course she is. Why would you think otherwise?'

'Because we're in a secluded car park, in the middle of lord knows where, and meeting up like a pair of seedy criminals.'

Richard let out a nervous laugh.

Rachel circled the trees at the edge of the clearing. She could see the rear wing of the car. The sun gleamed off polished orange lacquer. She withdrew her phone from her pocket. She was going to need a photograph of the numberplate.

The woman took the bag and opened it. Rachel stood to get a better view. She could see thick cylindrical bundles of bank notes.

'Phew. That's a lot of cash,' the woman said.

'It was different with the other deposits. They were much smaller. But this amount of money? It's safer this way.'

'Why?'

'Untraceable.'

The rear of the car was fully in view now. Rachel opened the camera app on her phone and pinched the screen to zoom in. The woman removed her sunglasses and Rachel felt a pang of familiarity once more. An image appeared in her mind's eye. Three people: two older, one younger.

'This will buy you a lot of favours, you know that?'

'I just want in.'

'Well, I think this might just do the trick.' The woman hitched the bag onto her shoulder. 'I'll talk to him.'

'Okay. Make him... see sense. Please.' There was a desperation in Richard's voice. It was unflattering. 'I need this. *We* need this.'

Rachel glared at her phone and watched as the numberplate came into focus. She stifled a little squeal of excitement. It was exactly as she'd hoped: TDevil666. The *tangerine-mobile*, the Lamborghini that Bea had seen parked outside the Penrose's home. But the woman? The woman didn't fit. Bea had said it had been driven by a big guy, and much older too.

'Please, Tara.'

Tara? Rachel thought. *That name. Where had she heard that name? And why did she look so goddam familiar?*

'Don't, Richard. Please don't.'

Richard approached the woman, arms outstretched. 'It doesn't

161

have to be this way. We could… make it better.'

Tara backed away. 'I don't think your wife would see it that way, do you? Terry certainly wouldn't.'

'But, Jonno?'

Rachel stopped in her tracks. Jonno? What did the kid have to do with this?

'Look, I have to go. I have a long drive back, and we have an important engagement this evening.'

'Don't go, please. Why don't you stay a while longer? We could talk some more.'

Rachel's brain was frantically scrambling through faded images and forgotten moments.

'I'll email you once I've spoken to him. Then, perhaps we can meet again.'

'Good. I'll bring Jonno next time.'

'Please don't.'

Rachel gasped and held a hand up to her mouth. The memory came back to her: a tiny photograph pinned to the noticeboard in Jonno's room; the screensaver on Richard's laptop. It was the same woman. A little younger back then, her hair a little shorter, but she was sure it was her. She was Jonno's mother.

'Tara, please! He's *our son*!'

The woman lifted the car door and threw the bag inside. She tossed her hair from her face and turned to him, a single tear on smooth milk-white skin.

'I'll be in touch.'

*

'Hey, you boys! Hey there! Yes, over here. Can I… can I have a word?'

Hattie was scraping mutilated bacon and egg remains into the food bin at the front of the cottage. She'd looked up just as Glanna's two sons crossed the driveway, towels and foam bodyboards tucked

162

under thick, suntanned arms. The taller one, Aaron, turned to her.

'Yeah? What?'

'Would you mind coming over here? Just for a second?' She waved them over. 'Don't worry. I'm not going to have a go at you.'

'Look, lady, we're kind of in a hurry.' It was the shorter boy with the cleft lip, Freddie.

'In a hurry? You mean, to get to the beach? Oh, come on now. It's not going anywhere, is it? It'll still be there in five minutes.'

'Yeah, true, but—'

'Okay look, I'll come to you.' She opened the gate. 'I just wanted to say... well,' she smiled as she approached. 'I think we got off to a bad start the other day and, you know, what you did for Jonno was really kind and much more than we expected.' She held out a hand. 'I just wanted to say thank you. And to say hi. I'm Hattie.'

'Er, okay,' Aaron grunted, raising an eyebrow. 'That's cool, I guess.'

'Yeah. That's what I thought,' she said. 'I can be cool sometimes, despite what the children might think.'

They stood that way for a moment, the two boys looking increasingly uncomfortable. Hattie's hand hung in the air.

'You going to shake it, or what? Just a little shake. I'm being friendly here.'

Aaron looked down at her palm and then glared at his brother. After a moment, he grumbled something under his breath and lowered his board to the ground, reluctantly taking her hand in his. It was a surprisingly soft grip. She pumped it twice and turned to Freddie. He paused for confirmation and received a reluctant nod from his brother. Hattie wasted no time in taking Freddie's hand, bringing a bright pink smear to his cheeks.

'Good. There, that's done. Now, I'll let you boys be on your way.'

Aaron collected his stuff. 'Okay, yeah. Thanks for that.'

Freddie grinned. 'Have a nice day.'

'And you, too. Have fun at the beach!'

They turned to leave, and she heard the bigger boy whisper, 'Stupid, demented cow,' in his brother's ear. She smiled. It was the least she expected.

As they disappeared behind the slope, she spotted Bertrand and Amy. They were by the ash tree and working feverishly on something in the dirt. It looked like a sort of painting or sculpture. She wiped her hands on her jeans and walked towards them.

She wore a big smile. She was feeling in a much better mood after getting everything off her chest. Yes, maybe she'd overreacted a little – she tended to do that when things got a bit much for her – but that was who she was. She'd never made any secret of it. It was her way of dealing with emotional claustrophobia. Once she got past it (and she almost always did) then she tended to relax. Today she'd promised herself a lazy, stress-free day. For twenty-four hours, at least. The weather was beautiful, it was peaceful, and she had her whole family by her side. Katharine had reminded her of that one luxury. She was lucky, *really* lucky.

She called out to Amy, who didn't appear to hear her. She called again.

'Morning, Amy! Bertrand!'

The pair were engrossed in their work. Bertrand was holding what looked like a long tool, maybe a chisel, and Amy was leaning over him, pulling on some kind of wire or string. The sculpture on the ground was an odd shape: a mixture of off-white and dark brown, with awkward-looking protrusions that jutted at strange angles.

Hattie was no more than twenty feet from them now, but their backs were to her, and she couldn't quite get a glimpse of their artistic endeavour. She entered the grey shadow of the sprawling tree and called out once more.

'Hi, guys, it's me, Hattie! Do you mind if I ask what you're up to? I'd love to take a look.'

Suddenly there was a shriek, like someone was in terrible

trouble, and then the strange object spasmed and jerked. Amy pulled on the tether as her head spun towards Hattie. Her eyes widened, and she shook her head, her eyes pleading for Hattie to leave. Her mouth was drawn downwards, her neck a thin shard of sinew and sweat. Bertrand grunted and drove his knee into the object's bulky mass. It was a goat, Hattie realised. Bertrand yelled and raised the chisel over his shoulder, except now Hattie could see that it wasn't a chisel at all. It was a machete; a large hunting machete with a razor-sharp edge. She ran to them.

'What the hell's going on here?'

'Blood of the beast, *feed us*! Nourish thy mighty vessel that we may all flourish in her solitude and protection!' Bertrand chanted the words, his eyes closed, and his head thrown back. She touched his arm, and he jolted.

'Bertrand?'

He glanced up at her for a split second, unseeing.

The goat screamed, its voice semi-human and childlike. Its muscles were taught and strained, its eyes bulging and bloodshot. Its swollen body jerked under the weight of Bertrand's foot. She could see it was pregnant. Amy yanked hard on the tether, and the animal's throat became immediately exposed.

Hattie gasped. 'Wait a minute—'

'Take this sacred beast, *oh Cernunnos*. This, our sacrifice to you, our *mighty saviour*!'

Bertrand let out a roar and the knife came down like a scythe, cutting through the animal's skin and tearing the ribbons of flesh around its throat. Amy fell backwards onto the grass as the blade severed the rope around the goat's neck. A jet of dark red erupted upwards and outwards, a splatter of crimson gloop and gore ejecting onto Hattie's chest and neck. Some of it landed in her mouth and its clotted ooze coated her tongue and teeth.

She screamed.

*

165

'Where are we going?'

'I want to show you something.'

'Is it the aeroplane again? Because that was pretty cool,' Jonno said. He was eager for a chance to see the Hurricane in the daylight. He'd showered in record time, even throwing on some of his dad's aftershave for extra measure. It felt hot on his neck.

'No, this is much cooler.'

'Well, I mean, I doubt it, but whatever. You do realise there's a World War Two aircraft, a historic artefact, just sitting there in the forest like it was nothing important. I only wish we had something like that back home. Me and my friends would be there every day, just hanging out and doing cool stuff. It would be so awesome, like an *Indiana Jones* movie or something. We'd turn it into a camp and stash stuff inside it, like things our parents don't let us have, and then—'

'Shh.' Evie held a finger to her lips 'You're being annoying.' She pointed. They were at the back of The Weary Traveller. A brick wall bordered the western tip of the property. Beyond that lay a small patch of lawn, a vegetable plot that had seen better days and a patio that spanned the width of the house. French doors opened to a room that was bathed in thick shadows.

'What am I supposed to be looking at? It's just a house.'

Evie approached the wall and vaulted effortlessly into the garden. She turned and beckoned him to follow.

'What? I—'

She hushed him once more, her hands pulling him towards her with invisible string. She removed her shoes and traversed the lawn. He thought she had the prettiest feet he had ever seen, small and delicate like porcelain. She reached into her pocket, removed a band and tied her hair back. With her neck exposed she appeared almost vulnerable, but she was tough, he was in no doubt about that. She rounded the patch of barren earth and crossed the patio in one smooth motion. Jonno, by comparison, tripped awkwardly on

166

uneven soil and staggered forwards. He almost landed face-first between two large plant pots.

'Where are we going?' he asked in little more than a whisper.

'In there.'

'But that's—' He attempted an objection, but before he could utter the words 'breaking-and-entering', she was inside. He looked back towards the relative safety of the trees and wondered whether he should just get up and leave. This wasn't his idea after all, and why should he risk getting himself caught intruding on someone else's property when he had absolutely no idea what they were doing there? He could only imagine how his dad would react when the police car pulled up at the cottage and he was there, sitting in the back, all handcuffed and red-faced. And Hattie? He couldn't even bring himself to imagine what Hattie would do.

'You coming, or what?' He felt Evie's pull on the sleeve of his T-shirt. 'We don't have long.'

'I don't know about this,' he said, but he was already stepping over the threshold.

It took a few moments for his eyes to adjust. They were in a wide, shallow lounge. It was gloomy inside, the heavy shades drawn across a large bay window. A brown leather sofa sat in front of an ebony bookcase. There was no TV.

'This way.'

'But, Evie, what about the owners? They could walk in at any minute.'

'Just come on, and be quiet, won't you?'

There was a low, repetitive thud coming from somewhere overhead. Jonno assumed it was a boiler or some old pipework making a racket, but that was odd because the place looked so modern.

Evie opened a door and stepped into a dark hallway. They turned left, the kitchen immediately to their right. Jonno could smell something meaty simmering in the oven. The dining room was next to the kitchen with an adjoining doorway. To their left

167

was a small study-cum-utility room, and the front porch lay straight ahead. The staircase to the first floor rose over and above the study. Evie pointed towards it, and Jonno felt his heart sink. They were going up there? He couldn't think of anything worse. He glanced to his right and spied a large silver-framed portrait of the owners. It was very recent. The mother, father and son were standing side by side in the garden and wore identical clothing: white T-shirts, beige shorts and open-toed sandals. The mother wore only one piece of jewellery, a silver necklace. Jonno took a closer look at the photograph. It was as though the kid's eyes were shifting and moving. He felt the hairs on the back of his neck start to flutter. The father's eyes were on him now too, his smile almost a cruel leer. Did the father's hand move? Jonno stepped away and bumped into the doorframe.

'Shh. Be careful.'

'I... I'm sorry.' He looked back at the photograph, but it was now no more than a picture. 'Where are we going?'

'Upstairs.'

'Are you sure about this?'

She nodded. 'You'll see.'

Evie rounded the corner and placed her bare foot on the first step. There was the hint of a groan, and she expertly shifted her balance to compensate. Within a moment, she was climbing the staircase with little more than the sound of skin pressing down on thick pile. Jonno followed, placing his own size eights in her size five indentations.

The repetitive thudding was louder now, and it appeared to be coming from somewhere up ahead.

On the first-floor hallway, Evie turned to him. Her face was a pale death mask in swirling shadows.

'Up there, on the left,' she said, smiling. It made Jonno anxious. Suddenly there was something forced about her; something untrue. 'You're gonna shit when you see this.'

There was a noise from behind him and he whirled around. A

hiss, a claw on skin, the hot sting of pain, the slick warmth of fresh blood.

'Ow!'

The cat dashed beneath his legs, and it disappeared into the doorway that stood ajar to his right. Evie suppressed a laugh.

'I think she likes you.'

Jonno dabbed at the wound on his shin. 'She has a funny way of showing it.'

'Don't be a wimp. Come on, let's go.'

Evie crept along the hallway, running her hand along the wall. The thudding was really loud now, resonating through the floor. The curtains were pulled across the window, meaning that everything was cloaked in an inky blackness. Jonno wondered why the owners kept the house so dark during the daytime. Evie stood outside the closed door. She suddenly turned, winked at him, and pushed.

The door swung inwards, and she was instantly bathed in an orange glow. It was as though the room was emitting some kind of radiation. She beckoned him, and Jonno stepped forward. He felt a deeply unsettling anxiety which lurked beneath his own fake smile, but he went to her regardless.

The room was small, with a window that had been carefully papered over. In each corner were incense burners, the scent of opium and jasmine wafting over him. Strange shapes were drawn on bare walls in black charcoal. There were numerous circles with what looked like petals inside them, and another, larger circle with an upside-down crescent hovering above it. A large statue of a creature with an open mouth and curved antlers, made from polished red stone, sat cross-legged against the rear wall. The floor was covered in a red and black hessian rug and, to Jonno's surprise, in the centre of the rug were the mother, father and son – each lying side by side, hands clasped together, eyes flitting and mouths moving soundlessly. Their palms slammed on the ground in a loud, synchronised rhythm.

169

Slam, slam, slam-slam-slam.

Jonno spun around. 'What the hell?'

'Be quiet, you'll wake them.'

'Wake them? Look at them? They're unconscious. I'm getting out of here.'

Slam, slam, slam-slam-slam.

'No, wait. This is the best bit.'

'Evie, this is too weird.'

She laughed. 'Just *stay here*. Please. You won't be disappointed, I promise.' She placed her hands on his cheeks, and he felt the warmth of her skin, the softness of her palms. She turned his face towards them. The three of them were shaking now, and the son started to convulse.

Slam, slam, slam-slam-slam.

'Is he having a heart attack?' Jonno asked.

'No, nothing as boring as that. Just look at him!'

Jonno's eyes widened in disbelief. He watched as the young man flailed around as if in the middle of a violent seizure, and then he slowly and gradually rose from the ground; little more than a few inches at first, but then rising higher and higher to around five feet in the air. It was as if he was being hoisted by an invisible hand.

Slam, slam, slam-slam-slam.

The floating boy spun around, his body now facing the floor. His arms and legs suddenly thrust out to the side, like a star.

'Whoa!'

'I know, right?' Evie said. 'Freaky, isn't it?'

'I don't even know what to think.' Jonno could feel the sweat on his neck, the terror leeching from every pore. How could the guy just be hanging in mid-air like that? 'This is some kind of trick, isn't it? It has to be.'

'It isn't.'

'Then how is this happening?'

Slam, slam, slam – slam!

The hands stopped moving, and the boy's mother and father sat up. Their eyes remained closed.

'Holy shit!' Jonno cried. He'd had enough. He tried to retreat but realised that Evie had disappeared, and the door behind him was now firmly shut. The floating boy's face turned to him, his eyes open. The orbs were black and fleshy, like liquorice. His parents rose to their feet as the boy spoke to him in a wet rasp, like heavy chains being dragged through shallow water.

'Welcome, oh special one. We've been expecting you.' His black eyes flitted from side to side. 'But tell us,' his face was close now, skin moving and sliding like a serpent, veins split and bleeding, liver spots like hard knots in timber, 'where is the child?'

*

Rachel jogged across the lane and edged along the perimeter of the cottage. She was still processing what she'd just witnessed: an exchange of a seriously large amount of cash between Bea's brother-in-law and his ex, Jonno's mother. Was Tara Deville really The Weasel? Could that be true? And if so, who was Quin? Was it Richard? Or Tara's husband, Terry; the same guy who had sent his goons to rough Richard up? It didn't seem real. It just didn't add up. Rachel had been tracking a seriously dangerous criminal – a premier league criminal – someone who sat at the top of an organisation that had once included the likes of Lyndsay Arthur. Could she really accept that at the apex of that pyramid of power were the Devilles, with the Penrose family in tow? A global, multi-billion-pound laundering operation, fuelled by drugs and violence, being run by middle class yuppies from the London suburbs?

So many thoughts were crashing around inside her head as she turned the corner, and she almost walked face first into Hattie.

'Whoa!' Rachel grabbed her by the shoulders. There was something wrong. 'Are you okay?'

'A goat.'

'A what?'

'They killed a goat.' Hattie's T-shirt was caked in something red and sticky. She had it on her lips and chin too.

'What have you got down yourself? Ketchup? Some sort of sauce? Is everything all right?'

'They just cut its throat, over there on No Man's Land, just a few moments ago.' Her skin was grey. 'It was terrified, the poor thing, pregnant too. It just screamed and screamed for its life.'

'Okay,' Rachel said. 'Okay, that's maybe what they do here – kill the livestock out in the open for everyone to see. It's odd, but you know, maybe it's not odd to them.' She thought it was strange, but then so was everything else about this trip.

Hattie looked down at herself. 'Oh, I've got blood on me.'

'Yeah, I can see that.'

'It must be from the goat.' She was now the colour of dried seaweed.

'Mm. I guess so.'

Hattie doubled over and threw up all over Rachel's boots.

'Ugh! Nice.' Rachel shook her head and let it happen. It was too late to move now, the damage had been done. She was going to have to hose herself down later, but what the hell. 'Let it out. Go on, get it all out. It's only natural. You've had a bit of a shock.' Suddenly the acid tang of last night's red wine rose in Rachel's throat, and it swilled around in her mouth. She sucked in oxygen, but it only served to fan the flames. The stench of freshly served vomit on her feet was doing nothing for her hangover.

'What's going on out here? Hattie?' Shit, it was Bea. 'Rachel, I thought you were still in bed.'

'I was, but your sister's not well.'

Bea grabbed Hattie. 'You okay, sis? Are you feeling the effects of last night's alcohol too?'

Hattie glanced up at her, half smiled and then placed a hand on her stomach and threw up once more. Bea jumped backwards.

'Jeez. What's going on?'

'A goat,' Rachel offered. 'She saw a couple of the locals

172

slaughtering one of their animals.'

'Ew! Gross.'

'Yeah. I think she got a bit too close to the action.' They both laughed.

'It's not funny, you two,' Hattie said. She was still doubled over. 'It went… *urgh*… in my… *urgh*… mouth.'

Rachel and Bea had the giggles now.

'It's probably good luck, you know?' Bea said.

'What, goat's blood in your mouth?' Rachel replied.

'Yeah, could be a thing.'

'You're sick, the pair of you,' Hattie groaned.

'No, sister dear. I think you'll find the sick's all over Rachel's shoes.'

'Hey, ladies!' It was Richard. 'Have you seen Jonno? *Whoa*, what's wrong with Hattie?'

'I'm fine.' Hattie pulled herself upright. 'It was just a little overwhelming, that's all.'

'What?' Richard asked. 'Have I missed something?'

'I'll tell you later,' Hattie replied, staggering towards the house. 'I'm just going to get a glass of water.'

Richard turned to Bea. 'What was all that about?'

'Oh, nothing, don't worry about it. She's fine. Anyway, where have you been?'

'Just for a walk along the clifftop.'

'What was it like? I bet it was pretty out there,' Bea said as Rachel eyed Richard.

'Yeah, yeah. Very nice.'

'Did you see anyone else?' Rachel asked.

'What, like other people? No, it was deserted.'

Rachel had to give it to him – he was a good liar. 'What's in the bag?' she probed.

'What, the rucksack? Nothing. I just took it in case I came across any rare rocks or pebbles.'

'And did you?' Rachel asked.

'What?'

'Come across any rare rocks or pebbles?'

Bea patted her arm. 'What is this, Rach? An inquisition?'

'I'm just taking an interest, that's all.'

'No,' Richard answered. 'They were pretty standard, actually. You know? Just flint and granite. Pretty dull. Anyway, have either of you two seen my son?'

They both shook their heads. Rachel thought he was probably out with that girl, the one with the dark hair and sneaky eyes.

'No, why?' Bea asked.

'Well, I was chatting to the owner earlier, Noah, and he generously invited us both out for a swim with him and his boys. I thought it would be fun.'

'I guess,' Bea said. 'Isn't he—'

'Isn't he what?'

'A little weird?'

'No,' Richard waved a hand dismissively. 'He's fine. Looks a little odd, but he actually seems like a thoroughly decent chap.'

'If you say so.'

'Bea,' Richard said, 'you've got to learn to be less judgemental. Not everyone's a bad person, you know.'

Rachel suppressed a sarcastic laugh.

'Daddy!' It was Sally. She was in a pink flowery dress and standing at the garden gate.

'Yes, my princess?' Richard went to her.

'Come and see.'

'Come and see what, my angel?'

'The children.'

He glanced at the two women, frowning. 'What children?'

Sally laughed and pointed towards the rear of the house. 'The little children in the woods. They're funny.'

*

174

'Where's JTB? Where's Jon?' Eli asked as Evie came into the barn. She reclined on a bale of hay and shrugged nonchalantly.

'How am I supposed to know?'

'I saw you with him.'

'Did you?'

'Yeah,' he slid down the ladder. 'At the Traveller. I saw you go inside.'

She turned away. 'So?'

'So,' he pointed with his good hand, 'where is he?'

Evie picked at a long length of hay and pulled out the seeds one by one. 'What happened to your nose?'

Eli raised a hand to his face. It was tender, swollen. He still had the taste of blood in his sinuses and throat. 'Noah.'

'Figures,' she said. 'He's an arsehole.'

'No he isn't!' he hollered. He loved his brother, despite everything. 'He takes care of me. Him and Sweet Mother. They love me!'

'If you say so,' Evie said, almost disinterested. 'But they don't hurt me the way that Noah hurts you, do they?'

Eli thought about that. He didn't know everything that went on in the big house, of course, but he'd never seen Evie bruised, had never seen her with marks on her face or on her arms, never with blood on her mouth or dried beneath her nose. 'I don't know,' he said, but he did really.

'Maybe they don't love you at all, Eli. Maybe they just pretend.'

'No!' he yelled again. 'They wouldn't!' He knew they wouldn't. He knew his sweet mother loved him, just like he knew his brother had saved him from their foster parents, the people that had really hurt him – for real.

'Whatever you say. I just know what I see.' She jumped up and took a step towards him. She raised a finger to the bridge of his nose and ran the tip along his shattered cartilage. 'And what I see is another human being who has been punished and beaten by the very person who should be taking him into his arms and telling him that everything is going to be okay.' She nodded slowly. 'That everything will be just fine.'

Eli felt his heartbeat slow to a dull thud, felt the blood flow become merely a trickle through his veins. She was soothing to him, like one of the strange poisons the Kid-Bastard boys sometimes smoked. He felt like a real person around her, a normal person with a normal life and a normal body. If only it were true, if only she could make it true. It had been all he'd ever wanted, to be just like everyone else. Maybe her gifts could help him. Maybe she could make him whole.

But then he saw it: the cruelty in her. It was just a moment; a slight glint in her eyes, sharp barbs shifting at the corners of her mouth.

'I know what you're trying to do, and it won't work,' he said, pushing her away. 'You've given him to them, and you know they'll do fings. Horrible fings. The fam'lee won't let that happen. They'll go looking for him.'

Evie turned away. 'Maybe, maybe not.'

'You know they will!'

'Then let them,' she tossed her hair and ran a finger along her lips. Eli could see the thrill in her eyes. She was excited by the prospect.

'I'll tell them!' he growled in defiance.

She was on him in a flash, her fingers at his throat, and the musty stench of death on her skin. 'You'll do no such thing, cripple. Because if you do,' she pushed a sharp fingernail into him, tearing a chunk of slippery skin from his neck, 'you know exactly what will happen.'

*

'There's no one there, Sal'. Are you really sure you saw someone?'

Sally laughed. 'You're silly.'

'Do you see anything?' Hattie asked, turning to her husband.

176

Richard shrugged. He was in the trees to the north of the garden. 'No. There's no sign of anybody out here.'

'And who did you say you saw, sweetheart?' Hattie sat on the ground next to her daughter.

'I told you already.'

'Well, tell me again.'

Sally pulled at her teddy bear's ear. 'Little children, all playing together. They were singing to me.'

'Singing?'

Sally nodded.

'Singing what?'

'I don't know. A funny song. Like a nursery rhyme.'

Hattie shook her head. A nursery rhyme like the one she'd heard in the woods, maybe. 'I don't like it.'

Richard walked over to her. 'She's probably just imagining it.' He grabbed her hand. 'You know, you really ought to get changed out of that T-shirt.'

He was right. She still had goat's blood and her own vomit all over her.

'Well, if we're done here,' he continued, 'I'm going to grab my swimming trunks and a towel. If you see Jonno, tell him to come down and meet us at the beach.'

'Are you sure about this, Richard? We hardly know these people.'

He pinched her chin tenderly. She hated it when he did that. 'Well,' he said, 'maybe it's time we got ourselves better acquainted.'

*

The beach was deserted, aside from the four of them. The two boys were already out on their boards. Noah stood by the waterfront, slipping off his sandals. He wore red speedos and goggles. His long, straggly hair hung down towards the small of his back.

'They're prescription,' he said, pointing to his goggles. 'I can't see a thing without them.'

'Really?' Richard said. 'I didn't know they were a thing.'

'It's the age of the Internet, Richard. Everything is a thing.'

'Where are we headed?'

'Out there,' Noah said, pointing towards the edge of the cove. The cliff to their right continued westward at a shallow slant and then curved back out towards the ocean, eventually taking a sharp right-angle and heading away from them and out of view. At its farthest point, where the tide was at its most fierce and the rock face turned into fingers of sharp obsidian-like daggers, there was a deep black crevice. 'It's a cave. It goes quite a long way back into the cliff. We have a little set up in there: torches, a picnic table, even a barbecue. It's our man-camp.'

'That's pretty cool,' Richard said, but he was still staring at the raging water crashing into the seemingly impenetrable cliff face. 'Is it safe?'

'Oh, quite safe,' Noah said as he stepped into the shallow tide, a waterproof bag tied to his waist on a long tether. 'We've only had a couple of near misses. Mostly our own fault of course. The boys, they can be quite daring. It's their age, you see. Oh, to be young again.'

'Mm,' Richard mumbled, thinking of a way he could politely back out and still save face. 'I… I can't be too long, you know. I promised Hattie.'

'We won't be.'

'And it looks quite rough out there. The water, I mean.'

Noah raised an eyebrow. 'I thought you said you were a strong swimmer?'

'Yes, I am, it's just…' He shook his head. 'Oh, what the hell. Let's do it.'

The paddle out was easy enough. Aaron and Freddie tore off ahead, while Richard followed in Noah's wake. Noah really was a good swimmer, his head dipping under the water, his arms coming over in shallow arcs before his face appeared once more, turning to the side, while his mouth effortlessly sucked in fresh oxygen. Richard was usually more of a breaststroke kind of guy, but he decided to attempt the crawl. He could feel the muscles in his back and arms groan and creak, but he was determined to keep up. He thought of the meeting that morning with Tara. She had looked good, like, *really* good. Life had obviously treated her well. He wondered whether she would have been in such good shape if she'd stayed with him all those years ago. He doubted it. I mean, you just had to look at his situation, out there handing over a bagful of cash that he'd had to scrape and borrow on the promise of a pay-off that he was banking on coming good. It had to, otherwise everything they owned, everything he and Hattie had worked together to build, would just get washed away like chalk paintings on the pavement. Or, perhaps more appropriately, like an overweight, middle-aged guy who was attempting, for some bizarre reason, to convince a bunch of strangers that he was able to swim half a kilometre in choppy water.

A wave crashed into him, and he swallowed a salty mouthful. He coughed and spluttered as most of it made its way into his lungs.

'You okay back there?' Noah turned.

'Yep. Wave just caught me off guard,' Richard spluttered, letting out a loud belch.

'They'll do that from time to time.'

'Are you coming, Noah?' It was Aaron. He was standing up on his board and balancing on one leg. 'I'm absolutely starving.'

Freddie leaned over and slapped at his brother's foot. Aaron flew backwards into the waves. 'Ha-ha! Did you see that?'

'Don't kill yourselves, boys.' Noah rolled his eyes. 'Your mother would never forgive me.'

As they pressed on, the waves began to increase in size and velocity, while the tide fought against them. Richard had to swim doubly hard. He could feel the pressure on his lungs and in his chest, and his calves and triceps were beginning to ache and throb.

Noah, by contrast, seemed to be slicing expertly through the water like a racing catamaran. Richard thought it would be just his luck to end up drowning out there, while Tara gave that crook, Terry Deville, all his money. The tragedy of it; the pathos.

Something brushed his leg and he jerked. 'What was that?'

'What was what?'

'Something touched my leg.'

'A rock, maybe. Or a jellyfish.'

He could hear the boys laughing up ahead. 'Or a sea monster!'

'Don't mock our guest, boys. He's just a little anxious.'

'I'm fine.' Richard was peering into the water beneath him. It was deep and dark, but he was sure there had been something there; something fleshy, something real. He strained his eyes but all he could see was his own pathetic reflection.

He looked up. They were quite close now, which was a relief. The cave was large and deathly black, but he could just make out the faint glimpse of a sandy shoreline that sloped down from the cavern's mouth like a yellow tongue.

'Come on, Richard. We've got lunch to cook.'

The final stretch was heavy going, and at one point, Richard had to stifle a yelp as his shin crashed painfully into a jagged rock. He was still fighting the waves as the boys made it to shore and climbed into the cave. They ascended the cliff face, bashing their chests and yelping like native warriors. Noah was next, gliding between two thick slabs of dark granite and rising to a standing position in one smooth motion. Richard, by contrast, barrelled onto the sand like a wounded walrus. He lay on the shore as the waves lapped over him, and he dragged in a great lungful of oxygen. He was exhausted.

'Well done, old boy. It's harder than it looks, isn't it?'

'I'm okay.' Richard said. 'I'm just a little out of practise.'

'Out of shape, more like,' Aaron said, running past them. 'You need to lay off the ice cream, mate.' The brothers giggled as they kicked sand at each other.

'Don't be rude, boys.'

'No, it's fine.' Richard said, leaning back on his elbows. 'They're right. I don't exercise enough.'

'Chuck us the matches, Noah!' Aaron yelled. 'We'll get the fire going.'

Noah untied the sealed flotation bag from his waist, reached inside and tossed them the box. 'Check to make sure the wood's dry. Stack it up like I showed you.'

'Oh, give us a break. We're not kids,' Aaron hissed.

'Yeah, Noah. It's not like we haven't done this like a million times before,' Freddie said as the two of them disappeared inside.

Noah shook his head. 'Does your boy give you this much trouble?'

Richard stood. 'Sometimes. I try to give him as much space as I can.'

'I wish we could do the same.' Noah took off his goggles and replaced them with his glasses. 'Where is he, anyway? Your son, I mean.'

'Do you know,' Richard said, 'I have absolutely no idea.'

*

'Where were you this morning?' Bea asked.

Rachel glanced up from her book. 'I was in bed.'

'No,' Bea glared at her, 'you weren't. I checked in on you.'

Shit, Rachel thought. *Busted*. She tried to think fast. 'I tossed and turned in bed for a while, but my head just hurt too much. I thought I'd go for a stroll, walk it off.'

'Where did you go?'

'Oh, you know, here and there.'

'Here and there? What's that supposed to mean?'

'What I said: here... and... there.'

'Like, where exactly?'

'Look, Bea!' Rachel feigned annoyance. 'Do I have to tell you

181

what I'm doing every second of every day? Have we got to that stage of our relationship already? The untrusting stage.'

'No, I—'

'Do you want to put a tag on me, maybe put one of those apps on my phone so that you can track my every movement?'

'No, I didn't say that. It's just—'

Rachel persisted. It wasn't fair on Bea, but it was the only way. 'I told you I went out for a walk to clear my head. You either believe that or you don't, it's up to you! I really don't give a shit either way!'

She stood up and stormed outside. Yes, the walkout was dramatic, but it was necessary. She could feel her pulse racing. She gripped the edge of the picket fence that bordered the boundary between Spriggan's Retreat and Excelsior Lodge, and tried to slow her breathing. That was way too close for comfort. She would message Eric later on. She'd get him to put the feelers out on Tara and Terry Deville and see where the breadcrumbs led. This balancing act was becoming treacherous.

She lifted her head to the sky and let the cool breeze waft through her hair and onto her face and neck. It felt good. She opened her eyes and spied the old lady in the wheelchair. She hadn't seen her before. She was seated in the sunny spot at the rear of Excelsior. She realised it was Glanna's mother, Dolly, and she was looking straight at her.

'Who are you?' Dolly asked. Her hair was white and balding at the sides. Her face was a mask of loose weathered skin and liver spots.

'Hi, I'm... I'm Rachel.'

'No, you're not.'

'Yes,' Rachel gave her a friendly smile. 'That's my name.' She laughed. 'Don't wear it out.'

'No, it's not.'

'Erm. Yeah, really, it is.'

Dolly appeared to become agitated. 'I said, it's *not*!'

182

Rachel leaned over the fence. 'Look, I don't know what—'

'You're a schemer, a deceiver.' She pointed a long, trembling finger. 'You're a gypsy's riddle.'

Rachel was taken aback. 'I'm… I'm what?'

Dolly closed her eyes, her head slumped forward. Within an instant she was snoring.

Rachel paused. What was all that about? What did the old girl think she knew? She had to talk to her some more. She went to climb over the fence when she heard another voice.

'Was my mother bothering you?' It was Glanna. She was standing at the old lady's side and dressed in a long, purple tie-dye dress with thin straps at the shoulders. 'She can be quite the character, I'm afraid. It's her age you see. And the dementia. Yes, I'm sad to say that terrible disease has really got hold of her.'

Rachel felt her muscles relax. 'Oh no, really. It's fine. We were just getting acquainted.'

'Well, as nice as it is, she won't remember what either of you said when she comes to.' Glanna closed the space between them. 'But I'm guessing that suits you, doesn't it?'

'What do you mean by that?'

'Some secrets are hard to keep, my dear. So, *so hard*. Especially keeping them from your friends and your family.' She glanced at the house. 'And especially your lovers. These little lies that you tell can suck at the very essence of your soul, can't they? They can make you agitated, sick. They can keep you awake at night and make you fret tirelessly during the day. I'm sure you have to watch your every step, carefully consider your every move. Deception really can be quite exhausting.'

'I don't—'

'I feel for you. I know what it's like – the pain that visits you; the loneliness you feel; the fear, even when you think that you're enjoying yourself, when you're laughing, even when you're crying. It's always there, isn't it? Never far away.'

Rachel nodded. 'It's hard.'

'You sense it, don't you? The futility of it? Eventually, everything you are will spill out from you like water from a burst dam. It's impossible to hold back for ever. And when that moment comes, when the vast volume of secrets and untruths emerge into the daylight for all to see, do you know what you will feel?'

'Relief?' Rachel offered in hope.

'No. That would be nice, wouldn't it? It really would. But I'm afraid not.' Glanna shook her head. 'You'll feel nothing, because that's all you'll have left.'

Rachel knew she was right. She closed her eyes. She could feel it. Everything she'd once been, the Beth Mckinley version of herself, was now diluted, tasteless. She wondered how long it would be before Beth just evaporated for good, and Rachel was all that remained. What would she do then? Continue the lie? Become somebody else? Vanish like a ghost? What would be the point? Was she beyond salvation? Was there really no way she could go back?

When she opened her eyes, Glanna and her mother were no longer there. She wondered if they'd ever been.

When she turned back towards the cottage, she found Bea standing right there behind her. She came to Rachel and held her tightly. Bea whispered in her ear as the tears came.

'I'm sorry.'

*

'We gave you quite the fright, I'm sure.' Bertrand said. He was standing at the doorway with Amy just behind him. Her eyes were fixed to the ground. Bertrand held a package, wrapped in brown paper.

'No, really,' Hattie said. 'It was my fault. I should have checked before I came rushing over. It gave me a start, that's all.'

'Let us pay for the cleaning bill, at least. Blood can really ruin good clothing if it's not treated properly.'

184

Hattie shook her head. 'Honestly, it's fine. I gave the stain a hand wash and then put the shirt in the machine. I'm sure it will come right out.'

'Well, if I can't convince you,' Bertrand conceded. 'Look, I know it might seem a little forward, but the meat is quite delicious, and we have plenty.' He glanced at the package in his hands. 'Will you take this? For your family?'

'Well, that depends on what it is,' but she knew. She knew exactly what was in that neatly wrapped parcel. Had Amy wrapped it? Was that why her eyes were transfixed on the gravel beneath her feet? Bertrand handed it to her.

'Take a look inside. I'm sure you'll be pleased. We gave you a really lean cut.'

As she pulled paper away from the sticky flesh, she felt her stomach flip once more. She could still taste the blood on her tongue. She breathed in through her nose and out through her mouth. *Keep it together*, she thought. *It's just a roasting joint, that's all, no different to what you would buy in the supermarket.* Except, of course, this particular animal had been alive and kicking just a few short hours ago. The goat loin sat in her hands. It felt heavy, like a severed limb. She knew as soon as the pair of them departed she'd be throwing it straight in the bin. She couldn't even bring herself to look at it.

'Thank you so much. That's,' she raised the back of her hand to her mouth, 'really kind of you.'

'No bother at all. Now, when your husband returns, please come over and let us give you the guided tour of the house. It really is quite a fascinating place, even if I do say so myself.'

Hattie couldn't think of anything worse, but she nodded. 'That would be wonderful. As soon as he returns.'

'That's a deal then. Very good. Well, we'll be on our way. Come on, Amelia,' he said, grabbing his wife's hand. 'That goat won't cook itself.' Bertrand turned just as Amy looked up. Her eyes were furtive, anxious. She glanced at Hattie and gave just a little shake of her head, as if to say, "Don't, please don't. For your own safety, don't come anywhere near the house", but before Hattie could respond, she turned and hastily departed.

Beyond them, a mud-spattered Land Rover sped in from the north. It rounded the circular common in a dangerously wide arc and pulled directly into the driveway at The Night Watchman. Hattie stepped out into the open to get a better look. She watched as Paz leapt from the driver's seat, his hair unruly, his shirt crumpled and hanging loose. He looked dishevelled, agitated. Hattie thought about going to him but decided against it. It didn't look like he was in the mood for visitors. Whatever it was, she had no business getting involved. If the incident with the goat had taught her anything, it was to stay out of local affairs.

There was something in the woods at the edge of her vision – hands, tiny hands, eyes glaring at her. She blinked and they were gone. Her own eyes narrowed for a moment but then she laughed at herself. It was getting to her now, the whole bloody place. She looked down at the slab of dead animal in her hands. *Do you know what?* she thought. *We're going to eat this thing, and we're going to like it. It's just a piece of meat like any other*. She chuckled as she headed back inside, the day suddenly seeming like it was less of a weight on her shoulders. She closed the door.

Above the awning, just out of sight and carved into the brickwork between the doorway and Jonno's bedroom window, was a rudimentary circle; a circle with six equally spaced petals protruding from its centre.

*

'Did you bring your camera?' Noah asked.

Shit, Richard thought. He'd completely forgotten. He'd been distracted by that business with Sally-Ann. 'Sorry, no. It slipped my mind.'

'Never mind. It's your loss,' Noah said. 'I mean, just look at

186

this place.'

Richard peered up at the glistening, blue-green mouth of the cave. 'Yeah, it really is quite something. How did you find it?' Richard asked.

'We didn't. It's been handed down through the generations. Glanna would come out here with her mother and three brothers, as would her grandmother and aunts and uncles, and her great-grandmother and great-aunts and uncles too. The Cormorans kind of stuck their family flag in this cave, hundreds – possibly thousands – of years ago, and it's been their secret garden ever since.'

'Pretty cool,' Richard said as he bit into his hotdog. It was doused in homemade hot sauce and was really quite delicious.

'It has its legends of course, this place, you know. About how the cave was originally formed.'

'Isn't that obvious?' Richard asked. 'It's science. A simple matter of coastal erosion.'

'Maybe,' Noah offered. 'That is one possibility.'

'And the other?'

Noah dabbed at his mouth with a napkin. 'That very much depends on your personal leanings, Richard. Do you believe in the mythical? The magical?'

Richard shook his head. 'You're kidding, right?'

'Okay, your answer tells me all that I need to know about you.'

'What's that supposed to mean?'

'That you're closed off to alternative ideas.'

Richard fought the urge to be offended. 'No, I think I'm pretty open-minded.'

'Well, let's see. Do you believe in sea dragons?'

'You mean, like dinosaurs?'

'Well, sort of. The word dinosaur is just Greek for terrible lizard. Do you believe in terrible lizards?'

Richard wondered where all this was going. 'I suppose we have komodo dragons. They're poisonous, aren't they? So I guess they

187

could be pretty terrible, as well as crocodiles and alligators of course. You wouldn't want to get bitten by one of those.' He laughed. Noah didn't.

'I'm talking about something larger than that, Richard. Much larger.'

'Like, how big?'

Noah looked around them. 'As big as this cave.'

'No way. That's impossible.'

'No, not impossible. Just improbable.' Noah swallowed the last of his hotdog. 'How does the saying go? If the universe is truly infinite—'

'Then anything is infinitely possible,' Richard said, completing the sentence. 'But that's just a speculation, a theory.'

'A theory based on science, Richard. Which means that science and theology are not as far removed as some people would have you believe.'

'I don't know. A giant sea dragon seems pretty far removed from modern science to me.'

'Well,' Noah stood. 'Believe what you will, I'm not here to convince you. I am, however, truly convinced that I need to take a piss.'

Noah disappeared into the gloom as Richard stood. The place really was something. What little light penetrated the oblique darkness glistened off wet dripping limestone. It emitted a green and bluish glow that shone from every surface. The cave ceiling was high and wide like a concert hall, and it stretched back into the cliffs farther than the light could reach. Richard decided to have a look around. The barbecue continued to sizzle and spit behind him as he walked into the depths of the natural chamber. The sand between his toes was dry back there and the echoes emanating from the stone walls and ceiling became resonant and enduring. Richard waited for his eyes to adjust, but there really was no light to adjust to. It was just darkness. Pure and utter darkness.

He heard the sound of shuffling feet in the sand, followed by the sound of scurrying on stone.

'Noah? Aaron?' His voice sounded eerily strange. 'Freddie, is that you?'

He cursed himself. He was being ridiculous. Something ran over his toes and his breath caught in his throat.

'What is that?'

He held his arms out in search of a rock face. There was nothing. He lurched forward but again found only cool, damp air. He was in a wide open space. He felt exposed, vulnerable.

'Noah? Are you there?

There was a chattering noise, fast and urgent, like teeth chomping. Richard swung a leg and instantly felt foolish. He turned but couldn't decide from which way he'd come. The cave mouth was no longer visible. How far had he walked? It seemed like only ten or twenty metres. Had he gone further than he thought, forty metres, fifty maybe?

Something clawed at his face. He held a hand to his cheek and touched something warm and wet. 'What the hell was that?' He started to panic. He flailed his arms around, trying to fend off the attack. His right hand struck something soft, and whatever it was must have flung backwards into hard rock because he heard the sound of bone crunching followed by an awful, high-pitched wail. That buoyed him.

'Come on, you fuckers, whatever you are. I'm ready.'

Suddenly there were tens of tiny teeth sinking into his calf, and he kicked out. The thing gripped on, incisors and claws now digging deeper and deeper. The pain was agonising, and Richard dropped to his knees. It was a mistake. Suddenly, one of them was on his back and clawing at his neck and shoulders. A third creature grabbed his arm and started gnawing at his fingers. Richard clapped his hands together, and the thing let go, but not before it severed his ring finger at the knuckle. He screamed out. He crawled around on the floor, blindly searching for his wedding ring. He couldn't lose it. Hattie would kill him. Two more creatures landed on him and

189

gouged at his scalp and forehead. Another bit into his side. He rolled onto his back and was instantly smothered. A mass of unseen creatures were now covering his face, pushing him down into the soft sand, tearing chunks of flesh away, gorging on blood and tissue, scooping out brain matter, severing bone from cartilage. He was going to die in this cave, alone and in the dark and surrounded by beings he couldn't even begin to comprehend. He hoped that they would find enough of him to bury. His kids deserved that, at least.

'What the hell is he doing?' someone asked, followed by the sound of cruel laughter.

'I think he's asleep.'

'He looks like a mental person.'

'Perhaps it was the physical effort of the swim.'

'Pussy.'

'Aaron, don't be mean. Help him up, will you?'

Suddenly there was a hand on his shoulder. 'Get away!' he heard himself shout. 'Get away from me or they'll get you too! *Noah*, get the boys out of here!'

More laughter. 'The guy's having a breakdown.'

'Richard, Richard.' A soothing voice. 'It's me. It's Noah.'

There was a clicking sound in his right ear, then his left. Richard opened his eyes, but sunlight blinded him. As his vision began to come back into focus, he started to make out the outline of magnified eyeballs, the wisp of a beard, and fingers snapping in front of his face.

'The creatures. Those things. Have they gone?'

'I'm afraid you must have passed out, my friend. Maybe that swim was just a little too far for you, after all.'

'What? But I'm wounded – badly. Look!' Richard tried to sit, but fireworks went off in his head, followed by orange and red sunbursts. It felt like someone was pushing needles into his eyeballs. He lay back down again.

Noah patted him. 'Nope, I think you're all in one piece, luckily for you.'

'Yeah, who'd want to eat you anyway?' It was Aaron again. Richard felt like getting up and punching the kid on the nose, but he knew it would only make matters worse.

'Don't worry.' He felt the air move as Noah sat down beside him. 'I always bring a phone for any such eventuality. I've called Pascoe, and he's agreed to bring the boat.'

'But no, wait!' The realisation dawned on Richard, and he let out a long breath. He didn't know what was worse: being eaten alive in a cave by strange creatures, or passing out from what was really only a middling swim. He was veering towards the latter.

'Richard, my friend, this little field trip is over.'

*

'And you what?'

'I passed out.'

'What, like totally out?' Bea asked.

'Yep, 'fraid so.'

'From the swim?'

'That's what Noah thinks.'

'But you're a good swimmer, love,' Hattie said, handing them all their dinner. It was pan-fried goat loin chops with mustard mash, peas and onion gravy. Rachel thought it looked and smelled delicious.

'Thanks, Hats. Well, that's what I thought too but, you know, maybe I'm not.'

'Good job you passed out after you'd made it to dry land,' Rachel said.

'Rach!'

'Well, you know, it would have been much worse if you'd fainted in the water. That's all I'm saying.'

'Yes,' Bea said. 'I think we know what you're saying.'

'It's okay, Bea. She's right. I think I'll stick to shallow water

191

from now on.'

'That's probably for the best,' Hattie said, smiling.

The front door opened and Jonno walked in.

'Hey, son,' Richard said. 'You wanna hear what happened to your old man today?'

'No,' Jonno said. 'I'm tired. I'm going to bed.'

'But Hattie's made us all dinner.'

'Not hungry,' he mumbled as he trudged up the stairs.

Rachel turned to Bea. 'Girl trouble?'

Bea laughed. 'If it is, he's in for a rough ride. That one looks like she could eat him for dinner.'

Richard spluttered. 'Bad joke, Bea. Bad joke!'

A newsflash appeared on the little TV screen, and the four of them turned towards it. There had been a car accident not far from the cottage. It was on a country lane leading from Pentewan to St Austell, maybe a fifteen-minute drive away. The whole scene was a smouldering disaster zone, the car ripped into scorched shards of torn and twisted metal.

'The poor driver. They didn't stand a chance,' Hattie said, but Rachel was transfixed. She could see that Richard was too. That colour – there couldn't be two vehicles in the area with that same garish hue. She placed her cutlery down on her plate, her appetite instantly spoiled. She could feel her stomach flipping. The picture zoomed in, and before the camera cut away, she saw the car's numberplate. It was as clear as day. She fought the urge to swear out loud, to throw something. She glanced at Richard, whose face had become ashen, the lines in his skin suddenly very visible. His mouth was hanging open, his eyes glistening. *If he had passed out before*, she thought, *this could finish him off*.

It couldn't be a coincidence, could it? It just couldn't be. That one car, in this one little corner of the country, in that one, absolute carnage of a wreck. What were the chances?

The numberplate was emblazoned on Rachel's retinas as permanently as the image of the fatal bullet that had struck Tommy. It was the tangerine mobile all right.

TDEVIL666

Alison wasn't impressed. 'It smells like mould,' she groaned. 'And old people.'

'Oh, it's not so bad.' Michael reached across her and shook the wooden handrail at the foot of the stairs. 'It's sturdy enough.'

'What the hell are these drawings?'

'Who knows? Who cares?'

'They're ugly.'

'Well, they're not as pretty as you, that's true, but then who is?'

Alison curled a lip and huffed. 'It's hardly the Seychelles.'

'It was never supposed to be. Come on, it'll be fun. Let's go and check out the beach.'

The little cove was quaint and secluded, and they spent the afternoon swimming in the cool waters. Later on, they made love al-fresco behind a sand dune, only to be disturbed by Michael's old school pal, Noah, and his pretty partner, Glanna. Michael spotted them first and leapt to his feet, clumsily pulling up his shorts and grinning. Alison, on the other hand, was left stranded in the sand in nothing more than the skin her mother gave her. Glanna spared her blushes by sliding in front of her and lifting her cream kaftan around them like a windbreak.

'There you go, my dear. We really don't want these men gawping at you, do we?'

'I'm sorry, we didn't think there was anyone around.'

'Oh, don't worry, it's not a problem at all. It's not like Noah and I haven't done it from time to time.'

I can see that, Alison thought as she eyed Glanna's baby bump.

From that moment on, the two of them grew close. Well, as

close as anyone could get in the few days they spent together. Alison found Glanna's personality inspiring, and a little addictive, too. Her lifestyle was so far removed from the hustle and bustle of their world back home. No rush-hour traffic, no early morning alarms, no difficult boss or bitching co-workers.

'I love it here.'

'It has its moments, I can assure you.'

'No, I get that. It's just...' They were sitting in the garden of Excelsior. Alison had already drunk over half a bottle of pinot. It was early evening, and the sun was starting to dip beneath the horizon. 'Well, it's just so relaxing. So liberating. I feel like I could do anything here, be anyone.'

'Everyone can be anyone or anything, my sweet. It just takes an openness to *be*, to simply exist in your own space in the form that you most prefer. Take Noah and I. Do I love him? Maybe. Does he love me? I think the jury's out on that one too. Do you know what keeps us together?'

Alison shook her head.

'Absolutely nothing,' Glanna replied, answering her own question. 'We're free to do as we please, with whomever we please and however we choose. We own our own space.'

'So, why do you live together in this house?'

'Well, it's my house. My family home, actually. I grew up here, as did my mother and her siblings, her mother and siblings too.'

'And Noah?'

'I allow him to stay, and he chooses to remain.'

Alison took another sip of her wine. It was cold and sweet and was going down way too easily. 'And what if he changes his mind?'

'That's his choice to make.'

'And would you care?'

'You mean, would I miss him? Perhaps. Would I get over it? Oh, of that there's no doubt. Just as I got over all the others.'

Alison was intrigued. 'All the others?'

'I'm not going to pretend, Alison. There have been lots of men.

Women too, from time to time.'

Alison blushed.

'I can assure you,' Glanna continued, 'I'm no slut or whore or whatever it is the villagers call me. I choose to be with whomever I choose to be with, and I give the companions in my life that same freedom of choice. My mother felt the same way, as did her mother and grandmother.'

'So, you don't have a relationship with your father?'

'I chose not to.'

Alison nodded.

'I've always wanted children,' she heard herself say. 'A little girl.'

'Oh, and why's that?' Glanna asked.

'I don't know. I've just always had this vision, this dream, of me holding my daughter in my arms, kissing her little cheeks, tucking strands of red curls behind her ears,' she sighed. 'I've always wanted that.'

'Then what's stopping you?'

'I don't know,' Alison said. 'Myself, I guess. I've never felt selfless enough to be able to care for someone so unconditionally. Maybe it'll never happen, I don't know.' She finished the last of her wine. 'Well, it's late. I guess I should go and see what Michael's up to.'

'Oh, I'm sure he and Noah are catching up on old times.'

'I'm sure.' Alison went to stand, only to find that her legs wouldn't comply. 'Woah.' She slumped back in her chair. 'Maybe I should have eaten more. This wine has gone straight to my head,' she giggled, 'and my legs too apparently.'

'Quite.' Glanna placed her glass of water on the table and stood. 'Why don't you make another choice?'

Alison peered at her through hazy eyes. Glanna looked radiant with the last of the sun at her back and her hair flowing over her shoulders like dark chocolate. 'Another choice?'

'Stay here. Be at one with yourself, with the air that you breathe,

196

the flowers in this garden, and the stars in the night sky.'

'Own my own space,' Alison said, but her voice seemed like it was coming from someplace else. Her eyes felt heavy, her muscles relaxed to the point of catatonia.

'It's everything that you have, my dear. Right here, in this moment, in our own little part of the universe. You, me, this house, these trees, the ocean, the horizon. It's all at one with us, and we are at one with it. Eternal, everlasting and—'

Alison barely heard Glanna's last few words. They were nothing more than scattered syllables, imprints on the thick, rolling wave of darkness that was now gently wafting over her.

When she awoke it was morning and she was in the double bed of the master bedroom at Spriggan's. Michael was snoring by her side. Everything was a blur, but she felt different. It was as if her brain had been removed from her skull, reorganised like the individual blocks of a Rubik's cube, and carefully replaced in a way that one might change a lightbulb or a battery. She pulled herself up onto her elbows, leaned over and carefully studied the face of her sleeping husband. She felt something stir in her stomach. Not hate, exactly, but not love either. Ambivalence perhaps. Things were going to change between the two of them. Change for the better.

Richard couldn't sleep. How could he? The image of the wreckage kept playing over and over in his head like some terrible snuff movie. The flames, the smoke, the twisted metal. Tara was gone – dead. And the money? What had happened to the money? He knew he had to tell Jonno, but what was he going to say? That the only reason his mother had been there in Cornwall, so far away from home, was because his dad was trying to buy his way into his stepfather's business with funds that weren't really his? Hattie would leave him, there was no doubt about that. And Jonno? Jonno would never forgive him. It would always be between them; the knowing, the resentment. Richard could just about handle being broke and destitute, but he couldn't be alone. He couldn't lose them. No, he would keep it to himself for now. He wouldn't lie, he just wouldn't let on that he recognised the car. The news would filter through to them eventually, of course it would, but by then he would have come up with something, some story that extricated himself from the situation in some way. It didn't have to be elaborate, just convincing. No, not convincing exactly. *Believable* – it just had to be believable. He would think of something. He always did.

He'd been distant with Hattie when they came up to bed, and she'd noticed. That had led to another one of their legendary rows, of course. She accused him of being cold towards her, which he guessed he had been, but how was he supposed to react after seeing what he'd just seen? It wasn't her fault, she didn't know, but that didn't change things. He'd never really fallen out of love with Tara, but that didn't mean he didn't love his wife. Of course he did.

He checked his watch. It was two in the morning and Hattie was fast asleep, curled up in a ball on the edge of the bed, facing the window. It wasn't because of their argument. She always seemed to sleep that way these days, as if even in a state of unconsciousness she needed to keep her distance. It was a chasm, the space between them, but he still believed he could build a bridge across that wide ravine. Her affair, that one little illicit secret she guarded so vehemently, had almost made that chasm too deep, too wide, but he still had faith. He had learned to love that faith, to cherish it. It was all he had, after all.

He let out a long breath. He needed some air. He carefully pulled on his shorts and a crumpled old AC/DC T-shirt and went downstairs.

The house was groaning in the way old buildings sometimes do in the middle of the night. It didn't frighten Richard like it frightened Hattie and the kids. He knew it was just the effect of decades-old timber shrinking and expanding over and over again in an endless, futile cycle. Eventually the building would collapse into so much dust and debris. It was inevitable. Everything died.

He cycled through messages on his phone. Work emails mostly. Nothing about Tara. Nothing from Terry. He scanned through his social media. Hattie's parents were on an overseas holiday again, somewhere in the Mediterranean. They didn't look happy, despite the sunshine. They never really did. Hattie's father was a cantankerous old git, and her mother was a fiercely opinionated hag. They didn't seem to care that they'd alienated themselves from their daughters. They didn't even seem bothered when they'd told Richard about what his wife had got up to behind his back. Their online posts were filled with comments from friends and clients wishing them both a wonderful holiday, telling them how much they deserved it, how great they looked, etcetera. He huffed and switched off his phone.

He looked out the window. He was surprised to see the lights on in Noah's workshop, who obviously couldn't sleep either.

Richard's embarrassing little episode in the cave now seemed inconsequential compared to the life-altering events of the past few hours. He needed his car, now more than ever, and Noah had promised to help. He slid into his flip-flops and unlocked the front door. As he pulled it open there was a sound like a child's soft whisper.

Save us.

The hairs on the back of his neck stood on end, and he glanced anxiously around the room. There was no one there. The driveway was dark, the sky bathed in thick inky clouds. He tentatively stepped outside, whirling his head feverishly, half expecting to see a killer clown holding the blood-soaked head of some unsuspecting passer-by. There was no one, of course. He was alone.

'Prat,' he murmured under his breath. He pulled the door closed behind him. The hinges creaked and squealed. He hoped he hadn't woken Hattie.

He crossed the driveway, shaking his head at the sight of his stricken car, and opened the gate to the picket fence. The path that led to the workshop at the rear of the building wound around the perimeter of the house. It crossed over a murky pond that looked like it had seen better days, and then zig-zagged between a pair of tangled, weed-infested rose gardens. Excelsior Lodge was dark, quiet. The only sound was the soft whisper of the wind.

As Richard approached, he caught sight of a tall, black, faceless figure standing on the path ahead. His heart leapt in his throat before he realised he was looking at his own shadow. It was cast low and long by the milky light of the moon that was just peeking out from behind the thick clouds. *Jesus*, he thought, *what the hell is wrong with me?*

He went to knock on the workshop's rickety tin door but noticed movement at the window. He walked towards it. A lamp cast a dim glow over the scattered objects in the room. He could make out dusty shelves stacked with haphazard boxes, tins and jars, tools and implements hanging from nails in the wall and ceiling, stuffed animals glaring back at him as if they were willing him to go in and retrieve them, moth-eared books and papers stacked on other boxes of books and albums. It looked chaotic, disorganised. The bench under the window was strewn with what looked like herbs and spices, tied bundles of plants and weeds bound together with hemp. Some sort of raw meat hung from several hooks, its blood dripping into vials containing colourful viscous liquids. There were sketches on the walls drawn with chalk and paint, circles of different sizes, petal-like shapes, a horse's head, and long curved horns.

The whole thing made Richard feel a little creeped out, but it was more than just the random collection of freaky objects that held his gaze. What really caught his attention was the sight of Glanna, naked and lying prone on a tatty sofa, her legs bent and open at the knees. Noah was crouched on the ground between them, his head lowered. Richard wiped a hand across his mouth, which was suddenly as dry as the sole of his flip-flop. He glanced around the garden. No one was there. He felt like a peeping tom. Shit, he *was* a peeping tom. He rubbed at the grime-covered window with the remains of a tissue from his shorts pocket. Glanna's mouth was open, sweat glistening on her forehead and cheeks. Richard thought she was either in the throes of ecstasy or in horrible pain. He was transfixed.

Suddenly, Noah raised his hands to his face. They were covered in something dark and glistening. Richard leaned closer to get a better look. His breath fogged the glass, and he lost visual for a few frantic seconds. When the mist cleared, he realised that a strange-looking object had appeared in Noah's hands, except this wasn't Noah at all. It was Pascoe. He was standing and holding a writhing, living thing. It looked almost like a baby, but this baby was deformed and unnaturally angular and crooked. Its spine was horribly curved, its head too big for its tiny body. Purple slime seemed to hang from its skin, the umbilical cord black and pulsing. Glanna was screaming, but Richard didn't think it was from the pain she'd just experienced while giving birth to this mutated thing.

No, she was angry, frustrated. She pulled a hunting knife from under the sofa, glared at it with a spiteful rage, and then lunged at the newborn. The child let out a terrible shriek, wrenching the umbilical cord from its own naval and tearing itself from Pascoe's grasp. It climbed over his shoulder, gnashing and biting at his open shirt. Paz released it and it jumped, landing awkwardly on the concrete. Glanna, naked and bleeding, made another lunge for it, narrowly missing with the blade's sharp point. The thing screamed once more and ran headlong towards Richard. He threw himself towards the ground as the glass above him shattered and the creature flew over his head, landing clumsily on the path. It then turned and ran through the rose garden. After a few seconds it was gone.

When Richard dared to look through the window, he saw Glanna sitting upright and staring directly at him. She looked pained, distraught. Richard peered through the broken glass, his heart thumping in his chest. He was confused and disturbed and yet morbidly intrigued. He couldn't look away. It was car-crash TV; a UFO documentary on steroids. The two of them held each other's gaze for much longer than he'd intended. Suddenly a blood-soaked hand gripped his shoulder. When Richard looked up, he saw a face in the moonlight, framed by long flowing hair.

'Richard, my friend,' Paz said. 'Let's talk.'

*

Hattie woke at around five. Something wasn't right. Her stomach, it was churning. She touched the area surrounding her naval. It felt swollen, tender. She reached for her glass of water and swallowed a mouthful. It didn't help. Where the hell was Richard?

She stood and looked at herself in the mirror. Her hair was all over the place, and yesterday's mascara was still clotted in her eyelashes and smeared on her cheeks. She peered closer at her reflection and let out a long sigh. Thin lines painted the skin at the corners of her eyes and mouth. She looked all of her thirty plus years and then some. Where had it gone, all that time? What had she achieved? Where the hell was her life headed?

Her thoughts were interrupted by a sharp pain in her abdomen, and she doubled over, dry heaving into thin air. She dropped to her knees and grabbed the waste basket. She heaved again and this time a thin line of snotty bile abseiled slowly from her lips. What was going on? What was this? Food poisoning? The effects of that strange meat? The memory of the gloopy blood spurting from the stricken goat's ravaged throat made her heave again, and this time everything she had inside her seemed to come out, liquefied into beige lumpy porridge that poured from her in thick clumps. It seemed to go on for eternity, the heaving and the retching. Tears ran down her cheeks as her body shook violently. Wave after wave poured from her, vomit streaming from her mouth and nose until she thought she couldn't possibly have anything left to give. Eventually it subsided. Her throat burned and her stomach hurt, but the evacuation left her feeling a little better. She slumped onto her side, holding her stomach, and wiping goo from her lips and chin with the back of her hand. She shook her head. She felt gross. She lay there for a moment, expecting the gurgling pain to return. Apart from a dull ache, she seemed to have a moment of respite.

Shit, she thought. *The others*. They had eaten the same meal too! She leapt up from the floor and ran to her daughter's room. She peeked in, but Sally was still sleeping. She went to her, pulled back the duvet and touched her head. It was a typical child's body temperature, warm but not too hot. Sally looked up, her eyes only half open.

'Mummy?'

'It's okay, bunny. Go back to sleep. Mummy was just checking in on you.'

'Can we go to the beach later?'

'Of course, my darling. We can do whatever you want,' Hattie whispered, bending down and kissing her daughter on the forehead.

Was it possible that someone could love another human being so unconditionally, so intensely? She would do anything for her, give herself for her without pause, without question. She was everything, there was nothing else. It made the whole mess with Richard and her make sense, despite everything. That one, tiny jewel they had created; their one little perfect pearl among a beach full of seaweed and washed-up rubbish.

She left her to sleep, grabbed the puke-filled waste basket and went downstairs. The living room was still bathed in shadows. The house creaked and groaned with what sounded like dozens of unsettled grievances. The place still wreaked of decades old dust and damp, almost overpowering the stench of vomit on her hands and lips. She sloshed cool water over her face and scrubbed her fingers with washing up liquid. She slipped into her sandals and unlocked the front door. Cool damp air poured in, and she thought she heard the faint whisper of a sigh on the breeze, as though the house was breathing.

The sun was already cresting the tips of the trees, and the warmth kissed her cheeks. It felt good. She tied a knot in the plastic bag that held her regurgitated dinner, and flipped it into the rubbish bin. She paused to listen to her stomach. It was grumbling a little but nothing more. She decided she was safe.

She glanced across No Man's Land and spied Amy. She was clipping the hedges at the front of her property. She was obviously an early riser too. She decided to go and ask her about the rancid meat. She thought it must have affected them also.

As she approached, she spied Katharine, Pascoe's wife. She appeared through the garden gate. Another early riser.

'Hi!' Hattie called out. 'I mean, good morning, ladies! What a beautiful day.'

Amy looked up from pruning, and then, oddly, she turned away. Katharine seemed to notice and interjected.

'Isn't it just. The gods are looking kindly on us this summer.' She approached Hattie and touched her arm. Her hands were cold.

204

'Blessèd be.'

'I guess,' Hattie said. 'Amy, how are you feeling? I mean,' she paused, 'it's just that I was sick this morning. Like, really, *really* sick. I wondered if it was the meat, the goat that we ate last night.'

Amy's eyes widened just a little. Her gaze flicked furtively to Katharine, and she shook her head. She began to sign.

'She says that she feels fine,' Katharine translated, 'and that the meat was cleaned and fresh and couldn't possibly have caused any sickness.' She smiled. Hattie thought the smile a little cold in her eyes. 'She asked how you're feeling now.'

'What? Oh, yes, it seems to have passed, and my daughter is okay too, which I guess probably means that the sickness was caused by something else, but I just wanted to let you know.' She glared at Amy who was still averting her gaze. 'You know, just in case you had it too? The sickness I mean.'

Amy shook her head once more and went back to pruning the hedge.

'Well, she seems to be fine,' Katharine said. 'And you seem to be all better now too, which is just perfect.' There was that smile again, a little firm, a little forced. Hattie decided to prod at it.

'I saw your husband yesterday, Paz.'

'Did you?' The smile was unwavering.

'Yes. He seemed a little agitated. Is everything okay?'

'Did he just? Well, that's unlike him. He's normally so placid, the poor fellow. I think senility is starting to bed in.' She attempted a laugh, but it never reached her eyes. 'I'm sure everything was just fine.'

'Mm,' Hattie mumbled. 'It was just that he came racing across the common in his Land Rover and almost hit the gatepost as he pulled into your driveway. When he got out of the car he seemed pretty upset, actually. Did he say anything to you at all? I know there was that awful car accident a few miles away, and I wondered whether either of you knew the poor woman. They say she died at the scene.'

There was a loud clatter as Amy's pruning shears fell from her hand, sending a spray of gravel over their feet. Amy stood motionless with her back to them. The smile never left Katharine's lips, but it certainly left her expression.

'No, dear,' Katharine said eventually. 'We have no idea who that poor girl was, and I can assure you,' she bent and collected the shears, 'that my husband and I are just fine.'

Hattie nodded and there was a moment of silence between the three of them.

'Be careful, Harriet,' Katharine said, glancing deliberately up at Excelsior Lodge. 'Be careful of what you notice around here, what you stick your nose into. You know, once a thing is seen, it can't be unseen.'

'What do you mean?' Hattie asked, taken aback.

'Just that, my dear.' Katharine's eyes narrowed, and Hattie felt a lump form in the back of her throat. 'Now, Amy, my love, I really must go and check on that fruitcake. If I leave it in the oven any longer, it will be nothing more than a fruity biscuit.' She turned and raced along the pathway, disappearing out of view.

Amy stood to face Hattie. There was the glistening dampness of tears on her cheeks and a reddening around her eyes.

'Oh, Amy, is everything okay?' Hattie said. She went to go to her, but Amy recoiled. She was wiping her hands with a rag as if she were trying to remove something horrid. 'Is there anything I can do, anything at all? You can tell me, I won't say anything, I swear.'

Amy picked at her nails, shook her head.

'Amy, please. Is there something I need to know? Something my *family* needs to know? It's just that, I've seen these things, these *strange* things, and Richard says I just fainted, but it didn't feel like a dream, it felt real, and then Sally was given this really scary-looking toy by some freaky kid, and she says she saw these strange children in the trees, and,' she took a deep breath, 'the tyres on Richard's car were slashed by God only knows who, and Jonno's

206

iPad was broken by those *boys*, and then that thing on the beach the other night. I mean, what the hell was that? And the house seems to have a life of its own, like it's breathing or something, and today I got this terrible sickness, and there's the *daisy wheels*. I don't even know what a daisy wheel is!'

Amy took a tiny step towards her, her glare suddenly resolute. She held out unsteady hands and began to sign furiously.

If you don't leave, they will take you.

'What? What the hell does that mean, take me?' A glacier of sharp ice raced up Hattie's spine. She suddenly felt the urge to get back to her daughter, to hold her close. 'Amy, for God's sake tell me! What do you mean?'

They will take all of you.

*

Rachel's sleep was broken at best. The accident, the wreckage, the melted tarmac; the image of that twisted, smouldering tangerine-coloured car, and the numberplate, blackened and charred but clearly identifiable, even on the cottage's crappy TV.

TDEVIL666

Tara Deville, Richard's ex. Jonno's mother.

She glanced at her watch – six-fifteen. It was no use, she couldn't sleep. Bea was curled up in a ball next to her and snoring like a foghorn, so she decided to sneak to the bathroom. She had to get back in touch with Eric.

The house was quiet, save for the constant creaking and groaning that seemed to seep from every joint of the rat-infested cottage. She closed the door gently behind her and turned the lock.

She logged into her account and checked her messages. The number one, next to an image of an envelope, sat there blinking at her. It was from Eric.

What the hell did you do?

207

Oh, obviously, she thought. After they'd lost such an important lead, Eric's go-to mode was to blame her. She was the obvious choice, really. Surely she must have had something to do with it. She had been the only one there, after all. She shook her head. She really was never going to wash that particular reputation away, was she? The reputation of being the kind of detective who gets her partners killed. Tommy, a single father of two. It had been her fault, and everyone knew it. She gave off a bad smell, a toxic smell.

She replied curtly, her thumbnails clicking hard against the screen.

Wasn't me. I'm disappointed that you think that.

It flashed silently. Maybe that was it. She'd let them all down: Eric, Tommy, Tommy's kids especially. She'd tried, she really had. She'd let herself go deep, deeper than with any undercover assignment before. Rachel Woodley, thirty-two, an aerospace engineer from Canterbury, ex semi-pro swimmer, good athlete, likes a drink and a laugh, even though her parents died in a boating accident when she was very young. Independent, strong-willed, if a little insecure. Falls in love easily. That last bit was true, of course, but the rest was all a badly conceived fallacy. A thinly veiled one at that.

Had this been The Weasel? Had he found out what Richard, or Quin, was up to with Tara and her husband? Rachel had thought Terry was The Weasel, but perhaps that was way off the mark. Perhaps Terry was somebody else entirely. If The Weasel was the fence for this particular deal, then had Richard and Terry tried to bypass him, to cut him out completely? If so, was Tara's death the result of The Weasel retaliating in the only way he knew how? Was he trying to get back at the two of them by murdering the woman they both loved? The whole thing left her head spinning.

Then there was Glanna and her creepy mother. What did they

know? Did they even know anything at all? And, even if they did, where the hell had they disappeared to? One thing was for sure, they'd freaked her out, which was completely out of character. She was rarely backfooted by anything at all.

Triple B, her father used to call her – his little Bethy Big Balls. Nothing ever shook her, not even when she was little: not her mother's death, not her brother's destructive spiral into heroin addiction, not even the sight of a shotgun suicide corpse at the tender age of thirteen. Her father, also a detective, had taken his little girl to the blood-soaked scene in a misjudged attempt to find out what she was made of, and perhaps to shake her up a little. It hadn't worked, of course. All she'd seen was a man's body with a hole in it, nothing more. She still thought of them that way, the victims. Just bodies to be tagged and bagged, cases to be solved. She had to be that way, particularly in her job. It was her mind's way of protecting itself.

This thing with Glanna though, a woman who she'd only spoken to once, twice even. How had she appeared to know her so well? How could that be? It made her feel violated in some bizarre, unexplained way. She realised she was going to have to find out what Glanna knew, if she even knew anything at all. It could only mean she was in on the whole thing; her and her crazy mother too. It was the only explanation that made sense.

Sorry, that email was an emotional reaction, and not a good one. I'll apologise properly when you're back at base.

The sudden appearance of Eric's crap attempt at an apology brought her back to the moment. She smiled. As much as she wanted to stay pissed off with him, Eric always had a way with words. He was a sweet guy, too. Like, wouldn't say boo to a goose, would sob at cheesy eighties movies, had had his heart broken way too often, sweet. She had a soft spot for him in a younger (much younger) sisterly kind of way. It wouldn't stop her from milking his apology though. No way. She was going to squeeze the juice from that particular lemon until there was nothing left but dry skin, so to speak.

We found something from a security camera on the edge of a large property situated half a mile along the same road. It's not a clear image, but it's something. We think this vehicle was involved in the crash.

She hammered out an eager reply. *Deliberate?*

We don't know yet, but we're scanning the cloud for security system feeds to see if we can find another sighting further along the road. If we can, we can estimate the speed the vehicle was travelling at.

Mm, she mused, *it was barely circumstantial*. No one was going to get questioned, let alone prosecuted, for being seen on a security camera somewhere close to a fatal motor vehicle accident, even if they were speeding. That wasn't what this was about though, was it? She felt bad for Tara Deville, she was Jonno's mother after all, but the truth was, no one was looking for a perpetrator involved in her death. It would just be written up by the overstretched local constabulary as yet another country driver failing to stick to the speed limit on these treacherously narrow country lanes. Operation Glow, however? Now, that was a different matter. Operation Glow would investigate the shit out of it.

Show me the picture.

Don't get your hopes up, Beth. As I said, it's fuzzy as hell.

Just pull your finger out of your arse and show me, Eric!

The little screen blinked some more, and then, thankfully, the progress bar started to creep to the right. She dragged the loading page downwards to refresh it, but at the speed the little blue bar was moving, she thought it was going to take until at least Christmas 2030 for the bloody image to materialise. Cheap, crappy, out-in-the-sticks Wi-Fi! She wanted to find the router, go to the top of the house, rip a hole through the straw roof and throw the flimsy little plastic box as far as she could, hopefully smashing it into a gazillion pieces. It wouldn't solve her problem, but she'd feel a hell of a lot better for it.

Suddenly the screen flashed again, and Microsoft asked whether she wanted to save or open the image. *Open it*, her head screamed. *Of course I just want to fucking open it!*

She clicked the icon as casually as her trembling finger would allow, and the grainy image started to appear. She leaned back on the loo seat and took in a deep breath.

'Well, I'll be,' she said, smirking. 'The little shits.'

*

'Come on, Sal. We need to hurry.'

'But why?'

'I told you why. There's something I want to show you, and it might not be there for very long.'

Jonno felt sick. It was a strange kind of sickness. Not the kind where you throw up or spend hours on the toilet. This sickness was different. It made his body ache and his eyes hurt. He couldn't remember coming home last night, or what had gone on after Evie had left him with the floating boy and his parents, but he knew that he had to go back, and with Sally, too. It was important. He just couldn't remember why.

When he went into her room she'd still been sleeping, of course. His dad and Hattie were out, and someone had been occupying the bathroom, for like forever, so he just threw on a pair of shorts and a T-shirt and coaxed his half-sister awake. She didn't mind, she'd

211

said. She liked an adventure.

'Can I bring Cross-Eye?' she'd asked.

'Cross-Eye? Who's Cross-Eye?'

'This!' She'd held out the little cloth ball with the funny face and the shaggy hair. 'It's what I call him.'

'Where did you get that thing from? I thought Hattie – I mean, your mum – took it away?'

'I just found it. It was under my pillow.'

Jonno doubted that. They all thought Sally was just a sweet little girl, but he knew different. She was smart. Like, devious smart.

'Okay. If you want. But don't tell anyone that I know you have it. Otherwise, the adventure is cancelled. You got me?'

'I got you,' she'd said, cocking her thumb and finger like a pistol.

'You promise?'

'Cross my heart, hope to die, stick a needle in my eye.'

'Cool,' he'd said, ignoring the irony. 'Then get moving, soldier.'

He just about remembered the way to the back of The Weary Traveller, and Sally skipped along behind him as if she didn't have a single care in the world. She was just a little kid, with little kid things to think about. He was much older, with much bigger problems. Such as, why had Evie abandoned him yesterday, without even saying a word? And why did he feel like everything he touched around this place infected him in some weird, itchy kind of way? And, more importantly, why did the big boulder of doom continue to press down on his head and shoulders and try to squash him into the ground like some sort of stupid, gross bug? The floating boy had made him feel different, like he meant something, like he *was* something. Nothing and no one had made him feel like that before: not his dad, not his mum and definitely not Hattie. Even Evie, who he'd thought he'd been kind of falling for, had turned out to be a big let-down. She was just the same as everybody else – selfish, mean.

212

'Ow!' Sally squealed.

'What now?' he said, spinning round. He felt angry, but he didn't know why.

'Ow, that really hurts!' Sally yelled. She sat down in the dirt and started to cry.

'What is it, Sal? What's the matter?'

'My leg. It's stinging.'

'What do you mean, stinging?'

'Like *stinging*, stinging, stupid!' She wailed again, and Jonno began to feel the mist of panic descend. What if somebody heard her? How would he explain why he'd taken her into the woods without his dad and Hattie's permission? What would he tell them?

'Do you think it's a bee sting?'

'I don't know, Jonno, but it really hurts, like baaad! Make it stop!'

Jonno touched the skin around her shin. It felt rough with little raised pimples. He could see a pink patch, as if the skin was raw. What was it? A fire ant? A snake? God, what if it was a snake?

'I'll get someone.'

'No! Don't leave me!' Sally was sobbing now.

'Sally, please, just try to—'

'I want Mum. I want my mum!'

'Look, I'm your brother, and I'm here. I'm right here. Let me help you.'

'You can't help me. *You're just a stupid boy*!'

'Please be quiet, Sal. Please!'

'It *huuurts*!'

'Here, try this,' a man said from behind Jonno. A hand reached out and passed Sally a large dark green leaf that was roughly the size of Jonno's head. The sobbing abated, and she looked up, her eyes red with tears.

'What is it?' she asked.

'A dock leaf,' the stranger said. 'It cures all nettle stings. Just spit on it. Yep, I know it's gross, but seriously, rub the wet patch

213

onto the sore area. I promise, the skin will feel as right as rain in no time at all.'

Jonno looked up and was startled to see someone he recognised; someone he'd encountered just the night before. The last time he'd seen that face, however, it was in a different orientation entirely. Horizontal, to be precise, and suspended about five feet from the ground.

'The floating boy,' Jonno said, unconsciously.

'What's that now?' the young man asked. 'Floating you say? What, like on the water?'

Jonno could feel his mouth hanging open like he was an awestruck little kid, and he instantly closed it.

'Do as the boy says, Sal,' he said. 'Spit on the leaf.'

'Yuk!' She screwed up her nose. 'And wipe it all over myself?'

'Just on the sting,' the floating boy said. 'You'll kind of have to trust me on this.'

'But I'll get *germs*!'

Jonno confronted her. 'Look, Sally, you either want to get rid of the sting or you don't. If you do, then do as he says. If you don't, then stop crying like a baby!'

That seemed to startle his sister into action, and with a look of mortified disgust, she dribbled gloopy spit onto the leaf and rubbed it into her leg.

'There,' the floating boy said, 'all better.'

'It really is,' Sally agreed, her mouth sliding into a lopsided smile. 'I can hardly feel it anymore.'

'My name's Sebastian,' the floating boy said. 'You can call me Seb. And you are?' He eyed Jonno.

'I… I'm Jonathon,' Jonno stammered.

'Ha-ha. That's not your name!' Sally yelled.

'It is *too*!' he yelled back, and then caught himself. 'It's just that everyone calls me Jonno.'

'Well then, nice to meet you Jonno,' Seb said, holding out a hand. Jonno shook it. It felt sort of funny shaking hands with the floating boy, but sort of cool too.

'And what about you, young lady?' Seb asked, lowering himself to one knee.

'I'm Sally,' she said, and pointed at Jonno. 'He's my brother. Well, kind of.'

'We're half-brother and sister,' Jonno said. 'We have the same dad.'

'Well of course, I can see that now,' Seb said, grinning. 'You have the same eyes.'

'Mine are prettier,' Sally said, and she stood. 'Jonno said he wanted to show me something at your house. What is it?'

Seb turned to Jonno. 'Well, did you now? Jonno, would you care to enlighten me?'

Jonno leaned in and whispered, 'Remember? Last night, you asked me to bring Sally. I can't recall why exactly, but it seemed important. There was something you wanted us both to see. It was when you were...' he held out his hands as if demonstrating a magic trick, 'you know, when you were—'

'When I was what?'

Jonno suddenly felt pretty stupid. 'I don't know really. Maybe we should just go home, Sal.'

Sally stomped her feet. 'But you said!'

'Breakfast,' Seb interjected. 'My parents are cooking it right now, and there's plenty to go round.' He turned and pointed towards the house. Jonno could see Seb's parents, but they looked different now. They stood at the French doors in their identical shorts and white T-shirts. They were both grinning, but there was something unsettling about their eyes. They looked cold, emotionless.

'Come,' Seb's father silently mouthed to them. 'Come in. We've been waiting.'

*

215

Eli watched from his spot behind the clump of tangled nettles as Kid-Bastard Aaron and Kid-Bastard Freddie climbed over the fallen tree and pushed farther along the path. He checked in his pocket for the notepad that Evie had given him. "Follow them", she had said. "Take notes, make drawings". He hated being at her beck and call wherever and whenever she pleased, but what were his options? Say no to her? Deal with her rage? Her terrifying thirst for violence? No, not likely. With Noah out to get him, Eli knew he needed friends, not enemies.

'You sure this is the right way, bro?' Kid-Bastard Freddie asked.

'Of course I'm sure,' Kid-Bastard Aaron replied. 'We were literally just here two days ago, dumb ass.'

'I don't know about this. I think the dead should stay, you know, buried and stuff.'

Aaron whirled on his brother. 'You heard Mother. With that bird up at Thatcher's Corner biting the dust, the police are bound to come knocking at our door. We can't be taking any chances. We've got to move him to the pit, and fast.'

Eli hastily scribbled a crude picture of a shovel and a corpse in his notebook.

'That pit's getting kinda full.'

'I'm sure we'll make room.'

'But I don't think—'

'Freddie, stop being such a pussy and get a move on. You're always whining like a little bitch.'

As the two brothers pushed their way through the dense woodland, Eli tried to stay close enough, while also keeping a safe distance. He knew he couldn't afford to lose them, but he also knew he couldn't get caught. If they saw him, then they'd make him pay, and the last time that had happened he'd been left bed-bound and semi-conscious for almost a week.

'It's this way, I'm sure of it!' Aaron yelled.

Even though it was just after noon, the sunlight was barely

216

penetrating the thick canopy, and the forest was cast in a dense, suffocating gloom. The day was humid and hot, and sweat was streaming down Eli's back and arms. Nevertheless, he kept pace with the boys, ignoring the hot sting of nettles and the sharp scrape of twigs and thorns on his shins and thighs. It was almost as if the forest was desperately trying to limit his every movement, as though it were allied in some sick way to Freddie, Aaron, Evie and Sweet Mother. He knew that was a ridiculous notion, but it kind of made sense. This was Sweet Mother's land, after all.

'Hold up, Aaron! I'm losing you!'

'Get a wriggle on, then! We haven't got all day!'

Eli watched as they disappeared down the other side of a steep slope and reluctantly decided to follow from behind a tight group of beech trees at the western edge of the natural bowl. As he huffed and puffed, dragging himself up the bank, he spotted the Red Man. He was perched on a moss-covered rock and watching the brothers' passage. His face was a vacant stare, his one remaining eye red and boiling.

'You can't do anything,' Eli said. 'You're just a ghost.'

The Red Man turned to him. He held out the shiny thing. Eli gazed at its finely polished surface and its beautifully ornate inscription. It was the most beautiful, magical thing he had ever seen. He wanted it almost as much as he loved Sweet Mother. Perhaps more.

'I... I can't. I... won't.'

The Red Man smiled. There was blood on his teeth and black slime on his chin. He nodded.

'You're starting to rot,' Eli said. 'You can't stay out here much longer. You're too far away from your real body. You need to go back. If you don't, you might never be able to see her again. Your wife, I mean.'

The Red Man shook his head. Eli could see his teeth through the hole in his cheek. He leaned towards him, the shiny thing dangling between what remained of his fingers. Eli felt its pull, like a strong magnet. He knew that if he did what the Red Man wanted, then he would be left on his own, probably for good. No Noah, no Evie, no Sweet Mother.

'They'll kill me.'

The Red Man's stare was impassive. A long, flaccid length of skin hung from the place in his scalp where the teeth had penetrated. Eli could see the remnant of the Red Man's brain through the jagged split in his skull. It looked like spoiled faggots. From somewhere distant, there came the sound of Kid-Bastard Aaron hollering at Kid-Bastard Freddie, followed by Kid-Bastard Freddie's howl of disapproval. They deserved it, they both did, for what they'd done to the Red Man and his pretty wife. Maybe Eli would be doing everyone a favour. Maybe it was the right thing to do. Maybe Sweet Mother would thank him for it. Yes, perhaps she would. Perhaps she would even think of him as a hero. And the shiny thing? It was so beautiful, so unforgettable. He would cherish it for ever.

He instinctively held out his good hand to touch its smooth surface, but the Red Man pulled it away, waving a split and bloodied finger back and forth. Eli's head dropped.

'Okay. Afterwards, then? You'll give it to me after?'

Eli knew he would. The Red Man always kept his promises.

*

It had been the boys. Those two hapless buffoons. They of the crumpled clothes, unwashed hair and bum-fluff chins. The body odour, the coarse language, the gruff bullishness – they hardly seemed smart enough. Jesus, she was amazed that either of them even knew how to drive. As unlikely as it seemed, there they were in all their grainy, pixelated glory: thick, grimy hands holding the wheel of a tatty brown Volvo, Aaron's eyes steely and determined, Freddie's furtive and anxious. Was it merely a coincidence that the pair of oafs from this strange little coven of a community had been

218

witnessed just a few hundred metres from the scene, at approximately the right time? Or, in fact, was it something far more sinister? If so, if the brothers really had been involved in driving Tara Deville's tangerine mobile off the road, then what bearing did it have on Rachel's case? Were the pair of them collectively The Weasel? Is that what this was? Was Richard now in danger too? What about Hattie and Sally? And Bea? What about Bea?

Rachel pulled on her trainers. She was suddenly very worried. Bea had headed off to the beach earlier that day for a morning swim and was still out there on her own. What if The Weasel got to her while she was in the water? What if the brothers weren't acting alone? This was a major global criminal enterprise after all, with billions of pounds at stake. They would do anything to protect their empire. If the events with Tommy proved anything at all, it was just that: they would stop at nothing.

Rachel heard Hattie crashing around in the bedroom across the hallway, and she went to her, leaning against the doorframe and trying to act casual.

'Hiya, Hats. Have you... have you seen Bea at all?'

'No,' Hattie replied, randomly throwing clothes into an open suitcase.

'What you doing? You going somewhere?'

'We're leaving.'

'Leaving? You mean, leaving today? We still have a few days left, don't we?'

'I don't care. These people are crazy. I'm done with all of them.'

Rachel felt her pulse race. Her case, her cover. They couldn't leave now.

'Don't you think you're being a bit—'

'I called them out!' Hattie whirled on her, her hair a tangle of kinks and curls, her eyes darting. 'I called them out on it, Rachel. Katharine and Amy, early this morning. I asked them about all this weird, crazy shit that's been happening. I thought I was being smart, maybe a little too smart for my own good, but so what? Do

219

you know what they said? Do you know what *Amy* said?'

Rachel shook her head, but the image of the two boys gripping the steering wheel just moments after a fatal accident was still clear in her mind. She then thought of Bea out there in the water. She needed to get to her.

'She told me to get out. To get the fuck out of here before Glanna and the others tried to *take us*. Do you believe that? *Take* us? I don't even know what that means, but I know it sounds really, *really* bad, and there's no way I'm taking any chances with my family. If it means we lose three days of this train crash of a holiday, then so be it. I want to go home, and I want to take my baby home, and I want to get back to normality, *my normality*, even if it is a screwed up, fucked-up version of what most people would consider normal. I don't care. It's my normal and I want it and I miss it, and I'm sick of this magical, tree hugging, pagan, goat-killing *shit*!'

Rachel went to her. 'I know, I know. I really do, honestly, and I'm sure that what you say Amy said is truly what you believe you heard, but I can't believe that—'

'That they're dangerous? These people? Really? Were you there at the beach? Did you see the blood on my clothes? The blood in my mouth? Did you hear Sally talking about those children in the woods? Or the tyres? Oh, God—'

'What?'

'Our tyres. Our slashed tyres. Our *car*!' Hattie grabbed Rachel's arm. 'It's them, don't you see?'

'Oh, come on. You don't really think they would—'

'Yes, I do! I really do. Richard,' Hattie went to the window. 'I need Richard. He said he'd speak to Noah. Have you seen him?'

Rachel shook her head. She hadn't seen him since last night. He'd looked more than a little green around the gills, and it was hardly surprising, was it? The mother of his son had just died in a tragic accident, not more than an hour after being there with him. What was he supposed to think?

'Jonno,' Hattie said. 'Maybe he's with Jonno.'

Rachel suddenly had a terrible thought. She raced along the hallway and burst into the bedroom next door.

'Hattie!' she yelled, suddenly very worried. 'Where's Sally?'

*

'So, Jonathon. Can I call you Jonathon?' Seb's father, Petra, asked.

'I prefer Jonno.'

'Of course you do. Yes, Jonno. A much cooler name. Well, Jonno, tell us again what you say you saw.'

Jonno was standing just inside the kitchen. He was holding Sally's hand as though her life depended on it. Petra and his wife stood in front of them, their arms hanging limply, their hair neatly combed. Seb was seated at the kitchen table, smiling.

'Look, I know it sounds crazy,' Jonno said. 'But you guys were all there. You were upstairs in the room at the back of the house, the one with the funky drawings on the walls and the papered-over window.'

'Dad's office,' Seb said.

'I guess.'

'And you said I was, what? Floating? Like levitating or something?' Seb asked, puffing out his cheeks. 'That would be way cool.'

'Well, you did, so maybe you are.'

'Am what?'

'Way cool,' Jonno said, but he regretted it as soon as the words left his mouth. He sounded stupid. A heavy mass settled onto his shoulders once more. 'I mean, I guess.'

'This all sounds very strange. Very strange indeed. I just don't know what to think,' Petra said. 'What do you make of it, Ger?' He turned to his wife.

'I don't know what to think, either,' she said, stooping. 'But I would very much like to meet this little one.' She placed the palm of her hand on Sally's head. 'She has pretty hair.'

221

'Her name is Sally,' Jonno said. 'You said to bring her over.'

'We did?' Ger asked, sliding a lock of Sally's red hair between her fingers. 'Well, if we did, then thank you for bringing her to us. She really is quite spectacular.'

'Thank you,' Sally said, but Jonno thought his sister looked really uncomfortable. Hell, he was uncomfortable too.

'I think we should go,' Jonno said. He'd wanted to show Sally the floating boy, but now he knew that the floating boy was just a teenager named Sebastian, it didn't seem to matter as much. He also suspected that Seb's parents were high on something illegal. He wanted nothing more than for the two of them to get away from there as fast as possible.

'Nonsense,' Seb said. 'You've just got here, and anyway, Mum's cooked us all a hearty breakfast.' He gestured towards the table, which was covered in plates piled high with smoked bacon, sliced sausage, blood pudding, thick cuts of steak and fried duck eggs. The delicious smell of salted meat and toasted bread wafted over Jonno. He felt his stomach growl with approval. 'We can't let it go to waste.'

'Can we have some, Jonno? Please?' Sally pleaded.

'Of course you can, my dear,' Ger answered, giving Jonno no time to politely decline. 'You can eat just as much as you want. We have plenty to go round.'

'I... I don't know,' Jonno said, but he knew it was too late. Sally had wrenched her hand from his, and was now being helped up to her place at the table by Seb's mum.

'There you go, my sweet,' Ger said. She placed her hands on her hips. 'Well, go on then. Get stuck in.' She let out a high-pitched giggle and glanced at her husband.

'She's a feeder,' Petra said, patting Jonno's shoulder. 'Now, while they tuck into that, I've got something I'd very much like to show you.'

'Me?' Jonno asked. 'Something to show me?'

'The very same, so if you don't mind, let's walk this way.'

222

Seb turned, grease running down his chin, a bloody chunk of charred steak clamped between his teeth. 'Oh, you need to see this, Jonno,' he said. 'You're gonna just die.'

*

'He's not answering his phone.'

Rachel and Hattie were downstairs in the living room.

'Try again.'

'I've just tried three times! There's nothing!'

'I'm sure they're fine,' Rachel offered unconvincingly.

'How could you know that? You can't know that.'

'I don't, but I guess, well, I just think—'

'She was there when I got out of bed this morning, Rachel! Right there! I talked to her. Richard was already out of the house by then.'

'Out of the house? So early?'

'We had a row, not that it's any of your business.'

'Well, maybe he came back to collect her?'

'And took her where?' Hattie asked. She was standing in the downstairs hallway.

'I don't know, but she wouldn't have left the house on her own. She's way too smart for that.'

'Where's Bea? Where's Jonno? Where the hell is everyone?'

Rachel had been wondering the same thing. It was as if the house had just swallowed everybody up.

'What the fuck is that?' Hattie shrieked. She was pointing at a framed picture on the wall. It looked new. Rachel stepped into the hallway, her hands on her hips. The picture was new all right, brand new. The paper was pristine white, except for the crude drawings. Six figures stood on what appeared to be yellow sand, a wash of blue waves and surf behind them. They were all drawn in exaggerated crayon technicolour, completely in keeping with the rest of the portraits. Hattie stood beside Richard, their hands not

223

quite touching. Rachel was with Bea, although Bea looked pretty mad. Jonno was sitting on the floor, building sandcastles with what looked like two halves of a busted iPad on the ground beside him. Sally was there too, but she was gazing up at a dark shadow that hung over the clifftop.

'I guess we've been added to the wall,' Rachel said. 'It's not bad, actually.'

Hattie glared at her. 'You're kidding, right? It's horrific! And how the hell did it get in here? It wasn't there when we all went up to bed last night, was it?' She paused. 'Wait a minute.' She touched the picture, running a finger along the yellow sand.

'What is it?'

'That's it,' Hattie whispered.

'That's what?'

'The beach.'

'What about it?' Rachel wasn't following.

'That's where Sally said she wanted to go today.' Hattie grabbed Rachel by the shoulders. 'Don't you see? She's at the beach! My daughter's at the beach!'

*

'I don't want to.'

'You have to.'

'But why?'

'Because otherwise you won't be able to see.'

'See what?'

Petra held a clam shell in his hands. It was filled with a blood-red powder, like brick dust. In his other hand he held a glass of water. 'This powder was created from the antlers of a mighty stag. The antlers represent Cernunnos, the horned god, our lord and one true deity. The antlers are chopped and crushed until they become this very fine silky texture. The antler powder is called Argen. The Argen is then mixed with the fresh blood of a still breathing doe.

The doe represents Artemis, the Greek goddess of the hunt.'

Jonno shuddered. 'It sounds gross and stupid.'

'I can assure you, it's no such thing.'

They were standing on the second-floor balcony, overlooking the ocean. The waves crashed noisily against the rocks below. Jonno imagined the ground giving way beneath their feet, and pictured the two of them falling into the raging waters. Part of him hoped they would.

Petra took a teaspoon of the red powder and poured it into the water, gently swirling the spoon until the liquid turned completely clear. The surface began to bubble and froth.

'It looks too hot,' Jonno said.

'No, no. It's quite cool. Don't let its appearance fool you.'

'I want to go back inside. I want to see my sister.'

'Oh, please believe me when I tell you she's quite all right. Ger is taking good care of her. She so desires a daughter of her own. Especially a red-head.'

'She's not for sale,' Jonno snapped.

'We're not purchasing.'

'She's only five.'

'We know.'

'We?' Jonno asked, although he found himself transfixed by the glass of bubbling, swirling water.

'Yes. All of us. We've been keeping a close eye on you and your family. All your secrets, all your quarrels. You fascinate us.'

'I don't know what you mean.'

'Oh, but you do, don't you?' Petra said. 'You know exactly what I mean. You're the one who sees everything, aren't you? The one who watches, who rarely speaks, but always pays attention. You don't miss a trick, Jonathon.'

'It's Jonno.'

'Nothing gets passed you.'

'I hold the power,' Jonno said, but his words were involuntary, spilling from his lips like smoke.

225

'You truly do.'

'They don't realise.'

'No, but they will.'

'They will,' Jonno whispered. He could barely hear the waves now, or Petra. He could barely even hear himself. He didn't feel the coolness of the glass as it caressed his lips, or the water that kissed his tongue. He didn't taste the sour liquid as it filled his throat and slid silently down his gullet. He didn't even feel himself slump into Petra's arms, or the dampness of the drool as it fell from his open mouth and slithered across his cheek. All he saw was the colossal beast as it appeared from the depths of the ocean, its eyes a yellow death, its hands rotting, its body swarming with locusts. It rose up into the clouds, its mighty form towering over them like a gigantic behemoth. It leaned towards him, its giant horns casting tree-like shadows. Jonno smelled the stench of festering waste.

'The child with the gift,' it growled with a voice like ancient gears grinding together. 'It's time for you to join us.'

*

Eli watched as the boys clawed clumsily at the shallow grave. At first, all he could make out was the sight of clumpy earth mixed with shards of flint, but then a hand was visible, a forearm, followed by a nose, and a mouth filled with leaves and dirt. Eli glanced back towards the hill where the Red Man had been, but he was no longer there. Perhaps he couldn't bear to watch. Eli thought it would be strange after all, watching your own body being dug up from its grave, even if it was a makeshift one.

He felt for the knife in his pocket. He knew he would have to be quick and decisive. He'd go for Aaron first. He thought he could fend off Freddie, but Aaron? That would be much more difficult. No, he would cut off the head of the snake. He might even enjoy it.

'I don't like it,' Freddie moaned.

'Oh, shut up and get on with it.'

'What if someone sees us?'

'They won't.'

'What about the family from the cottage? They might. Especially her. The mum.' Freddie dropped his shovel. 'She'll call the old bill on us for sure, and then what?'

'Just grab the wheelbarrow,' Aaron said, 'and help me lift him.'

'We'll have his DNA all over us.'

'What do you even know about DNA? You've been watching too much TV, mate.'

'No,' Freddie said. 'It's true. We touch that body, and we're as good as guilty.'

'Freddie,' Aaron said. 'We buried the body. We're already guilty.'

Eli moved as quietly and as quickly as he could. He edged towards Aaron's blind side. He watched as the two Kid-Bastards jumped down into the hole and attempted to hoist the broken and torn remains of the Red Man towards the edge of the grave. He almost cried out as the body slipped from Freddie's grasp and flipped backwards into the jagged hole.

'Watch what you're doing, won't you?' Aaron yelled. 'I don't want to have to take him back in bits.'

'He's heavy.'

'Then put your back into it. We got him in here, we can get him out.'

There was a movement to Eli's left and he whirled towards it. His eyes narrowed. They were here. He could smell them.

'Are you ready?' Aaron asked.

'I guess.'

Eli realised he had very little time. If he was going to do what the Red Man asked, then he needed to make his move, and quickly. Before *they* came.

'All right, after three. And this time, don't drop him.'

Freddie stuck out a tongue.

Eli held the knife and unfolded the blade. He would go for the

227

throat, dig the blade in and pull, like killing a chicken. It would be messy, but it would do the trick. He gulped. He'd never killed anyone before, especially not a Kid-Bastard, but he knew he couldn't let the Red Man down – not again – not after the little girl.

'One—'

Eli stepped into the clearing.

'Two—'

Freddie looked up and spotted him, his expression a mixture of confusion and revulsion. He mouthed, '*You*?'

'*Three*!'

Suddenly they were on top of Freddie – the Terrible Babies – dozens of them. Claws ripping, teeth tearing, and mouths devouring. Freddie shrieked.

'Freddie! What the—?' Aaron dropped the Red Man's body and leapt out of the hole. He swatted at one of the babies and turned to Eli. 'Stop them! Cripple! Whatever you've told them to do, you've got to stop them! They'll kill him!'

'I—' Eli went to speak but his eyes were transfixed. Freddie was trying to punch and swipe at his attackers but there were far too many of them. His face was a mask of crimson flesh and badly torn skin.

'Aaron!' Freddie yelled, but it sounded like his mouth was filled with blood. 'Help me, brusher! Pleashe! Help me!' He was crying. The Kid-Bastard was crying.

Aaron stooped to pick up the shovel, but he paused. He looked back at Eli who was still holding the knife. His eyes were filled with anger and hatred.

Freddie dropped to his knees as the Terrible Babies, all grey skin, bloodied fangs and red eyes, descended upon him. One blood-soaked arm protruded from their writhing mass, and trembling fingertips reached desperately for the handle of the pickaxe. Within an instant, one of the babies grabbed Freddie's hand and bit off two of his fingers. There was a yell of shock and terror from somewhere beneath the mound of bodies. The Terrible Baby closest to Eli, the one with a little tuft of yellow hair protruding from her scalp and with a twisted scar on her right cheek, looked up and smiled, the severed finger protruding from her grey lips.

When Eli turned back, Aaron was gone.

Damn it, Eli cursed. He knew Aaron would tell Sweet Mother everything, and then Eli would be for it, and not in a good way.

'That's enough!' Eli said. The gnashing and clawing ceased. 'Just... stop. Please. This was my job, not yours.'

'But... we help you,' one of the babies said.

'Mm,' Eli muttered, holding a hand to his face. He had a headache. 'Not really. I think this time you've prob'ly gone way too far.'

'But, we like you.'

'Well, I don't like you,' Eli said. 'Not really. You're just stupid forest kids.' He pointed at Freddie. 'Is he dead? The Kid-Bastard I mean.'

The Terrible Babies parted like the ocean, exposing Freddie's torn remains. He lay on his back, his eyes wide open, the shock and trauma still painted on his lifeless expression. There was a powdery trace of salty tears on his cheeks. Blood caked his face and body, his innards spilled out onto the dirt. He was dead all right, totally dead. Eli shook his head.

'What do we do now?' another one of the babies asked.

Eli shrugged. Things were about to get real tricky. Nothing would ever be the same again.

'We hide.'

Michael was angry with her.

'What do you mean, you need some space?'

'A time out, that's all.'

'You're breaking up with me?'

'No, not exactly.'

He threw out his arms. His cheeks and neck were bright red, his eyes blazing. 'What the hell's that supposed to mean? Not exactly? We're husband and wife, for God's sake! Doesn't that mean anything to you?'

'Glanna says that we should be free to be whoever we want to be, regardless of vows and traditions.'

'Glanna? Noah's lady friend? What the hell has she got to do with this?'

Alison sipped her coffee. She was trying to remain cool, focussed. 'We've been spending some time talking, that's all. She has an interesting perspective on things.'

'Oh, does she now?'

'Yes, she does. She's very forward-thinking. Very spiritual.'

She could see he was seething, but to his credit he paused and took a deep breath. He calmly and deliberately pulled a chair out from under the table and sat down. 'Look,' he said, attempting to take her hand in his. 'Ali, I love you. I do. All the way and back again. With everything I am. *Everything*. And I know you love me too.'

She decided to remain silent.

'This is just a stupid holiday, with some stupid people that are very different to us. Please don't let their New Age ways and New

Age ideals sway you from who you really are; the wonderful, kind, fun-loving person that is Alison Periwinkle, the woman I married. In two days' time we'll be back home, and all of this will just be a distant memory.'

She let the words hang in the air before answering him. 'I'm not coming home.'

'What?'

'I'm staying here.'

'Staying here? Where? With who?'

'Glanna said I can stay at Excelsior, if I like.'

'Why would you do that?'

'I don't know. Because I want to, I guess.'

He stood. 'This is crazy. I'm going to see Noah. His woman is filling your head with ideas that are nonsense. Pure gibberish.'

'His woman? What do you mean, his woman?' Alison leapt up from the table, no longer trying to remain cool.

'I—' he held a hand to his head. 'I didn't mean it like that. It's just that—'

'You don't get it do you?' she yelled. 'Glanna is no more Noah's woman than I am yours!'

'Ali, look. I know I don't own you, but you're my wife and you belong with me.' He reached into his shirt and pulled out a pendant that hung on a chain around his neck. It was in the shape of a half-heart, and was glistening silver, encrusted with tiny diamonds. 'These pendants we wear. They mean something. My heart is yours, and yours is mine.'

She could feel her own pendant, lying hot against her skin. It was scorching her, like a cigarette burn. She wanted to wrench it away, to toss it out the window.

'Our hearts are joined, Ali. They always will be,' his eyes narrowed. 'Look, I have something going down here. Something big. We can stay a little while longer, a few extra days. I'm meeting someone to help complete a transaction, and when I do…' He smiled sheepishly. 'Well, let's just say we'll be able to afford the

231

house we really want. The *home* we really want. Together. And then the baby, the daughter you've always dreamed about, our little red-headed princess. We can make it happen, we really can.' He went to hold her.

'Get your hands off me!' she screamed. 'Get your *fucking hands* off me!'

Michael pulled away, visibly shocked. She'd never spoken to him like that before. He stood there, just looking at her, wounded.

'I—' he said. 'I don't know what just happened here.'

He sighed wearily, before turning, grabbing his jacket and leaving, slamming the door behind him.

DAY 4
TUESDAY, 2ND AUGUST 2022

When Richard came to, he was in a bed. A strange bed. He was also naked. His head was thumping, and his muscles ached terribly. He sat up, but the room was swimming, so he lay back down.

'I would stay there for a moment if I were you.' It was a woman's voice. 'Just while your body and brain adjust.'

'Who—' he tried to speak but his throat was painfully dry. 'Where am I?'

'Excelsior Lodge,' the woman said. 'We had to bring you here. You saw something that you were never meant to see.'

'The child?' he said. 'That poor deformed child.'

'My child,' the woman said. Her fuzzy outline leaned over him, her dark hair caressing his face and chest. 'One of many I'm afraid. It's my curse. *Our* curse.'

'It smashed straight through the window and ran away. How did it—' His voice sounded terribly hoarse, and the woman, who he now realised was Glanna, held a cup of cool water to his lips. He sipped. It felt good. 'Thank you, but,' he started again, 'how did it do that? I mean, it had literally just been born. It can't possibly—'

'Hush,' she said, touching a finger to his lips. 'All in good time. For now, you just need to rest.'

An image came to Richard: Paz. He'd found him. A meeting in the house; a conversation, followed by a glass of wine, some food, a feeling of nausea. Had he been drugged?

'But Hattie? My children?'

'They're all being taken care of. I can assure you.'

'She'll wonder where I am.'

'And?' Glanna asked. Her face was gradually coming into

233

focus. 'Does that bother you? That she doesn't know where you are? Do you always know where the other is?'

'Well, I guess not, but—'

'Did you know where she was when she was sleeping with another man?'

'How do you know about that?' he scowled. He tried to push himself up once more, but the sharp pain between his temples forced him back down again.

'It's obvious, Richard. It's written all over your face, as clear as Amelia's tattoo. The hurt. It's right there.'

'I've forgiven her.'

Glanna laughed. 'You haven't even told her you know what she did.'

'What good would it do?'

She stood and struck a match. The smell of incense filled the room. 'Your family thrives on lies, Richard. Did you know that?'

'What do you mean?'

'Just that. Lies and deception. You revel in it. It's the one thing that binds you all together.'

Richard shook his head. 'No, I love my family, and they love me.'

'Mm.' Glanna sat on the edge of the bed. 'Family. It's a strange word, isn't it? Do you know the origin of that term?'

He shook his head.

'It's from the latin word, *familia*.'

Richard shrugged. 'And?'

'*Familia*. A much better pronunciation, I always thought. Do you know what it means?'

'The same as family, I guess. Your kin. Your blood.'

Glanna smiled churlishly. 'No, you'd think that, wouldn't you? Yes, based on our modern understanding, that would make sense, but it really doesn't mean that at all. Society's definition of family has changed over the years to suit the new normal, the new narrative. The ancient people did not limit their family to their

234

blood relatives alone. No. Servants, friends, guests, and even lovers were all covered by the same term. *Familia*. A much more inclusive definition, don't you think?'

Richard's head was pounding. 'Where are you going with this?'

'What would you call what you saw, Richard?'

'A monster. A mutation.'

'Yes, rather. I cannot carry normal children, I'm afraid. I'm cursed. Oh, I've tried, believe me. I've tried with many lovers, but every single time I've failed.'

'But your sons? Your daughter?'

Glanna gripped his hand with her own. 'My *familia*, Richard.'

'You mean, they're not your—'

'They belong *with* me.' She stood.

'So,' he said. 'You foster these children.'

'You could say that. In a way, I guess I did, but not by the official means of course.'

He felt his skin turn cold. 'What? You stole them? You stole those poor children?'

'I care for them.'

'The drawings, on the wall of the cottage. The boys, I saw them with their family. I didn't recognise them at first, but now that I think about it, it's them, isn't it? And the girl, Evie? She was there too, with her parents. What did you do to them?'

'We're all thrown together in this life, aren't we? By the fates. By the will of the gods. We're all pawns on this great big complicated chessboard. You didn't choose to come here, any more than the others did before you. We were brought here by higher beings. All of us.' She lit another incense stick and the smoke drifted across her face. 'And we'll all leave the same way.'

Richard swung his legs onto the floor and grabbed his trousers. He needed to get away. This woman was deranged.

'Where are my children?'

'They are safe.'

'I don't believe you.'

'They're special, your children, Richard. The little girl's hair, like cinnamon. Her imagination. She sees things, you know. Special things. And the boy, too. His unique ways. So sensitive, thoughtful, amenable. Petra believes him to have talents, and I happen to agree with him. Evie's really taken with him, too.'

'You leave my children alone.'

'Perhaps,' she shrugged. 'Do you know how to break this curse, Richard? The curse of the children?'

'The curse? I don't understand.'

'The blood of a Kernowyon. A pure breed.'

Richard stood. The ground felt like it was moving. 'You're crazy.'

'The mark. The daisy wheel. You've carried the mark from the moment you arrived. You've always carried it.'

He touched his forehead. He recalled the gathering on the beach, Pascoe tracing the pattern on their heads in invisible ink. And that scent? There was something about Glanna's perfume that was sparking a memory.

'I looked you up,' she continued. 'Your name: Penrose. It makes sense, really. Your parents. Did you know your mother and father both hail from Cornovii, what others now refer to as Cornwall? And their parents too. In fact, when I followed your bloodline, I found no hint of contamination, not a suggestion of cross-breeding. Cornovii bearing children with Cornovii, as far back as the genealogy thread can be traced.'

'I know my family originate from here, but we've been in Kent for so long, I assumed—'

'Never assume, Richard. You are a Kernowyon. Be proud of it.'

He reached for his shirt. 'This is all bullshit,' he said angrily, but he felt uneasy, and somehow unclean.

'Do you remember the early hours of this morning, Richard? After you came here, to this room?'

'I don't remember anything,' he said, but instantly that became a lie too. It was all coming back to him. A body, a woman's body;

236

skin on skin; anticipation, arousal. The smell of incense and that intoxicating perfume. Tongues touching, bodies writhing, frantic breathing, the sound of animalistic fucking. '*You*?' he hissed. He was suddenly distraught. Hattie – what would he tell Hattie?

'The seed of a Kernowyon man. Yes. You gave me your seed, Richard. But that alone is not enough.'

'I'm getting out of here!' he yelled.

'I'm afraid that isn't possible.'

'Well, we'll see about that!'

He took a step towards her, almost stumbling over a hefty object at his feet. He looked down and saw his duffel bag. It was stuffed full of cash. *His* cash.

'My money. How did you—'

'Another lie unravels, Richard. Did you really think we wouldn't know?'

'But... but...' he stammered. 'Tara? Her car, the wreckage? It was you?'

'Well, the boys, really. But, yes, it's true,' she said, laughing. 'That amount of money will do wonders for our little commune. These old properties take a lot of looking after, you know.'

Richard suddenly felt an intense boiling rage. This woman had murdered the mother of his son. She'd drugged and sexually abused him. She'd stolen children from their families, had ruined peoples' lives. His own family were in danger. She had to be stopped.

'You murderous fucking *bitch*!' he yelled, lunging at her.

Suddenly a strong arm grabbed him across his shoulders, pulling him back, a blade on his throat. He went to pull away, but felt a sharp, stinging heat as metal tore through his skin. He looked down and watched as hot, crimson liquid spilled onto his chest and torso. He felt his veins turn cold, his skin become plastic, unreal.

'Blood, Richard,' Glanna said. 'A pure seed, coupled with the pure blood of a Kernowyon. *Your* blood.'

She reached towards him, a bronze cup in her hands. His blood flowed rapidly into the metal vessel, instantly filling it. Glanna lifted it to her lips and drank greedily. Blood dripped from her mouth and ran down her chin. Her teeth and tongue were coated in him. Her image, the enigmatic woman with the silver streaks, dark eyes and blood-red lips, began to twist and fade. He felt himself lift up into the air. He looked down and watched as his assailant allowed his body to slump to the ground. It was Pascoe. Of course it was. He was still holding the bloodied knife. They were mad, this *familia*. Crazy, all of them. He wanted to feel fear for his wife and children, but his ability to experience emotion had all but disintegrated. He was smoke now. He was mist.

*

Hattie slammed her hands repeatedly on the hardwood door.

'Pascoe! Paz! I need to speak to you! Now!'

There was no answer.

'Perhaps they're out,' Rachel offered. She felt exhausted. She and Hattie had scoured the beach. They'd climbed the cliffs. Rachel had even swum out to the rock pool, but there had been no sign of either Sally or Jonno. Eventually they'd decided to try each of the houses, starting with The Night Watchman.

'They're here. I know it,' Hattie said. Her breathing was ragged, her eyes wild. Rachel thought she looked like she was in the middle of a panic attack. She looked sick.

'Let's think about this clearly,' she said, 'and rationally.'

'Oh, fuck rationally,' Hattie replied. 'She's my daughter. I need to find her.' She rounded the side of the house and climbed over the fence.

'Jesus, Hats,' Rachel said. 'You can't just break in.'

'Watch me,' she heard her say.

Rachel took a moment. She was a police officer. This was against everything she stood for. A citizen had a right to the privacy of their own home, didn't they? After a moment of quiet consideration, she decided she had no choice. She vaulted the

238

fence.

'Sally!' Hattie called out. 'Sally-Ann, are you in there?'

'Keep it down, won't you?' Rachel said. 'We're not supposed to be here.'

Hattie pushed herself up against the conservatory doors, her hands cupped over her eyes. 'There's someone in there,' she said.

'What? Are you sure?'

'I'm sure. I saw movement.'

Rachel joined her at the window. She felt eyes on her, the intense feeling of being watched. She leaned forward and waited for her vision to adjust. The room looked empty enough at first glance, but then the reflection in the living room mirror shifted. Hattie was right. Someone really was in there.

'Mr Tregeagle! Katharine!' she yelled. 'We need to speak with you urgently! It's about Sally!'

A hand on the door, the sound of a latch opening.

'What the hell is going on out here?'

'Katharine,' Hattie said. 'Thank God. Sally, have you seen my Sally?' Hattie pushed past her.

Rachel stood there on the step. Why hadn't this woman answered the door? Hattie had been knocking pretty loudly. Sure, she looked like a primary school teacher with her thin framed spectacles, mousey brown hair and a pear-shaped physique, but was there more to it than that? Was this woman what she seemed? Could anyone around here be trusted?

'Can I help you with something, my dear?'

'What?'

'You're looking at me like you might look at an interesting artefact in a museum.'

'Oh, really?' Rachel said, embarrassed. 'I'm sorry. I'm just worried about Sally, that's all.'

'Of course,' Katharine said. 'I understand. Well, as your friend has already made herself at home, you may as well come in.'

Rachel nodded and entered the conservatory. It was decorated

239

with thick bunches of loosely tied lavender, a hessian rug on the floor and large horns protruding from the apex overhead. Two statues were located either side of the rug. One creature sat cross-legged, its arms open, mouth grotesquely wide. The other statue was a green coloured stone depiction of a tree-like creature. The sliding door to the living room was open. Hattie was inside.

'What are you doing here?' Hattie exclaimed.

Rachel poked her head through the doorway.

'What's up?' She caught a gasp in her throat. Bea was in there. She was sitting with her legs tucked under her on a two-seater sofa and looking decidedly uncomfortable. 'Bea?' Rachel said. 'What—'

'Katharine invited me round for coffee, didn't you, Katharine?'

'That I did,' the older woman said, smiling. 'I took the opportunity to give Beatrice here the guided tour.'

'Of the house?' Rachel said. 'Why would you want a guided tour—'

'Oh, Rachel,' Bea said. 'It's like you told me. We don't have to be glued to each other every second of every day, now do we?'

Rachel blushed. She had said that, but only to cover her own tracks.

'We were hammering on the door for ages,' Hattie said. 'You didn't hear us?'

'We had music playing,' Katharine answered. 'And my hearing isn't as good as it once was, I'm afraid.'

Rachel didn't know what to think. Bea? Round here with Katharine? It didn't make any sense.

'Have either of you seen Sally?' Hattie asked. She was starting to look increasingly unwell. 'Bea. Do you hear me? We've lost Sally.'

'Jesus,' Bea said, standing. 'When did you last see her?'

'This morning, early.'

'And Richard? Could she be with him?' Bea grabbed her shoes from the hallway.

'I don't know,' Hattie sobbed. Rachel went to her. 'I don't know where he is, either. Or Jonno.'

'I'm sure they're fine. They're probably all out for a lovely walk somewhere,' Katharine said, smiling.

Hattie turned to her. 'It's you people!' she screamed. 'You, Glanna, Noah! You and your bizarre backwoods ways!' She grabbed Katharine by the shoulders. 'Since we arrived in this hell-hole, we've been plagued by bad luck and weird goings on. It's you, isn't it?' she yelled. 'It's all of you! You're all involved! I don't know why, or what you mean to achieve, but it seems to me that you're trying to take everything we have! Everything we love!' Hattie started to shake. 'Now, unless you answer me this instant, I'll be going straight to the police. Don't dare think I won't. What the hell have you done with my family?'

'What are you insinuating?'

'Hattie,' Rachel interjected. 'Perhaps we should just leave—'

'We're not going anywhere until this woman tells us what she's done with my daughter!'

Katharine pointed to the front door. 'I suggest you get out of my house. Now!'

'Katharine,' Bea said, trying to diffuse the situation. 'My sister's just distressed, that's all. She doesn't mean anything by—'

'Yes I do!' Hattie screamed. 'I mean *every damn word*!' She slammed her hands on the coffee table.

'Mummy.'

The four of them spun their heads towards the front door. Pascoe was standing in the hallway, Petra at his side. The girl, Evie, was standing beside Jonno. They were holding hands. The teenage boy looked sheepish, dazed. Sally emerged from between them.

'Bunny,' Hattie said, tears suddenly flowing. 'Thank God. My darling, you scared us. Where have you been?'

'Don't worry, Mummy,' Sally said.

'But I was worried, darling. I was so, so worried. Scared too.'

'There's no need to be scared,' Sally said, pushing past the others. 'He's coming to protect us.'

'Who is, baby?' Hattie asked, taking her daughter by the hand. 'Who's coming to protect us?'

'The man with the horns, silly,' Sally replied. 'He'll be here soon, and then we'll all be safe.' She grinned. 'You'll see.'

*

Eli watched from the trees as Aaron emerged from Excelsior. He had Sweet Mother with him, and Noah too. His brother looked mad, madder than Eli had ever seen him before. He knew if Noah got hold of him, he would pull him apart as easily as a stewed rabbit. The three of them entered the barn. Eli knew they would be rummaging through his things, but he didn't care. He had the only thing he needed: the shiny thing. He wore it around his neck and was comforted by its weight. The Red Man had given it to him, even though he hadn't really done what he'd asked him to do. The Terrible Babies had killed Kid-Bastard Freddie, not him. The Red Man wanted them all punished: Freddie, Aaron, and Evie too.

'I'm going to finish the job,' Eli said, fingering the pendant around his neck. 'For you. I owe it to you.'

The Red Man sat next to him and nodded, his head now little more than a bare skull, with patches of blackened skin and wispy hair clinging to yellow bone. He couldn't go home, not yet. Not until the job was done.

Eli gripped the handle of the knife and glanced over his shoulder. The Terrible Baby with the tuft of yellow hair was hunched behind him, the newest youngling suckling on her. The others were crouched farther back. She grinned at Eli. It wasn't their fault, what happened to the Red Man. Evie had made them do it. Evie could make them do all sorts of things, but right now they were with him. Eli thought they would fight to the death if needed. Everything had to die, after all.

242

*

Hattie carried Sally indoors. Rachel and the others followed close behind.

'Where the hell is your father?'

'I don't know,' Jonno said. 'We can't leave, anyway.'

'Yes, we can,' Hattie hissed. 'And we will.'

'And the car?' Bea asked. 'What are we supposed to do without a car?'

'I'll call a cab if I have to. We're getting the hell out of here. Things are getting out of hand.'

'I'm not leaving!' Jonno yelled, and stomped sulkily upstairs.

'Yes you are!' Hattie hollered after him. 'Bea, go pack your things.'

'We can't leave without Richard, Hattie,' Bea said. 'He's your husband. Aren't you even worried about him?'

'He does this. After a row like we had, it's not unusual,' Hattie replied. 'He'll turn up eventually.'

'Jesus Christ,' Bea exclaimed. 'You two have the weirdest relationship, you know that, right?'

'Whatever,' Hattie said, before heading up to the bedroom. 'Just get packed.'

As a semblance of silence resumed, Rachel let out a long breath. 'Phew. What a welcome to the family.'

'Sorry,' Bea said. 'For all of this. For everything. It must be so much for you to take in.'

'Yeah,' Rachel said, smiling. 'It can be a little overwhelming, that's for sure.' She delicately switched topics. 'What was that? That thing back there, with you and Katharine?'

'What do you mean?'

'You don't even know the woman.'

Bea turned away. 'She was nice enough to ask me over.'

'Why would she do that?'

'Why wouldn't she?'

243

Rachel considered her next question. 'Is there something you're not telling me, Bea?'

Bea opened the refrigerator door and started removing things, throwing them into a large bag. 'Don't be silly. I tell you everything.'

Rachel went to her, touched her arm. 'You can, you know. If there's something you need to offload, I'm here for you. Always.'

'I know that.' Milk went into the bag, then butter, followed by a huge slab of cheese.

'I mean it.'

'I get it.' Chicken slices, yoghurt, salad.

'Bea!'

'What?'

'I love you.'

Bea stopped then. She dropped the bag and lowered her head, her shoulders slumped forwards. Eventually she turned to Rachel. Her face was pink, her eyes moist. 'I can't.'

'What do you mean, you can't?'

'It's all gone so wrong.'

'What has?' Rachel held her close. 'Tell me. What is it? What's gone wrong, baby?'

Bea opened her mouth to speak, but the moment was interrupted by a loud rapping on the front door. They both ignored it, but the rapping grew louder.

'Just leave it,' Rachel said, but she knew the moment had passed.

'No, I'll get it,' Bea said. 'You go and take a shower. I'll deal with whoever this is, and then I'll sort out my emotional wrecking ball of a sister.'

Rachel smiled and nodded. 'Okay, if you're sure.' She reluctantly headed to the bathroom. She heard the front door open behind her, followed by the sound of Bea's voice.

'Hello, do I know you?'

'Hello there,' a man said in a coarse East London accent. 'The name's Terry. Terry Deville.'

*

Freddie was dead, killed by Eli and the others. Eli, the cripple. Evie hadn't thought he had it in him. She hadn't even suspected he'd been plotting against them, which was a failing on her part. However, as unlikely it was, the fact remained that if he was capable of taking out his anger on Freddie, he was more than capable of coming after her. Lord knows, he had the motive. She hadn't exactly been a loving, caring stepsister. He'd always been a means to an end for her; a tool she could use as she pleased. She'd been cruel and mean to him. She didn't regret it. These were just the facts. If Eli had truly flipped, then he was coming after her. There was no getting away from that.

'So, what do we do?' Aaron asked.

'What do you mean, *we*?' she replied, an eyebrow raised.

'He killed our brother, Evie. He could have killed me. We can't let that slide.'

'You both go and find him,' their mother said. 'You bring him here to me. I will deal with him.'

'I'll tear him limb from limb,' Noah said, raging. Evie stifled a laugh. Noah couldn't pull the wings off a moth.

'You'll do no such thing,' their mother scowled. 'He's my son, my blood. He's not your problem to solve.'

Aaron suddenly looked dumbfounded. Evie stifled her laughter a second time. The poor boy still didn't know anything, the imbecile.

'Your son?' Aaron asked, incredulous. He glanced at Noah. 'No, Mother, you're mistaken. He's Noah's brother, remember? The cripple's got nothing to do with us.'

'This is all inconsequential, Aaron,' their mother said, flapping an arm. 'Let's not use up precious seconds discussing it.'

245

'But—' Aaron tried to continue.

'I want him back *here*!' their mother yelled. 'I want him at Excelsior, and I want him in one *piece*! Do you hear me?'

Aaron nodded a reluctant agreement. Evie chose to look down at the ground. She had her own plans, and it certainly didn't involve the cripple walking back to Excelsior. It didn't involve him making it back at all.

'Good, now go, the pair of you. There's little time to waste.'

With the discussion ended, the pair of them trudged off along the path. After they'd made it someway into the forest, Evie stopped and turned to her brother.

'How old do you think Eli is?' she asked.

'I don't know. Thirteen, fourteen. I can't remember ever celebrating his birthday.'

'He's twenty-five, you idiot.'

Aaron stopped. 'What? No. That can't be right.'

'Mother had him when she was in her twenties.' Evie shook her head. 'We weren't even born yet.'

'But,' Aaron looked back towards the house, 'what about Noah?'

'Noah's got nothing to do with him. He's got nothing to do with any of us. He's just Mother's man friend. They're not even married, and she's certainly not faithful to him.'

Aaron took out his cigarettes, lit one.

'Holy shit,' he said. 'So, who's Eli's dad?'

'Oh, Aaron, you really don't know anything do you? The world must be such a wonderful, bright, shiny place to you. Where do you even think those monsters come from, the things that killed Freddie?'

'They live out here in the forest. They're woodland people, piskies, just like the ones in the stories that Mother used to read to us at bedtime. The scary stories.'

Evie shook her head and chuckled. She plucked the smouldering cigarette from her brother's mouth and took a drag.

She exhaled, stubbed the fag out on the sole of her boot and tossed it. 'Idiot,' she said, before turning away. 'Anyway, I'll see you later, dickhead.'

'Where are you going?' he asked. 'Evie, we're supposed to be doing this together.'

'You do what you do,' she said, walking into descending darkness. 'And I'll do what I do.'

*

'You must have got your wires crossed, Mr—' Hattie said to the man with the white hair and rugby player's nose. Bea had called Hattie to the door after the man had enquired after Richard. Hattie thought he looked familiar but couldn't quite place him.

'Deville. And I really don't think I have, Mrs Penrose. Your husband, Richard?'

'Yes,' Hattie confirmed. She felt herself forcing a smile.

'He met with my wife just yesterday, not half an hour prior to the crash that killed her.'

'That's nonsense,' Hattie said. 'Utter nonsense. He's been here with us this whole time, hasn't he, Bea? He simply couldn't have met with anybody without us knowing.'

'Her phone records suggest otherwise.'

'Well,' Hattie said, folding her arms. 'I'd certainly like to take a look at those when you have them to hand.'

'I'm sure that can be arranged,' he said. 'And where is he now, Mrs Penrose? Your husband, that is.' The man was persistent, she gave him that. 'Can I speak with him at least? Ask him a few questions?

Hattie huffed. 'I'm afraid he's out and won't be back for the rest of the day.' She had no idea where he was, of course, but that was beside the point.

'Mm,' he murmured, pursing his lips. 'Well, that is unfortunate. Look, I'll be staying nearby overnight, at a place called

247

Mevagissey. The pub's The Lookout. Do you know it?'

Hattie nodded. She didn't believe in coincidences, but if they did exist, there was a humdinger right there.

'I've heard of the place,' she replied.

'Well, that's where I'll be. Can you do me a favour? When he gets back from wherever he is, will you give him this?' The man thumbed a business card from his wallet and held it out to her. *Deville's Curiosities and Antiquities.* 'Don't worry about explaining who I am,' he said, barely concealing a sneer. 'We know each other.'

'I'm sorry for your loss,' Hattie said and closed the door.

Bea went to her. 'You know who that was, don't you, sis?'

Hattie nodded. She knew only too well.

'And you know who his wife is?' She raised a hand to her open mouth. '*Was.*'

Hattie nodded again. She leaned back against the doorframe and let out a long breath. There were only two things she didn't know about this horrible situation. One was why her husband chose to secretly meet his ex in the middle of the countryside, and the other was where the hell he was this very second?

*

Eli watched as Kid-Bastard Aaron stepped out into the clearing. He was holding a knife. Eli didn't care. He was holding his own. He placed it on the ground and grabbed the shiny thing. He held it up and let the moonlight reflect off its silver surface. A brilliant flare of white light shimmied across Aaron's face. He flinched.

'Is that you, cripple? You out there?' he called.

Eli crouched down behind the fallen tree. He was in no hurry.

'Mother wants you taken back in one piece, but that don't mean I can't hurt you a little in the process,' he said. 'And, oh, I do mean to hurt you. You better believe that, you murdering little shit!'

'I didn't kill Freddie!' Eli yelled.

248

'Oh, it is you out there,' Aaron said. 'I thought so.'

'I didn't do it!' Eli repeated.

'No, but you were there,' Aaron said. 'And you did nothing to stop it.'

Eli unfolded the knife. 'And neither did you. He was your brother.'

Aaron paused. 'Yeah, I guess you're right. But here's the thing,' he said. 'Turns out he was your brother too.'

Eli glared at the blade. 'What?'

'Yep,' Aaron chuckled. 'That was news to me as well. Unwanted news. You're older than you look, cripple. Older than you act, too. Mother's your mother, the same way she's my mother, and Evie's.' Aaron's voice sounded like it was getting a little closer. 'And Freddie's, too, of course. You killed your own brother, cripple. You killed your own flesh and blood.'

Eli was confused. Sweet Mother was his real mother? She was truly his? Could that be right? That meant that Noah wasn't his brother at all, and it also meant he hadn't been thrown down the stairs by the bad people; that he hadn't been beaten and battered until his spine cracked, his hand shattered into a million pieces and his head squeezed into this horrible seed-like shape. It meant he'd just been born this way, all twisted and broken like an old unwanted toy. Why would Sweet Mother lie to him all these years? Why not just tell him the truth? Why not let him stay in the big house, sleep in his own room, sit at his own seat at the dinner table, and have his own place at school? Why not let him celebrate birthdays, enjoy Christmas, have holidays? All of them, together, as a family. Unless, of course, she was ashamed of him, ashamed of the way he looked, of the way he acted; ashamed of the way he spoke, of the clothes he wore. Ashamed of him. *Ashamed*.

'You didn't know, cripple, did you? You had no idea. And now you don't know what to do with that information. It throws everything you thought you knew about yourself up in the air, doesn't it? Now you have to piece your life back together again, bit

249

by bit, piece by broken piece.' Aaron was laughing. 'Oh, it sucks to be you, doesn't it? Sucks to be Eli the cripple, the kid with the funny eyes, and the sticky-out purple vein and the little, useless T-rex hand.' He was revelling in it now. 'Oh, dude. Why don't you just do us all a favour and kill yourself already?'

Eli could feel the blood burning in his veins. The thick muscles in his arms flexed. They were all liars. All of them: Noah, Aaron, Freddie and Evie. Even Sweet Mother. *Especially* Sweet Mother. They'd been tricking him, all this time. Laughing at him, humiliating him. He pulled the blade across the palm of his good hand and relished the pain. He sucked at his own blood and let the salty liquid coat his lips.

'I hate you all,' he said.

'Found you.' A voice from above, a breath on his face. He looked up and saw Kid-Bastard Aaron glaring down at him. Eli gasped as Aaron gripped his throat with strong, clawing fingers. 'You're coming with me, you little shit!'

Eli lashed out with the knife in panic and cut a long gaping wound across Kid-Bastard Aaron's forearm. He let go.

'Ow!' Aaron yelled. 'You're gonna pay for that!'

Eli jumped up and ran north through the densest part of the forest.

'You're not getting away that easily, cripple!' Aaron yelled. 'You can't outrun me!'

Eli bounded over an old stone wall, splashed through a bubbling stream, and swung with one hand from a long loping branch and out into another clearing. He heard Aaron's boots pounding on the floor behind him and knew there was only a matter of feet between them. He sprinted across the open space and plummeted through a wall of nettles and brambles, the sharp thorns clawing at his face and arms. Beyond, there lay another dense area of woodland. Eli dodged from side to side, narrowly avoiding trees and branches, rocks and boulders. The ground was hard from the long hot summer, and Eli's sandals were worn and tatty, but he kept his footing, refusing to let his brother outpace him.

'I've almost caught up with you, Eli. And when I do, I'm gonna kick the living, breathing shit out of you!'

Eli felt Kid-Bastard Aaron's hand swish through the air, just inches from his shoulders. He knew he didn't have much time. He needed to make it to the spot. The spot they'd all agreed upon.

'Here I come, cripple! Here I come! Coming to hurt you! I'm gonna hurt you *so bad*!'

Eli leapt into the air at the last second, avoiding the hole that he and the others had carefully covered with fallen branches and leaves. Aaron had no such luck. Eli turned just in time to see his brother's eyes fly open in bewilderment as the ground beneath him gave way, his body plunging more than ten feet into the freshly dug pit. There was a sickening thud as Aaron's spine hit hard earth and his head crunched against stone.

'What the fuck?' Aaron said, but Eli could see he was hurt.

The Terrible Babies came out from the shadows and surrounded the hole. They peered in at Kid-Bastard Aaron, their teeth chattering.

'What are you doing, Eli?' Aaron said, his voice slurred.

'I'm finishing the job,' Eli said.

'What? What job?'

Eli glanced up at the Red Man and smiled. He was barely visible out there in the shadows, but Eli knew he was watching them. He turned to his little friends. They held out their hands, which were filled with hard flint and stone.

'Eli, you can't do this,' Aaron pleaded. 'I'm your brother. Your blood. We're family!'

Eli felt his words penetrate him like hot needles. All the years of denial. All the taunting, the humiliating, the torturing. He didn't hesitate. He turned and gave the signal. Within an instant, the rocks rained down. Sharp flint smashed into Kid-Bastard Aaron's skull, hard stone split his nose, jagged rock shattered his teeth, and large, fist-sized pebbles pummelled his broken body. The sound of

251

Aaron's screams echoed across the clifftops.

Half a mile away, in the rusted, burned-out cockpit of a fallen World War Two Hurricane, their sister Evie sat back in her chair and smiled.

*

'It's night-time, Hattie. Let's just wait until morning,' Bea said. 'By then, Richard could be home, and we might even have a way to get the tyres on the car replaced.'

The three of them were huddled in the living room and sharing a bottle of red wine. Sally was asleep on the sofa, and Jonno was in his room, listening to music. Aside from Richard being missing, the scene was almost normal.

'I guess,' Hattie sighed. 'I guess we could do that.'

Rachel thought she looked exhausted, sick too. In fact, she hadn't looked well all day. Her husband was AWOL, and her young daughter and stepson had spent most of the day out there in the wilderness. How would she have behaved in such a situation? She didn't really know. That world, the world that involved marriage and mortgages and kids and responsibility, seemed like such a long way off. How could she be expected to truly understand?

'Well, in that case,' Bea said, 'I'm going up. You coming, hun?'

Rachel nodded. 'Sure.'

'And don't worry, Hats,' Bea said to her sister. 'He'll be back in the morning, I know he will. He's a good man.'

'Yeah,' Hattie said. 'I'm sure you're right.'

'And that thing with Terry,' Bea kissed Hattie on the cheek. 'It's probably just one big misunderstanding.'

Hattie shook her head. 'How are we going to break the news to Jonno?'

'We'll do it later,' Bea replied. 'When Richard's home. It needs to come from him.'

'That poor boy,' Rachel said. 'That poor, poor boy.'

'We'll take care of him,' Bea said. 'We all will, just like we always have.'

Hattie lay back on the sofa. Rachel expected to find both her and Sally there in the morning. She didn't look like she had the appetite, or the energy, to climb the stairs.

When she and Bea lay down together in bed, Bea turned to her.

'That thing I said earlier, about everything going wrong.'

'Yes?' Rachel replied, hopeful.

'It was nothing, I was just being silly. This place, this situation, it just got the better of me.'

'Okay, if you're sure.'

'I'm sure.'

'All right, but you know, if you're not—'

'I know.'

'That's good. That's really good.' Rachel felt the disappointment seep into her. What else could she do? 'Night then.'

'Night, baby.'

When the lights went out, and Bea slipped into a deep, soundless sleep, Rachel lay there thinking. She thought about Tara and Terry Deville. She thought about Richard's disappearance. She thought about Bea's unexplained visit to The Night Watchman and her emotional outburst. She thought about Sally and the mysterious horned man.

When she eventually drifted off into her own fitful sleep, she dreamed of Tommy. She was running with him down a long green corridor. They were being chased by a tangerine coloured Lamborghini with Glanna's two boys at the wheel. Their throats were cut, and daisy wheels had been drawn on their foreheads in their own blood. A large stag charged towards them at full speed. Bea was riding side-saddle on its back, a holdall full of money slung over her shoulder. Before Rachel had a chance to react, Bea pulled a handgun and shot Tommy in the head. As his body fell, his daughters appeared at his side. They were laughing: laughing at Tammy Lush, guffawing at Rachel Woodley, rolling in the aisles at

Beth McKinley. The girls suddenly morphed into her father, except this version of him had maggots in his eyes and slugs in his mouth. 'Stop crying!' he yelled. 'You're not supposed to cry! You never cry!' He reached for Beth, grabbed her by her shoulders. His hands suddenly became branches, his face a mass of leaves, twigs and splintered bark. 'You're my baby, Beth!' he screamed, as pulpy wood filled his mouth. 'You're my Bethy! My little Bethy Big Balls!' His eyes became hard knots, his mouth a tangled bird's nest. He was laughing now too.

'Triple B! Triple B! Triple B!'

ALISON AND MICHAEL
JULY 2022

Michael confronted them.

'What the hell are you peddling to my wife?'

Noah looked taken aback. Glanna, on the other hand, appeared nonplussed, which only served to fuel Michael's anger.

'She's not your property, Michael,' she said. 'She can choose who she wants to be. You must know that.'

'I know that she was an entirely different person until you got your claws into her,' he hissed. He could feel his heart pounding.

'How dare you speak to my partner like that,' Noah growled, but it sounded unconvincing. 'She's just trying to be a friend to Alison.'

'Some friend,' Michael said. 'We were happily married. Now she's talking about needing a timeout.'

'Well, then you must allow her that freedom,' Glanna said. 'Give her some space. She deserves that much, doesn't she?'

'Fuck you,' Michael said, spitting. 'Fuck you and your New Age drivel. I came here for a relaxing holiday, not a lecture on the rights and wrongs of my marriage. If you two aren't happy, break up. Don't stain our relationship with your own dissatisfaction, your boredom!' He jabbed a finger at Glanna. 'I bet you're fucking around, aren't you?' And then at Noah. 'And I bet you're letting her do it, too.'

Noah glared down at his feet.

'I knew it! Jesus, you're a couple of hippy polygamists who think you can spread your free love, free-the-mind, free-the-body bullshit on anyone who dares to stay here. Well, we're not like that. *I'm* not like that!'

'I think you have us all wrong, Michael,' Glanna said, moving towards him. 'I believe we may have our wires crossed, and I'd dearly like to correct that.' She touched his arm.

'Get your hands off me,' he said, brushing Glanna's hand away. 'We're leaving in the morning, and we won't be giving you a review on Trip Adviser, I can tell you that for nothing. Noah,' Michael shot him the finger. 'Let's delete each other's numbers. You've changed, and not in a good way.'

As he turned, he spotted the girl in black: Evelyn. She'd been standing behind him all this time. As he walked past, her eyes followed him. He turned to her.

'What the fuck are you looking at?'

She shrugged.

This was his drop the mic moment, so he stomped off, leaving the family in his wake.

He decided to take a walk through the woods and head down towards the beach. He needed to cool off, and Alison had made it clear to him in no uncertain terms that she needed time to herself. What was he going to do, force himself back into the house?

The night was warm but overcast, and visibility was limited at best. Michael could just about make out the cream-coloured gravel of the path. The trees either side were gnarly black fingers, the ocean a carpet of ebony.

Who did Glanna think she was, with her words of fake wisdom and soundbite feminism? And Noah, too? He used to be so cool, so much fun. They used to get high together and chat up girls, talk for hours about the careers they were planning and how much money they were going to make. Never in a million years did Michael ever picture Noah living out here in the sticks, chained to a New Age hippy who shagged around and spouted theological bullshit. It was ludicrous, ridiculous. If it wasn't so tragic, it would be funny.

He thought about the trip. What had he been thinking, dragging them all the way down there? Well, that one was easy. He'd been thinking about the Belvedere Saints. He'd been thinking about the exchange. He'd been thinking about the ten million in transaction fees he'd pocket after the whole thing went down. And it *was* going to go down, despite the drama and the arguments. Noah and his flower power bitch could just suck on it, for all he cared. Nothing was going to come between him and his meeting with the mysterious Mr Quin.

Suddenly, there was a rustling in the bushes and dozens of little red lights appeared along the edge of the path. He stopped. The girl was standing not twenty feet in front of him. She was just a shadowy outline, but it was her all right. How the hell had she managed to get around him without being seen?

'Hello there. Hi,' he said. 'It's Evelyn, er, Evie, isn't it?'

The girl didn't speak. She didn't even move.

'Look, sorry about what went down back there, with your mum and Noah. We just had a little disagreement, that's all. It was nothing really. I'm sure it'll all blow over by the morning.'

There was the sound of a child's laughter from somewhere beyond the treeline. The red lights started to jitter and scramble.

'I'll walk you back if you like. It's dark and you really shouldn't be out here on your own. It's late.'

Tiny footsteps, twigs snapping, high-pitched voices yammering.

'You can come back to the cottage. My wife will make you some hot chocolate if you want some?' he said, trying to sound parental. His voice seemed to have lost its air of authority, which annoyed him.

A pebble suddenly hit him in the side of the head, another in the mouth.

'Hey! What the hell's going on here?'

More laughter, more rustling, more pebbles.

The girl held out her arms. Despite the darkness, he sensed she was smiling.

'What are you doing?' he asked, but still she offered no response. 'I'm going back. This is crazy.'

There was a loud snap as the girl clicked her fingers, and in an instant, dozens of tiny squirming bodies descended upon him. He yelled as he was driven to the ground. He felt skin being peeled from flesh, flesh being peeled from bone. His earlobes were wrenched away, his nose bitten off, his cheeks splayed open by savage, unyielding claws. Blood filled his mouth and lungs. A sizzling pain rippled through his body. It felt like burning electricity. He knew there was no way out. As the lights began to fade, he thought only of Alison. She was back there in that creaky damp-ridden cottage, and she was alone. He wanted to be there with her. They'd been meant for each other. He still believed that, despite everything that had happened. They would have had a beautiful future together, had beautiful red-headed children. He felt sadness, remorse, desolation, but he clung to his rage. They would pay for this, these people. He didn't know how, he didn't know when, but they would pay. Even if he had to make a deal with the devil himself...

Save us.

Save us.

Please, save us.

Hattie sat up sharply. Lingering voices beckoned to her from the dark, and she had the sensation of something looming close by, an unwavering certainty that she was being watched.

It took a moment for her to recognise her surroundings. A small TV, a latticed window, curtains open, a coffee table with three empty wine glasses. She glanced at the other sofa. Sally was curled up in a ball with her comfort blanket pulled up around her shoulders.

Hattie peered through the open door to the hallway. The corridor was dark, but the orange light from the digital microwave in the kitchen illuminated a shadowy form. A human form. Tall, slender, head tilted to the side. It reached out an arm and beckoned her forwards.

Follow me, Harriet. Come with me. I have something to show you.

Hattie found herself standing and moving slowly towards the unseen thing in the darkness. Her stomach hurt and her skin felt like it was on fire, but she couldn't help herself. She wanted to scoop Sally up in her arms, climb through the living room window, and run with the wind at her back and the moonlight on her face.

She entered the hallway which glowed with a green-blue hue. She gazed at the crayon drawing of her family. The six of them together, except now Richard's face had been erased. She felt an emotional pull. Was it sorrow? In the background of the picture the

259

giant shadow had grown bigger, much bigger. It rose from the ocean and hung in the sky like a monstrous storm cloud. It had ghostly arms that were outstretched and grasping, and a long beastlike head with twisted horns that spanned the horizon.

She spied another familiar face in one of the other pictures too. The faint outline of a colourful lily on an ashen cheek. She knew that face, but she couldn't remember why. The features were barely visible, the lily smeared and blotted.

The silhouette in the hallway moved silently. It opened the front door and stepped out onto the driveway. Hattie followed. There was no moon tonight; no light. Just the sound of footsteps on gravel and crickets in the trees. Hattie felt the hot sting of terror building in her lungs and throat, a bilious nausea in her stomach.

The thing was just up ahead. A dark robe, slender arms and long, flowing hair. It crossed the common as if it were floating, drifting. Hattie could feel the damp grass between her toes, the cool night breeze on her face. This was like no nightmare she'd ever experienced before.

We killed the rat, Harriet. Just like you asked.

The ash tree loomed ominous ahead, mighty limbs reaching across No Man's Land with sharp, impenetrable fingers that flexed and clawed. The silhouette moved beneath these long ensnaring branches and turned to face her. The moon peeked out from between the clouds, and the milky light caught the thing's face. Hattie gasped. It was Glanna, and it was the old lady, Dolly, too, except this must have been the Dolly from many years ago, not the old, infirm woman who sat in her wheelchair all day long and rambled nonsensically. The thing's face flitted and shifted: at once Glanna with her long slender nose and narrow eyes, and then Dolly, with her pointed chin and her high cheekbones. The Dolly-Glanna thing smiled through blackened teeth. It licked its dry lips, tilted its head upwards, and raised a long spindly arm towards the tree's canopy.

Hattie's view was impaired by the heavy foliage, and so she

moved closer. She could hear creaking and groaning, like the sound of a child's swing. Standing this close to the Dolly-Glanna thing, she could smell its scent. It was a sickening mixture of incense, musty perfume and blood. It made her want to throw up. She followed the line traced by its arm. There was something hanging, not five feet above them. She could make out light-brown moccasins, a cream-coloured smock, a slight frame, lank silver hair, and a pretty tattooed face. Hattie cried out. It was Amelia. The face from the picture. She swung back and forth, a thick rope tied around her neck, her tongue black and lifeless, hanging limply from split purple lips.

No humane traps, Harriet. Not for this giant rat. But there's more. There's so many more.

Hattie heard herself sobbing. She tried to grab the Dolly-Glanna thing, but it crumbled beneath her fingers like the smouldering embers of a fire. She fell to the floor as the ash filled her throat and lungs, and the soft earth pulled her downwards. She felt herself sinking into a cool, damp quicksand of mulch and clay. She couldn't breathe, she couldn't think. She was helpless.

Kill the rats! Kill the rats! Kill the…

*

What was that smell? The cottage smelled like faeces mixed with festering food waste.

'That's disgusting,' Bea said, opening a window. 'Jesus,' she held a hand to her nose. 'Oh, God no! If anything, that's worse.'

Rachel was only half awake. Her sleep had been filled with images of her dead father, and of Tommy being repeatedly killed.

'Close the window, Bea. I'm sleeping here.'

'Can't you smell it?' Bea asked. 'Really? Are you trying to tell me you can't smell that? Are your nostrils dead or something? It smells so bad. It's like someone's smeared diarrhoea all over the walls.'

261

'I got it,' Rachel said, but she was in no mood for toilet conversation. 'Look, I'm tired, and it's only—' she held her phone up to her face, 'Jeez, It's only eight thirty in the morning. We're on holiday for God's sake. Can't we have a lie-in at least once?'

'I guess,' Bea said. 'But we've got to do something about that smell first.'

Rachel sat up, defeated. Yes, the smell was gross, but she had far more important things on her mind, like the conversation they'd started last night, for example. She shook herself awake.

'Bea, I have to talk to you.'

Bea sat down on the edge of the bed.

'Look, I know you said it was nothing,' Rachel continued, 'but I really need to know whether you're involved in anything bad here. Something that maybe you wished you hadn't started, or that you wish you could get out of.'

Bea's eyes narrowed, her lip curled. 'What the hell are you talking about? Are you joking with me?'

'No, Bea,' Rachel said. 'No, I'm not. I'm serious. I'm deadly serious. You have to be totally, no bullshit, honest with me. I mean it.'

'I've never bullshitted you,' Bea said, offended. 'I am totally, *totally* honest with you, always.'

'That's not true, is it?'

'Oh, really? Is that where this conversation is going? Are you ever really, totally honest with me? Could you put your hand on your heart and say that? Really? I mean, take that incident the other day, for example. Telling me you needed to sleep off a hangover, and then disappearing for hours. And then when I asked about it,' Bea stood, 'woah! You would have thought I'd just called you a thief or something. You wouldn't even give me a half-arsed explanation. Nothing!' Bea said, red-faced. 'You gave me nothing!'

'Then I didn't lie,' Rachel muttered, whispering.

'What?'

'You said I gave you nothing, which theoretically means I didn't lie.' She couldn't meet Bea's gaze. She knew her answer was pathetic. Of course she'd lied. Even her name was a lie.

'Theoretically?' Bea threw out her arms. 'Theoretically? That's your answer, is it? Well, if that's what you call honesty, Rachel, then I'm out.' She opened the door. 'I'm so *out*!'

'Bea, wait!'

The door slammed shut, followed by loud footsteps and another groan of hinges. There was a loud crash as the front door closed. Rachel rubbed furiously at her eyes. She cursed her crap way with words. There she was, supposedly the big-shot undercover police officer, and yet when it had been time for her to tactfully ask the detailed questions, she'd turned into Little Miss Pedantic.

'Shit,' she said. 'Shit, shit, *shit*.'

How could she have got it so wrong with Bea? She was just clutching at straws, wasn't she? She had nothing. No leads, no clues, and a series of disastrous dead ends. This whole field trip was just one long ridiculous mistake. The only thing she could have possibly salvaged from it, the one and only thing that would have made the whole job even remotely worthwhile, was her relationship with Bea. And now it looked like she'd blown that too.

'Great job, Rachel,' she mumbled to herself. 'Great job.'

She got out of bed and threw on a pair of shorts and a grey top. She glanced at herself in the mirror. Her hair was almost passable, her face probably not. She couldn't be bothered to shower. She couldn't be bothered, full stop.

'Ugh,' she grunted, holding a finger to her nose. Now that the discussion with Bea was over, her senses were entirely distracted by that godawful smell. She went to the window. Bea was right, it was worse over there. She threw on her sandals, headed downstairs and stepped out onto the driveway. There was a noise like a pump whirring. She remembered something Glanna had said on their first day. Something about the cesspit, about not putting anything except toilet paper down the loo. "The smell can be downright repugnant",

263

she'd said. *Well*, Rachel thought, *as weird as the witchy woman was, she was on the money about that.* It was rotten. Had Jonno thrown something down the loo without thinking? That was where she'd place her bet: on the teenager with the attitude.

She heard raised voices coming from somewhere along the track that curved to her right. It snaked between the barns at the rear of Excelsior. Rachel thought the whirring noise was coming from that direction, too. Had Bea marched over to the main house? Was she planning on giving the crazy family with the stinking cesspit a piece of her mind? In the mood she was in, that was likely to turn ugly. Rachel didn't want that. She didn't want Bea ending up in a stupid senseless row, just because she'd managed to annoy her by getting everything so damn wrong.

She opened the gate. She had to stop her.

*

Eli watched as Kid-Bastard Evie entered the cafeteria at Dozmary Point. He knew she'd be headed this way, especially after the way it had finished up with Kid-Bastard Aaron. Eli had been pleased. The whole thing had gone exactly the way he'd expected it to.

The lady who ran the café called herself Hilda. She was a witch-lady. Evie and the witch-lady were friends, good friends. Evie spent more time with her than with her own mother; with Sweet Mother.

Eli followed close behind. He knew not to trust the silence. Evie would have a plan. Evie always had a plan.

He watched from the hillside. Evie hugged the lady who called herself Hilda, except this early in the morning, the lady didn't look like Hilda at all. She looked like what she was, which was a witch, like Grandmother Dolly. The witch opened a trapdoor behind the counter. Inside was a large rectangular hole. Evie kissed the witch-lady on the cheek, hugged her tightly and then descended into the dark opening. Eli placed a hand on the shiny thing. He needed his lucky charm. How was he supposed to make it past the witch-lady

264

and down that hole without being spotted?

The Red Man was suddenly seated next to Eli, although he was barely there now. He was just bones, gristle and gloopy stuff. He didn't say anything as usual. He just pointed a skeletal arm towards the right-hand side of the café. Eli looked. There was a wire-framed cage with large blue and red cylinders inside. Of course, Eli remembered, there was a camping ground just over the hill. The café made a lot of summer money selling camping equipment to all the other faraway people. There were lots of different things: tent poles, pegs, sleeping bags, battery-powered lamps, and gas – camping gas.

Eli smiled. If he couldn't make it down that trapdoor unnoticed, he was going to have to go the other way. The loud way.

*

'Come on, Sally. Mummy needs to speak with the lady.'

Hattie was tired and she was upset. Richard still wasn't home, she hadn't slept a wink, and now the whole place smelled like a sewage works.

'Are we going home, Mummy?'

'Yes, we are, sweetheart. Very soon. Right after I talk to the nice lady next door about whether she's done anything to fix the tyres on our car.' *And then we will be gone*, she thought. *Long gone*.

Hattie strode up to the front door of Excelsior Lodge and rapped it hard. She was trying to calm her temper, which was now a raging inferno. She was also trying to pacify her gurgling stomach. All through the night she'd been hot and clammy, and she now felt decidedly unwell. She couldn't throw up again. She wouldn't. Her sickness could wait until after she'd got her family back home.

The door opened. It was Glanna.

'Hattie. What a nice surprise,' Glanna said, but her painted smile faltered. 'Oh, my dear, you don't look well at all. Come on in, I'll grab you a glass of water.'

265

Hattie pushed past her. 'I'm not here for pleasantries, Glanna. I want my car fixed, and I want my deposit back. We're leaving.'

'I see,' Glanna said, gesturing towards the kitchen. 'Well, why don't you take a seat, and we can discuss what it is that's making you feel so unhappy.'

Hattie shook her head. 'I don't want to sit. I want things fixed. Right now!'

'Well, as I said. Take a seat. I'll make us some drinks, and I'll call Noah. I'm sure he'll have the car roadworthy in no time at all.'

Hattie didn't want to stay in the Cormoran house any longer than she had to. It smelled of death. The living room was bleak, unwelcoming. It felt old and outdated, as though it had been frozen in a time long ago and was now somehow separated from the outside world. Dust mites hung in the air, and a thin layer of grey coated every surface. The carpets were threadbare, the dark wood furniture chipped and scratched, the wallpaper curled at the edges, stained.

'I need it sorted, Glanna. This morning. I mean it.'

'I'm sure you do. And I truly want to make sure you get what you want. Now, please,' she motioned them on. 'Follow me.'

Sally pulled at Hattie's sleeve.

'Not now, Sal.'

Hattie tailed Glanna through a doorway that led down a long dark hallway. Shadows lurked in every corner, the ceiling a patchwork of yellow and grey plaster. Hattie gripped Sally's hand. She was relieved when they were ushered into the kitchen at the rear of the house. Haphazardly hung cupboards littered the walls, and a large rectangular island occupied the centre of the room. A picture window opened onto the overgrown garden that separated Excelsior from Spriggan's. An old lady sat at the island, a bowl of cereal in front of her, dribbled milk on her chin.

'You know Grandmother Dolly?'

'Not really,' Hattie said, although she knew the old lady's face from her terrifying nightmare. 'Very pleased to meet you, Dolly.

My name's Harriet, but everyone calls me Hattie.'

'Whore!' Dolly exclaimed.

'I beg your pardon?'

'Oh, don't mind her,' Glanna said. 'It's dementia, I'm afraid. She says whatever's up there in her little confused head. She can be quite offensive at times.'

'Okay,' Hattie said, still shocked. 'I guess.'

'Mother, wipe your chin,' Glanna said. 'You look a state.'

'A little girl!' Dolly cried, suddenly grinning. 'A pretty little red-head. Come over here, princess. Let Dolores get a good look at you.'

Sally went to go to the old lady, but Hattie pulled her back.

'The car?' she asked.

'Yes, yes,' Glanna nodded. She grabbed a napkin, leaned across the island, and wiped milky drool from Dolly's face. 'I'll get one of the children to fetch Noah. *Evie!*' she hollered. '*Aaron*! Will you go and fetch Noah from the barn, whichever one he's hiding himself away in today!' Glanna smirked.

'Are they even at home?' Hattie asked.

'One of them will be, I'm sure. Now, that drink. I can offer you water, juice, tea, or something stronger if you like.'

'A water will be fine,' Hattie replied. Her face was burning hot, her arms sticky.

Sally tugged her sleeve again. 'Mummy!'

'Not now, Sal,' Hattie said, suddenly feeling quite faint. She reached for the back of a chair to steady herself.

'Oh, Hattie, your ear.' Glanna reached for her.

Hattie felt something trickling down her neck. She placed a finger to it, and she felt a sticky liquid. Her finger came away covered in blood.

'I was trying to tell you, Mummy,' Sally said. 'Your ear. It's bleeding.'

Glanna dabbed at it with the drool-covered napkin. 'Here. Let me clean it for you. You need to sit down.' She pulled a chair from

267

the island.

'I don't understand,' Hattie said, taking the chair. 'Why do I feel so ill? Why the hell am I bleeding?'

'Come to me, little one,' Dolly cooed. 'Let's go outside and look at the fishies.'

'No,' Hattie said, but she could barely see. Her vision was swimming.

Glanna approached her, her face now merely a blur. 'Oh, don't worry. Grandmother Dolly will take good care of little Sally-Ann, won't you mother?'

'Of course I will. What do you take me for?' Dolly hissed, wheeling her chair through the open door.

'I'd rather you stayed here, Sally,' Hattie said, but she knew it was useless.

'I'll be fine, Mummy. I want to see the fishies.'

'Well, that's only natural,' Dolly said from someplace outside. Hattie thought her voice sounded different. It had the pitch and tone of a much younger woman. 'That's what all kids want, isn't it? To do exactly what their parents *don't* want them to do. To go exactly where their parents *don't* want them to go.'

'Don't listen to her, Hattie,' Glanna said. 'Just focus on drinking your water.'

Hattie took the glass and sipped eagerly. The liquid was cool and slightly sweet. 'What is this?'

'One of my own concoctions. Trust me, it will clear that sickness of yours, and more besides.'

'And more besides? What does that mean?'

Glanna touched Hattie's face. Her palm was silky smooth, her skin warm. Hattie tried to pull away, but for some reason she couldn't. Glanna's face was just a swirl of colours, a smudge on a smeared cloudy backdrop. There was that smell again. It was the scent from her dream. Incense, perfume, blood.

'The car?' Hattie asked, but she couldn't remember why it was important to her. 'Something about the car?'

'You've been looking for Richard,' Glanna said. 'Haven't you?'

'Yes,' Hattie replied.

'I saw him.'

'You?'

'Yes, just yesterday morning. He was spying on us.'

'Spying?' Hattie started to laugh.

'Yes,' Glanna said. 'Intruding. We had to bring him here. To Excelsior.'

'Of course,' Hattie agreed. She suddenly felt much better. She was relaxed, floating. Her mind was a smooth ocean, her thoughts now a straight line, calm and serene. 'What did you do to him?'

'Do you really want to know?'

Hattie nodded.

'I fucked him,' Glanna said. 'And then I killed him.'

Hattie felt a warm tear trickle down her cheek, but she didn't feel angry. She didn't feel anything. 'Why did you do that?'

'Because you don't need him. And I only needed this one little thing. Now I have it.' Glanna rubbed her abdomen. '*We* have it.'

'We do?' Hattie asked.

'Oh, Hattie,' Glanna said. 'We have everything.'

*

Rachel saw a movement between the barns. She approached cautiously. She was trespassing after all, and she didn't even know if Bea had come this way. She listened keenly for the sound of her voice, but there was nothing except the whir of a motor. She took a moment to consider her options: give up, go back to the house and wait for Bea to return home, or press on and hope for the best. Her impetuous nature got the better of her, and she continued.

She could hear the sound of a male grunting and something heavy being dragged. The smell up here was much worse than back at the cottage. She held a finger to her nose. *The cesspit must be*

269

really backed up, she thought. God knows how many weeks' worth of human excrement was down that hole. The image made her gag.

When she reached the corner of the second barn, she pressed her back against the rusty tin wall. She couldn't hear anyone talking. If Bea was around that corner, she was either standing, watching in silence, or she was helping. Neither of those scenarios seemed likely to Rachel. Bea had been mad. If she'd come here at all it would be to vent, and when Bea vented, it was like a geyser.

'Ugh!' The sound of another grunt, and of something else being dragged. Rachel thought of the job; of The Weasel and Mr Quin, and of Tara burned alive in that wreckage, followed by the sudden appearance of her husband, Terry. She exhaled slowly. What was she doing trespassing on the Cormoran property, searching for her pissed off girlfriend? This was a distraction. This was senseless, pointless. This wasn't getting revenge for what happened to Tommy. This wasn't achieving anything at all.

She went to leave, and that's when she saw it. It just flopped to the ground ahead of her. A hand, a man's hand. It was grey, swollen and covered in brown sludge. Rachel felt her pulse start to race. *A body*, she thought. *Is that hand attached to a body? A dead one?*

She paused to calm herself, and then slid along the barn's wall. She could hear a man breathing heavily, could smell the tangy odour of sweat and hard labour, mixed with the increasingly strong scent of faeces and decay.

She counted to three and peered around the corner. The hand was indeed attached to an arm, and the arm was protruding from a black, plastic sack. Noah was there. He was facing away from her and leaning over the open mouth of the cesspit. A large pump whirred next to him, and a thick pipe was thrust into the hole in the ground. He was wearing a full body medical suit and a face mask. He looked out of breath and out of sorts.

'Why the hell do I have to do this?' he muttered to himself. 'She still has four grown-up kids, for heaven's sake, but oh no. They couldn't possibly help, could they?'

Four? Rachel thought. She didn't know Glanna had four kids.

'No, get Noah to do it. The lackey, the hired help. Someone blocks the cesspit, and I'm the one that has to clear it out, like I have nothing better to do.'

Rachel craned her neck. There was another body, and another. She couldn't believe what she was seeing. Who were these people? What kind of sick, crazy family was she dealing with here?

Noah turned, and Rachel quickly spun out of view. She caught her breath. What should she do? Confront him? Arrest him? Reveal herself as a police officer? Blow her cover? Should she contact Eric and hit the panic button? That would be the end of Operation Glow, so she couldn't do that. Not yet. She needed more time to think.

She chanced another peek. Noah had vanished. He'd left the pit open and exposed, with the four bodies lying there alongside it. She glanced inside the barn. It looked empty. She peered towards the house. Had he gone back inside to fetch something? Should she take a closer look? Did she even have time? A million thoughts whizzed through her mind at a thousand miles an hour. She decided to take a chance.

She rounded the corner and stepped towards the pit. It smelled so bad. She had to bury her nose in the crook of her arm and breathe slowly through her mouth. She could taste the toilet waste, could feel the decay entering her lungs. All four bodies were bagged. She leaned over the one closest to her. She had to get a photograph. She needed evidence. She pulled her phone from her pocket with her free hand and then stooped down, pinching the edge of the black plastic sack between her fingers. There was a wet, sucking noise as she pulled, and then the thick plastic detached itself from dead, flaccid skin. Vacant eyes glared up at her. Female eyes, a slim face, blonde hair, and a colourful face tattoo

'Holy shit,' she heard herself say. It was Amelia, the mute woman. She had a black and purple welt around her throat. 'Oh, Amy.'

Rachel backed away and almost stumbled over the body behind

271

her. She spun and looked down. The face was partially exposed.

'Oh no,' she said. 'Oh no, no, *no!*'

She pulled frantically at the plastic sheet, revealing dark hair, dark eyes, and a little scar on a rounded chin. The man's throat had been cut, and dried blood covered his clothes. She brought her hand to her mouth and shook her head back and forth repeatedly. She thought she was going to be sick. How was she going to break this to Bea, or to Hattie for that matter? What about Sally? How could she tell them? He was just lying there on the ground, covered in his own blood and swimming in a pool of excrement.

Richard hadn't run out on them after all. He'd been murdered.

The Cormorans had killed Richard.

*

When the gas canisters exploded, the earth seemed to shudder and shake, just like when the tractor motors came to life in the fields each morning. It was loud and it made Eli's chest vibrate. The wall of the café just evaporated; brick, mortar and timber flying in every direction. The witch-woman was screaming like a cat on fire. The horrible shrieking sound hurt Eli's ears. He hadn't realised that a sharp, twisted piece of projectile timber had wedged itself into Hilda's upper thigh, and blood was pouring from the wound. Eli didn't stop to help her. He slipped in the open door and headed around the café's counter. The hatch in the ground was unlocked, and so he yanked it open. It wasn't so heavy. The hole underneath was dark and damp-smelling, but Eli didn't hesitate. He'd made a promise to the Red Man, and he intended to keep it. Kid-Bastard Evie had to die.

He thought about what Aaron had said. He didn't know whether the story about Sweet Mother being his mum in real life was true or not, but he knew that Aaron wasn't smart enough to come up with the lie himself. It was either completely true, or Kid-Bastard Evie had convinced him it was true. Either way, he hated her for

272

who she was and for what she did. Maybe he always had. She seemed to have a way with him, a way to get him to do whatever she wanted. He knew he had to try to resist it now. He had to block his ears, close his eyes, and shut off his brain. She was poison. She was acid.

The ladder that led down to the basement was slippery and cold. Eli could smell Evie. He could feel her eyes on him. His skin itched. He'd never been down in the basement of the café before, but he knew exactly where to go. He followed his nose, followed her scent. There was a staircase at the end of the wide chamber, and it descended steeply down a winding tunnel, through granite and limestone. A dull light emanated from lamps hanging from the tunnel's ceiling. Eli wondered how he didn't know about this place. Evie must have kept it a secret from all of them. It was her and Hilda's little hiding place. He wondered what else she'd been keeping from them. Sweet Mother would not be pleased.

From above, Eli heard the wailing sound of sirens approaching. It would be chaos up there. Whatever happened, he knew he couldn't go back that way. Too many questions would be asked, questions that he was in no rush to answer.

The tunnel seemed to go on forever, a continuous right-hand curve that sloped downwards on an ever-increasing gradient. Twice Eli slipped on the damp ground, almost tumbling bum first onto the hard rock. He held onto the shiny thing, praying it would bring him good luck. He needed all the luck he could get. Kid-Bastard Evie was no idiot. She would have set a trap for him, and he knew he was probably walking head first into it.

Suddenly there was the smell of wood burning, the crackle of an open flame. There was cool air on his face, a soft breeze through his frizzy crop of dark hair. Daylight seemed to be peeking around the corner. Eli crept along the tunnel wall, half expecting Kid-Bastard Evie to come rushing towards him, a bloodied knife in her hand.

'Come on, Eli!' he heard her yell. 'I haven't got all day.'

'I—' he went to answer but stopped himself. What was he thinking? He had to remain in control here, he had to be in charge. 'Don't give her what she wants,' he muttered. 'Don't do what she says.'

As sunlight crept up his leg, bathed his shirt in orange and then kissed his cheeks, he saw her. She was standing on the sand, the ocean at her back. She was wearing black jeans, a long black hoodie and black boots. The tunnel had led him straight down to Sweet Mother's cave. How did he not know about this? All those times he'd been half-drowned, tied to one of the Kid-Bastard boys' surfboards like a captive, because they knew he couldn't swim. Eli hated the water. It was salty and it was wet, and it made him want to throw up. That's why Evie had led him here. He suddenly felt the hot prickle of fear creep up his spine. He wanted to leave.

'Come over here, already,' she said. 'I'm cooking your favourite – Cumberland sausage. I've even brought rolls and ketchup. You know you like ketchup, Eli.'

'I… I'm not hungry,' he said. He sounded stupid.

'You're always hungry, mate.' Mate? She never called him that. 'I can't remember you ever saying no to a hotdog.'

'Fings have changed,' he said. 'You're not who I thought you were.'

'Oh, Eli. I don't know how to take you at times. You're so difficult to please. So bloody difficult. And after everything I've done for you, too. You know, you should be thanking me.'

'Fanking you? For what?'

'For finally revealing the truth.'

'You're all liars,' he said. He could feel hot anger burning in his belly.

'No, Eli. I'm not a liar.' She smiled. 'I'm your sister.'

Eli shook his head. 'I don't believe you. Sweet Mother would never lie to me.'

'Oh, wow,' she exclaimed, flipping a sausage. 'You're even dumber than I thought. You ever wonder why Noah beats up on

274

you so much? Why Mother keeps you so close? I mean, why would she even keep you around? You're practically no use about the place with your one good hand and your funky, twisted bones. You're not smart, you've got no skills.' His anger was bubbling now. 'Come on, Eli! Don't be such a fuckwit. You're her son. Her *real* son! Her no-shit flesh and blood. Not like Freddie. Not like Aaron.' Her eyes suddenly became glassy. 'And not like… me.'

The lance of her truth suddenly pierced him. The Kid-Bastards weren't Sweet Mother's children. Eli wasn't Noah's brother. But how?

'It doesn't make any sense.'

'Doesn't it?' Evie said. 'Really? Think about it. What happened to the Periwinkles?'

Eli thought of the Red Man, his festering body in the hole.

'You think that hasn't happened before?' she continued. 'Seb, Freddie, Aaron? Me? We're all stolen goods, Eli, taken by Mother so she could create the family she couldn't have naturally. She picks the ones with the gifts, or at least, they start out with them. Aaron and Freddie lost theirs long ago, not long after they were taken. That's why she never really cared what happened to them. Seb still has some of his. That's why I showed him to the boy, Jonno. He seemed to like it, and Mother likes the idea of him. The little girl too. She thinks they're blessed.' She glanced over her shoulder. 'Me, on the other hand,' she gazed at her palms. 'My power just seems to get stronger and stronger, like tea in a pot, it keeps brewing. You know what I mean?'

Eli gulped. 'But if all that's true,' he said, 'about you being 'ducted by Sweet Mother, then what about your parents? Your *real* parents?'

'Well, let's see. Those drawings, Eli. The ones you have all stacked up in the barn. You ever noticed some of them go missing from time to time?'

'Yes,' he said.

'You wanna know who takes them?'

He shrugged.

'She does,' Evie said. 'And she sticks them up on the wall of the old cottage. You've seen them there, haven't you?'

He had.

'And you know why she does that?' she asked.

'Because she likes them?' he offered. She did. She'd told him so. She'd said he was an artist. She'd told him he had talent, like those people on the TV who sometimes put things in large rooms with colourful displays.

'Because they're her memories, Eli. You draw her memories.'

'But I—'

'No, you don't know you're doing it. I've always believed that. I don't even think you're fully conscious when you sit there with your little pack of crayons and your notebooks, drawing for hours on end, sketching all the terrible things that you've seen. But think about it: the geeky kid; the little girl with freckles; the fat kid with shaggy hair. Haven't they ever looked familiar to you?'

He shook his head, but now that he thought about it…

'They're us, Eli. You drew us. We were much younger of course, much smaller, but it's the four of us all the same, way back when we were kids. You were younger too, but you were old enough to see, and to know. You would have been ten or eleven, maybe, when I first came here. I was with my mother and father. People who loved me.' Her voice cracked.

'You have people who love you now!'

'I don't mean the kind of fake, self-serving love that Mother gives us. I mean real love, Eli. Real, deep-down, truthful love. The kind of love that only a real mother and father can have for their real children.'

Eli was transfixed, completely absorbed. He didn't realise he'd shuffled towards the centre of the cave, now no more than ten feet from Evie.

'And where are they now?' he asked. 'Your real mother and father? Did they just leave you behind? Did they leave you here alone with Sweet Mother and the others? That doesn't sound like real love to me.'

Evie shook her head. Her cheeks were damp.

'Check the cesspit,' she said. 'You'll find all the truth you need right there.'

*

'Bea! *Bea*!' Rachel yelled as she entered the cottage. 'For God's sake, where are you?'

Her mind was a blur. Amy was dead. Richard was dead. How many others had been murdered? She reached for her phone. Eric would know what to do. Eric would send a team down here immediately and make damn sure the Cormorans would never get the chance to kill again. Of course, The Weasel and Mr Quin would disappear, probably for good, and her case would be screwed, but did that even matter now? Wasn't this more important? 'Tommy,' she heard herself say. 'I'm sorry.'

Where the hell was Bea? She bounded up the stairs three at a time and plummeted into their bedroom. Clothes littered the floor, make-up bags were spilled open, and hair dryers and hair straightener cords lay in a tangled heap. It looked like a disaster zone, but Rachel knew this was normal. Neither of them were the tidiest.

She crossed the landing and entered the master bedroom. Hattie and Richard's room. She realised she would never be able to say that again: Hattie and Richard. There was no Richard anymore. A phone had been tossed onto the bed. It didn't look familiar. She reached for it and instantly the screen came to life. The phone's wallpaper was blank, a simple blue background. Rachel realised it was unlocked. All thoughts of the bodies in the cesspit evaporated. She glanced around her to check that no one was watching. She pressed the email icon.

haribe@gmail

Rachel heard herself gasp. haribe@gmail. That was Mr Quin's email address, the address that had sent the messages that were intercepted by Eric. That could only mean one thing, couldn't it? That Harriet was Mr Quin. Could Bea's angry, pissed-at-the-world sister be a multi-million-pound money launderer for a major drug and human trafficking cartel? It didn't seem possible, let alone plausible.

She opened the last sent message, and sure enough, there it was.

What the hell's going on? I haven't heard from you in four days. Is this deal still going ahead or not? I'm ready to blow the whole thing and walk. Suggest you get your shit together and sharpish. We've worked way too hard on this to see it collapse at the last minute. You said I could rely on you, so do yourself a favour – be reliable.

That was it. That was the final message Eric and the Operation Glow team had intercepted from Mr Quin, and it had been sent from this very phone. Hattie's phone. Rachel let out a long, tired breath and collapsed onto the bed. The whole thing with Richard, Tara and the tangerine mobile had been a complete red-herring. She'd been chasing the wrong lead all this time. She felt so stupid, so bloody incompetent.

'Whatcha doing?'

Rachel sat up sharply. It was Bea. She tried to hide the phone but it was too late.

'Whoa, you made me jump! Where—' she thought fast. 'Where the hell have you been? I've been looking all over for you?'

'I had to cool off. You really made me mad, you know that, right?' Bea eyed the phone in Rachel's hands. 'What you got there?'

'Oh, I just found it on Hattie's bed. I—' Rachel tried to steady her voice, 'I thought she may have tried to contact you.'

'And?'

'And what?'

'Had she? Tried to contact me?'

Rachel found herself stumbling over her words. 'I... I don't know. It's locked, so—'

'Let me see.'

Before Rachel had the chance to yank the phone away, Bea snatched it and read the open email. She frowned, and her eyes narrowed into thin slits.

'This phone isn't locked, Rach.'

'No, I guess not.'

'Then why did you say it was?'

Rachel shrugged.

'What do you think this message means?'

'I... I don't know, Bea, but it doesn't look good, does it?'

'No,' Bea shook her head. 'It doesn't. It really doesn't.'

'Look,' Rachel stood. 'I don't know what your sister's got herself into, but if it's something illegal, and the people she's dealing with are bad people, then I suggest we confront her together and somehow convince her to go to the authorities. She needs to make things right.'

'Yeah, yeah,' Bea glanced up at her. She looked upset. 'But she's my sister, you know?'

'I know, Bea,' Rachel touched her arm. Bea flinched. 'But letting whatever this is run its course will only mean she'll get into even more trouble than she's already in. And she will get caught eventually. People like Hattie always do.'

'People like Hattie?'

'People that play way out of their league.'

Bea nodded, her lips thin. 'I need to think. This is too much.' She left the room.

'Bea, wait.' Rachel went to go after her but decided against it. Bea had had a huge shock, and there was so much more she didn't even know yet. Jesus, how was Rachel going to tell her about the

Cormorans and the bodies in the cesspit? Richard's body?

Rachel gripped the doorframe and took a beat. Hattie was Mr Quin that much was obvious, but who the hell was The Weasel? When was the transaction due to take place? Could she convince Hattie to play along with the ruse, maybe under some promise of a reduced sentence? Could she use Hattie to get to The Weasel, to uncover his links with whoever was now running the Belvedere Saints? This thing was much bigger than a money laundering deal going down in Cornwall. This was about bringing down the whole murderous enterprise. Could Hattie be Rachel's key to unlocking the door to the secret kingdom? Could she help her crush everything that Lyndsay Arthur and his cronies had built? Its foundations were created by so much blood, so much death and sorrow.

'Let's go, Rach,' Bea said.

Rachel spun round. 'Bea!' she cried out. 'What…?'

'Downstairs, now!'

'What are you doing? Why are you…?' she was suddenly reeling, confused.

'Why did you have to find that phone, Rach? Why did you have to go and look at those emails?' Bea shook her head, her eyes filled with tears. 'Why you? Why did it have to be you?'

'I don't understand,' Rachel said, but she was beginning to. Bea had a knife, and she was pointing it directly at her. It could only lead her to one dreadful conclusion, and it was the one outcome that Rachel had feared more than anything.

Bea was in on it too.

*

'But if Sweet Mother can't have any children, how can I be her son?' Eli asked. He and Evie were sitting on a picnic blanket. He was taking a huge bite from a freshly grilled hotdog. She'd offered it to him, and despite his feigned reluctance, he hadn't refused. She had been right: he couldn't resist. He hated himself for giving her control of the situation, and for the measly price of a greasy sausage and stale bread roll too, but there it was. He groaned with satisfaction as fatty oil and ketchup trickled down his chin. What did it matter? The things she was telling him had turned his whole life topsy-turvy. He didn't even know if she was the one he should be angry at any more. Maybe the Red Man had it all wrong. Wasn't she just a victim, the same as him? Freddie and Aaron too? Had he made a terrible mistake in killing the two of them? Was he the one who should be being punished, not them?

'You were her one and only success, Eli, and look how you turned out.'

'What do you mean?' he asked through a mouthful of bread and ketchup.

'Well, you know. You're not quite the finished article. Not that it's a bad thing, and I don't mean it in a horrible way. But look at you. It must be hard being—' she shook her head, 'the way you are.'

He nodded sombrely. It was.

'Yeah, I thought so. But even then,' she continued, dabbing at her mouth with a napkin, 'you turned out better than all the others.'

'The others?'

Evie smirked. 'Yeah. What is it you call them again? The Horrible Kids?'

'The Terrible Babies.'

'That's it. The Terrible Babies.' She laughed.

'What? So, they're just…?'

'They're just you, Eli. I mean, they're just the same as you, except—' she paused. 'They didn't come out quite so well, so to speak.'

'But… but why am I—'

'Better?'

'Yes. Better. Like this?'

'That would be down to your father,' she said. 'He had cleaner

281

blood.'

'I don't understand.'

'Look, Eli. Glanna, your mother, is a Cormoran. The Cormorans have been here, in this village, for like for ever, since even before records began, or whatever. Apparently, way back when this land was just trees, rocks, dirt and sand, the last of the Cormoran women, a witch named Eseld, got into some trouble with another local tribe, the Viguns. The argument was over the rights to this place, Bodhmall's, if you can believe that. I know, who would fight over this shithole? Anyway, the Viguns' had laid claim to it, and the Cormoran family didn't take kindly to a tribe coming in and trying to take land they saw as being rightfully theirs. The two tribes quarrelled and eventually fought a long, bloody battle. After three weeks of fighting, the Cormorans emerged victorious. The Vigun men were slaughtered, and the women were beaten and raped. When the last of the females was sent off to the stake to be burned alive, she turned to Eseld and cast an eternal hex on her and any Cormoran woman who came after her.'

'She killed Eseld?'

'No, worse.'

'Worse than death?'

Evie nodded. 'She cast the piskie hex.'

'She turned her into a piskie?'

'No, idiot. Aren't you even listening to what I'm saying? The spell wasn't about Eseld. It wasn't even about the Cormoran men who'd raped and killed. No, that wasn't it at all. The spell was intended to kill off the bloodline, to stop it dead in its tracks. The Cormoran women would no longer be able to bear normal, living and breathing human children. Their offspring would now be horribly deformed, vicious savages that existed only to kill and maim.'

'The Terrible Babies?'

'Yes!' she cried. 'Hallelujah, he gets it.'

He didn't know what to think. He was the same as them, those violent, bloodthirsty things. How could that be? He didn't kill people, didn't hurt people. Or did he? Was that really true? He recalled Kid-Bastard Freddie's terrible cries of agony as his skin was torn away, and he remembered the horrifying sound of Aaron's face collapsing in on itself as rock after rock rained down on him.

'But you said my father almost solved the curse. Is that true?' he asked, clinging to a thin slither of hope.

'Well, not exactly. The loophole is all about how Cornish the bloodline is. If the conception is with a male who is a true Cornovii man, truly Kernowyon with no contamination from the outside world, then the child will be born full bodied and of sound mind. However, if there's any hint of an unclean bloodline, any hint at all, then the greater the contaminated content, the more affected the baby will be. And, even then, the female needs not only the seed from a Kernowyon man, but also the blood.'

Eli felt a small amount of sick rise in his throat, and he fought to keep it in check.

'And,' he gasped for air, 'my father. Who was he? Where is he now?'

'A friend of Noah's,' Evie said. 'Everyone thought he was Cornish through and through. The right name, the right lineage. The only thing is, the records just don't go back far enough. Not all the way. Not back to the beginning. His family must have mixed, just once, and that one little drop of migrant blood led to you.' She pointed at him. 'Glanna was furious with Petra, but how could he possibly know?'

'Petra,' Eli cried. 'What's Petra got to do with this?'

Evie raised an eyebrow.

'He—' he shook his head. 'He's my father?'

'I'm afraid so. That's why she let him stay here. That's why they built him that house. He'd at least given Glanna hope, if not the pure born child that she craved.'

Petra was his dad? His flesh and blood? He'd never said anything to him, never shown any sign of affection. How could he just ignore his own son like that? Forget about him? Eli felt his rage begin to boil once more.

'This is crap!' he said. 'If this is true, then what was the problem? Back in olden times when there were fewer people, surely everyone in the village was Cornish.'

'Yes, they were,' Evie agreed. 'But as the years went by, and more and more people migrated into the area, cross-contamination occurred, and that contamination worsened and worsened until almost no pure Cormoran were born.'

'What? You mean they were wiped out?'

'Almost,' Evie said, finishing her meal. 'But one of the women had the good sense to seek out the one rare spell that could at least pause the Cormorans' inevitable extinction.'

'To fix the curse?'

'No, the curse is unfixable. Jesus, if it were that easy we wouldn't even be having this conversation. No, she scoured the globe for the rare ingredients that were needed to complete the charm, selling her own body to pay pirates, cutthroats and thieves, prostituting herself to get exactly what she wanted.'

'And the spell? What was the spell?'

Evie let out a long breath.

'The spell of the eternal soul.'

Eli huffed. How ridiculous. It all sounded like a stupid fairy story; a story like the ones that Sweet Mother used to tell him to get him to sleep. It couldn't possibly be true. It was nonsense.

While he sat there with Evie and ran everything over and over in his mind, he failed to hear the scurrying of tiny feet on the rocks behind him, and the urgent chattering of a thousand sharp teeth.

'No. I don't get it,' he said. 'And I don't believe it.'

'Oh, come on, Eli. It's right there in front of you. Glanna isn't forty years old, or fifty years old, or whatever it is she wants us to believe. She's hundreds of years old, maybe thousands. And she keeps her family close by.'

'Her family? You mean me?'

'And Paz and Bert too. They're distant cousins. Their families have lived here with her ever since she cast that spell. They're sworn to be her protectors. Who the hell do you think built these crumbling old houses? They're not pure blood, but they're Cormoran descendants, and they're dedicated to the cause.'

'She wants to mend the bloodline,' he said, not hearing the loud clatter of loose stones falling from the ledge overhead.

'Exactly. A revival of sorts.'

Eli paused as another thought occurred to him. 'What about Grandmother Dolly? Where does she fit into all of this?'

'Ha, well that's the best bit,' Evie said. 'You see, the spell requires an outgoing body to become the vessel for the ageing soul, and a younger body to carry the soul's regeneration. Glanna's body carries half of that soul, the young half.'

'And Dolly carries the part that's dying,' he said.

'That's right,' Evie grinned. 'Glanna and Dolly. One and the same.'

Everything came crashing in on Eli, then. It was all too much. He couldn't bear it. He felt like a lie, like a made up version of himself. Nothing he'd ever thought to be true was real. He felt the tears come and heard himself sobbing.

Evie leaned forward, and to Eli's surprise, hugged him. 'I know, it's a lot to take in.'

'I just—' he tried to say. 'I just feel really sad.' He looked up at Evie's dark eyes, the freckles on her cheeks, her long, silky hair. She looked like a child. 'How do you even know all of this? How could you?'

'Because I see things, Eli. I see lots of things. They didn't reckon on that when they took me in. They didn't check who I really was, and who my mother and her mother really were. My family has the knack. We've always had it. Glanna didn't do her research, but I did. My mother might be buried in that pit, rotting away along with the bones of my father, but she left me something far more valuable than Glanna can ever give me.' She smiled, but her eyes were steely. 'I can see everything. I see who Glanna is, who she truly is. I know what she wants, what she needs. I've used that against her, I've *been* using it against her since I was a little kid. I see the blood that they've shed. I see the way they abduct and torture people. I saw what happened to the Periwinkles. I see what's going to happen to the Penroses.' She stood and gestured towards the cave. 'And I also see that while we've been sitting here chatting away like old pals, my other little friends have been busy gathering themselves.'

Eli looked up. She was right. The Terrible Babies. They were everywhere. He heard their feral growls, the grinding of teeth. Their bodies twitched, and their red eyes screamed hunger and hatred.

'They might be your brothers and sisters, Eli, but they do what I tell them.' She held out her arms, her black hoodie billowing like a long cape behind her. 'They just can't help themselves.'

'But—' Eli leapt up. 'The fings you told me? We've been talking like brother and sister! We shared a hotdog! You hugged me!'

'Oh, Eli,' she said. 'When are you going to learn about the art of manipulation?'

'But—'

'People hurt people, Eli,' she said in little more than a whisper. 'That's just what they do.'

She touched her fingers and thumbs together and winked.

Snap.

*

'So, what happens now?'

'We wait.'

'For what?'

'For Hattie.' They were seated in the living room. Bea was sitting upright in the armchair, while Rachel was perched uncomfortably on the edge of the sofa. Bea looked anxious, upset.

286

'I wish you'd never found that phone,' she said. 'I told Hattie time and time again to be more careful, always leaving it around the way she does. We even found Sally with it a couple of times. I mean, Jesus.'

Rachel was still taking it all in. The two of them, in it together. Bea and Hattie – Mr Quin. *The Mysterious Mister Quin*, no less. She'd even seen a dog-eared paperback copy of the famous Agatha Christie novel in Bea's flat, but she'd never even considered the connection.

'Even that crappy email address,' Bea continued. 'It's a dead giveaway, but oh no, she likes it so of course we have to keep it. She thinks it's cute. Haribe? Harriet and Beatrice? It's corny, not to mention obvious.'

Of course, Rachel thought. She cursed her crap detective skills. 'But why, Bea?' she asked. 'Why get yourselves tangled up in this mess? You're a good person.'

'Do you know my parents? I mean, of course you know them, you've met them a few times, but do you really know them? Who they really are? What they represent? Dad's businesses? You know how much money gets funnelled through those companies on a weekly basis? It's obscene, really. Like, totally gross. You know how much he gives to charities? To the poor, the needy?' she scoffed. 'Or to his kids?' She shook her head. 'We get nothing, Harriet and me. Trust fund? Savings account? University subs? Zero, zilch, sweet eff-ay. We've had to scratch and scrape our way through life without even an ounce of support from our not-so-caring father. His money just sits there, digits on a bank account, numbers on a balance sheet, buried deep in multiple investment funds that just ratchet more digits, so that he can look at his numbers grow and grow and feel his ego swell to supernova size. Mum even eggs him on, encourages his all-consuming thirst for mind-blowing wealth. I've always imagined them, just sitting there night after night, sipping Cristal and laughing to each other as the pound signs spin up and up like the second hand on a clock, only

287

this one's on steroids.' She grunted. 'And then there's the gay thing. That's not going away, is it? Their disgust. It couldn't possibly be true. Their little Beatrice Jane Piper, a lesbian? What would they say at the golf club? Or the masonic lodge? Or, and here's the best one, the church? Father Harold probably had a heart attack when he heard, what with the amount of money Dad throws at that old ruin of a building. You think I'm getting a penny of their savings now, Rach? You think Daddy dearest will be putting his hand in his pocket for me now? Not a chance.'

'I get it, Bea. I really do. You've got shitty parents.' Rachel shrugged. 'But lots of people do. It doesn't justify crime. It doesn't justify this.'

'I told you how they treated Hattie, right?' Bea continued, increasingly animated. 'She went to them for help. Her and Richard, they really needed help, not just for them, but for Jonno and Sally too. They were approaching financial ruin, bankruptcy. I mean, this was serious shit. You know what Mummy and Daddy did? They laughed at her, Rach, like it was some sort of joke. I mean, who does that? Their daughter, in a real financial crisis, and they have millions in the bank, and all they could say was, "Ah, that's a shame, love. How awful for you. Another tea?".' She huffed. 'I know it sounds like I'm being a diva, complaining that my rich parents won't sub my lifestyle, like I want something for nothing, but it's not just about the money. It's about them. Who they are. *What* they are, and how they've treated their two daughters, not just once, but all of our bloody lives!'

Bea took a breath. Rachel considered everything she'd told her. Bea was being a spoilt brat, that much was obvious, and Hattie had been at the point of desperation, but how did any of that lead to the Belvedere Saints? How did it result in the pair of them agreeing to launder millions?

'So, I get how you feel, Bea. How your parents make you feel. But how did it move on from there? I mean, being angry at your mum and dad is one thing, but becoming involved with bad people, the type that you're involved with? I mean, how does that even happen? How do two middle class women from Kent suddenly get hooked up with a multi-national criminal enterprise?' As soon as it came out of her mouth, Rachel knew she'd made a mistake. She'd pretty much come out and confirmed that she knew about the Belvedere Saints.

Bea laughed. 'I know. It sounds ludicrous, right? Like something in one of those tacky novels?'

'Yeah.' Rachel feigned a laugh, but she'd slipped up and she knew it. 'I guess it does.'

'Well, you'll laugh at this. It was through one of Dad's connections, actually. Ha, that sounds ridiculous, doesn't it? This guy, he fancied me. This was in 2019, way before I came out, so it wasn't a bloke hitting on a lesbian in some kind of fetishy way. He was a young guy, and he'd been round the house a few times, and I guess he just took a liking to me.' Bea smiled. 'He was Jewish, which was also a difficult thing for my God-fearing mummy and daddy. Now, what was his name again?'

'Zef?' Rachel offered, hoping she was wrong in her suspicion that the man Bea was referring to was Zef Abraham, Lyndsay Arthur's chief accountant and the guy that had fired the bullet that killed Tommy.

'That was it!' Bea clapped her hands together, almost dropping the knife. Rachel could have made a move then, of course, could have disarmed Bea at any time. It was the type of thing they trained you to do, but how could she? Why would she?

'Anyway,' Bea continued, 'you're right. Zef Abraham. That was his name. We got chatting, we even went out for a drink or two as I recall, and we got talking about my mum and dad. He really seemed to relate. His parents were arses too, or so he said, and we eventually got onto the subject of money – inheritance money, or lack thereof – and whether I had access to the comings and goings of Dad's various businesses. He basically wanted to know whether I was interested in making a shedload of cash for doing what

289

amounted to not a lot. Of course, I said I was. I didn't know he was talking about anything illegal at that point. I thought we were just talking about an innocent little scam. It seemed like an easy way of solving our problem – mine and Hattie's. She would get out of the hole Richard had dug them, and I would get some funds to set me on whatever life path I chose, so to speak.'

Rachel shook her head. An innocent little conversation, maybe, but Bea hadn't realised who she'd got herself involved with.

'I discussed it with Hattie,' Bea continued, now on a roll. 'She was against it at first, of course. That's Hattie. She's afraid of her own shadow at times. But when she realised how much money we could make, the *huge* amount of money we could bag ourselves, then she was in. Richard didn't know. Still doesn't as far as I'm aware. He would never go for it. It's more of a pride thing for him, but Hattie knew it was the only way to get them out of their mess. I gave Zef the nod over a gin and lemonade, and it was all in the process of going ahead. Unfortunately, then we hit a snag.'

'He stopped making contact,' Rachel said, recalling the events of that fateful night in the club.

'That's exactly right. He just seemed to vanish into thin air. He just stopped coming round. I didn't take it personally. It wasn't like I was attracted to him or anything. I was just pissed off about the money. As I said, I had plans for it.' She paused and shook her head. 'Anyway, it was like that for a couple of years. Hattie and me, we thought the whole thing had died on the vine. Eventually we just forgot about it and got on with our lives. Then, all of a sudden, I get an anonymous letter through the post. I was intrigued. When I opened it, I found a simple list of instructions on how to set up an untraceable email address. It was signed "your very wealthy friend". I guessed it was Zef, so I showed Hattie and she agreed that we had no choice, we had to go through with it. Nothing had changed. We'd just had a little pause in proceedings. Anyway, the instructions were easy enough. We bought a burner phone from the trader listed in the letter. Once that was done, they sent another letter with the email address of the person they identified as The Weasel.'

This is it, Rachel thought. *This is the jackpot.*

'I have no idea who he is, this Weasel, just that he has an equally stupid call-sign. The Weasel was our fence, the middleman. We were to have no contact with Zef, or whoever had sent the letters – just with The Weasel. I guess it gave them, erm, what do they call it again?'

'Plausible deniability?'

'Yeah, that's it! Plausible deniability. They get to distance themselves from the transaction, and we get to do the deed.'

'So why are we here, Bea? All the way down here in the middle of nowhere? How does this place have anything to do with laundering obscene amounts of money through your dad's books?'

Bea smirked. 'Because The Weasel's here. Or, at least, he was.'

Okay, Rachel thought. *Now we're getting somewhere.* 'What do you mean, *was?*'

'Booking this place was no accident, Rach. The Weasel put us in touch with the Cormoran family, and they made space in their schedule to fit us in.'

'So, The Weasel knows Glanna and Noah?'

'Well, that's what he made us believe. He told us this was the perfect spot to sign off on everything. It's so out of the way, so unexpected. He'd bring the encrypted laptop, we'd bring all of the access codes, bank account numbers, and passwords. Hattie managed to get copies of everything from Dad's study. Don't ask me how. She can be a devious little so-and-so at times.'

'But The Weasel never showed up.'

Bea shook her head. 'You saw that last email, right? We haven't heard from him in days. Hattie's going out of her mind. I'm just disappointed. It seems like the whole thing was for nothing, like it was just a big waste of everyone's time.' She sighed. 'Anyway, you know they know about you, right?'

Rachel winced. 'Well, you didn't flinch at me slipping up just a moment ago,' she shrugged. 'So I'm guessing that means—'

'That I know about you, too? Yes. I know about everything, Beth.'

Rachel let out a long breath. This was the moment she'd been dreading.

'Yep,' Bea said, forcing a smile. 'I know about how you trailed me to that bar, how you deliberately started up a pre-scripted conversation, took me to dinner, got in with my family, and wormed your way into coming on this holiday.' Bea's voice cracked. 'And made me fall in love with you.'

'I—'

'Don't bother,' Bea said. 'Don't bother apologising or trying to make excuses. I think we're way past that now. And, anyway,' she shook her head, 'it was my fault, really. I let it happen.'

'We both did.'

'Please don't try to convince me that this wasn't just a game for you, Rachel. Or should I call you Beth? Or Tammy? I mean, who the fuck are you really?' She waved the knife at her. 'Do you even know yourself? You must get confused, looking in the mirror every morning and wondering who the hell is standing there, staring straight back at you.'

'It was real for me, Bea. I swear it.'

'Yeah, right.'

'It was unprofessional, it was idiotic,' Rachel said. 'But I couldn't help it. The more we saw each other, the more I grew fond of you, and then that fondness became affection, and that affection became attraction, and eventually—'

'Don't!' Bea yelled. 'Don't you fucking dare say it! Don't you *fucking* dare!'

'But I do, Bea! I do! I really, truly… do.'

Rachel tried to wipe away the tears, but she couldn't. They just kept coming. The two of them sat there, swimming in the silence, both crying, both wishing they'd met in different circumstances, in a different time, when they weren't on opposite sides of the same game. If only things had been different; if only they'd found each other before, before this, before everything.

'We could run,' Rachel said, but she didn't even know where that came from.

'What do you mean?'

'We don't have to do this,' she continued. 'We don't have to let it play out this way. We could just—' she ran ideas over in her mind. 'We could just make ourselves disappear.'

'I can't. What about Hattie? I can't.'

'Look, Bea,' Rachel leaned forward, acutely aware that the knife was still a thing between them. 'I was going to tell you this, and, well—' she paused. 'This seems like the right time. The people here at Bodhmall's. They aren't what they seem.'

'You mean Glanna and—'

'Noah. Pascoe. The lot of them. They kill people, Bea. They're murderers. I don't know why, or what's in it for them, whether The Weasel or the Belvedere Saints are involved, but I do know that there are bodies in that cesspit, at least four of them anyway, and the lady with the face tattoo, Amelia?' She recalled her cold, lifeless eyes. 'She's one of them.'

'The mute woman?'

'Yes.'

'My god.'

'I know. But there's more, Bea.' She didn't know how to say it, so she just blurted it out. 'Richard. They killed Richard, too.'

'What?' Bea stood. 'You're lying!'

'I'm not. God, I wish I was, but I'm not, I swear. I saw him, wrapped up in a plastic bag, his throat cut. There was blood all over him, Bea.'

Bea was shaking. 'If this is some way of trying to distract me, Rachel, then… then it's sick!'

'I'm not trying anything here. Look—' Rachel jumped up.

'Sit down!'

'Okay, okay.' Rachel held out her hands and sat back down.

293

'Sorry, look. Why would I lie about that? I mean, I could come up with a million ways to distract you, so why would I pick one that's so outlandish, so cruel?'

'I don't know, you tell me?'

'Because it's true, Bea. It is. Please believe me.'

Bea pursed her lips. 'Richard,' she said. 'Gone?'

'Yes. I know it's horrible, but he's gone and there's no bringing him back. But we could use it, Bea. To our advantage, I mean.'

'What the hell are you talking about?'

'Look, I'm thinking on the fly here, and clearly I'm not great at that, but just hear me out.'

Bea sat back down and gestured with the knife. 'Go on.'

'We grab Hattie and the kids, you can tell her that your little secret's out, and we can talk that through together if we need to, but we'll have to get past that pretty quickly.' Rachel pointed to the ceiling. 'The loft, the thatched roof. Glanna already told us it's a fire hazard, right?'

Bea nodded. 'I guess, but what's that got to do with anything?'

'We set it alight, Bea. We burn this whole fucking place down, and we leave clues to suggest it might have been arson, that Glanna and her goon family might have caused the whole thing. Hopefully, that will lead the police and the fire crew to the cesspit – we can make sure it does – and in the melee that follows we just—' she opened and closed her fingers, 'disappear.'

Rachel didn't know what she was doing, but she knew she was terrified of losing Bea. She couldn't just let it end like this. If the trail to the Belvedere Saints had really gone cold, if The Weasel wasn't going to show, and if Glanna and Noah were involved in some way, then getting them arrested for arson, for murder and whatever else the investigation turned up, wasn't that a pretty decent compromise? A fair trade? Eric wouldn't like it, but Eric wouldn't need to be involved. Rachel could handle it all from here – with Bea.

'I don't—' Bea started to say.

294

'Think about it. A new life, a new us.'

'But the money? We don't have any money. How will we even survive?'

'Didn't you just say you have complete access to your dad's accounts?'

'Yeah, I do. I have everything, but—' Bea shook her head, the weight of Rachel's suggestion dawning on her. 'Wait a minute. Are you suggesting we steal from my parents?'

'Sorry, am I missing something here? Weren't you and your sister on the verge of laundering millions through your dad's books without him even knowing?' Rachel smirked. 'I mean, what's the difference?'

'I… I guess there isn't any, is there?'

'Absolutely none.'

Bea's expression softened. She placed the knife on the table and wrung her hands together. 'Do you mean it? Do you think we can do it?'

Rachel did. She really did.

*

'Wait!' Eli yelled. The babies paused in mid-flight. 'Just wait a minute!'

Evie snapped her fingers again. The creatures began to resume their furious charge, but Eli held up an arm and hollered. 'Just… *hold*!'

They stopped.

'Weren't you listening to what she just said?' he called out. 'We're fam'lee, all of us! You're my brothers, my sisters. We're the same!'

The baby closest to Eli cocked its head. He could smell its awful breath, could see the remains of fresh blood on its lips. He stepped towards it.

'Look at my face. Look at my skin,' he said. 'Look at the way I

295

walk, how my back curves, and my hand.' He pointed at it. 'Look at it. Then look at her.' He pointed towards Evie who was scowling back at him. 'She's not like us. She's not one of us.'

'Not us?' the creature said.

'Do you really fink she cares about you?' Eli continued. 'Do you really fink she'll take care of you? Understand you? Love you?'

There was a grumbling among the other babies, a scrambled muttering.

'Don't listen to him,' Evie said. 'He's trying to confuse you. He's just a horrible, hateful thing that wants to trick you into doing what he wants. He hasn't been there for you all this time, has he? Hasn't helped you the way I have. Hasn't let you do the things I've let you do. Kill the people you've killed.'

Another scrambled conversation, the sound of claws on stone, and the urgent gnashing of teeth.

'And where has that left you?' Eli asked them. 'You're still out here in the forest, feeding off whatever you can get your hands on. Berries, nettles, the odd rabbit. More of you die each year than are born. If you keep on trusting her, then within a few years there'll be none of you left. You want that, do you? Because I don't. I want you to survive. I want *us* to survive.'

'S'vive?' the creature said. 'S'vive, s'vive, s'vive!' .

Eli placed his hand on the baby's shoulder. It flinched.

'I will never use you, never hurt you,' he said and pointed at Evie. 'She will.'

'*Hurt* them?' Evie cried, outraged. 'Hurt them? I've fed them. Given them freedom to satisfy their desires. I've allowed them to be what they really are.'

'And what are they?' Eli asked her. 'Why don't you tell them what you fink of them? What you *really* fink of them.'

'*Yes, yes, yes, yes, yes…*' the babies cried.

Evie shuffled uncomfortably. 'Well, I—'

'*Tell us, tell us, tell us, tell us…*'

'Oh, come on!' she yelled. 'Don't you see what he's trying to do?'

'*Tell us, tell us, tell us, tell us…*'

'He's trying to turn you against me. That's all. It's just a trick.' She pointed at Eli. 'He might look like a dumb cripple, but he's clearly smarter than I thought.'

'*Eli, Eli, Eli, Eli, Eli…*'

'Oh, this is nonsense.' she said, turning to the darkest corner of the cave. 'Boys, this appears to be going nowhere. You're on.'

From behind an outcropping of black rock, two human-shaped silhouettes emerged. As the black figures stepped into the light, Eli's mouth fell open. It was Sebastian and Jonno the Turd Boy. What was he doing here, with them? It looked like a sickness had taken hold of him. Sebastian, however, was grinning. He was also holding a gun.

'Sorry, Eli old mate,' he said. 'I'm afraid there really is no other way.' He turned to Evie who nodded. 'See you on the other side.'

And, with that, Seb pulled the trigger.

*

It took them a couple of hours to rig the thatched roof with enough flammable liquid to make sure the whole place would be scorched to nothing more than a pile of smouldering embers. Bea had the idea of using the fuel from Richard's car. It seemed like a perfectly good plan to Rachel. The car wasn't going anywhere anytime soon, after all. Bea cut off a length of garden hose, pushed it into the fuel pipe, and sucked until petrol gushed from the open end. They filled half a dozen empty water bottles and shoved torn lengths of petrol-soaked bedsheets into the open tops, creating makeshift Molotov cocktails. Rachel's job was to tuck each bottle beneath the eaves in the large loft space, and then connect them with one long length of linen that would dangle through the loft hatch and onto the first-floor landing. When they were ready, they would light the fuse and

297

watch from a safe distance as the flames engulfed the bone-dry straw covering the top of the building.

When Rachel stood on the landing and opened the loft hatch, she immediately felt a cold breath float over her. She gazed up into the rectangular black hole, and she shivered as an icy tendril crept down her spine. She glanced back at Bea, who nodded eagerly.

'Looks a bit creepy,' Rachel said.

'You're a copper, aren't you?' Bea asked. 'Then get yourself up there.'

Rachel hoisted herself into the loft. She paused for a second to let her eyes adjust to the minimal light. Sunshine peeped through tiny gaps in the eaves, and dust and straw powder floated in the thick air. It was hot up there, and close. Everything felt cramped, claustrophobic.

'It smells of damp clothes,' Rachel said.

'That'll be the rat's piss,' Bea laughed.

'Just shut up and hand me that bottle, will you?'

As Rachel proceeded to place their little homemade bombs into the loft's dusty corners, she became convinced someone was sitting next to her in the darkness, watching everything she did, eyeing everything she touched. It felt like an untethered soul, an energy. She felt a soft finger touch her arm, and then trace the line of her cheekbone. She whirled around with a start, only to grab at sticky cobwebs and stray strands of straw. She thought she saw luminous eyes peering at her from the gloom, and she frantically pushed herself away before realising it was just beams of stray light reflecting off an old mirror. She shook off what she realised were merely irrational, baseless fears and swore under her breath. Bea was right, she was supposed to be trained for this kind of thing.

'Done,' she said, and wasted no time in shuffling towards the welcome embrace of the light that was pouring through the open hatch. She dragged a long length of damp bedsheet behind her and dropped it through the hole. 'There, that should do it.'

When the loft was completely rigged, they cracked open a

couple of beers in the kitchen, and they sat there with Bea's laptop fired up.

'So, we transfer the money, fetch Hattie and the kids, place the spare bottles by the mouth of the cesspit, light the touch paper, steal a truck, and head off into the sunset,' Bea said, boiling their little plan down to six short bullet points.

'That's it,' Rachel confirmed. 'Sounds simple, doesn't it?'

'I suppose it does. Almost too simple to be true.'

'These things never are, I'm afraid,' Rachel said. She knew that was true, too. There were a lot of things that could go wrong. Not least, Glanna and Noah catching them in the act, or Hattie refusing to go along with the plan.

'Then I guess we'll have to be flexible,' Bea offered. 'Roll with the punches.'

'You're so cliché,' Rachel said, laughing, but she couldn't help but feel a little sick inside. She was going against what she believed in, and against Eric and the team. She was letting everyone down. Letting Tommy down. Then again, if Glanna and her family really were connected to all of this, then there was at least some hope that the trail would lead to the Belvedere Saints. She had to believe that, had to cling to it.

'Okay,' Bea said as the screen sprang to life. 'We won't be greedy. We'll take just enough to set us up somewhere far away, and to give the kids the life they deserve. Three mil' ought to do it.'

'That seems like a lot,' Rachel replied, once again feeling the sharp pang of guilt eating away at her. 'Can't you lower it a little?'

'You're right,' Bea said. 'Let's make it two.'

'I tell you what, sweetheart.' A man's gruff voice boomed from the open doorway behind them. 'Let's make it twenty, and we'll say no more about it.'

Bea whirled around. 'Mr Deville!' she cried, shocked.

Rachel turned, and suddenly a switch flicked inside her. Three years of recurring nightmares came flooding back all at once. She felt herself gawping. She couldn't believe it. She was staring at a ghost, a real-life ghost. His name wasn't Terry Deville, which was obviously just another false identity. No, this was somebody else entirely; somebody she knew very well; somebody that everyone at Operation Glow believed had been assassinated by the Belvedere Saints as retribution for the fuck-up that night in the club. The night he and his crony killed an undercover police officer.

'Hello, Lyndsay,' she said.

'Hello, Tam. Long time, no see.'

BEFORE RACHEL
FRIDAY, 6ᵀᴴ SEPTEMBER 2019

'I don't see it.'

'Try the safe.'

'The safe's locked, Beth. Do you have the combination?'

She did, but this was costing them time.

'Move over, Tommy. I'll open the safe. You try the panel on the east wall.'

'Got it.'

Beth could feel her heart pounding. She fumbled for her phone, retrieved the safe's code from her internal notes, and entered it into the digital keypad: 061286. Lyndsay Arthur's date of birth.

She pulled the handle on the safe's door, but it didn't budge. She entered the code again. She thought perhaps she'd mis-keyed, but again the door didn't move. She checked her phone, and yep, she'd been right: 061286. That was the code Eric had given her. She tried one more time, but she already knew the result. Lyndsay had changed his passcode.

'Anything?' Tommy asked.

'No, I think he's changed it.'

'What?'

She shook her head. 'The code, I think he's changed it.'

'Shit.'

'I know. Anything with you?'

'Nothing.'

Tommy looked worried. He knew, as she did, that they didn't have much time. She needed to come up with something, anything. She thought fast. They'd tried the desk, the two pedestals, the filing cabinet, the overhead panel, and the panel in the wall. The only thing they hadn't tried was the safe. The laptop had to be inside.

'We're taking it,' she said, eventually.

'Taking what?'

'The bloody safe.'

'Isn't it bolted to the ground? How are we supposed to…?'

She grabbed the small steel box. Tommy was right, it was screwed to the concrete floor, but not securely. She thought the two of them together could pull the fixings free if they shook it hard enough.

'Come over here,' she said. 'I think we can lift it.'

Tommy knelt down beside her. He set his gun on the ground and grabbed the box, placing his hands just below hers.

'Right, first your way and then mine, and we pull upwards at the same time,' she said. 'We keep repeating that exact action until this bloody thing comes free.'

'Sure thing, boss,' he said, but he didn't look convinced.

'It's in there, Tommy,' she reassured him. 'I know it.'

Suddenly, Beth heard movement in the corridor, followed by male voices. She realised it was Lukasz, Lyndsay's chief bodyguard, and one other. She raised her hand to signal Tommy to pause, and then held her breath as the voices approached and stopped outside the office door.

'That fucking Zef is pissing me off, man. Who does he think he is, screaming at me like that?'

'My suggestion to you? You swallow your pride, and you do exactly as he says. Lyndsay puts a lot of faith in this guy. You try to go against him, bad things will happen to you.'

'I'd like to make bad things happen to him, I can tell you that. Really bad things.'

'You watch your mouth, Ishmael. You do something stupid, it looks bad on me, and that's not happening. You get me?'

'I just—'

'Just do as you're fucking told. You get paid good money for this job, better than you'll get loading boxes at the docks or working at another club. Don't ruin a good thing.'

'Yeah, I suppose you're right.'

'Of course I'm right.' There was the sound of bullish laughter from both men. 'Now, go and get the cars. Lyndsay's leaving in thirty minutes, and you know he hates being late.'

The voices faded as the two of them moved away. Beth turned to Tommy.

'Now.'

They shook the safe for what seemed like for ever, and at first it barely moved. They repeated the motion over and over again. Left, right, left, right, and pulling upwards with all their collective strength. Tommy grunted as his own hands worked the safe back and forth. Beth had all but given up hope when she felt the box come away from the ground, just a little.

'Keep going,' she said. 'Come on. Keep pulling.'

There was the sound of metal on concrete, and then the other side of the safe broke away. Within seconds they were falling backwards as the box came completely free and fell straight into Tommy's lap.

'You bloody beautiful bloke,' she said and kissed him on the lips, causing him to blush. 'We've got it. We've got it.'

He shook the safe, smiling. 'There's something in there, all right.'

'Well, let's not hang around,' she said. 'Let's get out of here.'

Beth stood and turned towards the exit, and that's when she saw the two men. They were standing in the doorway. Her heart sank. How had she not heard the door open?

'Tammy,' Lyndsay said. 'What are you doing in my office?'

'I—'

'She appears to have our safe, Zef.'

'That she does,' Zef said. He was a tall, slim man with a neatly trimmed beard and a moustache, waxed at the tips. He always wore a tailored suit and tie. He was also holding a gun.

'And who the hell is this bloke?' Lyndsay asked. 'Norman out

303

front says he was giving him trouble earlier, and you rescued him from a beating, Tam. A beating he well and truly deserved. You want to fill me in? You know, you being the front of house manager, an' all?'

Beth was reeling. What to do? What to say? She felt for the gun that was hooked in her waistband. How quickly could she draw it?

'We're SOCA, Lyndsay,' she said, trying to sound assured. 'That's the Serious Organised Crime Agency to you. The police. You understand? You and your mate here, you're both under arrest.'

Lyndsay doubled over, laughing. 'That's brilliant,' he said. 'That's fucking priceless, that is. What do you think, Zef?'

Zef was impassive. 'It's downright hilarious, Lyndsay.'

'Yeah, yeah,' Lyndsay said, slapping Zef on the back. 'That's the best... that's the best fucking joke I've heard all day. Just bloody hilarious. Really, *really* bloody good. You're a funny girl, Tam, a really funny girl.'

'There's nothing funny about this, Lyndsay. Nothing funny about what your organisation gets up to either. The illegal trafficking of human bodies, young girls and boys, all sold to the highest bidder. And the drugs. You know how many lives have been lost because of the shit you peddle? We're taking you in, and the world will be a better place for it. We have all the evidence we need to put the both of you away for a very, very long time.'

'Evidence?' he said. 'What, you mean in that safe? You think there's something incriminating in there? Open it up, Zef, go on.'

'Gladly,' Zef said, moving towards Tommy.

'Whoa there!' Tommy yelled. 'You okay with this, boss?'

'Boss?' Lyndsay smirked. 'You're the boss, Tam? What, of the po-lice? You're a big boss copper? You mean I screwed a big boss copper? Oh, this just gets better.'

'What?' Tommy exclaimed. 'He's lying, right? Tell me he's lying.'

Beth groaned. 'Now's not the time, Tommy.'

'Oh, Tommy mate,' Lyndsay sneered. 'Didn't she tell you? Yeah, we had a good time, didn't we, Tam? We had a real good time. Twice, if I remember rightly. Yeah, that's right. I tapped that sexy little arse two times. Tapped it real good.'

'Don't flatter yourself, Lyndsay,' Beth said, recalling the disgust, the shame. It had never left her. 'It was all in a day's work for me.'

'You're a prossie then,' Lyndsay said, a wry smile on his lips. 'A prossie boss copper.'

Tommy was glaring at her.

'Just let him open the safe,' she said. 'Let's see what's inside.'

Tommy shook his head and handed the safe over. Zef placed it on the desk, still gripping his gun. He tapped in the code and instantly the lock buzzed into life. He opened the door and pulled out a package. It was a box, wrapped in glossy red paper.

'Doesn't look like what you expected?' Lyndsay asked. 'What, you thought my laptop was in there? You did, didn't you?'

'I—' Beth found herself lost for words. 'Open the package.'

'Could be a bomb,' Lyndsay said. 'You sure you want to risk it?'

'Doesn't look like a bomb.'

'Oh, Tammy love,' he growled. 'Not everything's what it seems. You, of all people, should know that.'

'Just fucking open it, Lyndsay!'

'You sure are giving a lot of orders, given the situation you're in,' he replied. He nodded at Zef. 'Open it.'

Zef hooked a finger under the loose end of the paper and pulled, revealing a blue box. 'You want me to show her what's inside?'

'Oh, please do.'

Zef removed the lid, and there, nestled on cream-coloured silk, was a gold necklace, a diamond pendant hanging from its centre.

'It was going to be for you, Tam,' Lyndsay said. 'Something from me as a little—' he shrugged. 'I don't know. Romantic gesture, I guess. I suppose I'm a softie at heart, really.'

Beth was shaking her head. No, *no, no*! This couldn't be right. The intel, the information. Everything they had on Lyndsay suggested he kept it here. The incriminating evidence, the put-him-behind-bars-for ever kind of proof. Not some cheap, tacky reward for letting him get inside her knickers. She wanted to throw up, to run screaming out of the club, and to hideaway from everyone, especially from Tommy, who was shooting her a glare of angry disappointment. She'd let him down, let everyone down. She hated herself.

'Oh well. Zef's got the receipt,' Lyndsay said. 'I could always take it back. Or—' he moved towards Tammy, 'not.'

'Stay the hell away from me.'

'It doesn't have to end this way,' he said. 'You know, in fisticuffs like this. We could just pretend this never happened and go back to where we were. You working for me and being with me. We'd have to get rid of Tommy here, of course, but whatever. I could make that happen pretty easily.'

'You know that's not the way this is going to go, Lyndsay.'

'Well, what's your alternative, Tam? What? You think we're just gonna stick our hands up and come in quietly? What do you think about that, Zef?'

'I think that's very unlikely, Lyndsay. Very unlikely indeed.'

'It's not just us here,' Beth said, feigning confidence. 'We have back up.'

'Of course you do.' Lyndsay nodded towards the open door. 'And so do I.'

Beth slowly moved her fingers towards her waist.

'I wouldn't do that if I were you,' Zef said, pointing his gun at her. 'This thing's loaded and the safety's off.'

Beth glanced at Tommy who glared back at her. They both knew if they were going to make a move, they were going to have to do it quickly. Zef was right, his gun was trained directly on them. Beth's, on the other hand, was tucked in her belt and Tommy's was still lying on the floor. They might not be outgunned, but they were outflanked.

'You're not thinking about charging him, are you Tommy mate?' Lyndsay asked, grinning. 'You've got no hope. Zef's a dab hand with that thing. You wouldn't get within six feet of him before that gun went off. Tammy, please,' he said, turning to her. 'See sense, will ya? Just give it up. Your little operation here is a fuck-up. It's over. Don't let your pride get in the way of good judgement. As I see it, you have two options. You either give up and come back to work for me, or you try and fight it out with the two of us. Either way, your mate here has got to go.'

Beth eyed Tommy. She wasn't going to let him down like that, and he knew it. He winked at her, and she knew then that he was going to make a move. She started to shake her head, but he was already on his heels and hurtling towards Zef. Lyndsay was wrong. He did get within six feet of the wrong-footed accountant. In fact, his shoulder connected with Zef so hard that Beth heard a rib crack and the accountant grunt in agony. They both went tumbling onto the floor as Beth reached for her gun.

Everything from then on seemed to happen in slow motion. Her gun was in her hand. She crouched and took aim at Lyndsay. He was diving for cover behind the desk before she could pull the trigger. Tommy was pummelling Zef on the ground, raining down punches on the accountant's bloodied face. Beth circled the desk, looking for Lyndsay, and found him pulling a gun from one of the desk drawers. He whirled around and fired. She felt the cold hiss of the bullet as it whistled past her ear and buried itself in the filing cabinet behind her. She fired her own gun and watched as her bullet struck Lyndsay high in the shoulder. He fell backwards, a look of betrayal on his face. Zef slammed a knee into Tommy's testicles, and she heard her partner cry out in pain as he rolled sideways. Zef crawled out from beneath him, his nose shattered, his cheekbone collapsed. He reached for his gun, but Tommy swung a leg and kicked it away. Beth shifted her gaze back to where Lyndsay had fallen, but he was gone. She spun her head, frantically searching every corner of the room, but the only visible sign of him was a trail of fresh blood leading towards the open door. Zef was on his knees, and Tommy was gingerly getting to his feet, ready to swing a punch into the stricken accountant's midriff. What Tommy hadn't realised, what neither of them realised, was that Tommy's own gun was just inches from Zef's hand. Before they could react, Zef grabbed it, rolled onto his back, and fired three rounds, hitting Tommy's arm and chest with the first two. Neither of those on their own would have mattered much – Tommy was wearing a standard issue Kevlar vest, after all – but the one that hit him in the face, just to the left of his nose, did all the damage. Tommy's eye socket shattered as the bullet entered his frontal lobe and exited through the back of his head. The wall behind him was immediately splattered in blood and brain matter. As Tommy crumpled forward, Beth screamed. She aimed her gun and put four bullets into Zef Abraham's stomach and head.

As far as she could remember, she was still screaming when the backup team arrived.

DAY 5
WEDNESDAY, 3RD AUGUST 2022

'I don't think he's dead,' he heard a man's voice say. He realised it was Seb. 'Shall I finish him off?'

'No,' another voice said. Eli was pretty sure that one was Kid-Bastard Evie. 'Now that he's out of action we may as well take him back to Mother. For some reason she wants him alive. You and the boy will have to tie him to the board and drag him back to the beach.'

'In the water? What, like swim? Really? Why can't we just go back the way we came?'

'Because our little crippled friend here decided to blow up the café. You want to explain to the police and the reporters why you're carrying a man with a bullet wound up from the cellar of a building that just exploded? It might look a little suspicious, don't you think?'

There was a groan of disappointment. 'I suppose you're right. What about those things?'

'They won't be a problem,' Evie said. 'They're scared of their own shadows most of the time. I sent them away.'

Eli thought of his brothers and sisters. They were on the verge of helping him, he really believed that. It proved everything to him. Despite the power Evie held over them, the spell she'd cast, it couldn't beat blood; couldn't beat family.

His side was stinging real bad. He felt like throwing up, but he knew if he did that then Kid-Bastard Evie would realise he was awake, and she would probably fire the gun at him again. He could use his knife, but he didn't think he had the strength. He'd lost a lot of blood. He suddenly felt sad. He didn't want to die. His family

309

needed him. It felt good to be needed.

'The sea's pretty rough today, Evie. Why can't we just leave him here and swim back to get him when the waves calm down a bit?'

'Because Mother wants him for the offering, fuckwit. I thought you were supposed to be the smart one.'

'Ah, right. Yeah, I got it. That's tonight, isn't it?'

Eli felt the warmth of a human palm on his cheek. It was Evie's palm. He caught the scent of her perfume.

'Yep, it sure is. And Eli here is the guest of honour.'

*

'I already told you, I don't have it.'

'I'm sorry, sweetheart. I don't believe you,' Lyndsay said, the muzzle of the gun pressed into Bea's chest.

'She's telling the truth, Lyndsay,' Rachel cried. 'She hasn't got it. If she had, she would have given it to you already.'

'Oh, is that so, Tam? You know that, do you?'

'I've been living this fake life for over a year now. I've spent every waking minute with her, so yes, I think I'd know if she was lying.'

Lyndsay's eye twitched. 'Then we have ourselves a little predicament, don't we? A right little bugger's muddle, so to speak. What's the options then, Tammy my love? What's say I shoot your little girlfriend here, and you and me run off into the sunset like Bonnie and Clyde?'

'You kill her, and you get nothing.'

Lyndsay swung his arm at her. The butt of the pistol connected with her right cheek with a loud crunch. She cried out and tumbled to the ground, feeling the hot pain in her face as it started to swell. The taste of blood filled her mouth.

'Please don't tell me what I can and can't have,' he sneered. 'You tried that once before and look where that got you. Oh, and

310

by the way,' he massaged his left shoulder, 'that was for shooting me.'

'I guessed as much,' Rachel scowled, spitting blood on the floor.

'What about that idiot, Mike?' he asked, his attention returning to Bea. 'I lost contact with him a few days ago. You trying to tell me you don't know where he is either?'

'Mike?' Bea said. 'I don't know a Mike.'

'Oh, give me a break, love.'

'I swear, I don't.'

'So, you all just came way down here for a little family break, did you? Is that your story?'

'I don't understand,' Bea said.

Rachel pushed herself up to a sitting position. 'He's talking about The Weasel, Bea. I'm guessing they're one and the same.'

'You got it, Tam. You always were bright.'

'But we haven't heard from The Weasel, either,' Bea said. 'He just seemed to disappear. We thought he'd got cold feet.'

'That idiot wouldn't dare,' Lyndsay said. 'He knows better. He owes me.'

'Owes you?' Rachel hissed. 'He was mediating between those thugs you employ and these two civilians. Is that what you call payback?'

'You still think this has something to do with the Saints, don't you?' Lyndsay smirked. 'It doesn't. Those fools tried to gun me down in cold blood for what you did, but you know I'm smarter than that. I had a lookalike attend that dinner in my place. Paid him three hundred quid for the privilege. I told him to just show up and act like me. He didn't even know the risk he was taking. I already had my new identity by then. I had a nice-looking woman on my arm too – Tara. She thought I was in love with her, the sweet little thing. I wasn't really. Well, maybe a little. What I really wanted was a life I could hook onto. No one suspected a thing. Terry Deville? Old school antique tradesman?' He ran a hand through his

311

freshly dyed platinum hair and matching goatee. 'What an upstanding citizen. But then that prat Richard made contact through Tara, his ex of course, and wanted to earn himself a few bob. Seemed like he'd got himself into some serious hot water. Of course, he didn't know back then how hot the water could get. When I researched who he was, I realised he was married to your sister-in-law.' He gestured towards Bea. 'And what a nice surprise that was. The very same family that my newly deceased accountant,' he shot a glance at Rachel, 'had been trying to launder money through on my behalf. Do you believe in fate? I do, and I also believe in payback. Mike Periwinkle, my old mate from way back in the day, agreed to be my fence, and all of a sudden we had ourselves a little plan. The icing on the cake was when you, Beatrice, hooked up with our little nightclub manager friend here, Tammy Lush. Or should I say, Beth Mckinley?'

Rachel sneered. 'So, this was just some twisted plot to get back at me? For what? For defending myself? For avenging my partner's murder? That's sick.'

'Not only did you kill my friend,' Lyndsay snarled, 'you screwed me over in the process.'

'You screwed yourself over when you admitted to sleeping with a copper. I'm guessing that your senior partners in the organisation watched the CCTV tapes and heard everything.'

'Something like that,' he said. 'I don't regret it, though.' He leered at her. 'Do you?'

'Every... single... day.'

Lyndsay lunged for her again, but Bea intervened.

'Wait! Wait! Tell us what happened next. What happened to Tara? What happened to this Mike?'

Lyndsay glared at her. 'Well, Tara was supposed to collect the money from your prat of a brother-in-law and bring it back to me. It was gonna be double bubble, a nice little earner. Then Mike was to come back here, trick you and your sister into giving him access to your father's bank account, and then transfer twenty million into a little fund I have offshore.'

'Except Tara was killed in a car accident, and Mike disappeared,' Rachel said. She shook her head. It had all been a set up, and she'd fallen for it.

'Exactly. And now you two are going to help me find out what the fuck happened.' He pointed the gun at Rachel. 'Or else.'

'The family that runs this place,' Rachel said. 'They're not what they seem. They have dead bodies in their cesspit. Human bodies. Maybe your pal Mike is one of them. I'm pretty sure they were involved in Tara's death too.'

'Jesus, Tam!' Lyndsay said, suddenly furious. 'You really come up with some pretty out-there nonsense at times, you know that?'

'Look, look!' Bea said, her hands raised. 'I don't know about this Mike, or your wife, but the last code? I know where it is. I can get it for you, just don't hurt us. Please don't hurt us.'

'I'll make the demands round here, love. Now, why don't you just tell me where it is?'

'My sister. She's an infuriatingly risk-averse person by nature. She would never leave all of the account numbers and access codes in one place. She has the last one, I'm sure of it.'

'Bea, no!' Rachel said. 'You give it to him, he'll kill us both.'

'Shut your fucking mouth, Tammy!' Lyndsay said and struck Rachel with the back of his hand. She grit her teeth, determined not to show him how much it hurt. 'You're being so rude,' he said. 'Your friend here is trying to tell me something important, and all you keep doing is butting in.'

'Please, please!' Bea pleaded with him and placed a hand on his arm. 'I'll give it to you. I'll give you anything, but please, *please* don't hurt her again.'

Lyndsay grabbed her face, her cheeks squeezed between his fingers, his palm pushed hard into her chin. 'Then give me what I fucking want.'

'It's not here,' Bea said. 'Hattie has it, I know it. She'll have kept it close. We just need to find her.'

Lyndsay moved his face to within an inch of hers and exhaled. 'Then what are we waiting for?'

*

Hattie watched as Sally played with some old toys that Glanna had given to her. She seemed happy, which was good. Hattie wasn't. She felt dizzy – dizzy and sick – like she'd had too much to drink on top of too much Valium. Her body was numb, her mind a swimming mass of soft melted cheese. She was alive in body only. Her soul was floating somewhere in the ocean, or out there on the breeze like a bird. She was air, she was vapour.

'Look, Mummy,' Sally said. 'It's my ball thingy.'

The little crudely stitched face with the woollen hair gazed up at Hattie from its cushioned spot in her daughter's hands. It smiled at her and winked. Hattie wanted to eat it.

'Mummy… Mummy's tired, bunny.'

'Oh. You're always tired.'

'Mm… you're right.'

'I want to play in the garden again. With the old lady.'

'No… no, not a good idea.'

'But I want to!' Sally stomped her feet, which she never did.

'I… said… no.'

'Where's Daddy? I want Daddy!'

Hattie had a vague memory of a man she once called her husband. He was short… no wait… he may have been tall. He had dark hair, sometimes wore two days of stubble, and could be a bit flaky. She had another memory, a terrible memory. She pushed it away.

'Don't know.'

'I want him!'

'Shh, bunny. Mummy has a headache!'

'Mummy's boring!' Sally yelled and stormed out of the room.

Hattie tried to get up, but her muscles were useless. She could barely turn her head.

'What's happening to me?'

'It's the transition.' It was Glanna's voice, but it sounded like it was coming from the end of a very long tube. 'It can be difficult at first, but it gets easier. Believe me, I speak from personal experience. It's my cousin, you see? He needs a new partner. The previous one became more trouble than she was worth, so we had to leave her behind. A terrible shame. He likes you, though. He likes you a lot. He gave you some meat from his own livestock, and he hardly ever does that. You will become his.'

'His? What do you mean, his? I don't—'

'Oh, you will adjust in time. They all do, eventually.'

'They all do? Who are... they?'

'Amelia, Katharine, Ger, the others who came before. So many others. You will be renamed of course, as they were. I think Talwyn is a beautiful name, don't you?'

'No, I don't need a new name. I'm quite happy with—'

'Save your breath. You can't stop it now. The wheels are in motion.'

Hattie tried to feel afraid, to feel angry, but she felt nothing. A cloud of resignation descended upon her; an acceptance.

'When?'

'Tonight. It happens tonight.'

ALISON AND MICHAEL
JULY 2022

Alison had to get away. The things she'd seen, the things they'd done. These people, they were crazy. She'd thought Glanna was her friend but then she'd told her about who she was, who she truly was, not the fake version who gladly welcomed visitors into her home. What she'd done to the children was unforgiveable. She'd taken them from their families. Alison had to do something about that, had to let somebody know.

Michael hadn't come home after their argument. It was now a little after three in the morning and he still wasn't back. She was worried about him. Yes, she'd acted like an idiot, pushing him away like she had, but God, he could piss her off sometimes. Then things had changed. Glanna had showed up at the door with her words and her promises. Alison was planning to stay. She really was. She thought this could be her new universe, her new Zen. How wrong she had been. The Cormorans had blood on their hands, terrible, *terrible* blood. She had to leave.

She threw some clothes in a rucksack and grabbed the front door handle. It was jammed. The lights suddenly went out, and she cursed. 'Shit! That's bloody typical.' As she sought frantically for the fuse box, she heard the awful sound of a child's terrified scream. It came from somewhere upstairs. Alison cried out. A dark shadow ran across the kitchen and clattered into the knife rack. Something slammed into her hard, and she fell onto the tiled floor.

'Who's there? Who the hell is that?'

Another child's laugh, the pattering of tiny feet on wooden floorboards overhead.

'Jesus,' she heard herself say.

She leapt up and tried the door again. It was still jammed. She tried the light switch but there was nothing. She went to the living room window. A face glared back at her through the glass. It had the complexion of moonlight: yellow eyes, fractured skin. When Alison jerked her head away, the face disappeared. She tumbled over the sofa and gashed a shin on the coffee table. The back door stood open, and she ran towards it. Another shadow confronted her, but she shut her eyes and pushed through it. She had to get away.

'Michael! Michael, goddammit! Where are you?'

She trampled over the flowerbeds and staggered down the broken path. She barely noticed the heavy downpour.

Glanna stood on the driveway, Dolly at her side. Their images fizzed and blurred, their bodies at once apart, and then together.

Stay with us, Alison. Stay with us. We have a place for you. You are needed here.

Alison couldn't answer. She could barely breathe. She glanced at the road. It was cloaked in ominous darkness, save for that bloody girl. The emo girl, standing out there in the middle of the tarmac, still and soundless, seemingly oblivious to the rain that was soaking her hair and clothes. Her head was bowed, her hands open, palms out.

'Who the hell are you people?' Alison yelled as she turned and ran in the opposite direction. Her only route out of this place was the path through the forest. She didn't like that idea any more than the idea of staying in the house, but what choice did she have?

'Michael!' she yelled once more. 'Michael!'

As she pushed through the darkness, slamming into wet tree after wet tree, pulling herself through brambles and nettles, she thought of what she'd learned. The kids had been abducted. Glanna seemed to take what she wanted, regardless of the consequences. She thought of herself as some kind of mystical New Age sorceress, blessed with powers of regeneration, of immortality. It was ludicrous, really, laughable. Michael was considered an obstacle, a distraction. Glanna wanted him out of the way so she could partner

317

Alison up with the oddball guy, Petra. She now knew she was being indoctrinated, groomed for Glanna's freakish cult, and she'd almost bought into it too – almost. And those creatures, those horrible, childlike creatures that Glanna had shown her in the garden. Had they even been real?

Something grabbed at her ankle, and she fell.

'Shit! *Shit*!'

The clasp of her sandal had torn in half, and the shoe was now hanging limp, useless. She grabbed it and threw it angrily into the undergrowth.

'Bloody cheap crap!'

She unclasped the other and tossed that too. She was crying now, tears rolling down her cheeks and mingling with the rainwater. She wiped her forearm across her eyes and stood, almost slipping in the mud once more.

'Michael! Where the hell *are* you! I'm out here in these bloody woods, all on my own! This is so like you, just abandoning me like this! You're such an arsehole!' She was shaking with rage, but she was afraid too, like, really afraid. Her voice became a hoarse whisper. 'Michael? Please. I'm… lost out here.'

It was hopeless. She sounded hopeless.

That bitch; those monsters. They'd called themselves neighbours, friends even. She'd fallen for it, been taken in by the woman's charm and her fake promises. What the hell had she been thinking? How could she have been so naïve, so pathetically foolish? Michael had tried to tell her, but had she listened? No, she hadn't. She'd allowed herself to be seduced. To be… well, to be bloody groomed.

Suddenly there were eyes all around her: red and orange, hundreds of them floating in the black, glaring at her, malicious and hungry. She heard the sound of sniggering and scowling, like a thousand hissing snakes – the *babies*.

The air had turned putrid and dense, like a toxic fog. She backed away and turned on her heels, retreating the way she had come,

318

stumbling and staggering. She could hear a wailing, a sobbing, but she couldn't place it. She realised with a growing sense of despair that it was her. The sound was coming from *her*.

Childlike voices drifted from within the darkness.

Alison. We can see you. We can smell you. Come back to us, Alison, come back home.

'Stay the fuck away from me! I don't want you anywhere near me, you fucking freaks! I—' Tears continued to pour down her face. Rain ran from her slick hair and into her eyes. 'I don't believe in you!' She pushed through a dense thicket but tripped on a rock. She cried out but managed to keep her balance by pin-wheeling her arms and spreading her legs. She slid down a muddy slope, her body gathering pace at a frightening speed. She reached out and found a hanging strand of ivy that she clung onto in grim desperation. Her feet continued to slip and move in the mud, but she wedged them onto a slug of limestone. She began to laugh hysterically as her uncontrolled journey came to an abrupt halt.

She glanced over her shoulder. The eyes had gone, as had the cruel laughter. She was getting out of this. She was now so determined to make that her truth. Surely it had all been just a crazy hallucination, a nightmare. When she eventually woke up, she was going to slap Michael for being such a dream idiot, and then they would have coffee in bed, and maybe they would make love. She needed him close to her. She needed to feel the warmth of his skin. It had been so long.

She stepped through the wall of ivy, pushing it aside like a heavy drape, and gasped. She was at the cliff's edge. The land fell away sharply towards ferocious waves that roared savagely beneath her feet. It was that place; that terrible, blood-soaked hellhole. The ocean ravaged the rocks with an unyielding onslaught. The sky was black, the water charcoal-grey. A sweeping, silver beam from a distant lighthouse flitted across the undulating waves. The swell rose and fell with a growing intensity. The horizon appeared endless, her route to escape just a distant promise. The hiss from the ocean sounded like a desperate scream. Alison slipped at the edge, almost tumbling feet-first into the darkness.

That was when she saw it. It was gargantuan, a giant behemoth rising from the depths. Pounding waves lashed over enormous, heavy hooves. Its hands were encased in a swarm of black locusts, its huge equine skull resembling something from a freakish horror movie. It leered down at her. Drool hung from its teeth and lips, elastic and yellow.

'Oh... oh, *God*!'

She turned her head, only to be confronted by the sea of red and black once more. The eyes – they resembled a twisting loop of grotesque Halloween decorations. The laughter resumed. She heard her own voice from a million miles away, frantically reciting a once forgotten prayer.

'I believe in God, the father almighty, creator of Heaven and Earth, and in Jesus Christ, his only son, our lord, who was conceived by the Holy Spirit, born of the Virgin Mary...'

Something warm and wet fell onto her shoulder and she raised her head. Her vision was obscured by a huge, terrifying face: the skin cracked and bleeding, black, soulless eyes unmoving, dark crimson teeth hanging with festering skin. She smelled its breath. It reeked of death.

The beast smiled.

'Give yourself to him, Alison. Give yourself to Cernunnos, completely and totally, before it's too late!'

Alison whirled around. It was the Dolly-Glanna mutation. Glanna's head protruded from a twisted, bulging shoulder. Dolly's head was buried in its chest. It had four arms, crooked, angular legs, a hunched spine, skin that boiled and pulsed, and black and orange eyes. It was surrounded by dozens of those terrifying babies.

'Leave me alone!' she yelled, but she was barely audible through the sound of the pouring rain. 'This isn't real! This is some hellish nightmare! You're not real! None of you are *real*!'

'Your fate is already written, Alison. It is cast in rock. You'll

320

be at one with us, for ever! You shouldn't feel afraid, you should feel blessed.'

'I won't have anything to do with you or your... sick, murderous freak show of a family!' She heard herself sobbing once more. 'I want Michael. I want to go home with my husband!'

'I'm afraid that's impossible, my dear,' the Dolly-Glanna thing said, gesturing with its many fingers. Suddenly a pair of figures emerged from the shadows. It was the two boys, and they were carrying something heavy. The big one, Aaron, smirked at her as they tossed it at her feet. It was a body. A dead body. As the bloodied head became visible, she realised with a sickening certainty that she was staring at the face of her husband.

'Michael!' she yelled. 'You bitch!' She sobbed and trembled, as her world began to fall away.

She saw the Dolly-Glanna thing move one of its hands through the air, smelled the scent of incense and firewood, watched as the gigantic horse-beast began to dilute and fade, and felt the soft carpet of wet leaves as her head connected with the ground.

When she awoke, she felt different, better somehow.

A man was there, illuminated by an orange glow from a papered-over window. He looked down at her, a sympathetic smile on a smooth, bespectacled face.

'Hello, Ger,' he said. 'Welcome to your new home.'

DAY 6
THURSDAY, 4TH AUGUST 2022

It was the early hours of the morning. The cove at the little idyllic hamlet of Bodhmall's Rest was at peace. The water lapped gently onto the soft sand and a delicate night breeze kissed the long grass that flourished at the base of the cliffs. The beach was bathed in a silky darkness, save for the silvered gilt of moonlight and the orange glare of lit torches. A metal cage was placed close to the water's edge, large bunches of heather placed around its perimeter. Eli crouched within this cage like a stray, wounded dog, his good arm in a bloodied sling.

He scowled at the group and glared at Sweet Mother. They stood in a wide semi-circle that surrounded the cage. The water was at Eli's back which made him feel sick and very, very anxious. Eli hated the water. JTB and the little red-headed girl were part of the group, which was confusing to him. Their mother, the angry woman, stood in the middle. She wore a black mask, her eyes and mouth covered. She wasn't moving.

Eli let his eyes wander towards the tree-lined hill. He was searching for the Red Man. Where was he? He'd done everything he'd asked, except kill Evie of course. What had the Red Man expected? The boys had been easy, but Evie? She'd always been the smart one.

'We gather here this sacred morning, brothers, sisters and friends, for a covenant,' Sweet Mother said. She was eyeing the angry woman. 'And for a blessing. A blessing to our lord, master and redeemer.'

'*The horned one*!' the crowd yelled.

'He feeds us, nourishes us, and holds us eternal. We live

because he lets us live. We breathe because he gives us air. We love because he gives us hearts that beat and eyes that see.'

'Blesséd be!' the crowd hollered. 'Blesséd be!'

'Blesséd be!' Sweet Mother agreed. 'Blesséd be! Blesséd be the one who cares for us, and who holds us in his arms unconditionally – his children, his imperfect creations.' She approached the angry woman. 'Harriet, are you ready to let go of your earthly existence, of the name your life-givers gave to you? Are you ready to join with us, to embrace what you will inevitably become?'

The angry woman was silent. Eli thought she had fallen asleep or passed out standing up. He guessed that was possible. Suddenly she spoke in a little mouse voice.

'Yes, I am.'

'Will you swear yourself to him for all of eternity?'

'I will.'

'Will you forego all sin, all privilege, and all selfish thoughts?'

'I will.'

'Will you take the name Talwyn of Cormoran, she of fair hand and selfless soul?'

'I will.'

'And will you devote yourself to Brother Bertrand? Will you obey his wishes? Will you be his devoted servant for as long as you draw breath and your veins run red?'

'I will.'

Eli gasped. What about her husband? What would he have to say about all this? Wouldn't he be furious? Wouldn't he come after Sweet Mother? Or had he already tried and ended up the same way as the Red Man? Eli thought he already knew the answer to that question, without really knowing.

Bertrand approached the angry woman. He was wearing a lilac dress robe, a sprig of lavender woven into his single plait of hair. He appeared to be crying.

'These are tears of joy, my angel,' Bertrand said. 'Tears of joy, love and pure, utter happiness.' He removed the angry woman's mask. She was crying too, but Eli guessed hers weren't happy tears. 'Come, Talwyn,' Bertrand said. 'Join with us in the circle. You are an important piece of it now.'

'I betroth myself to you,' the angry woman said, but her eyes were black, unseeing. 'I am yours, eternal.'

'Talwyn, Talwyn, Talwyn, Talwyn…' the group chanted as Bertrand led her to her place alongside him.

'Our circle has grown, my friends!' Sweet Mother yelled, the wind suddenly gathering force. 'We have become whole once more, like the essential pieces of life, welded together in an unbreakable embrace. We must call to him!'

'Call to him!' the group hollered.

'Let us yell at the top of our lungs, my friends, for he will listen to those who would wish to be heard! We must call for him as one, our voices a harmonious crescendo of love, devotion and servitude! Will you join me?'

'We will!' The group bowed their heads.

'Will you help me?'

They stomped their feet. 'We will!'

Sweet Mother's face melted and transformed into the face of Grandmother Dolly before shifting back again. 'Will you give yourselves completely and utterly for me?'

The trees at the summit of the cliff parted in the middle, and Eli heard a low guttural growl. The air was filled with the stench of death.

'We will!'

'Then come to us, oh horned one! Come o come! Be one with us this moonlit night! Through the blessed waters, the green o' this sacred forest, over the mighty cliffs that protect us from the non-believers. Be with us, be upon us, do not forsake us. Come, o come! Come, o come!'

'*Come, o come! Come, o come! Come, o come!*'

Eli had heard this chant before, and it never ended well. He glanced nervously behind him at the growing tide, and pushed himself towards the front of the cage as the water began to encroach at his feet. He swung his head and looked up towards the cliff top. There was a loud crack as earth shifted, rocks tumbled, and trees split in half. He knew what was about to happen.

He was coming.

*

Rachel crouched behind the large dune at the western entrance to the beach. Bea was beside her, Lyndsay at her rear, the muzzle of the gun pressed into her lower back.

'What the fuck is going on here?' he said. 'I mean, I knew these people were weird, but this is a whole other level.'

'I told you,' Rachel said. 'It's Glanna. She's not what she seems.'

Lyndsay huffed in disbelief. 'Which one's your sister?' he asked, pushing Bea forward.

'The one who was just wearing the mask.' She turned to Rachel. 'I have no idea what she's doing.'

'I think Glanna has some sort of hold on her,' Rachel said. 'The kids too.'

'But how could that be? You know Hattie. She's no pushover.'

'Drugs would be my guess,' Rachel said. 'That and some kind of mind manipulation. I think Glanna and the others are well rehearsed at it.' She recalled her encounter with Glanna and her mother in the garden. They seemed to be able to make you see things, to believe.

'We've got to help them. They're getting wrapped up in something dangerous, Rach. We need to get them out of here.'

'Keep it together,' Lyndsay said. 'Remember what we're here for.'

'And what's your plan, genius?' Rachel sneered, turning to him. 'Go in all guns blazing?'

'If I have to.'

'And shoot anyone who gets in your way?'

'That's the general idea.'

'There are innocent people out there, Lyndsay,' Rachel said. 'I'm not going to let you roll the dice on whether they get out of this alive or not.'

Lyndsay shoved her to the ground. 'I don't think you have much option in the matter, and even if you did, you think I'm gonna let you stand in the way of me getting my hands on twenty mil?'

Rachel gritted her teeth. 'Then you'll have to put a bullet in me.'

'Gladly,' he said, aiming the gun.

'Wait!' Bea cried. 'I'll go.'

'You'll what?' Rachel said.

'I'll go.' Bea turned to Lyndsay. 'I'll do it.'

'That's my girl,' he said. 'Well, go on then. Off you trot.'

*

Ger didn't see him at first. She was too engaged in the ritual, too absorbed in the calling. Cernunnos was coming – the horned one. He would provide them all with absolution. They would repent and he would listen, Glanna had told them so. She was so thrilled, so energised. They all were.

The little red-headed princess was with them too. The angel. The daughter she'd always dreamed of. Her hair was like fire. It reminded her of another time, recalled to her something beautiful, something she'd let slip away. The memory was foggy, like a loved one standing in so much smoke.

Glanna had promised her the girl. She and Petra would have a child, a crimson-haired blessing. It would be her reward for her devotion, her dedication. She felt like it was her missing piece. She would cherish her.

When the man touched her shoulders, it felt like cool water on skin. With a shudder, she smiled and turned to see who it was. He was barely recognisable at first. His face was mainly bone and

326

gristle, but his eyes… It was those two beautiful pastel-blue orbs that brought her back. Like elegant marbles or cherished jewels. She could never have forgotten them. She knew instantly who was standing before her. It was her love.

He gave a slight nod of the head, raised an emaciated arm, and held a bony finger towards the shoreline. She realised he was pointing towards the disabled boy in the cage. The boy was wearing a jewelled silver pendant around his neck. A half-heart pendant. She looked down and saw the other half of that pendant hanging around her own neck. How had she not noticed it before? She suddenly knew everything. Evelyn had carried out the deed of course, but the conductor, the orchestrator, was standing just a few short feet in front of her. It had been Glanna who had manipulated Alison (she remembered that was her real name). It had been Glanna who had deliberately driven a wedge between her and Michael. And, it had been Glanna who had maliciously ordered her husband's execution.

Vis-a-vis, it was Glanna who had to pay.

*

Something was beginning to happen. The trees were bending and twisting, the earth was shaking like jelly, and the storm clouds were drifting in from the south like giant black balls of cotton. Eli knew if he didn't get out of this cage, the storm would build and then the waves would come barrelling towards him, drowning him in so much salty, silt-riddled sea water. It would fill his mouth and lungs with filth and slime. He retched and spat out bile, which was stupid. He had more important things to worry about.

He could see the Red Man standing in the shadows. He was talking to the pretty lady. *Maybe*, he thought, *she will remember now*. The lady glanced at Eli, and he placed a hand instinctively on the shiny thing. She'd probably want it back, of course, but that was okay. She needed it more than he did.

The Terrible Babies were gathered at the base of the cliff. They were trying to hide among the grass and sand. He could see the confusion on their faces. Why was Eli now in a cage? Why had Kid-Bastard Evie almost tricked them into attacking their own brother? And why did Sweet Mother have everyone gathered together on the beach in the middle of the night?

Eli glanced at Evie. She had her eyes closed and seemed to be muttering to herself. If he was going to get out of this, he was going to have to out-think her. He knew that was going to be difficult. She was tricky.

He nodded towards the eldest baby, the one with the grey hair hanging over thick ears. She raised her eyebrows which was a sign she was listening.

Not yet, Eli said without words. *We need to wait, just a little while longer.*

Whatever Kid-Bastard Evie was up to, Eli knew he needed to let her make the first move. Evie had taught Eli this. It was called distraction. The other thing Kid-Bastard Evie had told him about was adaptability. When things didn't go according to plan, you needed to think fast and adapt. When the lady with the freckly face suddenly stepped out into the open from behind the dunes, Eli knew that was exactly what he needed to do.

*

Evie had a clear bird's-eye view of everything as it unfolded. She called it her bubble-eye, a little trick she had to use sparingly as it sucked the air from her lungs like a tyre with a puncture. In this situation, however, she considered a little lost oxygen to be a small price to pay. There were too many factors at play here, too many interlopers.

Firstly, there was Eli. The cripple was out to get Evie, which she thought understandable, particularly as she had got him in this mess in the first place. That was okay. He was just a pawn after all,

328

a pawn that had its uses. Then there were those little toothy fuckers. They were allied with the cripple, she knew that now. They were all out there, hiding in the shadows in the mistaken belief that they couldn't be seen – idiots. The guy with the gun was new and interesting. He would have to be dealt with, as would the female police officer with the fake name. Evie wasn't stupid enough not to realise that if the detective had deemed it necessary to go undercover in Bodhmall's, then there had to be a whole team behind her. The new lady, the one bedding down with Petra, had been acting odd, so Evie was keeping part of her bubble-eye on her too. She was talking to herself and gesticulating wildly as if trying to communicate with someone close by. Whoever it was, they were invisible to her. And then there was Glanna, her fake mother, the woman who had killed her parents.

Evie could see her pet, Morgawr, too. She was swimming way out there in the deep water, waiting patiently to be summoned. Her scales were shimmering blue, her tail long and silken. *Not today, my darling*, she thought, *not today*. Morgawr had been her back up plan, but Evie knew it was way too late for her to help her now. Things had gone too far for that. Evie had to do this on her own. She had to do this for her mother and father.

It had been Hilda – or Morai, to be more precise – who had filled her in. Hilda was just her human moniker. Morai was the name of her soul eternal. She'd seen it all unfold over many centuries: the killings, the abductions, the failed births. Glanna had killed her husband too, many decades ago, over the border between Dozmary Point and Bodhmall's Rest. Morai had been biding her time ever since, waiting for the right moment, the right person to exact her revenge. She had sought Evie out, she knew that. Evie wasn't so naive as to believe their meeting had been by chance. Who better to take out the head of a rival family than an insider? An insider with beef. Morai had told her all about how Glanna had manipulated Evie's mother and seduced her father, only to dispose of him when she'd obtained all she needed – namely his seed and his blood. Evie thought this was pretty gross. Her mother, Tilly, had remained at Bodhmall's for some time after her husband had disappeared, but then the spell on her had worn thin, and she had started to remember things, like who her daughter was. When Tilly tried to sneak Evie away (although her name hadn't been Evie then – it had been Rebecca), Glanna had confronted her. There had been a fight, of course – Tilly was also blessed with the knack – but Glanna had been around for so much longer. Eventually, she'd proven too powerful, and her mother had become just another one of her victims.

As it turned out, Morai knew some secrets her mother hadn't known; some pretty useful information about Glanna's weak spot, her Achilles heel. It was very interesting. Evie planned to exploit it to the fullest extent possible. She would avenge her parents, her lost childhood, and all the years of having to do Glanna's dirty work, too. More than that, she would lay claim to Bodhmall's Rest: the properties, the land, and the roads in and out. She knew it would go for a pretty hefty sum. Ten, fifteen million, maybe more, and she'd earned it. She'd earned everything.

*

'Sorry, sorry,' Bea held up her hands. 'I'm really, truly sorry to interrupt your... thing here, but I really need to speak to my sister, Hattie.'

Glanna looked up. 'There is no Hattie here, Beatrice. I'm afraid you must be mistaken.'

'Oh no, I'm quite right, actually. I can see her. She's standing just over there, see? And my nephew, Jonno, and niece, Sally-Ann. There they are. Hi, guys.' She waved.

Paz approached. 'I'm afraid you need to leave. This is private property.'

'Whoa there, fella,' Bea said, laughing. 'It's me here, Bea. You know me, right? We had a drink together the other night. You must

330

remember.'

'You need to leave now, dear, before things get out of hand.' He grabbed her by the arm, but Bea swiftly yanked it away.

'I suggest you get your hands off me, old man,' she said, irritated. 'That's my family, and they look pretty uncomfortable. Come on, guys. Let's get out of here.'

Glanna nodded to Bertrand, who immediately stepped out of the circle. 'You're leaving, young lady, whether you like it or not.'

'Well, I don't,' Bea said. 'And I won't.'

Bertrand lunged for her, but she skipped out of the way. Rachel laughed. *That's my girl*, she thought, fighting the urge to go in after her. Lyndsay's gun was still pressed into her spine.

'Too slow, old man,' Bea said, ducking under Pascoe's arms. 'I'm afraid you're gonna have to do better than that.'

'You're outnumbered, Beatrice,' Glanna said, unmoved. 'Eventually you'll be extracted, and the longer this goes on, the more chance there is of you getting hurt. Or worse.'

'Oh, you mean like Richard?' Bea said, spinning behind a copse of bracken. 'You mean like him? I know all about what happened to him, you know.'

'I don't know what you mean,' Glanna said.

'Okay. Well, we'll see if the police agree, shall we? They're on their way, by the way. I called them earlier. I told them all about the cesspit, and what you keep in there.' Bea glanced at Hattie who was staring into the middle distance. 'I'm sorry, sis. I won't say anything in front of the kids, but I promise I'll fill you in later. Just—' she paused. 'Ready yourself.'

'It sounds like you've concocted some sort of mistaken fantasy, my dear,' Glanna said, interrupting. She glared at Pascoe. 'You really do have quite the fertile imagination.'

Paz took the hint and dived for Bea's feet, but she skipped away again, dancing between Paz and the onrushing Bertrand. 'Oh, you guys are way past your best, aren't you?' Bea said, laughing. 'You need a couple of younger bodyguards, Glanna. I think these two are

331

beyond their sell-by date.'

As Bertrand doubled over and Pascoe leaned against a tree to catch his breath, Bea walked confidently towards her sister.

'Now,' she said. 'Hattie and I have some catching up to do.'

As Bea approached, a figure rushed at her from her blindside. Rachel saw it happen in an instant. It was Jonno, the kid. He had a large, jagged rock in his hands, and he swung it towards Bea's exposed skull. As rock struck bone, Rachel heard a sickening crunch, and she watched helplessly as Bea's body collapsed to the floor.

'Jonno!' she cried. 'What the hell have you done? What have you done?' She leapt from her place behind the dune, ignoring Lyndsay's grasping hands. 'Bea!' she yelled. '*Bea!*'

'Oh, for fuck's sake,' she heard Lyndsay huff from behind her. She dived instinctively on top of her partner's body as he fired off two shots into the night sky. 'Okey-dokey! Now I've got your attention,' he said. 'Everyone just get down on the ground before I blow your carrot-crunching brains out. Well, go on then! Straight away, not tomorrow!' Glanna and the others gingerly lowered themselves towards the sand as Lyndsay turned to Hattie. 'Right,' he said, holding out a hand to her. 'To be clear: the blonde one's coming with me.'

*

Eli knew it was now or never. He slipped his arm from its sling, pulled the knife from the pocket of his shorts, and shoved the blade into the cage's rusty lock. He knew it wouldn't hold. The thing had been in the family for decades and had been used more times than he cared to mention. While everyone stood mesmerised by the freckly-faced woman dancing around like a rabbit being chased by a fox – two old, out of shape foxes, for that matter – he twisted the knife and heard a satisfying crunch as the latch disengaged.

He let out a smug chuckle and went to pull the door open, but just at that exact moment, an unusually large swell swept towards the shoreline, immediately covering the sand around his feet. He felt cold sea water creep up his ankles.

'Ugh!' he yelped, as he felt his throat begin to close. He gagged. 'Get off me!' he yelled at the water. 'Get, ugh, get away from me!'

In his haste he tripped over his own feet and fell face first into the waves. Frothy, salty liquid entered his mouth and nose. He gasped for air, but in the process, he sucked more water into his lungs. He tried to drag himself along the wet sand, but his hands only grasped sodden, slimy seaweed instead, and he pushed it away. More water rushed over his flailing body. He was drowning. Idiot! He thought he'd escaped, but he'd left it too late and now the tide had come in and he was going to die there on the beach like the fool that he was, bobbing in the water like a dead fish. He hated fish.

Suddenly he heard two loud cracks, like lightning striking the ground. It was followed by shouting and cursing,

'Come on, cripple,' he heard a familiar female voice whisper in his ear. 'We've got work to do.'

He looked up through wet, stinging eyes. 'Evie?'

'We both want her dead, don't we?' she said, glancing furtively over her shoulder. 'Well, now's our chance.'

*

As the man with the gun went to pull Talwyn – no, Hattie – towards him, Alison made her move. Michael had told her this was going to happen, so she was well prepared. She knew that the dangerous criminal, the man who Michael had shady business with, would emerge from the dunes just as the boy, Jonno, struck the pretty woman over the head with a rock. She knew the man would be carrying a gun, she knew that he would unload two bullets into the sky, and she also knew he wanted Hattie. She didn't know why – Michael didn't seem to know why, either – but it didn't matter.

What mattered was there was going to be a gun in easy reach, and the man holding it wasn't going to suspect that the little woman with the vacant stare was going to reach out and grab it. But grab it she did.

'What the fuck?' Lyndsay yelled in surprise.

Alison pointed the gun at his knee and fired.

'Aargh!' Lyndsay fell to the ground in a heap, bone and bloodied flesh now visible through the newly formed hole in his leg.

Alison then turned to Petra and unloaded a bullet into his face. His head exploded instantly as his body was thrown violently backwards into the onrushing tide. He would no longer be able to lay a single hand on her body. He was scum.

She heard the ghostly yelp of encouragement from her husband. He was standing beside her, his hand on her hip. He was at one with her, as always. Her guardian.

'You people are sick,' she said, turning to Glanna. 'Sick and disturbed.'

'Jonno, Seb,' Glanna said. 'Will you take the gun from this woman? She seems to have lost her senses.'

Alison heard movement from her left, and she swung the gun towards the approaching pair. 'Move, and I'll blow your fucking brains out.'

'No!' Rachel yelled. 'No. It's not their fault. They've been brainwashed, drugged. They're confused.'

'He didn't seem too confused when he smashed that rock into your friend's skull,' Alison said.

'He didn't know what he was doing. The real Jonno would never have done that to his auntie, would you, kiddo?'

'I—' Jonno shook his head. 'She was intruding.'

'See what I mean?' Alison cried. 'Now sit, the pair of you, or you'll be joining that sick son of a bitch in the water.'

'Ger,' Glanna interjected. 'This is foolish.'

'My name's Alison, Glanna, but you already know that. You

really are something, you know? You drug people, manipulate them, murder their husbands, and steal their children. And for what?'

'You don't understand,' Glanna said. 'You'll never understand.'

'I don't think I will. Only a lunatic can understand lunacy.' She turned to Hattie and then to the older woman, Katharine. 'You two need to wake up from whatever spell she's put us all under. She's taken your family, or at least tried to, and eventually she will tire of all of us. We'll all go the same way as Amy, hanging from a tree like a ragdoll. You want that, do you?'

Hattie stood motionless, but the sharp remark seemed to spark Katharine into life.

'Amy's... dead?'

Alison nodded. 'I saw her, last night. They'd hung her like a piece of raw meat. They'd strangled the life from her, Katharine.'

'You killed Amelia, Glanna? But why?' Katharine's face turned the colour of spoiled milk.

'She was talking,' Glanna said. 'To the Penrose woman. She broke our trust.'

'She was our friend.'

'She was no friend of mine.'

'But she was a friend of mine!' Katharine yelled. She approached her. 'She was my only friend in this terrible place!'

'I suggest you take a step backwards,' Glanna said, her face impassive. 'You've been turning for weeks, I've sensed it. Your time was coming too. Don't let it be now.'

'I've been seeing things,' Katharine continued. 'I've been remembering things. It's been foggy, blurred, but gradually it's been coming together. That's why I spoke to her.' She pointed to Bea's prone body. 'I was trying to remember, to reconnect with other humans. My brain has been such a mush, such a mess. You—' she paused. 'You took my husband too. I remember that now. The baby you were carrying, it was his, wasn't it?'

335

'He was contaminated,' Glanna huffed. 'He was such a disappointment.'

'And now you have *her* husband's seed inside you, don't you?' Katharine yelled, pointing at Hattie. 'I bet he's dead too, am I right?'

'What?' Jonno said with a start. 'My dad?'

'He had seen too much,' Glanna sighed.

'My dad's dead?' Jonno started to cry. 'You killed my dad?'

'He intruded onto our property and saw me birthing. He had no right. I still have high hopes for him, though. Our line can be strong once more.' She turned to the others. 'The Cormorans will no longer be cast in the shadows, hidden in this little unseen corner of our once great county. We can grow, we can breed.'

'I have no interest in your family or your breeding,' Katharine sneered. 'Frankly I couldn't care less if she puts a bullet in your head. I was Mary, Mary Elizabeth Gordon, and I was a happily married woman with a nice house, good job and a loving husband. You! You crazy bitch!' She thrust out a wavering finger. 'You took that from me!'

'If you mean I removed the bonds that tied you to a life that was beneath you, then you're right, I did, and I'd do it again, too.'

'That thing you made us see, that awful, giant creature. You told us it was our God, our great protector, but it was a lie too, wasn't it? A vision brought on by whatever it was you were drugging us with. That, and your manipulative words, too.'

'You only saw what you wanted to see, Katharine. If he wasn't already inside of you, inside all of you, then he would have remained invisible. You wanted to believe, and you wanted a piece of this life.'

'All I want is my dad,' Jonno said, suddenly standing between Alison and Katharine.

'And my mother and grandmother,' Seb said. 'I want them, too.'

'I'm sorry, boys,' Alison said. 'I'm so sorry, but they're gone.

She took them.'

'Then shoot her,' Jonno hissed through gritted teeth. 'Kill her!'

Seb nodded. 'Blow her murdering brains out.'

'Gladly,' Alison said, and aimed the gun at Glanna's face. 'This is for all of them.'

There was a loud bang, followed by the acrid scent of spent gunpowder. Glanna didn't even flinch, which was hardly surprising because the trigger hadn't been pulled. When Alison looked down at her own chest, she saw the red blossom of blood spreading across her white T-shirt. The energy suddenly left her legs. She glanced back at Michael who was trying to reach for her. She touched the pendant hanging around her neck as the world faded into darkness.

'You stupid bitch!' she heard a man's voice shout from somewhere above her. 'You thought I'd only carry one gun?'

*

Hattie watched everything happen in fast-forward. It was as though her life had been sucked from her, transferred to a VHS cassette, and played at superfast speed. She only caught snippets of what was going on: Jonno was angry; the lady, Ger, had a gun and was pointing it at Glanna; a man on the ground was bleeding but reaching for something strapped to his ankle; the crippled boy and the girl were up to something, but she couldn't make out what; Rachel was holding Bea, who seemed to be bleeding from a wound in her head; Sally was sitting in the sand and crying.

Why did she feel like this? Why did she feel so obsolete? She glanced up at the forest and saw the emerging shape of Cernunnos: the head of a horse, the shoulders of a mighty beast. Glanna was right, he was coming, and that meant the reckoning was about to happen. She needed to be good. She needed to obey. She needed to repent, repent everything, or her family would die. They would all die!

337

'Bea,' Rachel said. 'Bea, wake up. Please, Bea!'

She turned to Sally who was sobbing.

'Sally, sweetheart. Come over here. It's too dangerous over there.'

Sally looked up. 'She said my dad was dead. Is it true?'

Rachel didn't know what to say. 'I don't know, sweetheart, but I'll find out what happened, I promise, I really will, but first you need to walk over to me.'

Sally stood. 'Is Aunt Bea okay?'

'She's really hurt, baby. Really hurt. We need to get her to the hospital.'

'But what about Mummy and Jonno?'

'I'll come back for them.'

Sally shuffled towards her. Rachel swept her up in her arms and hugged her. 'Good girl. Now, I'm going to lift your auntie up, okay? And we're going to walk up that path and back to the house. You'll need to walk beside me, but stay really close. You understand?'

Sally nodded.

'And no noise, okay? We need to be really quiet.'

'Like a mouse?' Sally suggested, her finger to her lips.

'Exactly,' Rachel said.

However, before she could make her move, Lyndsay pulled a gun from an ankle holster and unloaded a round into Ger's chest.

She grabbed Sally. 'We need to go, now!'

'Back to the house,' Evie yelled at Eli. 'We need to get back to the cottage, to Spriggan's.'

'I don't understand,' Eli said. 'She's right there in front of us.'

Evie stooped down to him. 'We can't finish it at the beach, Eli.

338

We need to use it against her.'

'What? Use what against her?' Eli asked. He was still reeling from his terrifying experience at the water's edge.

'Her weakness, stupid,' Evie replied. 'Hilda told me all about it. That's why she hates the roof of that cottage so damn much.'

'I don't get it.' Eli was panting now. His lungs were still filled with salty liquid. Why was he doing what Evie asked? Hadn't she tried to kill him, at least twice? He glanced over his shoulder and was relieved to see his brothers and sisters skulking in the bushes along the edge of the path. He knew they were there if he needed them.

Evie grabbed him by the shoulders.

'Fire!' she said, her eyes ablaze. 'Glanna's afraid of fire!'

*

'This is getting out of fucking hand!' Lyndsay yelled. 'Getting right out of hand. All I want is the blonde woman. That's all. Now, if someone else tries to stop me or grab my gun, then I'm going to shoot the lot of you, one by one. You hear me!' He was limping badly from his shattered kneecap.

'You'll get no trouble from us,' Paz said, holding up his hands. 'Bert? Glanna? Do we agree?'

'Reluctantly, but yes,' Glanna said, eyeing the hills.

'And you boys?' Lyndsay asked. 'You gonna give me any trouble?'

Jonno and Seb looked at each other and shook their heads.

'Okay, good. That's good.'

As Lyndsay approached Hattie, she saw the look of a man slightly unhinged. He was at the edge of a precipice, she realised. He would do anything to get what he wanted. She would go with him, but with the satisfaction of knowing he would come unstuck. The Horned God was coming, and the man had committed terrible sins, sins for which he had not atoned. She didn't fear him as he

339

grabbed her arm and twisted it painfully behind her back; she wasn't concerned as he pushed her up the hill towards the house; she wasn't afraid of the smouldering gun pushed into her ribs. She could hear Cernunnos following them from his place within the forest.

She knew she would be protected.

*

'I need my phone,' Rachel said, laying Bea carefully on the sofa and rushing up the stairs. 'Stay with your Aunt Bea, Sal.'

She barged into the door of her bedroom and ran to the bedside table.

'Shit!' she yelled as she grabbed her phone. Her battery was dead. She looked around for her charger. She knew it was probably buried in the mountain of clothes that were scattered across the bedroom floor. 'Shit, shit, *shit*!'

She went to the dresser on her side of the bed, pulled out a drawer, and reached for the secret phone that was taped to the inside. This one didn't have the ability to make calls, but it had access to email, namely Operation Glow. She opened it and tapped in her password. She checked incoming emails but there weren't any.

I need immediate extraction, she typed, and then paused. *Extraction and rescue. There are at least six civilians in immediate risk. I repeat, six civilians in immediate risk of death, and four casualties. I also have one civilian requiring immediate hospitalisation. Bring medics.* She paused again. *I have located Lyndsay Arthur.*

She hit enter. *That last little bombshell should do the trick*, she thought.

As she headed back towards the stairs, she heard the front door open.

'Bea?' she yelled. 'Sally? Is that you?'

340

'Afraid not,' she heard a young woman say.

'It's Evie, isn't it?' Rachel enquired, descending the stairs. 'And... I'm so sorry,' she said, turning to the man with the twisted arm and albino eyes, 'but I don't know your name.'

'Eli,' he said, sheepish. 'My name's Eli.'

'That stuff that's happening down there,' Rachel said, peering into the living room and attempting to remain calm, 'it's crazy, right?'

'That's par for the course around here,' Evie replied. 'Glanna's quite mad, I'm afraid.'

'I can see that.'

'She'll be coming for you. Us too.'

Rachel raised an eyebrow. 'The last time I looked, Lyndsay, the man with the gun, seemed to have taken control.'

Evie laughed. 'Not for long.'

'But she's unarmed, isn't she?'

Evie huffed and pushed Eli up the stairs. 'If you say so.'

'Wait, where are you going?'

Evie turned. 'Look, lady. You want to get out of this or not?'

'Of course, but—'

'That's what I thought. Eli here has agreed to be the bait. And you three?' She smirked. 'Well, let's just say that you get to be the distraction.'

*

'I need your codes,' the man with the gun said. 'All of them. I've got the ones your sister gave me, I've got your laptop, but there seems to be two codes missing, and I'm reliably informed that you have them.'

Hattie didn't speak. She didn't think she was able. Her head hurt and her mind was a mash of anagrams and colours. It was all she could do to put one foot in front of the other.

'Can you talk, lady?' the man growled, shoving the gun into her

341

side. She thought it would hurt but she couldn't feel a thing. 'You hold out on me, and I promise things won't end well for you, or your family.'

Hattie started to laugh. She couldn't help herself.

'What are you laughing at, bitch?' he yelled. 'Stop laughing. This isn't funny.'

He cracked her across the head with the butt of his gun, and she fell to the floor. She was still laughing. The whole thing seemed hilarious.

'Get up!' he screamed at her. 'Get up before I put a bullet in your fuck-ugly face!'

This made Hattie laugh even louder. In the old days, she would say that she was laughing so much that her sides hurt, but nothing really hurt anymore: not the murder of her husband, not the fact that her daughter had been taken from her, and especially not the impact wound on her head. It was all just so funny.

When she looked up at the angry man, she saw the Horned God looming behind him. Fire leapt from its nostrils and its breath created a swirl of billowing clouds around its head. Its hooves were so big they created giant craters in the earth. Its eyes swam with the undead souls of the eternal, and its locust-encrusted hands grasped a mighty sword that she knew had been smelted in the molten lava of spewing volcanoes. It leered down at the man and judged him.

'You either get up and come with me, bitch,' the man hissed, pointing towards the cottage, 'or I'm going in there and killing every single living thing I see.'

That was when the babies rushed out from the shadows, their tiny feet making little pattering sounds on the earth, and their high-pitched voices cawing and shrieking. They covered the man in seconds.

'*Argh*!' he yelled. 'Argh! Get off me. Get the hell off me!'

He fired the gun, but it was useless. The bullet simply scattered gravel from the path. There were too many of them. Hattie heard the ripping of flesh, the splatter of blood as it spilled onto the ground. The man fell to his knees, his hands attempting to pull the creatures off him, but more and more of them rushed out from the shadows. They clawed at his eyes, bit chunks from his throat, and gorged in his warm blood. He was dead before his face hit the ground.

Hattie stood. She turned to the cottage and smiled.

*

Eli sat in the darkness of the damp, musty attic. He could hear the whispers of the lost, the misery of the taken. The cottage reeked of it, stunk of the stench of despair. These were its dying moments, this cursed place. Eli didn't think it would fight it. The cottage was tired, exhausted. It had once been a place of hope, of joy. Then the bloodshed had started, and the rot had set in. Once it had taken hold, it was irreversible. No chemical treatment or replacing of beams could save it now. It was drowning in the blood of the dead.

The Red Man was gone. *At least he's with his wife now*, Eli thought. He touched the pendant that hung around his neck. He would lay it with her, the pretty lady, when she was buried. He could do that much. He would also do the last thing that the Red Man had asked of him: he would kill Evie. He would go along with her plan, but she would have to pay eventually. Her story was sad – everything that happened to her had been sad – but she'd had a choice, just like Eli had had a choice. She had chosen badly, selfishly.

Sweet Mother wanted Eli. He could feel her thoughts crawling all over him, swimming inside of him. They burrowed under his skin like tics, squirmed into his ears like slugs. She knew where he was, just as Eli knew that the man with the gun would fail. It would take more than bullets and hate to bring his Sweet Mother down. She had survived this long for a reason. She was cunning. She had talents.

Eli felt the sting of fear. How could he even believe he could

343

defeat her? It was impossible, wasn't it?

Evie planned to burn Eli alive along with Sweet Mother. She hadn't said as much, but it was implied. She acted like she understood him, empathised with him, but she valued him even less than she might value a bramble in her hair, or a stain on her clothes. He wasn't going to let her win. Firstly, he would make sure that there was no way out for Sweet Mother. She needed to be stopped for everything that she'd done, but then he would turn the table on the Kid-Bastard. Her time was coming too.

*

'Hattie,' Rachel exclaimed, 'how did you…?'

'He's dead,' Hattie said. 'The Horned One took him. He is coming.'

'What? What did you say? Lyndsay's dead?'

'You need to repent,' Hattie said, approaching her. 'You are not who you say you are. You must forsake your sins, repent your lies.'

Rachel turned to Sally. She was sitting cross-legged and staring oddly at her mother. 'Go into the other room, Sal.'

'I don't want—'

'Now, please.'

The little girl stood and reluctantly stomped into the dining room.

'Close the door.'

Just as the words left Rachel's mouth, Hattie was on her, clawing at her face and pulling her hair. Rachel whirled to the side and swept Hattie's legs away. She crashed into the coffee table.

'Just cool it, Hattie,' Rachel said, readying herself for another attack. 'You're confused. I think Glanna has been drugging you or something, but you need to shake it off.'

'You will perish in the eternal fires of hell,' Hattie sneered, launching herself on all fours and wrapping her arms and legs around Rachel's upper body.

Rachel was caught off guard. 'Jesus, you're freakishly strong.' She tried to pull her from around her neck, but Hattie held her tight, her legs almost crushing her ribs. 'I don't want to do this, but—' Rachel twisted and dropped forward onto the floor, crushing Hattie under her full body weight. She felt something crack in Hattie's chest and heard a grunt as air was pushed forcefully from her lungs.

'Look,' Rachel said, standing. 'Bea's badly hurt, and the kids are in danger. I've called for help, but I've no idea how long that will take. We need to help ourselves, I think.' Rachel looked around the room. 'We have to find something to arm ourselves with. Knives, metal bars, bricks, anything.'

'It's futile,' Hattie said, grinning. 'If you do not repent, you will be weighed, judged and reckoned. You cannot escape.'

'Oh, this is bullshit,' Rachel sighed, as Hattie leapt up and swung a wild fist towards her. Unfortunately for the older woman, Rachel had hundreds of hours of unarmed combat training under her belt, and she easily avoided the blow, stepping to the side and bringing a powerful sidekick up into Hattie's jaw. Hattie's teeth crashed together as her jawbone fractured, and her eyes rolled up into her head as she went sprawling face first onto the carpet.

'Sorry about that,' Rachel said, crouching down and turning Hattie onto her side. 'No hard feelings.'

By the time the front door crashed open, Rachel had already seized the opportunity to hide both her and Sally, leaving Hattie and Bea unconscious in the living room. She'd calculated that if Hattie had somehow managed to shake off Lyndsay Arthur, then Glanna and the others wouldn't be too far behind.

Glanna entered the house, her black kaftan billowing around her. Her hair was sleek, immaculate, her red lipstick just so. She looked like she was about to attend a funeral. Perhaps she was. She eyed the two unconscious women.

'They're here,' Glanna said, turning to her two male accomplices. 'Find them.'

Jonno, Seb and the woman, Katharine, stood silently in the barn. Noah was standing in the doorway, the gun trained on all three of them.

'You know what she told me to do, right?'

Jonno did. He'd heard every word. "Clean up the mess, dispose of them".

'I do, but you can't do it, Noah. They're just kids.' Katharine was shaking, the smear of tears on her cheeks.

'She doesn't care,' he said. 'And... and neither do I.'

'You're not a murderer.'

'I've done some pretty bad things.'

'Yes, you have. But only at her behest.'

Jonno didn't know what behest meant, but he knew he didn't want to die. Petra had done something to him, that much was obvious, and it had made him do something awful to Aunt Bea. He hoped she was okay, and that Rachel had got her some help, but more than anything, he needed to make sure Hattie and Sally were safe. He was the man of the house now, after...

'I'm an accomplice, Katharine, in the eyes of the law. I enable her fantasies. I threw those people into the cesspit. I might not have actually killed anyone, but I didn't stop it either.'

'Then stop it now,' Katharine implored him. 'You can end this, right here, right now. Let us go, call the police, and give evidence against her. They'll look kindly on you, I'm sure of it. We'll say you helped us escape, that you saved our lives.'

'She can be cruel, you know?' he said.

'No shit,' Seb sneered.

'She took care of you,' Noah replied, turning the gun on him.

'She stole us, robbed us of our childhoods,' Seb replied, his lips a hateful scowl. 'She drugged us and filled us with lies and crazy ideas. And why? Because some of us have gifts? I can levitate, Evie can control the weak-minded, Freddie could predict the future, and

Aaron could once move inanimate objects. So what? Did that justify her snatching us and killing our parents?'

'She wanted to help you fulfil your true potential.'

'Oh yes, that's right,' Seb continued, 'fulfil our potential. And, remind me, where did that leave us? Walking around like zombies, with images of monstrous demons terrorising our every waking thought and wondering when Glanna would tire of us. With Aaron and Freddie dead, only Evie and I remain, and now she's told you to finish us off, too.'

Noah paused. 'You're just a mess that needs tidying.'

Seb glared at him. 'Well, thank you very much. I appreciate the compliment.'

Jonno was only half listening. He was mentally pushing away the boulder that had been weighing down on him ever since he'd heard of his dad's murder. He knew he needed to shift it before he did what he was planning to do next. Seb had spotted it first, and he'd signalled Jonno with his eyes. Jonno had ignored him initially – he was too terrified to think straight – but once he took a breath and calmed himself down, he slowly followed the line of Seb's glare. It was obvious. Aunt Bea had already mentioned it, just before he'd cracked her across the head with that rock. "I told them all about the cesspit", she'd said. The cesspit; the place where Noah obviously planned to get rid of their dead bodies once he'd killed them all. Noah had already removed the metal hatch covering the pit's mouth, and he was now standing right in front of it. Close enough for Jonno to...

'Why are you so quiet, kid?' Noah asked Jonno, now pointing the gun at him. 'These two have got plenty to say, but you? Not so much.'

'I... I don't know what you want me to—'

'You've got a strange look on your face, like you're planning something.' Jonno felt his mouth turn bone dry. 'I wouldn't if I were you. I'm still considering my options here.'

'You could just... walk away,' Jonno said. 'Leave us the gun if you like. You could just disappear.'

'Mm,' Noah said, glancing towards Excelsior. 'She wouldn't like that.'

'She's not going to like what I'm planning to do to her, either,' Jonno scowled. 'She killed my dad.'

'Ha,' Noah laughed. 'You? You're just a kid. You think you could get one over on her, and the others too?'

'I know I could,' Jonno said.

'Huh, you certainly seem serious enough.' Noah paused. 'I tell you what. I like the idea of getting out of here, I really do. I've done my time, and with Petra gone, there really is no reason for me to stay.'

'Good,' Katharine said. 'That's good. You're thinking clearly now, Noah. Really clearly.'

'However,' Noah said. 'You three are witnesses and could testify against me if it came to that.'

'But we wouldn't,' Katharine assured him. 'Why would we?'

'Oh, there's plenty of reasons, and plenty of evidence too.' He glanced at the cesspit. 'I don't like it, I've never liked it, but I really have no choice.'

'No choice?' Seb said. 'What do you mean?'

Noah pulled the trigger and there was an *oof* as Seb slumped to the ground. Blood was spurting from a wound in his stomach. Seb glanced up at Jonno, his face suddenly a deathly grey.

Jonno nodded an acknowledgement, took a breath, and charged.

*

Evie sat in the shadows as Pascoe walked past. He was such an idiot, he couldn't see a dinosaur if it sat on his lap. Bertrand was no better. He'd literally opened the door of the airing cupboard where she was hiding, looked around and closed the door again. He hadn't thought to look up, which is where she'd crammed her body, jamming her feet into the sidewalls and pressing her hands into the

348

frame of the door. She literally could have dropped a phlegmy spit all over his bald head, and had to stop herself from laughing at the thought.

Paz and Bertrand had to be taken out if her plan was going to work. Glanna had to be put in a position where she had no choice but to go up into the attic on her own. The two men couldn't be allowed to go up there to fetch the cripple for her. That was okay, because they would never make it that far. The babies couldn't hurt Glanna, she was their mother after all, but they sure as hell could do a job on the two old geezers. All Paz and Bert had to do was enter one of the bedrooms. They were waiting; waiting to be fed.

*

Jonno heard the gun discharge again, but he didn't care. He ran shoulder first into the soft spot just beneath Noah's ribcage. It caught the older man off guard and his legs buckled. Jonno pushed, imagining his own legs as giant steam pistons, and he let out a loud *urgh*! as he shoved as hard as his thin arms would allow. At first, he thought he was going to miss the target, but when he stood back and glared into Noah's wide eyes, he saw a look of grim realisation. Gravity did the majority of the work, and Noah's head struck metal and concrete as the rest of his body disappeared into raw sewage. The stink was horrendous. Jonno didn't hesitate. He grabbed the hatch, slammed it shut and locked it in place. Noah was no more.

He turned to face the others. The stray bullet had struck Katharine in the shoulder, and she was slumped against the barn wall.

'You okay?' he asked.

'I'll be fine. I'm not sure about Sebastian, though.'

Jonno went to him. There was a lot of blood, and Seb's face was now the colour of soft cheese.

'I don't think there's much you can do here, mate,' Seb groaned. 'I think he got me pretty good.'

349

'No,' Jonno said. 'I'll get you help. I'll find Rachel and Aunt Bea, and we'll call an ambulance. You'll be fine, honest, you'll be fine. After all that's happened, you have to be okay.'

Seb tried to laugh, but there was blood in his mouth. The sound was like someone gargling soup. 'Just stop her, Jonno. Promise me, you'll stop her.'

'I… I promise.'

'For my mum and grandmother, your dad too. And the others.'

'I know. She's gonna pay, Seb. I'll make sure of it.'

'Good,' Seb said, his voice cracked. 'That's good. Really, really goo—' His head lolled forward, a thin line of blood falling from his lips. Jonno wiped away a tear and turned to Katharine.

'Wait here. I'm going to finish this.'

*

Eli heard the dreadful sound as the Terrible Babies pulled Pascoe and Bertrand to shreds. He didn't like the fact that Evie had once again manipulated them into doing awful things – surely there was only a fine line between that and what Sweet Mother did – but he knew they didn't really have any choice. If their plan was going to work, then Sweet Mother had to be alone.

He peered into the four corners of the loft space. The two women had already placed bottles of petrol under the eaves, and rags soaked in fuel were jammed between the roof joists and the thick thatch. All Eli had to do was light one end of the petrol-soaked sheet that lay at his feet, and *woof*, the whole place would go up like a Roman candle.

He swallowed sticky saliva and called out.

'I'm up here, Mother!' he yelled. 'I'm in the attic. I'm… I'm all alone!'

He heard footsteps on the floorboards below, the sound of small, soft feet pressing on threadbare carpet. He sensed Sweet Mother standing just beneath the loft hatch.

350

'And why would you be all the way up there, boy?' she said, her voice soothing, calming. 'Why not come down here? I'll take good care of you, like I always have. I've always looked after you, haven't I? Even though—'

'I'm not yours?' he offered.

'That's right,' she said. 'Even though you're not mine. That has never bothered me. I've always treated you the same as the others. I've fed you, bathed you, clothed you.'

'And yet,' he said, 'I slept in a barn. I ate leftovers. I froze in the winter and baked in the summer.'

'And weren't you grateful? A roof over your head, and food in your belly?'

'I know some fings, now,' he said. 'Some horrible fings.'

'Such as?' she asked.

'About who my father is, who my mother is.'

'Really? And may I ask who gave you this information.'

'Evie,' he answered. It didn't matter if she knew now.

'She was always a manipulative liar,' she hissed.

'She told me that you are my mother.'

'Lies,' she said.

'And that Petra was my father.'

'Also lies.'

'And that you stole Evie and the others from their real parents. That you killed them.'

'Huh. One day, when this is all over, I'll tell you the truth, Eli. The real truth.'

'Evie's already told me the truth.'

'And where is she now?' she yelled. 'Where is Evie? She's abandoned you, hasn't she? She's left you up there in the attic all on your own! Doesn't she realise you're afraid of the dark? No, of course not. She doesn't know you like I know you, Eli. She has always been a cruel, wicked child. You want to know the truth about Evie?' she sneered. 'Do you want to know why her parents abandoned her, why they left her here on her own with strangers?

351

Because they hated her. They couldn't stand the sight of her. An ugly, pasty-faced little girl with frizzy hair and little brown dots all over her like flies. She was always crying and never did as she was told. They begged me!' She was almost screaming now. 'They pleaded with me to take her! I didn't want to, of course. I mean, why would I? But then I relented, because they really were desperate. I truly believe if I hadn't taken her in, then they would have killed her with their own hands.'

'*Liar*!' he heard Kid-Bastard Evie scream as the cupboard door crashed open. 'You liar, you killed them! *You killed my parents*!'

*

Rachel heard the commotion upstairs and ushered Sally back into the living room. Bea was sitting upright now.

'What the hell happened?' she asked, holding her head.

Rachel held a finger to her lips and gestured towards the stairs. 'You need to get Sally and your sister away from here. Head towards No Man's Land, and if I'm not out in the next ten minutes, start walking, you hear me?'

Hattie was beginning to come round too. 'Rachel?' she said. 'Sally?'

'What happened to her?' Bea asked.

'Long story,' Rachel said. 'We had a little disagreement, but she seems to have come round to my way of thinking. Just do as I ask, please.'

Suddenly there was the sound of a woman shrieking. '*You killed my parents*!'

'What's happening up there?'

'It sounds like it's all coming to a head,' Rachel said, ushering them towards the door. 'And I'm going to make certain that the head gets cut clean off.'

*

Evie had heard enough of the bullshit streaming from Glanna's poisonous mouth. She dropped from her place above the closet door, kicked it open and charged.

Sure, this wasn't her plan. She wasn't even thinking particularly clearly, but what did that matter? Sometimes rage was the only answer.

As she sped across the landing, Glanna turned to her and smiled. Too late, Evie realised she'd been duped. Glanna had been planning this exact moment all along. She'd goaded her, prodded her, and she'd taken the bait. True, the babies couldn't hurt their mother. They couldn't even hurt Evie when she was thinking clearly and exercising control over them, but she wasn't thinking clearly, and she certainly wasn't exercising control. A red mist had completely obscured her judgement.

When the first creature attacked, she barely felt it, but when one became two, two became three, and three became a dozen, she felt every single claw, every razor-sharp tooth. She smiled at the irony of it all as she became buried beneath their squirming, rampaging onslaught. She'd get to see them again, her parents. There was justice in that, at least.

*

Rachel heard the sound of a woman screaming in agony, and the terrible cacophony of flesh being ripped, of blood spattering on walls. She couldn't see what was happening, but she knew that whoever had tried to get the jump on Glanna had come unstuck, possibly terminally.

She pressed herself against the wall of the staircase and tried to make herself as small as possible. Rachel was unarmed, except for her hand-to-hand combat skills, but she doubted very much that that was going to be a factor here. Something unnatural was at play, that had been clear from day one, but even if she didn't know what she was up against, she had to at least try to stop Glanna. The killing had to stop.

When she was level with the top of the stairs, she chanced a peek. What she saw made her stomach turn. The young woman, Evie, was now just a shredded mass of blood, flesh and torn skin. Her head was pulled back so that her dead eyes were staring directly at Rachel, a grim smile on bloodied lips. Rachel gasped and held a hand to her mouth. What the hell had happened to her?

Something emerged from beneath Evie's body and stood upright. It was tiny, no more than two feet in height. It had grey skin, a tuft of black-grey hair, blood-red eyes, rows of tiny teeth, and fingers that ended in hooked claws. It was naked, exposing its sex. It was male. He walked towards Rachel, who instinctively stepped backwards, almost tumbling down the stairs.

'Beth?' A familiar voice from further along the landing. 'Don't worry, Beth, he won't hurt you. Well, not unless I ask him to, of course. Why don't you come up here where I can see you?'

Rachel took a deep breath. She peered back at the door, which was firmly shut. She stared at the unholy creature standing before her, and at Evie's shredded corpse. She decided her only option was to be bold. She took the steps one at a time.

'Sorry about the mess,' Glanna said as Rachel mounted the landing. 'I had some… housekeeping to take care of. I still have a little—' she glanced at the loft hatch, 'tidying up to do, but after that, I would very much like to sit down with you and the others. I think we could help each other, you and I.'

'What could we possibly have to talk about?'

'You had a little bother with that criminal fellow,' she said. 'The one that Ger's ex was so besotted with. Well, my children took care of him.'

'Your children?' Rachel asked, shocked.

'Yes, my real children. You can leave us now, dear,' she said to the creature. It nodded and ran down the stairs. 'Anyway, with that man taken care of, I believe you have free access to all that money.'

'How... how did you know about that?'

'This is my house, dear,' Glanna said, laughing. 'I know everything that goes on here.'

Rachel looked around her at the landing. Cameras – there had to be cameras.

'Anyway,' Glanna continued. 'It stands to reason that I could also use a little of it, the money I mean. All I ask for is a little share of what's rightfully mine. Then you and the others can leave without any further trouble.'

'And what makes you think we won't just do that anyway?'

'Because I'll kill you,' she said, as cold as ice. 'Or, at least, I'll have you killed.'

Rachel considered her options. She knew she had to stall the woman. Eric and the others would be on their way, and once they arrived, Bea, Hattie and the kids would be safe. They would all be safe.

'Oh, you're thinking about your email,' Glanna said. 'That didn't send I'm afraid.'

'What?'

'Your email, to your friends in the police. I only ever allowed you to send the emails that were helpful to me. That last one, I blocked it.'

'How did you...?'

'No matter, dear. Just remember that I'm holding all the cards here.'

Shit, Rachel thought. She really was.

'We just want to go home.'

'And go home you will,' Glanna said, smiling. 'Just after you do as I ask. I can't be any more accommodating than that, I'm afraid.'

Rachel glared at the woman's face. It was starting to move, seemingly of its own accord. Strange bulges appeared, then the eyes shifted, the mouth became thinner. At first she was Glanna, and then she was the old woman, Dolly. The younger version of Glanna looked no more than twenty-one, but then the face would change and morph into a young Dolly, pretty lips, curled blonde hair, and dark eyes.

'Who are you?' Rachel asked.

'I am everything you want to be,' she answered. 'And so much more.'

Suddenly there were dozens of the little creatures at Rachel's feet. She could smell their festering meat-breath and could hear the urgent chattering of their teeth. One trod on her foot and she jumped.

'He is coming, Beth. There's nothing you can do to stop that.'

'You're talking about this horned god of yours. You know that's ridiculous, right?'

Another creature clawed at her shin, drawing blood. 'Ow!'

'If you remain a non-believer, if you do not do as I ask, then you will perish, just like the others.'

'You're crazy,' Rachel cried, but she couldn't explain away the horrible beings now swarming all around her, and she couldn't block out the squirming, moving features of the woman standing before her.

'You're in a bit of a pickle here, Beth, my dear. What's your next move?'

Rachel didn't have a move. She was all out of moves. She could feel terror rising in her chest like poison. She was either having a really bad dream, or she'd somehow walked onto the set of a surreal horror movie. She just had to buy Bea and the others enough time to get away. She owed them that much.

Suddenly Glanna doubled over as if in pain, and her face seemed to lock itself in a space somewhere between Glanna and the old woman. The right side, the older side, started to blacken and peel. The eye started to disappear, like something was eating away at it. The mouth sagged and drooped, as if the muscles there had been unattached from the bone.

'*Aargh*!' Glanna screamed, although the sound was muffled. 'It can't be! This can't be!'

The creatures around Rachel's feet started to approach, spitting and furious. They seemed spurred on by the agony their mother was experiencing. Confused, Rachel started to back away. As she bit down on her lower lip and braced herself for what she was sure would be thousands of tiny teeth and claws tearing at her face and body, a boy swung down from the loft hatch and kicked Glanna in the back of the head, knocking her to the ground.

Jonno landed in the hallway and screamed at her.

'Run, Rachel! *Run*!'

*

Jonno left Katharine in the barn and ran towards Spriggan's. *That's where they would be*, he thought. If this was going to end anywhere, it would be there.

'Where are you going, young man?'

Suddenly, there was the dark silhouette of a woman; a woman sitting in a wheelchair.

'Dolly?' he said, suddenly very afraid.

'Dolores to you, you impudent child,' she scowled. 'I suggest you stay away from there.' She pointed at the cottage. 'Bad things are happening there.'

'I'm going to stop her.'

The old lady let out a loud cackle. 'She is me and I am she. To stop her you must stop me.'

'I hardly think that would be difficult,' Jonno said, picking up a spade from the garden.

'You'd be surprised,' Dolly said, and launched herself at him with the sprightliness of a woman a quarter of her age. Jonno fell backwards onto the ground, dropping the shovel. Dolly was on him, her fingers gouging at his eyes and mouth. He suddenly felt all his anxiety, his self-doubt, filling his body like festering water. Pinpricks of terror rippled across his skin.

'Stupid, pathetic, feeble child!' Dolly yelled, her saliva falling onto his face and lips. 'No friends, no girlfriends. Just sitting in your room listening to crap music and playing baby games. No one loves you. No one likes you. You'll die alone, Jonathon. All alone in a crappy bedsit with no job, no family, and no life. This is a mercy killing,' she yelled, slamming the palms of her hands into his face. 'I'm doing you a favour, you pathetic little—'

'No!' Jonno screamed, shoving her away from him. 'I'm not that! I'm not! You're the old pathetic hag, and it's me that's doing you a favour!' He picked up the shovel, and in one swift motion, swung it with all his might at the old woman's head. The sharp edge of the spade connected with her neck, just below the jawline, and sliced through skin, cartilage and bone. Her head was severed completely from the body. It flew through the air, spinning and whirling like a football. Finally, it came splashing down into the pond, nestling in the thick weeds and algae. A goldfish quickly approached and started nibbling at the old lady's eyeballs.

Jonno, breathless, threw the spade on the ground and spat.

'That's for my dad.'

*

Eli was caught completely off guard when Jonno the Turd Boy emerged from the gap in the eaves.

'Jonno, what are you…?'

Jonno held a finger to his lips. 'Noah's dead,' he said. 'I killed him. Dolly too.'

'You did what?'

'She's decapitated, and Noah's in the cesspit.'

Eli smiled. If ever there was a fitting end to someone's life that was it.

'Sweet Mother is down there,' Eli said. 'We're going to burn her.'

'She's not coming up here, Eli,' Jonno said. 'Evie's dead, and she's got Rachel surrounded with some freaky little creatures. We have to do something.'

'But, what?' Eli asked.

'We catch her off guard,' Jonno replied. 'It's the only way.'

Jonno crawled towards the open loft hatch and gripped the wooden frame in both hands. 'Wish me luck,' he whispered, before he disappeared.

Eli was too dumbstruck to move. What the hell had JTB just done? He heard his feet connect with something hard, followed by the sound of Sweet Mother crying out. Then he heard the urgent chattering of his brothers and sisters. Eli looked at the containers filled with petrol and the lighter in his hand. He thought of the Red Man and the pretty lady. He thought of what Sweet Mother had put him through, of the beatings he'd taken at the hands of Noah. The house spoke to him.

Do it, Eli, finish it, let us be at peace. Destroy this place, burn it to the ground, free us once and for all...

He held the lighter up as the flame flickered into life. He took a breath, touched it to the drenched sheet, and suddenly everything around him turned into a sea of orange.

*

'Get him!' Glanna yelled, but the creatures were too confused. Jonno grabbed Rachel by the shoulders.

'We have to get out.'

Suddenly smoke was billowing through the loft hatch and the whole place was blistering hot.

'He's lit the flame,' Jonno said. 'Go on, Eli!' he yelled. '*Go on*!'

Rachel turned and saw Glanna rise to her feet. Half of her face had disappeared, the bone visible beneath. Her right arm hung limply, and her right leg dragged useless behind her.

'Kill them!' she screamed, just as the ceiling above collapsed and flames scorched the walls and floor. The creatures ran, scrambling over each other to get out of the burning building. The smoke was dense now, suffocating. Rachel could barely breathe.

'The [*cough*] door,' Jonno said. 'We [*cough*] need to get out, [*cough*] and lock her in.'

Rachel stumbled down the stairs. The living room was now just a black cloud, the hallway a swirling tunnel of smoke and heat. Rachel glanced at the pictures on the walls. They were curling at the edges, the crudely drawn figures starting to blister and bubble. Their picture was now just a yellowed, faded blur. *Would they disappear too*, Rachel wondered, *Bea, Hattie, Sally, Jonno and her*? What about Beth Mckinlay? She'd only wanted to avenge Tommy's death. That seemed so long ago now, so irrelevant.

'Come on!' Jonno hollered, just as Glanna emerged from the smoke.

'You're going nowhere,' she said, and pulled a knife from the kitchen counter. The blade was red-hot and smouldering.

'Jonno!' Rachel cried out. She pushed the boy to one side as Glanna slammed the knife into her chest. Rachel felt the blade penetrate skin and flesh, and she dropped to her knees.

'Rachel! *No*!' Jonno yelled, and punched Glanna in the nose. What was left of her face seemed to compress like a rubber ball. Her left eye drooped like she'd just suffered a stroke.

'You little shit!' she screamed. 'You cocky little—' She swung the knife at Jonno as he ducked and brought his elbow round, striking her in the chin. She staggered backwards as he turned and grabbed Rachel under her arms.

'Come on,' he said. 'You can do it. We're getting out of here.'

The flames had made it to the bottom of the staircase now, and the room was so hot it was making Rachel's head spin. She couldn't breathe, couldn't think, and now there was blood all over her shirt and a terrible, burning pain in her chest.

'I can't,' she said.

'Yes you [*cough*] bloody can,' Jonno replied. 'And you will!'

'I don't think so!' Glanna yelled. She clasped her arms around

Jonno's chest and held the blade at his neck. 'We're walking out of here together, boy. You and me. One false move and I'll slit your throat.'

'Just go with her, Jonno,' Rachel said. 'I'm not [*cough*] getting out of here alive, but you, you have a chance. Just tell Bea—'

'Shut up, Rachel,' he said.

'Do as the nice lady says.' Glanna's gruff voice was coming from within shattered teeth and a collapsed face. 'And you might even live.'

Suddenly a shadowy form dropped into the kitchen. The strange silhouette was crooked, misshapen. It had a bulbous head, one good arm, and tufts of wispy hair.

'Let my friend go!' Eli yelled. 'Mother.'

Glanna turned. 'I thought you were dead, son.'

'No such luck.'

'You tried to kill me, you thankless child. I should have thrown you in the pit when I had the chance.'

'Well, guess what?' Eli said, shooting Rachel and Jonno a glance, 'you missed it.'

He let out an almighty scream and charged headlong at his mother. Jonno took the opportunity to slip out from within Glanna's grasp as Eli's body connected with hers, throwing them both into a giant wall of ferocious flames and billowing smoke.

'Now!' Jonno yelled, and he pushed through the front door, hauling Rachel out with him, before slamming it shut behind them. Within an instant, the roof of the cottage collapsed in on itself, and flames as high as the trees erupted from the building's structure. Rachel and Jonno dived for cover as the walls collapsed, and brick and timber fell in smouldering clumps. The front wall of the house gave way and fell forward onto Richard's car, crushing it.

Rachel glanced over her shoulder and spied two black silhouettes thrashing around within the inferno, apparently locked in an epic battle. She guessed the fight would go on for a long time, maybe long after death. Immortality was like that.

EPILOGUE
FRIDAY, 26TH AUGUST 2022

Beth's debrief was challenging, but uneventful. The story was simple, really. Lyndsay Arthur had duped all of them into thinking that the Belvedere Saints were arranging a huge money launder, but it was just a way to get his revenge after the shoot-out at the club. The only problem was, he hadn't counted on coming up against a dangerously violent family, the Cormorans, who had been conducting a campaign of murder, extortion and abduction for decades. They'd killed him, as well as many others – Hattie's husband Richard included – before they'd all perished in a fire that had started, possibly due to faulty electrics, in one of their buildings. The wiring in the properties was outdated at best. It was a wonder that it hadn't happened sooner.

Bea had almost fully recovered from the crack on the skull her nephew had given her (something he apologised for daily), and Hattie was back to being her old self, if a little less angry. The sisters had even reconciled with their parents, almost. Not embezzling them out of tens of millions of pounds obviously helped matters. Almost dying at the hands of a bunch of lunatic hippies did the rest. Hattie missed Richard dearly, but as she said, what could she do? She had to move on.

The only fly in the ointment was that the woman still lived: Glanna. She was a burnt, half-human mess, but she'd miraculously survived the blaze. What was more of a shock was that the baby had also survived. It was still alive and healthy in Glanna's womb.

Hattie demanded to see her, and despite her angry protestations, Beth had made the arrangements. It was only on the understanding that Hattie allowed Beth to accompany her.

The day was overcast, and a heavy storm threatened. As they pulled into the hospital car park, Beth adjusted the heavy bandage on her chest and turned to Hattie.

'You sure you want to go through with this?'

'I'm sure,' Hattie replied. Her expression was unmoving.

'I still think it's a bad idea, you know,' she said.

'I know, but it's my choice.'

When they entered the room, Glanna's one good eye opened. The rest of her face was obscured by heavy dressings and a ventilator mask.

'You *hsssss* came,' she said.

'I did,' Hattie replied.

'I'm *hsssss* pleased.'

Hattie approached the bed and placed a hand on Glanna's bulging abdomen. 'The baby,' she asked, 'is it his?'

Glanna nodded.

Hattie smiled. 'That makes me happy.'

'Me *hsss* too,' Glanna said. 'It will be *hsss* a true Cormoran.'

'Perhaps.' Hattie replied. 'I think I'll raise it.'

'Hattie!' Beth objected, but Hattie shooed her away.

'And so *hsss* you should.'

'It was a shame, the cottage burning to the ground like that,' Hattie said.

'A *hsss* real shame.'

'I could have been happy there.'

'There is *hsss* always Excelsior.'

'Maybe,' Hattie replied. 'Maybe I will.'

'You can take *hsss* care of the baby there.'

'Yes,' Hattie said. 'I'd like that.'

'And *hsss* you'll come and visit me too?'

'Ha,' Beth laughed sarcastically, but once more Hattie raised a hand to silence her.

'I could do that.'

'Dolly is *hsss* dead.'

363

'I know.'

'It needs a host. Perhaps *hssss* that could be me.'

'Perhaps,' Hattie responded.

'I think *hssss* you know what he wants.'

'I do.' Hattie nodded. 'One body for the departing soul.'

'And one *hssss* for the new,' Glanna acknowledged.

From where Beth was standing, she couldn't see the wry smile on Hattie's lips, or the silver streaks now visible through her tangle of blonde curls. She also didn't see Hattie's face shift and morph. It was fleeting, but it was there just the same.

Outside, the winds began to swirl, and the sky darkened. Dozens of tiny grey creatures huddled together in the bushes at the edge of the grounds, and a giant black cloud with twisted horns and an equine skull reached over the roof of the building, its arms held wide in a grotesque embrace.

Blesséd be…

Blesséd be…

A WORD FROM THE AUTHOR

I started writing this book during the latter part of the dreaded pandemic. You might ask why that's still a relevant point given I don't even mention the C word during the novel, and in fact, I deliberately shied away from including it, believing we'd all had enough of hearing about face masks, social distancing, lockdowns, and the constant hypocrisy of politicians. However, the fact remains that without that awful disease this book might never have happened. 'Why's that?' I hear you ask. Well, in the summer of 2021, my wife and I had been planning to pack a tent into the back of our VW Golf and head off around Europe. However, with the virus still lingering, and countries still ruminating on what their border policies might be, we decided to head down to south Cornwall instead and give our ageing Bassett Hound, Lily, what would prove to be her last big holiday. It was during that two-week break at the western-most tip of the UK, and particularly in the early hours of the morning when the sun was just starting to peek over the picturesque horizon, that I forged the idea of a little Cornish commune harbouring murderous intentions, a fractious family with their own intricate riddles to solve, and angry pixie-like beings lurking in the dankest, darkest parts of the forest. Cornwall always seems to give me such a creativity boost, particularly when it comes to writing horror and fantasy. After all, as Bea says, 'everywhere you look there's a stone monument, witch's cauldron, or crop circle'. Okay, that's not really true, but you get my drift. We visited Falmouth and Mevagissey on that trip, so I thought it was appropriate to namecheck them. Bodhmall's Rest is a made-up place though, so don't waste your time looking – or at least that's what I told the publisher.

I often wonder what would have happened if I'd kicked the novel off while sitting in a tent beside Lake Garda or hiking up a snow-capped Matterhorn. I guess it would have made for a very different book, and perhaps one for a later time.

People often ask me where I get the inspiration for my characters. I think every writer will tell you that their literary babies are forged from little bits of everyone: people they've met, people they've watched on TV, people they've read about, and more importantly, people that have left a lasting impression on them, good or bad. The character of Glanna Cormoran began after an initial meeting with our very lovely host during that holiday, but she obviously morphed into something altogether different. Hattie and Richard were a mash-up of people I've known over the years; married friends and acquaintances who always seem to be approximately thirty seconds from a blazing row. Bea and Rachel were inspired by those energy-bunny type characters who seem to have boundless amounts of enthusiasm to spare, coupled with a slightly reckless sense of fun. You know the ones I mean, right? Jonno was taken from the A-typical awkward teenager template, but I wanted to combine his fragility and self-doubt with an underlying strength. I also didn't want him to be defined by his condition, so I purposefully didn't name it. The character arcs of both Jonno and Eli are my favourites of this book.

I have a few people to thank, as you would expect. My wonderful wife, Jo, the other half of me, and the real reason I started writing again after so many years sitting behind a corporate desk. She constantly drives me to do this stuff, even though at times I feel like the industry has beaten me into submission. Our children, Jayden and Harley, who inspire me every day. They've forged their own respective creative paths in the world and have made such a success of everything they've taken on. My mum and dad, who support everything I do. My dad tells everyone he reads everything I write, and he really does. Our best friends, Phil, Sam, Shell, Kev,

Matt and Lena, for just being there at the right times and continuing to be such a massively important part of our lives. The team at Cranthorpe Millner – Kirsty, Shannon, Vicky, Lauren and Sue – for supporting me with two books now. I'm sure I can be a pain at times. The immensely talented Dan (@DansMonsters) for creating such a stunning and eerily terrifying piece of cover art. And lastly, to you, the reader. Most writers say that first and foremost they write for themselves, and I guess we do, but of course we also write for you, the people that read. I get fed up hearing about the growth of AI and the imminent death of human creativity. I don't believe it and I never will. People love books, and people love to connect with other people on an emotional level. That's why the robots will never win. The formula is simple: good readers = good writers.

Anyway, I hope you enjoyed The Faraway People and found something in there that made you happy. If you've come this far, I'm guessing it at least kept you engaged. I'll be out on the road in 2024, so if you happen to be at a show where I'm exhibiting, please come over and say hi. In the meantime, if you feel like catching up, you can contact me on any of the below platforms. Keep an eye out for my next release, more news of which will be on my website in the coming months.

Take care of yourselves and each other, and above all, happy reading.

SD

CONTACT ME:

Website: www.staceydighttonstoryteller.com
Instagram: @staceydightonauthor
Facebook: stacey.dighton.509
Twitter: @Stacey_Dighton